Going Medieval

Going Medieval
When Reality TV and King Arthur Collide

Neil Silberman and Michael Rosenblum

CONTENTS

CHAPTER 1
STAIRWAY TO HEAVEN

Monte Levine was a storyteller. And his story was, in so many ways, too good to be true. Standing in a brilliant circle of light at the center of the enormous American Icon soundstage, with fifty million eager viewers on their sofas, recliners, and easy chairs all over the country rooting him on, he had suddenly become America's latest superstar.

Blinded by the stage lights, he squinted out into the darkness listening to the excited murmurs of the packed studio audience. How many people were out there? A thousand? Ten thousand? He had no way of knowing, but he did know that somewhere out there, near the front row was the love of his life. As multicolor laser beams twirled around him and a climactic drumroll began, he heard the voice of Simon Cornwall—the arrogant, wise-ass spokesman for the judges—calling out his name. Monte stepped forward to the front of the stage, holding his beloved '57 Stratocaster tightly, ready to play.

But before he did, Monte raised his right hand, clutching his guitar pick between his thumb and index finger, signaling to the crowd he had something to say. The audience grew still and Monte leaned toward the glistening chrome microphone stand.

"Before we start, Simon," Monte said, almost daring Cornwall to insult him or mock him in his trademark condescending way. "I want you to just take a timeout from your usual wisecracks while I get serious for a second. I have to offer my deepest thanks to someone who is here in the audience tonight."

Cornwall's eyes widened. Nobody had ever dared to upstage him in this way. But he remained silent as Monte continued. "Thank you, Simon. I just want to take a moment to offer a great big shout-out to my wife—my lover, my best friend, and an awesome life partner." He raised his hand to his brow to squint through the brilliance of the stage lights into the darkness. "Without her love and support I never could have made it. That woman—that woman," Monte almost choked up as he continued his expression of love. "I'm here because she never stopped believing in me."

The audience burst into cheers and sighs, and then thunderous applause. Simon Cornwall recognized that he had been bested. And he knew that 170 million people from Key West to Fairbanks, Alaska had texted, called, or voted online for Monte Levine. That was more than the votes cast for both candidates in the last presidential election. Even Simon Cornwall knew how was dangerous for anyone in the public eye to challenge popularity like that.

"What a beautiful tribute, Monte," Simon said through gritted teeth, quickly changing the subject and reading the lines off the teleprompter. "And now we have come to the moment everyone has been waiting for," Simon announced. "This year's American Icon will perform for one last time on this stage. Are you ready Monte? Off you go!"

The houselights suddenly went dark. The audience fell silent. The stage was bathed in brilliant light as Monte took a step forward and picked out the first few notes on his Stratocaster. The sound was hypnotic, slowly picking up steam and growing in volume. His left-hand fingers effortlessly glided up and down the fretboard and his right hand played the melody of what sounded at first like a medieval troubadour's tune. But the audience recognized it right away. Stairway to Heaven, one of the most famous rock songs of all time.

The amps were all the way up. The music vibrated, resonated, shook the stage. Monte could feel it pulsing in his veins as he cranked out the song. This was Monte's moment, his crowning achievement. He had fucking won this year's American Icon competition, and nobody could ever take that away from him.

He was about a third of the way through the song when a bloodcurdling screech from somewhere above stopped him cold and cut to his very core.

"Monte! Monte! Do you hear me?! For Christ's sake turn that stupid thing down. I can't even hear myself think!"

It was Sylvia.

Sylvia Levine.

His wife, standing at the top of the stairs.

His bliss suddenly vanished. The music went dead and the studio audience—along with Simon Cornwall and the rest of the judges—vanished into thin air. Monte Levine, 44 years old, was not the winner of American Icon. He was not standing in the brilliant lights on a Hollywood soundstage, performing for an adoring national audience; he was playing all alone in the finished basement of his home in the New York City suburb of Scarsdale. And Sylvia Levine was his only audience tonight, an unwilling audience, as she was every night.

"Will you please put that goddamn guitar down and call your boss?" she shouted in exasperation. "He's already called three times and he doesn't sound happy. If you ever lose that fucking job of yours, I just don't know what we'll do."

"Don't be ridiculous, Sylvia. Brinkman's not going to fire me. He needs me too much. In fact, I'm pretty sure that I can convince him to give me a big raise."

Sylvia shook her head in frustration. "Jesus Christ, Monte. When are you ever going to grow up and get your head out of the clouds?"

"Listen, Sylvia," he shot back with a smile, slowly tapping his forefinger on the side of his forehead. "It's this head and those clouds that have made a very nice living for us. And I have a strong feeling that it's going to get a lot nicer soon."

Monte Levine was a compulsive spinner of fantasies—not only in his own mind, not only to vainly try to pacify Sylvia's worries, but also for the rest of America, or at least the ones who watched his TV shows. As a producer for a Reality TV series that aired on Fox on Thursday nights, and a veteran of the Reality TV business, he had come up with hundreds of story ideas that entertained, titillated, and fascinated hundreds of millions of viewers in just over a decade. And the six Emmys that stood side-by-side in a bookcase in his office at TrulyTV in Manhattan proved that the stories he dreamed up were sometimes very, very good.

As far back as he could remember—even from his earliest childhood, making up stories was his sword to slay his inner dragons, to outsmart school bullies, and to charm the girls he wanted to impress. All the way from grade school to college, he had honed his uncanny ability to anticipate the kinds of stories that people wanted to hear. It was both a talent and a curse to be able to create alternate realities that people believed in; it was obviously a talent, because his wild, sometimes funny but always entertaining stories, regularly got him out of tough scrapes and unpleasant situations; but it was also a curse, because to keep peoples' attention and be taken seriously by the listeners, the stories he told had to get continually more engrossing and vivid over time.

That was exactly what had happened with Sylvia. She just didn't believe his stories anymore. When they first met, she was swept off her feet by Monte—an offbeat, charismatic character on the Hunter College campus, a longhaired communications major with a knack for communicating his own quirky and amusing perspectives on life. Sylvia herself had grown up in a very strait-laced neighborhood in Scarsdale, the daughter of a prominent corporate lawyer, for whom very little in the world was a joking matter. She had been trained to become a dutiful wife to a successful but boring professional man. A doctor or lawyer was what Sylvia's parents naturally had in mind. But Sylvia fell in love with Monte's stories about his own exploits and adventures in the hippest clubs and recording studios in Manhattan. It was not long before she fell in love with Monte himself. When he got a job in television, they got married. She longed to escape from her stifling suburban upbringing and in Monte, she felt she had found both a funny and charming man who would bring excitement into her life. But she had been wrong.

When it finally dawned on Sylvia that nothing much ever came out of Monte's stories about his own fame and fortune being just around the corner, she gradually grew cold and distant. Their marriage, like so many others, was not particularly happy, yet not terrible enough to detonate—with all emotional upheavals and lawyers' fees that involved. She was always telling him that he lived in a dream world. It became the major source of friction between them. Where Sylvia longed for travel, adventure and exciting experiences, Monte preferred to make them up.

And the problem with Monte's stories, Sylvia realized too late to make any difference, was that no matter how exciting or amusing they might be, they were not real and never would be.

For the past twenty years, Monte had been spinning dreams for the millions of people in America with basic cable and a desperate desire to escape from their own harsh daily realities. Lenin may have called religion the opiate of the masses, but in 21st century America, the opiate was Reality TV. It seemed to make them feel better—or at least get them to watch more and more Reality TV. And that was really all that mattered to the man who paid Monte's salary and made their comfortable life possible.

That man was Sam Brinkman, a titan of the television world. He was the founder, CEO, guru, sales manager, and public face of TrulyTV. But Sam was not an easy person to work for; he was especially merciless when it came to matters of the bottom line. In the industry, they didn't call him "Sam the Wizard" for nothing. He had, long ago, pretty much invented and discovered the profit potential of the Reality TV genre. Real Life Cops? That was him. Horror in the ER? Yup, him too. The bloodier the better. Sam had his finger on the zeitgeist of the moment. When the 2008 real estate crash came, he quickly pivoted from Home Hunting to Make Over Miracles. While others suffered in the financial crash, he made a fortune.

Why pay for actors, sets, and a full camera crew when one minicam could catch drunken family fights and wedding disasters? Brinkman's secret was that it was all about the story—and that's why he liked Monte so much. If you needed a quick idea for a pitch to network execs, Monte was the guy you wanted at the meeting. You never knew what he was going to come up with, what crazy ideas would tumble out of his mouth. But after the polite introductions and small talk was over, Monte would unfailingly offer the perfect pitch. Outrageous. Funny. And always with some kind of happy ending. The network execs ate it up. Monte was Brinkman's secret weapon. And over the years Brinkman became something of a father figure for him.

Things had been going pretty well at TrulyTV, Monte thought, at least until earlier that evening. He had received a quick text from Brinkman's assistant, informing him that the boss wanted to meet him early the next morning. Very early. That was so uncharacteristic of

Brinkman. He liked to start his days slowly—making phone calls and going through all the trade papers in the comfort of his own Upper East Side apartment—seldom appearing in the TrulyTV offices before eleven am. It was clear that something was up, but Monte had an amazing capacity to favor fantasy over worry. He quickly tapped out a return text that he would be at the meeting. Whatever it was about, he would deal with it tomorrow. In the meantime, the judges and excited audience of American Icon were waiting for him downstairs.

* * *

While Monte bathed in the stage lights and the admiration of the masses, Brinkman himself called three more times. The first time, Sylvia didn't bother to pick up Monte's cellphone. But when Brinkman called on the landline and his name popped up on caller ID, Sylvia panicked. He was not a man to be trifled with. Should she answer? Should she just let it ring? By the time she finally reached for the phone, the high-pitched beep sounded from the answering machine and Brinkman's impatient, gravelly voice could be heard telling Monte to call him right away.

So when Monte bounded up the carpeted stairs torn away from his American Icon visions of adulation, fame, and fortune by Sylvia's strident voice, he faced the usual tirade.

"Listen, Monte, I'm not your personal secretary," Sylvia said in a mixture of fear and exasperation. "Brinkman has already called three times. And when Brinkman calls, you've got to answer. And when he asks you to call him back, like he did an hour ago, you've got to call him back immediately. You can't afford to lose this job. You have no idea what shaky ground we are on financially."

"Shaky ground? You think 300k a year is shaky ground?" Monte innocently countered. "That's ten times more than my old man ever made."

Sylvia was right. Monte had absolutely no idea what their real financial situation was. She loved him; she was dependent on him. But she couldn't help marveling at the fact that someone who made his living as a Reality TV producer was so utterly divorced from reality. And so, while Monte dreamed up Reality TV ideas for Sam Brinkman,

Sylvia took care of the bills and household expenses. She watched over their IRAs and other investments. She prepared all the paperwork for their accountant every year at tax time. And she knew exactly how far $300,000 a year could go.

A few weeks before, Sylvia sat down in the kitchen breakfast nook and wrote out all the calculations on a yellow legal pad. Her neatly handwritten figures told a sobering story: First off, nearly half of Monte's salary went federal, New York State income taxes as well as Scarsdale's notoriously high real estate taxes. So, their after-tax income was about $150,000 a year. Then came the big-ticket items: mortgage payments, utilities, and insurance for their five-bedroom, five-bath house on posh Tryamon Drive in Scarsdale; college tuition for their two daughters, Sylvia's Range Rover lease payments, the payments for Monte's beloved Porsche, the monthly bills from landscaper and the pool company, the hefty credit card payments, food, clothing, restaurants, cable, internet, the cleaning lady and the dog walker and a dozen other things (not to mention yearly vacation trips to Cabo). Sylvia sat and stared at the bottom line for a long time. On $300,000 a year, they were barely keeping their heads above water. They were, like so many of the American families they mocked and looked down upon, actually just one paycheck from being out on the street.

"Oh Monte," Sylvia pleaded, her anger and frustration turning into a kind of emotional breakdown of suburban self-pity. "Please don't do this to us. We've built a nice life here in Scarsdale. Please don't fuck it up."

It would have been enough if Monte had shown some sign of understanding what Sylvia was saying. It would have been enough if he promised to be more attentive to his phone calls—and immediately gone off to another room to call Brinkman back. Of course, Sylvia knew that those simple gestures wouldn't have changed anything. Monte would have quickly returned to his world of opiate-like fantasies about the way things should be.

In fact, Monte had already come up with an irresistible story in which no apologies, no promises, no acts of contrition were needed. It was Monte's usual tale of rags to riches, of anonymity to fame and fortune, but this one was not for a TV show but for Sylvia and himself.

"Trust me, Sylvia," Monte reassured her. "I know what I'm doing.

I've got Brinkman wrapped around my little finger. The guy knows that he needs me. Without me, he's nothing. Just last week, I gave him pitches for five new series, and I understand that he's already got network commitments for three of them. Where else would he get talent like that from a simple line producer. Sure, he takes me out to lunch, and he acts like I'm his private idea machine. But does he offer me a piece of the company? When was the last time he offered me a raise? He keeps calling because he wants something from me. I give it to him without fail. I mean *Wife Swap Extreme* was all my idea and it's been running for three seasons. Do you have any idea what that means for TrulyTV and Brinkman's bank account? And what do I get from him? A fucking W-2 form at the end of the year. It's time I get some recognition, Sylvia. And tomorrow I'm gonna lay it on the line with him. He's got to give me what I deserve.

"And what is that?" Sylvia asked

Monte smiled. "Partnership. I'm sick and tired of being just an employee."

Sylvia stared into Monte's face and noticed how much it had changed. A few minutes before, he was a balding, overaged stoner banging on his cherished Stratocaster guitar. Now he had transformed himself into a skillful, intense pitchman, spinning a vivid tale about how everything would be ok. At moments like this, even Sylvia believed Monte's stories. In a strange way, she felt she had to. Her own future, and the futures of their two daughters, Lauren and Wendy, depended on   them.

CHAPTER 2
THE QUEST

Early the next morning, Monte pulled his sleek black Porsche into the underground lot beneath TrulyTV's offices on West 26th Street in the fashionable, if slightly rundown Chelsea neighborhood. As Monte pulled the car up to the Stop Here line, Manny the morning attendant came over to him right away.

"Hello Mister Levine. You're early today."

"Got a big meeting. Manny," he said, getting out of the car with the engine still running. Even though Sylvia dutifully paid steep monthly parking fee by check, Monte felt he still had to tip Manny $5 every day to take "special care" of his car.

"Don't bury it," he said. That was what Monte said every day as he slipped the cash into Manny's hand. It was a kind of ritual.

"Don't you worry Mister Levine; I'll take good care of your baby. How about a wash? She's looking kind of dirty."

Every day it would be something else: shampoo the interior carpets; polish the fancy rims; buff and clean the leather upholstery. That would be another $50 every day, but Monte couldn't help himself, despite Sylvia's constant warnings about money.

"Go for it," he said with a smile. He was so damned easy to play, and he knew it. But it was all part of the urban aristocracy game. Besides, he was about to take one of the biggest gambles of his career and he felt lucky.

"You got it Mister L."

As Monte walked out of the garage and into the Goldberg Building on 11th Avenue, home of TrulyTV, he was still polishing he mental script he had prepared for his meeting with Brinkman. When the elevator doors opened on the eleventh floor, Monte strode through the floor-to-ceiling glass entrance doors of the TrulyTV offices ready to make the pitch of his career. But Jane Hanson, Brinkman's executive assistant intercepted him before he even had a chance to drop off his coat and laptop on his desk. "He's already in there waiting to see you," she said. "You better go see him immediately." Then putting her hand to her mouth, she said in a theatrical whisper, "I think he's in a bad mood."

She led him into Brinkman's office. Brinkman was standing by the window on the phone with a client, but he waved Monte in and pointed to one of the two leather seats in front of the glass table that Brinkman used as a desk.

When the call was over, Brinkman put down the phone but did not take his seat. Brinkman puffed silently on his cigar.

"Let's take a walk," he said.

They took the elevator down to the ground floor and walked a bit up West 26th Street, not saying a word. When they got to Lou's Deli, they slid into a booth.

"Coffee," Sam said. "And a bagel with a schmear."

Monte waved off the waitress. "Just coffee for me."

Brinkman leaned across the formica tabletop. "Monte," he said, "We've got a problem. We've got a serious problem with your show *Wife Swap Extreme*. Let me give it to you straight: It's dying. And the bean counters over at Fox want to pull the plug."

"Dying?" This came as a total shock to Monte. Yes, sure there had been a slight dip in the ratings but Monte wasn't expecting the show to be cancelled. Plenty of hit shows have their ups and downs. But Brinkman would hear none of it. Sylvia was right. If *Wife Swap Extreme* were cancelled, that probably meant that he would be cancelled too.

Back in 2004, the original Wife Swap had been a big hit for ABC and every TV producer in America began to tinker with their own version of it. Monte had tried out a few pilots himself, hoping it could become the next national sensation. Gay Swap. Lesbian Swap. Polygamy Swap.

But none of those shows did well with focus groups. So Monte kept trying.

"How about Wife Swap meets The Bachelor," Monte had suggested to Brinkman at one pitch meeting. "We'll turn it into a contest. In each episode, the husband gets to pick a new "wife" from a lineup of contestants. There will be cat fights and nasty texts messages between all the wife candidates and one by one they'll be eliminated from the game. And at the end of the season, he gives a rose to the swapped wife he liked the best. Just think of it as Wife Swap meets the Bachelor meets Survivor."

Brinkman liked the idea and for the first two seasons, it had been a big hit, a big success. But now in the third season, the ratings were down. Monte knew that. But the real fact of the matter was that *Wife Swap Extreme* wasn't that extreme anymore.

"The show is tired," Brinkman moaned as he bit into his bagel, and continued to recount the bad news as he chewed. "Fox is talking about cancelling the order if we can't come up with something much more outrageous that will bring the 18-34 viewers back in."

"I'm not quite ready to fire you, Monte, but I'm close," Brinkman told him. "Fox is willing to give us one more shot, but you've got to make the show much edgier. Much edgier! You've got to bring the ratings way, way up or it's over.

He gave Monte one episode to make the big change. One episode.

And this one had to be a blockbuster. No half-way measures.

"OK," Monte countered, "and if I do give you—and the Fox bean counters—a smash hit, "I want something from you."

"Like what?"

"A full partnership in TrulyTV."

Brinkman put down his bagel and cream cheese and stared into Monte's eyes for a moment of uncomfortable silence.

"OK, it's a deal" he said finally. "But if it's a flop, you're history at this company."

Monte smiled broadly. Though Sylvia might have been terrified at the gamble he was taking, he saw it as a challenge, one he would rise to and win, no matter what it took.

All he needed now was a good story idea.

That night, back in Scarsdale, Monte had to muster every bit of his imagination to transform *Wife Swap Extreme* from a corny, soft-core gameshow into a hard-core hit. He had one shot and one shot to save not only his job, but also his heavily mortgaged house, his marriage, and his family. Admittedly, they were all living way beyond their means, like suburban royalty, but were actually just barely squeaking by. If either Sylvia or Monte had admitted this to themselves years before, they could have made some changes. But it was too late to do anything about it now.

Monte picked up the Stratocaster. This always helped him concentrate. Normally when he felt like this, he would turn the amp all the way up, but Sylvia would be on his case, and he had no time to get into another unpleasant conversation with her about money right now. He could hear her upstairs in the den, watching TV and talking on the phone with her friends. He couldn't quite make out her words, but she knew by the tone of her voice and her occasional shrieks of laughter what she was talking about with her friends. Sex. Adultery. BDSM. But those women had come a long way from gossiping about afternoon soap operas or even romantic movies. And when he thought about it, Monte realized that it all began with a new kind of entertainment that targeted explicit women's sexual fantasies.

Back in '86, Kim Basinger and Mickey Rourke had torrid sex in *9 1/2 Weeks*; in '91 Barbra Streisand was drawn into an adulterous affair with Nick Nolte in *Prince of Tides*. But those were just the beginning; the *Fifty Shades of Grey* made the others look tame. Sylvia and her friends snapped up the novels and were transfixed by the movies; that was almost all they talked about for months. *The Girl with the Dragon Tattoo* gave them a new focus for intimate fantasies, and the sequels only made them long for more. Netflix made them endlessly rewatchable. Upstairs, the bursts of laughter and joyous shrieks of Sylvia's conversation with her friends about vicarious sex and illicit affairs was disturbing Monte's brainstorming about the new, edgier version of his show.

So he plugged his expensive Bose noise cancelling headphones into the amp and slipped them onto his head. His guitar riffs were silent to everyone but him. He began to pick out the opening notes of Led

Zeppelin's classic The Immigrant Song, which they always played to start their live performances.

Suddenly, the idea came to him. The Immigrant Song was used in the title sequence of *The Girl with the Dragon Tattoo*. He was now playing that throbbing rhythm as he pounded the strings of his guitar. That was the beat—the same dangerous, erotic vibe that seduced Sylvia and her friends. Even their local gossip in Scarsdale had grown more hardcore over the years. When the rumor spread that Mortie Goldblum had been sleeping with his brother's wife, or when Annette Wilson had been caught with a young handyman in her pool house, Sylvia and her friends could not stop texting about it. Adultery, in all its explicit, erotic details, was an irresistible subject for them.

Bang! That was it. The idea came like a lightning bolt to him. The edgier idea he needed for *Wife Swap Extreme* was a real on-camera adulterous relationship revealed on TV!

Of course, he would have to find two couples, couples who understood that this was not about who cleaned the house, not even about who would win a stupid reality competition. They would have to agree to engage in an extramarital affair. They would become mass-market reality stars in front of millions of viewers. It would make TV history.

And he knew just the right person to help him find the perfect couple—and to help him save his job and career.

CHAPTER 3
KATHY

Kathy White had made a name for herself in the business as the "Queen of the Bookers," a combined talent scout and scheduler who could turn an otherwise tedious half hour of television into a national spectacle.

But that reputation didn't come quickly or easily. Born and raised by a single mother in the prosperous seaside town of Avalon, New Jersey, she was always determined to escape from the petty gossip, greed, and jealousies of Avalon to make a career in the dreamworld of TV. Graduating from Rutgers with a degree in communications, she, along with thousands of others, entered the race for a place in the media industry. And like so many of those starry-eyed diploma-toting communications grads, she had ambitions of being an on-camera reporter. But the competition was brutal. She applied to every TV station in New York and New Jersey, and later expanded her search to Pennsylvania, Maryland, Delaware, and eventually everywhere else.

She didn't give up, though, and by working every connection she could think of—including calculated flirting with the uber-rich New York TV execs who came down to Avalon with their wives and kids every summer—she eventually collected contacts and some helpful phone calls that led to a minimum wage job as a production secretary in the labyrinth of office cubicles in the midtown Manhattan network offices of America's most popular breakfast show, *Good Morning USA*.

With that first real job, Kathy had gotten her foot in the door, but not very far. The title of "Production Secretary" with a well-known show at a national network may sound impressive to friends and relatives, but it's really the lowest of the low TV jobs, pure entry level, and the work pretty much involved making coffee, running errands, and arranging the muffins and bagels on a platter for the guests as they waited in the green room for their three and a half minutes of fame. Despite the fact that she was a complete naïf in the TV business, an attractive young woman at the bottom rung of an operation run by frustrated and potentially lecherous middle-aged men long before "sexual harassment" was a ground for career-destroying lawsuits, Kathy achieved just what she wanted: amazing professional success.

Another fledgling production secretary would have learned to keep her mouth shut and her head down. Not Kathy. She was always on the lookout for an opening, an opportunity, to make herself not just an office decoration, but an invaluable asset to the show.

That opportunity came just a month or so into the job, when the news broke that the President of the United States had been sexually involved with an attractive White House intern less than half his age. That titillating news was the talk of the nation, and even though it was leaked by a rightwing media source with the intention of embarrassing the President, the TV networks became obsessed with identifying the intern and once identified getting her on the evening news for an interview.

It figures, was Kathy's reaction to the whole sordid affair. President or pool boy, men were all led around by their dicks. But when the name and picture of the intern was eventually revealed, she had an entirely different reaction: Marci Lewis had been her best friend at Rutgers; they had often double-dated. And Kathy had often consoled Marci when a boyfriend had suddenly dumped her. Marci admired Kathy—and always told her so—for her imperviousness to the treachery and dishonesty of men.

Kathy couldn't believe it. She had a direct connection and even the private cellphone number of the young woman that every news organization, every on-camera reporter in the country was desperately and unsuccessfully trying to interview. *Good Morning USA* was not, strictly speaking, a news show except for headlines and weather at the top of every hour. Most of the show's viewers had little interest in news anyway. They preferred the playful banter between the Ken and Barbie hosts, tips on how to prepare a Thanksgiving turkey, what makes a great Super Bowl party platter, how to lose weight without exercising, how to look great for only $29, and other TV fluff. But if the show could lasso the President's lover, Marci Lewis, for an exclusive interview, not only would the show become must-see TV for tens of millions of new viewers, but it would also guarantee a big bump in ratings over the other networks in the dog-eat-dog breakfast time slot.

Kathy tucked away her feelings of friendship and compassion for Marci and coldly did what was necessary to advance her career. She looked up Marci's contact card on her cellphone and tapped in Marci's number. Ring… Ring… Ring… Ring… Kathy was thinking about what kind of message she'd leave when suddenly Marci answered in a subdued and trembling voice.

"Oh my God! It's so great to hear from you, Kathy! You're finally someone I can trust. You have no idea what kind of living hell I'm going through…"

"Would you like to talk?" Kathy asked.

Marci had always trusted Kathy and she was now in a helpless and desperate situation where the press was camped out outside her DC condo and her parents' phone was ringing off the hook. Kathy agreed to take a day off to come down to Washington on Amtrak to offer sympathy to her old college friend. She spent a long teary afternoon with Marci, laughing about the old times and commiserating with her about the present bad times—and returning to New York with Marci's agreement that the only way to reclaim her self-respect and dispel all the ridicule and rumors was to tell her side of the story on *Good Morning USA*.

The next morning as she arrived for work at the *Good Morning USA* offices, Bob Rosser, the show's executive producer who had been relentless in tormenting her, caught her eye. She was still pretty much the staff laughingstock, and everyone assumed that it was only a matter of time before she quit.

"Hey White!" Rosser yelled. All eyes turned to see what torture he was about to inflict on her. Everyone needed a bit of entertainment today. Across the newsroom, the producers and reporters were nudging each other. "This should be good," some whispered between cubicles and across desks.

Kathy froze in her steps and glared at Rosser.

"How would you like to step inside my office and be my little Marci Lewis?" he taunted. A few people in the office tittered at the mention of what had by then become a national joke.

Kathy stood her ground. "What if I told you I can get the real Marci Lewis for an exclusive interview on this show?"

Rosser stared at her for a long time, not knowing what to believe. "Stop shitting me and get to work!" he finally said, dismissively concluding that Kathy's incredible claim was just a joke. She assured him that she was not shitting him. And she explained how she had done it. Rosser was shaken and suddenly realized what this would mean for the show.

So, the schedule for the next day was cleared, and a crew from Good Morning USA traveled down to Washington with Kathy to set up a satellite link. In the blink of an eye Kathy went from zero to hero. A morning show had snared an interview that the most prestigious evening news programs and the country's most prominent journalists had sought. Rosser was already running on-air promos: AN EXCLUSIVE TOMORROW MORNING ON GOOD MORNING USA with a picture of Marci Lewis juxtaposed against a background shot of the White House.

The interview went off without a hitch and the President's declarations of innocence took a major hit. Nielsen reported that 20 million people had tuned in for the 8am interview. The ratings for *Good Morning USA* went through the roof.

When Kathy returned to the offices later in the afternoon, Bob Rossner was all smiles, standing at the door of his corner office. "White, get in here," he said.

And so, Kathy White was invited into Bob Rosser's office, offered a seat at the same table where Rosser met only with his hosts, Dave and Jane and his senior producers. No more taunts, no more harassment. He closed the door, reached into his desk drawer and took out a bottle of Johnny Walker Black and two glasses.

He poured two inches of scotch into each glass and offered one to White.

"Congratulations on a great get," he said.

And from that moment forward, Kathy was no longer a production secretary but a senior booker for the show.

*   *   *

Good Morning USA had to fill three hours every day and booking just the right guests was the key to making the show work. Not everyone could do that, but in the months that followed the exclusive interview with the notorious Presidential intern Marci Lewis, Kathy White proved that she could.

In fact, Kathy White did it masterfully, show after show. She knew how not just to find the best doctors, authors, cooks, and offbeat personalities, but to cajole them into being on the shows for no money at all. Most did it, for the fame and publicity, and strangely, from a genuine desire to make Kathy White happy and show their gratitude for the attention she had lavished on them.

She hunted for interesting guests the way someone today would scroll through Tinder sizing up their pictures and descriptions of themselves. When she found someone she thought would make a great segment, for whatever reason, for whatever the show required, she contacted them, she flirted with them, she seduced them, she entered into a kind of relationship with them so that in the end, they were so flattered they wanted to please her, to make her happy by doing the best performance they could do.

Her seductive manipulation of would-be TV guests paid off. As her reputation rose, other networks flooded her with offers in the hope that her magic could work for them. Rosser was aware of the offers. To keep her with *Good Morning USA*, he kept raising her salary and expanding her perks until she was the best paid booker anywhere.

That didn't deter Sam Brinkman. He knew that great characters made great stories —on Reality TV no less than on breakfast time chat shows. So, it was after the article came out in Broadcasting and Cable and he read about Kathy's uncanny talent, that Brinkman set his sights on poaching Kathy White away from *Good Morning USA* and hiring her for TrulyTV.

He did it by giving her an offer she couldn't refuse. Not only did he offer to double her salary, but also gave her a cut on the profits on every show she cast. For Kathy this was a dream come true. No longer just an employee, she would be a partner. And in the two years that followed, she shared a fortune with Brinkman, brilliantly casting reality shows, game shows, hidden camera shows, home video shows, and death-defying stunt shows, all peopled with the most amazing characters she could find.

The money rolled in and Kathy achieved all that she had ever hoped for in the world of TV. But during the two years she worked with Brinkman she had also developed a dangerous addiction that she was completely unable to shake.

*   *   *

Despite, every promise she had made to herself, Kathy White had fallen in love.

She was in love with Monte Levine.

Deeply in love.

No one would have thought that a twenty-something rising star of the talk show-reality TV world would have surrendered her soul and very possibly her future to the balding, forty-something, head-in-the clouds producer of Wife Swap Extreme? They came from such different backgrounds—from different generations, in fact.   They behaved differently; they even dressed differently. Where he was casual, she was stylish. Where she was career-driven, he was a daydreamer, a spinner of seductive fantasies.   But they were so damn entertaining: whether he was chatting over drinks or pitching a new show, Monte's enthusiasm was infectious. He effortlessly created tales with happy endings and hilarious twists.

Maybe it was Monte's weirdly wonderful imagination that fascinated Kathy. She had had a long string of relationships, but her approach to romance had always been as calculating and clinical as her booking. In fact, until now, all of her prior relationships had, in fact, been a kind of booking.   A smile, a seduction, an appearance and then the show as over and time to move on. But with Monte it was different.   It was she who had lost control.   And, like a character in one of Monte's reality TV shows, she could never be sure exactly how the story would end.

And ironically for Kathy, she was well aware that this relationship was going nowhere if its plotline didn't dramatically change—soon...

"When are you going to leave her?" Kathy would ask Monte.

The answer was always the same, with a few minor variations. "I can't until the girls go to college," he had said. But when they both had left for college, Monte's delaying tactic changed. It had to wait until both girls graduated. After all, they kept coming home for the holidays. When Lauren finally graduated, well, Wendy was still at Boston University.

"Just tell me the truth," Kathy would say as they lay together in bed in a midtown hotel during one of their regular afternoon trysts. "I know you're never leaving her."

Monte would close his eyes and just wish this conversation would go away.

His relationship with Kathy was a bit like his private dream of being a superstar singer-songwriter; a bit more real perhaps, but it was primarily a comforting emotional escape with very little risk—or so he thought. Kathy had, over the years, and it had been nearly four years now, come to gradually accept that this relationship was not good for her. If she had the courage, she would leave Monte, leave him to his wife and make a normal life for herself. But she could not bring herself to do it.

Things could be worse, she would tell herself. Despite the secrecy, despite the endless excuses, there was something profoundly exhilarating that they shared. Oh, the sex was fine, though as time passed it gradually grew more routine and less exciting; it was rather the dreams that the two of them wove into stories, sharing of their feelings and private triumphs with a hilarious detail or bizarre twist. Despite their obvious differences, Kathy and Monte spoke a common language and shared a perfectly compatible pride in each other's creative talents. Neither of them had ever before experienced such a close connection with another person. The attraction between them was irresistible. Some days, when Kathy recounted a casting idea or a character she had recruited, Monte listened with a combination of pride and amazement. That kind of intimate attention was for Kathy like a drug- induced high, an adrenaline rush. For his part, Monte's tales to Kathy were not about the characters, they were about the audience. And his shows had an audience of millions, at least the good ones did.

When he came home to Sylvia after a particularly good day at work, overwhelmed with pride by what he had just shot or cut together in the editing suite, she did not care. He could not make her care. And the more he tried to share his excitement, the more annoyed she seemed to get.

"Please Monte," she would say, "Stop. Enough with the fucking television. Can't you just leave it at the office?"

With Kathy, it was totally different. She listened with the same mix of pride and admiration that Monte shared with her. She was always ready to talk about the amazing Hells Angels biker she had found for *Wife Swap Extreme*, and Monte was always ready to describe what crazy things happened at yesterday's shoot—and how the viewers would love it. For both of them, the sex was just a bit of carnal foreplay. The real climax came when they shared stories of the creative triumphs, however fleeting, that each of them had achieved—and the crazy dreams about happiness-right-around-the-corner that both of them shared.

No, none of the men that Kathy had ever really understood her. Monte did. And so Kathy White was both attracted and trapped.

* * *

Over lunch at a trendy new cafe in midtown Manhattan, Monte shared a painful admission with Kathy that Brinkman had not revealed to her. Monte painfully confessed that Wife Swap Extreme was in deep shit, and so was he.

"I need to take this thing to the next level," Monte told her. "What I am thinking is something like *Indecent Proposal* for reality TV."

"That's a great name!" said Kathy.

Monte frowned. "It's already taken. *Indecent Proposal* was a movie that came out in 1993."

"It was?" said Kathy. "Never heard of it. Who was in it?"

"Robert Redford and Demi Moore."

"Who?" asked Kathy. There were times when their age difference was a problem.

"Robert Redford. You know, that old guy who does the Sundance Film Festival. Woody Harrelson was in it too. The guy from *Cheers*."

Kathy shrugged her shoulders. She was a millennial after all. "Never heard of them."

"It doesn't matter," Monte continued. "In the movie, Harrelson is a failed architect with a big dream, and he goes with his beautiful wife Demi Moore to Vegas hoping to bet his way into making enough money to build his dream house. But when they get to Vegas they meet Robert Redford, who is a millionaire, and he offers Woody and Demi a million dollars if he could sleep with Demi for one night."

Kathy took it all in. "Wow! What a fucking great concept for a Reality TV series. It's like the *Who Wants To Be A Millionaire* of adultery. Now THAT would rate."

"That's what I'm thinking," said Monte. "Kind of a proven concept. But in the show I'm thinking of, the participants only get the million-dollar prize if they consummate the act on camera. It probably won't happen all the time. And, we pay the million out over twenty years so we really just amortize the cost. It's actually not that expensive. And I even think we can probably get away with a hundred grand. That should be enough. How's this for a title: Wife Swap Extreme: Adultery Edition."

Kathy thought for a minute. "Yep, adultery is certainly a proven concept." She could see an opportunity here both to make a boatload of money as a part owner of TrulyTV and to make Monte happy, maybe happy enough to leave his wife.

"I get it," she said. "Let me get to work."

* * *

It didn't take long. A week later, she walked into Monte's office with her iPad.

"Sit down," she ordered Monte. "We've got some decisions to make." She put the iPad in front of him.

"There are two elements to this show. The married couple and the home wrecker."

"Prospective home wrecker," Monte cautioned.

She smiled and proceeded to present Monte with the digital folders with photos and info on the possible participants she had identified.

"Let's start with the happily, until now, married, couple," she said, thumbing through photos on her iPad. She already knew who she wanted, but she had to give Monte at least the appearance of participating in the choices.

"Tom and Susan Millstone from Tulsa Oklahoma. He's an architect, just like in the movie, and she's an elementary school teacher. Both in their early 30s."

"Very good looking," Monte said. "Could work."

Kathy rolled her eyes. "They're all good looking, no one wants to watch ugly people have sex. And they all know the deal. I could have had a million people sign up for this thing, but we need something different here, something with a twist." She kept scrolling through the photos, barely giving Monte a chance to settle on one until she got to her own choice.

"Now, here we are," she said. "Danny and Krystal Locovita. She's 28 and a real stunner, as you can see. Former Miss Topless New Jersey. He claims to be 42, but I think he's probably closer to 62."

Monte examined the photos. "She's a winner, but he's fat and balding."

Kathy smiled. "Exactly! He's known as the Tire King of Monmouth County in Jersey. Trophy wife. Number 3. He's loaded and she's a gold digger. It's perfect. Also, he's really in love with his wife. Told me that about a million times. She doesn't work but she really wants to be a Reality TV star, which she'll do almost anything to become."

"But he's so short, fat, and ugly," Monte said.

"And that's what makes him so perfect," Kathy replied.

"I thought you know all about audiences," Kathy continued, "Because guys who watch this show will think to themselves, if he can have a hot young wife like that, maybe I could too. It's guaranteed to make them feel better about themselves, if only in their fantasies."

Monte could see once again why they called Kathy the Queen of the Bookers.

"And this couple, they're cool with the concept?"

She's a *Real Housewives* addict. In fact, I nearly cast her for it a few years ago. That's how I know her. She'll do anything to be on TV."

"And the husband?"

"He is madly in love with his wife. Madly. Insanely. And he'll do anything she wants to make her happy, and this is what she wants."

23

"And what about our candidate for homewrecker?"

Kathy brought up his picture.

"Meet Tommy Noonan. Davenport Iowa's most popular fireman. 32 years old, incredibly nice guy, and take a look at that body."

Noonan was stripped to the waist as Mr. February on the Davenport Fire Department's fundraiser beefcake calendar.

Monte was delighted.

He reached out and hugged Kathy. "What do you say we go over to our   favorite   hotel   and   celebrate?

CHAPTER 4
THE TIRE KING

Danny Locovita loved his wife. Or at least he loved the idea of having such a hot piece of ass as his wife. It made him feel better about himself and was a clear demonstration of his success and virility to the world at large.

That would be his third wife, Krystal.

Tall, bleached-blonde and beautiful in a siliconed kind of way, she was young enough to have been his daughter, if he had let his daughter work at the Cavern of Love in Hoboken, the strip club that he owned, as one of his many "investments" throughout New Jersey. The Cavern was where he had first laid eyes on her through the smoke-filled glare of the pink spotlight as she snaked her beautiful body around a silver stripper pole. She was only 18 and he was sixty and still married to the soon to be former Mrs. Locovita, who now lived in a condo in Parsippany.

Danny and Krystal did not live in a condo. They lived in a mega mansion built on the largest lot on Royal Way in Summit, New Jersey, an enclave of the very rich and the very successful. Danny was both. He called it The Castle. King Danny's Castle. And it was like a castle. Big. Bigger than life.

Tonight, the magnificently cut and manicured green lawn behind the Castle would be the scene of a big celebration. The Hoboken chapter of the Knights of Columbus had chosen him as New Jersey Businessman of the Year. He and Krystal had invited 300 couples to witness his coronation as an honored and respected entrepreneur.

White coated waiters and waitresses bustled in and out of the mansion's oversized kitchen delivering drinks and hors d'oeuvres to the arriving guests. A large stage had been set up on the patio. Dozens of tables with flickering candle globes and enormous flower arrangements filled the lawn. Inflatable lighted crowns bobbed in the Olympic sized pool; bartenders popped open champagne bottles and mixed elaborate cocktails to slake the thirst of anyone who wanted more. Mountains of shrimp, lobster tails, and caviar were arranged around towering ice sculptures of the Coliseum, the Leaning Tower of Pisa, St. Peter's Basilica, and near life-sized ice sculptures of Danny and Krystal themselves.

When the sun had set and the band started to play, the waiters and waitresses politely ushered the guests to their tables. Spotlights were flipped on to bathe the stage in brilliant illumination as a procession of priests, knights, and other New Jersey dignitaries solemnly mounted the platform and took their seats. And when Danny and Krystal appeared to take their own places beside the rostrum, the assembled crowd erupted in cheers.

They rose to their feet almost in unison, glasses raised high, and chanted "Long Live the King! Long Live the King!"

"I love you guys, each and every one of you," Danny croaked through his tears. Krystal quickly rose from her place at the head table on the dais and shimmied in her tight dress toward her husband to give him a kiss and big hug.

Danny beamed with pride as they embraced, and he turned back to the mic. "How about a big hand for my lovely wife who I love more than anything else in the world." The crowd enthusiastically obliged. "I do it all for you baby. All for you," he said, staring intently in her heavily mascaraed and long, fake-lashed eyes, loud enough so everyone could hear.

The audience rose to their feet for a loud standing ovation. They were his people, his loyal subjects, his vassals, his army. Among them were the owners of the more than 200 King Danny Tire franchises, the biggest and most successful auto franchise in the state.

The Tire King of New Jersey, like any king, was personally

responsible for the lives of his subjects; their businesses, their mortgages, their wives, their children, their homes and their very lives. King Danny had made it all possible, by making his tire franchises convenient covers for a wide range of activities, some legal, some ethical, and others not so much. Before Danny came along, most of them had been lowly tire salesmen working for the major chains like Bridgestone or Firestone, earning a base salary of $24,000 a year, plus commissions. They were in dead end jobs, with dead end careers, dead end lives, and they knew it. But Danny showed them a different way. He taught them a new way to do business and had lifted them up and made them the successes they were today.

"I would take a bullet for that guy," Sammy Ioria, one of Danny's most successful franchisees told the reporter for the Newark Star-Ledger who was there to cover the festivities.

"He's a total business genius," added Bobby Feldman, the franchisee who covered Camden County. "If you're loyal to Danny, he's loyal to you."

*　*　*

Danny was what you would call a people person if you weren't too choosy about the people you did business with. Organized crime and the tire business proved to be a perfect match. From his days as an enforcer, he knew all the right people who ran trucking companies, taxi garages, and solid waste disposal outfits—and they knew him. He also knew all the wrong people who could pay a visit to tire factory managers and make them offers they couldn't refuse.

He knew what all of those people needed—kickbacks, bribes, drugs, or "special friends in high places"—and he always made sure he delivered. Once he delivered, they owed him, and he knew how to extract a debt. But he always made sure that if he made money selling factory-reject tires called "blems" at inflated prices, all his people got to wet their beaks too. And word of his success, Danny's uncanny ability to turn a buck and give you fifty cents for your help spread far and wide.

Soon, every taxi not just in Jersey but also in Manhattan was crossing over the Hudson to have their tires changed at Danny's. Then, rather inexplicably, he got the contracts for city buses in Jersey City, in Hoboken, and then in Trenton, the state capital that the big companies like Firestone and Goodrich had held for years. Danny knew how to wheel and deal, and when that didn't work, he knew how to threaten. But sometimes even that was not always enough. Taxi drivers or bus companies that did not frequent a King Danny's often mysteriously found themselves in need of new tires in the middle of the night, or the drivers arriving early in the morning to a school bus depot might suddenly find that quite a few of their yellow buses had flats.

"You gotta do what you gotta do," Danny would say. And he did. And so did his faithful men.

*   *   *

Only two of the people in attendance at the party that night were new to the group. Monte Levine and Kathy White sat next to each other, trying but not always succeeding to make polite small talk with the strange collection of couples at Table #3. The fact that they were seated there was a high honor, even though they may not have realized it at the time. The closer you were to Table #1 on the dais, the longer you had known Danny, the more important you were to him and Krystal, or the more franchises you owned.

"This is a hell of a party," Kathy said as she turned to one of the other guests at the table, "it must have cost a fortune. "Are Danny's parties always like this?"

Marilyn O'Shea, her hair in a lacquered beehive piled high and topped by a sparkly tiara, her long fingernails manicured and intricately painted, her face the product of the best plastic surgeons in New Jersey, nodded her head emphatically, as she filled herself another crystal flute of Dom.

"Oh yeah. Every one of them. Danny is the best!"

"How do you know Danny?" Kathy asked.

She poked the fat balding man seated next to her.

"Freddy's got four of Danny's franchises. Parsippany, Paramus, The Oranges and Tom's River."

Freddy was trying to focus on his wife as she spoke. His head swayed drunkenly as he tried to agree. He raised his oversized tumbler of scotch, spilling some as he leaned toward Kathy and Monte. "Here's to King Danny. May he live forever! Long live the King!" he slurred.

Just then all the chit-chat at the table stopped abruptly and Kathy felt a gentle tap on her back. Throughout the meal, Krystal had kept fluttering down to table #3, to make sure that Kathy and Monte were enjoying themselves. She motioned to a passing waiter and gave him stern instructions "Make sure you give my friends here anything they ask for and for God's sake keep their glasses filled!"

For Krystal, no one else on the lawn that night mattered, except of course, Danny. When she scanned the assembled guests, with their laughing, drunken faces, she thought to herself what losers they are. Especially the men. They were the kinds of losers, weaklings and gavones who would reach up and tuck dollar bills into her G-string at the Cavern of Love, thinking that they were bigshots. "Shmucks on wheels" she would call them, even though Danny didn't like it whenever she did. They were his friends, the Tire King's royal court, his collection of half the tire salesmen in New Jersey, all of whom owed Danny their success and their livelihoods. He could count on them to do anything for him, but to Krystal they were just low-rent schlubs. Tonight, there were only two guests that mattered to Krystal, guests from Manhattan—not New Jersey. TV people! Real live TV people.

And they were here to make her lifelong dream come true. She was going to be a national celebrity. She could feel it in her bones. Her moment had come at long last, and Danny had made it all possible.

Since the first time she had seen The Real Housewives of Orange County on Bravo, she knew that that was what she wanted to be. A TV Reality Star! She could do it. She saw how they walked, how they talked, how they dressed, how they did their hair. They were bigger than movie stars. That was what she wanted more than anything else, and here, right now, right in her own house, were the two people who could make it happen.

* * *

The party wound down around 2AM, and Kathy appeared again at Table #3, insisting that she personally accompany Kathy and Monte to their room.

As Krystal led them up the thickly carpeted stairs, she noticed for the first time that Monte wore a wedding ring, but Kathy did not. Monte said a polite goodnight, thanked Krystal again for her hospitality, and walked into the room.

As soon as Krystal left, they closed the door and, trying to stifle their giggles, tumbled onto the huge king-size-plus bed.

"You are a fucking genius," Monte said to Kathy with a wide grin. "A genius! This show is gonna be a big hit. Bigger than anyone can imagine."

"I love you," he said.

"Love you too."

Kathy rose to undress.

"I have something I've been meaning to tell you, Kathy."

Kathy spun around and faced Monte. He didn't usually make big announcements, but the emotional catch in his voice seemed to suggest that this would be one.

"I've decided to leave Sylvia."

Kathy was dumbstruck. "Why now? What happened?"

"This show," Monte said without any hesitation. "I just know that this fucking reality show we've dreamed up together is going to change both our lives."

* * *

Phil Eagleburger, President of Fox Entertainment loved the concept but hated the title.

"*Fuck Wife Swap Extreme*. It's already damaged goods" Eagleburger had said over lunch with Brinkman and Monte to finalize the deal. "Let's call it *Thou Shalt Not*. As in, thou shalt not commit adultery."

Monte actually loved this new title. It was what every producer in the country dreamed of: a whole new reality TV franchise. Thou shalt not commit adultery. That could be followed by a spin off, like, thou shalt not steal, then thou shalt not bear false witness…

"Or thou shalt not kill," Eagleburger said over lunch, his mouth filled with the $129 lobster salad at The Lobster Club in Manhattan.

"Thou shalt not make graven images," Brinkman quickly chimed in.

Eagleburger immediately got it. "False Gods! Bring it on baby!!!"

"And honor thy mother and father. I LOVE it!"

In a country that talked so much religion and wallowed in so much sin, there was no way that a reality show about violating the Ten Commandments could lose. Visions of millions swam before their eyes. Monte realized that he would be able to re-negotiate his deal with Brinkman when this hit the air.

The concept for the pilot was dead simple. It would all be shot at the Tire King's castle in Jersey. Danny would be Danny, with his friends, his unbelievable cars, his tire business. He just had to do what he always did. The crew would follow him all day long. Danny loved the idea. He would get to be the King in primetime, not just paid thirty-second spots on local cable. He could promote his tire business to a massive national audience. It was, he figured, ten million dollars' worth of free advertising, maybe more. With a national TV show like this he could take the franchise across the country and would cost him absolutely nothing. In fact, if Krystal played ball, he would earn a quick hundred thousand. What a deal!

As for Krystal, all she had to do was do what she did every day, which was next to nothing. She could lounge by the pool. She could lounge in the spa. She could have her girlfriends over, which they were all delighted and excited to do. The only rule was she could not leave the house, which was fine with her. But she and her friends could do as much shopping as they liked. The show had arranged for Gucci, Prada, Henri Bendel and a few other selects to send over options for her to try on.

But the foundation of the show, of course was, Adultery.

The star of the show was going to be Tommy Noonan, the hunky Iowa fireman. He was going to come to work at the Castle as the pool attendant. Of course, like all reality shows, it was entirely scripted, 100% fake.

In the beginning, when Kathy and Monte first sat down with Danny and Krystal to lay out the pilot and explain how it would work, Krystal was more than a bit confused.

"You mean it's really all fake?"

"Let's not say fake," Kathy had said. "Let's say directed. Yes, it's all directed. Nothing happens by accident."

Danny could only smile.

31

"What the fuck is not fake in the world baby? Like your boobs…"

"It's television, Krystal," Kathy said. "We can make all fantasies come true…."

"If we just let things happen on their own, well, nothing might happen. And the viewers will be disappointed."

Krystal suddenly identified with the Reality TV viewers, of which she was one of the most loyal ones. "Oh, I can make things happen," she said.

"I bet you can baby," Danny interjected.

"But we have a tight production schedule, so we have to shoot the whole show in just three days—and make it look like it took weeks. So there'll be lots of costume changes…"

At the mention of this, Krystal perked up immediately, already dreaming of the many sexy outfits she could wear.

"No shit. Just three days?" asked Danny.

"That's it. That's all it takes," Monte replied.

Danny smiled. This deal was looking better and better all the time.

The plan was pretty simple. The seduction would take place in the jacuzzi on the third day of the shoot, after a long buildup of sexual tension between Krystal and Tommy, with Danny pretending not to notice. It was all in the script.

"Aren't you worried about your wife being seduced by a fireman?" Monte had asked Danny over a few drinks.

Danny laughed.

"Are you kidding me? Krystal? She was a stripper when I met her. She was Queen of the Lap Dance before she was ever Queen of the Castle. She knows how to play a mark. She once got ten grand out of some sap just for lap dances. Trust me, she'll be in total control the whole time, and she'll give you TV guys exactly what you want. Don't worry about my reputation, I'll be cheering her on. She's always wanted to be a TV star—and besides she'll be right back in my bed when it's over, giving me the best blowjob of my life. Don't worry. We're gonna make sure this show is a number one hit. We both want it to succeed."

Danny took out a large cigar, a Cuban Monte Cristo and casually snipped off the end.

"Want one?" he asked Monte, who waved a pass as Danny lit up.

"Look, I wasn't born yesterday. I know exactly what you people are looking for. And lemme tell you something, so does Krystal. She and I are a team. We're both in this for the money, and I am not talking about your chickenshit hundred grand, nothing personal."

At this, Danny took a long drag on his cigar and smiled.

"Well, Monte, I gotta tell you, based strictly on my back of the envelope calculations, if this show is a big hit, it could make for Krystal and me somewhere in the neighborhood of $10 million, based on my ability to use your show to expand my tire franchise nationally. Nationally."

"So what's a little nookie for ten million, right Monte?"

And at this, Danny reached over and smacked Monte on the back. His thick hairy hand should have conveyed a warning to Monte to be careful. It was a lot harder than a friendly smack.But Monte, being Monte, was too busy dreaming of his new life with Kathy and his promised part-ownership at TrulyTV that he didn't stop to realize the consequences of the deal with the devil that he and Kathy had just made. And as happens so often in life, the devil was standing right in front of him, but Monte never saw it until it was too late.

CHAPTER 5
BETRAYAL

Monte was at home with Sylvia when the phone rang. It was Brinkman.

"They're dancing in the halls!" Brinkman yelled into the phone.

"Fox loved the pilot. They absolutely fucking love it."

"We've hit the mother lode," Brinkman screamed into the receiver. "They are ordering a full season." Thirteen shows at $750,000 per episode. In an instant, nearly ten million dollars slid across the green velvet into the hands of TrulyTV. But that was only the beginning, Brickman said. "They're going to do a ten million dollar spend on advertising and promotion. Can you fucking believe that?"

"Plus, they want to lock us up for five years and they want all international, digital and product rights." Product rights meant toys, books, games, online junk. This deal could be worth more than $100 million before it was over.

DING DING DING

It was a once in a lifetime moment for Monte, the thing he had been waiting for his entire life. "And that deal we discussed, you remember?" Monte asked.

"Do I remember?" Brinkman snapped back sarcastically. "What am I, some kind of schlemiel? A deal is a deal, and a hit is a hit. I'll have the papers drawn up to make you a full partner just as soon is the deal is finalized and the first episode airs."

Monte cupped the phone in his hand, turned to Sylvia and said, "Buy the house in the Hamptons."

This had been Sylvia's dream come true. Maybe it would make the divorce a bit easier, Monte thought to himself.

A rising tide lifts all boats, but this was more than a rising tide, this was a tsunami. A massive flood of money that was going to change everyone's fortunes forever.

The pilot was set to air on Thursday, at 9 PM on premium cable. Total prime time. The primest of prime time. It was heavily promoted on network TV and on all the social networks. It was slated to follow the season finale of *The Naked Bachelorette*, which was projected to have one of the biggest audiences in cable history, and that would provide it with a gigantic lead-in audience, projected to be in the millions. Fox itself had now pushed all its own chips to the center of the table, betting everything on Thou Shalt Not.

And why not?

It was a ground-breaking show in every way.

The actual show had far surpassed even what Monte and Kathy had hoped for. Krystal had played the seductress perfectly and Tommy looked great around the pool and in the house, shirtless with his broad shoulders and tight six-pack abs. Krystal had been in total control throughout the whole production, turning cold and uncaring to Tommy when the camera stopped shooting, and Tommy took it in stride, wandering off to sit down and play video games or scroll through porn sites on his phone. But in the final scene something very strange happened.

Krystal, wearing a tiny string bikini, was in the hot tub with Tommy and they were supposed to simulate heavy petting and groping as if to suggest they were about to have sex. But something came over her. Something came over both of them. The breathing got progressively heavier, their tongues intertwined, and Tommy began to fondle Krystal's large silicone-filled breasts. She obligingly slipped off her bikini top and reached down between Tommy's legs. Pretty soon they were actually fucking on camera – hot, passionate, real. Splashing, gyrating, and moaning, they were lost in their own unlocked desires.

The scene was as shocking as it was unexpected. As Krystal and Tommy made love in the hot tub, the cameraman had turned to Monte with a questioning look. This was not in the script, should he keep shooting? Monte knew TV gold when he saw it and signaled the cameraman to keep rolling. Pornography met Reality TV at that moment. A new standard for reality television was set.

But if that was not enough, the day after filming wrapped, Krystal had announced to Danny that she was leaving him, packing up and moving back to Iowa with Tommy the hunky fireman. That also was not in the script. She was in love, Krystal told Danny. Really in love for the first time in her life. She was filing for divorce. Monte and the cameraman caught that moment too.

*   *   *

When they saw the first rough cut of the *Thou Shalt Not* pilot, Fox's publicity department could not believe their luck. They had already advertised the crap out of what they were now calling The Season Opener of the most exciting new series to ever be seen on no-holds-barred cable TV. They were now also busy calling the tabloids, calling in their debts for the celebrity gossip they had leaked over the years. Monte, Kathy, and Brinkman did the same, urging the tabs to go all out with stories of the show's passion, adultery, and divorce. Reality TV finally met reality.

For their part, the tabloids were delighted, more than happy to piggyback on what was clearly going to be a mega hit. Their tacky covers with photoshopped pictures of the triangle of Krystal, Danny, and Tommy, flew off the supermarket checkout line racks. The NY Post even got into the fun with a full front-page picture of a scowling Danny and the Post's trademark punny headline: "New Jersey's Flat Tire King."

The Enquirer found photos of Danny, apparently obtained for a large fee paid to Krystal, on the beach at the Jersey shore with a bathing suit a few sizes too small and a spare tire of blubber overhanging his crotch. Tommy, on the other hand, looked like Adonis lying on a lounge chair with Krystal sitting cozily next to him by the side of the Castle's pool. Tommy and Krystal looked like the perfect sexy couple. Danny came across as an old rich guy who had no business—except for his filthy money—for being with such a beautiful girl.

The Enquirer had a still photo of the Love Birds entwined in the hot tub, provided by Truly TV. "Hot Hot Hot Tub" ran the headline. The story went on to speculate how much alimony Krystal could wrangle out of Danny, the Tire King.

This was the kind of free advertising that TV executives dreamed of, and they were just getting started. Only a few hours later, Oprah called. Oprah herself. Direct to Monte. She wanted to book Krystal, Tommy, and Danny on her show. Monte swore he would get them. No sooner had Oprah hung up than Ellen and Dr. Phil called with the same request.

This was going to be the biggest thing Monte had ever been involved in.

Ever.

Monte's cellphone did not stop ringing all day. One call after another. Radio talk shows wanted them on the air. Literary Book agents wanted them for a tell-all. Talent agents wanted to book them for made-for-TV movies. Other TV production companies wanted to hire Monte away from Brinkman. It was a whole new world for Monte, a story too good to be true., but it was. Monte had once again turned fantasy into reality.

Then, at 4:12 PM, Monte's phone rang again.

This time it wasn't a reporter or a TV show or a tabloid or an agent. It was Danny.

And Danny was pissed.

Really pissed.

This was not the Danny that Monte had seen before. Scheming Danny. Agreeable Danny. This was scary Danny. Very scary Danny.

Monte had barely said hello when Danny let him have it.

"Listen to me you little motherfucker. You're gonna make this stop right now. Do you hear me? You're gonna make this stop or you're gonna be sorry that you were ever born. You have no idea how much pain I can inflict."

Danny wanted the stories killed now. Now! He wanted the tabloids to stop. He was being made a laughingstock not just all over New Jersey but all across America. He had never been so angry in his life. Krystal had betrayed him, that little bitch, after all he had given her. He told Monte plain and simple that he wanted the show killed. Dead. Dead.

Do you know what dead means you little fuck? I want this thing dead. Now."

He not only wanted the tabloid stories killed, he wanted the show killed. He wanted it never to air, never to see the light of day.

"No one should ever see that fucking travesty, do you hear me? No one!"

Monte tried to explain to Danny, to talk him down a bit, that he, Monte, had no control over whether the show aired or not. He didn't own it. The Fox network owned it. Danny would have to talk to them.

"Gimme their fucking number," Danny demanded.

Monte did, then hung up. He silently replayed the angry conversation with Danny in his mind and his heart started to beat faster. "I have to sit down," he told Sylvia.

"Exciting, huh?" she said

He looked at her.

"You have no idea. That was just Danny Locavita threatening to whack me," Monte said with an uncomfortably forced smile. "All in a day's work when you have a monster hit on Reality TV, I guess."

Sylvia looked at him and visibly paled.

Monte tried his best to be reassuring. "Oh I'm sure he's just being dramatic, He's upset. Believe me I've dealt with this kind of reaction a thousand times."

Monte focused on Sylvia. He made eye contact and saw the fear in her eyes. For perhaps the first time in Monte's life, reality was starting to intrude on a life spun largely of fantasy and storytelling.

"He's not kidding, Monte," Sylvia said. "I heard the sound of his voice screaming you on the phone. That's not 'disgruntled' in my book. This guy is a gangster—a real gangster—the tire stuff is all a big front."

Sylvia glared at him.

"Oh Monte, what the fuck have you done to us?" She took a few steps around the kitchen, thinking deeply, then she said, "Monte, listen. If he calls back, record the call. On your phone. Record it."

Monte shrugged. Maybe, just maybe, that might be a good idea.

It did not take long for the phone to ring again. Monte recognized Danny's number on the screen and he pressed the "record" button. His heart beating wildly, he answered.

"Hi Danny," he said.

"They told me I can go fuck myself," Danny wasn't yelling now. His voice was deep, slow, and very, very serious.

"What did they say exactly?" Monte asked. He was playing at being Danny's friend now, trying to calm him down. He had done this God knows how many times for Wife Swap Extreme. Husbands could get upset, but Monte had always been pretty good at talking them down.

"They said that I had signed the release you gave me and now it was theirs. I could go and fuck myself for all they cared. That release was watertight."

"Well, we can always seek legal advice," said Monte, with mock confidence, hoping to seem like Danny's ally in this mess. But he knew that there was nothing that could be done to get Danny out of a hole that was sealed like a cement grave.

There was a long pause.

Then, Danny spoke very slowly.

"Listen to me you little Jew piece of shit. You gave me the fucking release to sign. This is on your head. Either you get this fucking show pulled in 24 hours or I am going to kill you. Did you get that? I have people who will break your legs, cut off your balls, and then kill you. Believe me I have given my crew the orders to do just that many, many times before. Are you ready to die, you fucker?"

And with that, Danny hung up the phone.

*　*　*

Monte poured himself a drink, went upstairs and plugged in the Stratocaster. Fuck Danny, he thought to himself. Fucking Tire King of New Jersey. Big fucking deal. Sylvia was just being hysterical. Thou Shalt Not was going to earn Monte millions, freedom to marry Kathy, and a piece of TrulyTV. Sylvia would get her house in the Hamptons, which, he increasingly acme to think, was what she most cared about. As for Danny, he would get over it. Big-talkers like him always did.

The next morning, Monte was confident and cheerful when he came down for breakfast. Sylvia was up early. "I think you should call that real estate agent out in the Hamptons," he told her. "We're going to live a different life from now on."

"But what about the gangster?" Sylvia asked.

"Oh, he's not a real gangster," Monte replied. "A little shady maybe but definitely not dangerous. I'm going to let the lawyers handle if he hassles me again. Anyway, thanks to you, I've got him on tape threatening to kill me. I bet our lawyers can scare the crap out of him with that. Besides, I have a big day ahead of me, talking up the show on the Breakfast Club, on Howard Stern, Dave and Chuck the Freak out in Detroit, and Heidi and Frank for morning drive time out in LA.

As Sylvia answered a call from the realtor out in the Hamptons, Monte picked up his briefcase and went into the garage. Funny, he thought, the garage door was open. He would have to be more careful about that. He got into his Porsche and pulled out into the street. He loved the purr of the engine, the thump of pure power. He leaned back in the leather seat and slipped into first. He was going to drive down to the TruTV offices in Chelsea, but first he would pick up Kathy at her condo in White Plains. He had been thinking about her all night. His life was going to change forever and he had finally made the decision she had been waiting for.

Kathy was waiting outside her condo, slid into the Porsche and gave Monte a big kiss.

"We did it," she said, "We did it as a team." She smiled broadly and tapped her watch. "We better get moving or we'll be late for the first interview."

As he shifted into first gear and headed for the Bronx River Parkway that would take them to Manhattan, Monte imagined to himself what his new life with Kathy would be like. Of course, the divorce settlement would be painful and disruptive, but money would now not be a big issue if the revenue projections for Thou Shalt Not panned out. He would pay Sylvia a generous alimony, let her have the house in Scarsdale and even another one in the Hamptons. And he could definitely benefit from some downsizing. He'd move into Kathy's two-bedroom condo—at least at first.

As usual, he was spinning a new story for himself, this one a carefully scripted happily-ever-after tale about him, Kathy, and Truly TV. Here was a woman—now sitting right next to him in the front seat of his Porsche—who understood him, who appreciated his achievements in the TV business, who understood the value of a 17 rating and a 29 share. It made a great story, a great made-for-TV movie even. This was all going to work out just fine. Another happy ending. Another great Monte Levine production, he told himself as they drove along.

Kathy leaned over and kissed Monte's cheek gently as they reached the entrance ramp of the Parkway. Nothing could have made her happier than to be with Monte this morning. celebrating their love and their shared success. For her as well, for the first time perhaps, her life seemed complete.

When they reached I-87 and merged into the Manhattan-bound traffic, Monte gently put his foot on the gas. There was the usual morning truck traffic, but he was driving his Porsche and felt confident with his lover by his side. As he began to weave among the eighteen-wheelers, he felt a slight ping, heard a pop on the passenger side. It was unusual; they both heard it and looked at each other.

Maybe they hit something. There was always plenty of litter on the road the closer they got to New York. And the car seemed to be running fine. These Porsches were so delicate, always some problem. He would take it into the Porsche dealership on 11th Avenue this afternoon. It cost $500 just to walk in the door, but now, who cared?

As they got closer to the George Washington Bridge and the junction with Cross Bronx Expressway, the traffic began to slow down and jam up. Monte suddenly saw the red taillights of the huge trailer truck he was following dangerously closely and slammed on the brakes. As soon as he did, there was a large boom on the car's front right side and then the terrifying sound of metal screeching along the pavement as Monte lost complete control of the car.

The front right wheel separated entirely from the car and rolled down the highway on its own.

The Porsche careened forward. It all happened very fast after that.

Monte saw the back of the tractor trailer coming up fast. "Get down!" he yelled to Kathy just as the Porsche slid into, and then partially under, the back end of the giant Amazon delivery truck, with a sharp-edged hydraulic loading platform at the rear.

There was a deafening bang and sound of shattering glass as the car came into contact with the steel back of the truck, the front end of the car slipping underneath the back of the truck. The hydraulic lift sheared off the windshield of the car until the laws of physics brought it to a halt.

It had all happened so quickly, Monte was barely aware of what had occurred. The car, or what was left of it was neatly pinned beneath the back of the Amazon Prime delivery truck. The top of the Porsche had been sheared off by the impact. It was dark in the wreckage of the car. The truck was on top of them. Slowly, he began to focus.

He was alive. He was trapped in the car but he was alive. But Kathy?

"Kathy!" he called. "Kathy, are you OK?"

At first there was only silence and darkness. Then, he heard a low moan from next to him.

"Kathy!" he cried out, and reaching over, turned on the interior lights, which still worked.

It was then that he saw her, still alive, but barely, tightly pinned between the back bumper of the Amazon truck and her passenger seat. He reached for her hand.

"Kathy!" he cried. "Oh my God, Kathy! You've got to hold on."

She could barely breathe, but she was still alive. Outside the car, he could hear the wail of the sirens, and then, a man's voice.

"We're gonna get you out of there buddy," the man said. "Just hold on..."

Monte tried to reassure Kathy, who was drifting in and out of consciousness.

"Just hold on," he cried. "Just hold on." He held her hand tight and felt her squeeze his hand in response. "There are people here to help us. They're going to get us out."

Then, the car began to move. They were pulling it back and out from under the Amazon truck, and as they began to move it, the truck's jagged metal released its grip on Kathy, but as it did, it ripped open her chest, leaving a ghastly open wound of torn flesh and exposed bone.

Torrents of blood began to stream out of her mangled body. Her hand went limp in his. It had only been the pressure of the back of the Amazon truck that had been keeping her alive.

But   now   she   was   gone.

CHAPTER 6
REBIRTH

"Monte!" screamed Sylvia.

"Kid, can you hear me?" pleaded Brinkman's gravelly voice.

Another figure pushed his way between them and placed an ice-cold stethoscope on Monte's chest.

"Mr. Levine, can you hear me?"

It was the voice of someone that Monte did not recognize.

"I hear you," Monte whispered, suddenly feeling pain rippling through his entire body and the needle pricks of the intravenous drips that were held by tape to both his arms.

A bright light danced from one eye to the other. "Yes, he seems to be fully conscious," said the stranger who was holding the light.

"Where am I? Monte demanded.

Then, it all came back to him in a flash. The car, the crash, seeing Kathy. Jesus Christ Almighty. He had been in a terrible accident. The sound of the sudden crash played over and over and over in his mind, like some horrible, grotesque video loop. Poor Kathy. He had killed her. He had killed her. He had killed her. He had killed the woman he loved. The woman who loved him. He would never be the same person again.

"Mr. Levine," the man said, interrupting Monte's private nightmare. "I am Dr. Meyer. I am an attending physician here at Lenox Hill. You have been seriously injured and have suffered a severe concussion. We are here to take care of you.

Sylvia approached and put her cheek gently next to Monte's. He flinched almost instinctively. He always hated that perfume. Brinkman patted him lightly on the shoulder. Monte could sense the stale smell of cigars. Gradually, Monte regained full awareness of what had happened and where he was.

Dr. Meyer stepped forward again. He held up his hand in front of Monte's face and asked him to follow his finger as he shifted it from eye to eye, observing how well Monte could follow it.

Meyer ran a few more cursory tests, and then, turning to the assembled group in the hospital room said, "I think you can talk to him now."

A tall stranger stepped forward and pulled up a chair next to Monte's bed. Another stranger turned to Sylvia and Brinkman. "I'm afraid I'm going to have to ask you to step outside for a few minutes. Mrs. Levine and Mr. Brinkman." Sylvia gathered up her Gucci handbag and iPhone as Sam put his arm solicitously around her expensively silk-scarved shoulder and led her out into the hall.

"I'm Tim Gannon, special agent FBI," said the tall man sitting next to Monte, flashing his badge. "This is Detective Anthony Damasio of the Organized Crime Unit of the NYPD," he said motioning to the other man. "Do you feel well enough to talk to us? It's pretty urgent."

Monte nodded silently, fearful of what they wanted from him. Did it have to do with Kathy's death?

"I don't understand how it could have happened," Monte volunteered. "There was this loud noise and I just lost control." The horrifying sound of the crash, images of Kathy's mangled body covered in blood, it was all too overwhelming. Tears welled up in Monte's eyes.

"The forensics team knows exactly what happened to your car." Agent Gannon slid a glossy 8 x 10 photo out of a manila folder.

"I presume you know this man." In the photo was Danny Locovita speaking from the podium on the night of his big celebration, shot with a long telephoto lens.

"Yes, I know him. He's the star of my new show *Thou Shalt Not*.... He's...."

Gannon interrupted him again. "Yes, we know who he is."

"Mr. Levine, Danny Locovita is one of the most powerful organized crime bosses on the East Coast. He is involved in drug dealing, money laundering, prostitution, and human trafficking. And murder. Lots of them, we believe. We've been on his trail for years."

"Did he ever threaten your life?"

Monte remained silent, not knowing exactly what to say. "Listen," Monte finally answered, "Danny was upset with me, but I swear he signed all the releases. He had no legal grounds to do anything to me."

"Well, your friend the "Tire King" apparently had a different opinion," Gannon retorted, "He had dangerously defective tires mounted on your Porsche. A definite match with some others we found at his Newark shop. That was what caused the crash."

"Tires? On my car?" Monte always made a point of only having his car serviced at the Manhattan Porsche dealership on 11th Avenue. He had never given his car to Danny or anyone else in his crew. Then suddenly he remembered the mysteriously open garage door on the morning of the accident. The heart monitor behind his ICU bed began to beep faster and a shudder of terror shot through his body.

"I repeat, did Danny Locovita ever directly threaten your life?" insisted Agent Gannon.

Monte nodded silently.

"And do you have any proof of that?" Detective Damasio interrupted.

"Play the messages on my phone," Monte said, "That is, if it wasn't completely destroyed in the crash."

* * *

The trial held in the Federal Courthouse in Lower Manhattan, was as sensational as it was short. The US Attorney, with evidence from the FBI and from the NYPD and the New Jersey authorities made it an open and shut case, despite the endless objections and courtroom maneuvers of Locovita's six-person defense team—the best that money could buy. The federal prosecutors had Danny dead to rights on a 132-count indictment, enough to put him away until the end of time. Not unexpectedly, the seamy stories that the trial generated made Thou Shalt Not an even more colossal ratings hit. Fox re-ran the pilot for four consecutive weeks, and Brinkman even convinced them to go

Comcast with a pricey On Demand "special director's cut" of the show.

The star witness for the prosecution was of course Monte Levine— or to be more precise, Monte Levine's phone. After two weeks of circumstantial evidence about how Danny had used his tire business and his faithful franchisees to wreak murder, mayhem, and havoc across the Tri-State area, Monte Levine mounted the stand.

Monte was sworn in, and Danny seated in shackles and an orange jump suit at the defense table stared at him with murder in his eyes. Monte recounted the whole story of how the idea of Thou Shalt not was developed and how both Danny and Krystal had willingly signed the releases to cooperate. He was also shown photos of some of the guests at Danny's award ceremony, and they were identified as lower-level soldiers in the Locovita crime family, who were already behind bars and awaiting trial.

The courtroom fell silent when the message on Monte's cellphone was played. It survived the crash for the simple reason that Monte had forgotten it at home in his rush to pick up Kathy and drive down to Manhattan for their appearance on the Howard Stern show. The voice on the message was unmistakable as the enhanced recording was played:

"Listen to me you little Jew piece of shit. You gave me the fucking release to sign. This is on your head. Either you get this fucking show pulled in 24 hours or I am going to kill you. Did you get that? I have people who will break your legs, cut off your balls, and then kill you. Believe me I have given my crew the orders to do just that many, many times before. Are you ready to die, you fucker?"

The case was now open and shut. Danny's own words, his own mortal fear of appearing impotent in public, had been the source of his downfall.

The jury vote of 12-0 to convict him on 132 counts was just a formality.

* * *

Now that the trial was over, all Sylvia wanted was to return to her old life in Scarsdale, as miserable as it could sometimes be. She assumed that Monte would resign himself to their marriage and no longer chase after skirts. She had an inkling about Monte's deep feelings for Kathy but didn't want to know all the details. She vowed to herself that she would take a greater interest in his work and not be so intolerant when he played that stupid guitar. Besides, they had put in a bid on a beautiful beach house in the Hamptons and she would be spending her summers shopping, going to glamorous parties, and sitting on the beach with her friends.

Monte, for his part, was heartbroken over losing Kathy. A happy future with her had skipped beyond his grasp. In fact, every part of his pre-accident life had been stripped away from him. Ever since he had been released from the hospital, he and Sylvia had been stuck in an FBI-rented apartment in Lower Manhattan, conveniently close to the US Attorney's offices and the federal court. The security provided for them by the marshals was stifling; all their food was delivered to the downstairs reception desk, they were instructed to keep all the drapes drawn, and heavily armed marshals were on duty down in the lobby and right next to the elevator on their floor twenty-four hours a day.

As the victory celebration was breaking up in the Attorney's lounge in the courthouse, Monte approached his original contact FBI Special Agent Gannon and tapped him on the back. Gannon spun around, distracted from an intense conversation with an attractive assistant US attorney, and burst out in a big smile.

"You did a terrific job, Monte. You and your phone nailed that bastard and now he's going to pay—and pay—and pay." Monte took that as a rave review for his performance on the witness stand. He nodded and smiled.

"I have only one question to ask," he said, thinking longingly of his house in Scarsdale, his finished basement and his beloved '57 Stratocaster and full bank of high-powered speakers and amps. "When do we get to go home?"

"Home?" Gannon replied quizzically. "I thought when you and your wife signed the papers for US Marshal Service protection, you understood what you were agreeing to. You have testified against a very dangerous person and even though he's going to be spending his time in some federal supermax prison, he still has plenty of friends who would love to make good on his threat to you: to break your bones, cut off your balls, and kill you in some horrible way. No, there's no way you can ever go home again."

Monte's eyes widened in surprise. This was not in the script. "So where are we going?"

"They didn't tell you?" Gannon answered in surprise. He stepped away to confer with a nearby marshal, apparently the chief of the detail. After a few minutes of hushed conversation, he came back to Monte. "It's all arranged," he said.

He guided Monte back to where Sylvia was sitting and pulled up a chair next to them. "Mrs. Levine, I've just had a word with your husband, and I apologize if the preparations for your post-trial life weren't made clear."

"Exactly what kind of 'post-trial life' are you talking about?" Sylvia asked in a tone of surprise, even panic. "But we have perfectly respectable lives and responsibilities that we have to return to, now that the trial is over."

Gannon tried to stifle a chuckle. "Well, if you just go back to your house in Scarsdale, those 'perfectly respectable lives' are likely to be very short. We are pretty sure that one of Danny's lieutenants will come back to kill you and Mr. Levine. As long as Danny Locovita is alive, even if he is in jail, he is still capable of giving orders to his lieutenants to kill you, and we know he has already done that.

"Well can't you just station marshals outside our house? The same guys that have been keeping us safely cooped up in the apartment you got for us?"

"I'm afraid we simply don't have the manpower for that. There's no way we can provide you with round the clock security for the rest of your lives. We have another way of taking care of you. We're going to give you new identities, a decent car and a nice house to live in, though maybe not as extravagant as your house in Scarsdale. You'll live in a place where Danny's violent friends will never be able to find you."

"So where will we be going?" Sylvia was clearly outraged.

"I'm afraid I can't reveal that to you right now, Mrs. Levine. But I'm confident you will be comfortable there."

"And what about the summer house in East Hampton we've already made a deposit on?" Sylvia was still intent on putting up a fight.

"Well, I can't make any promises," Gannon assured her, "but I do know some higher-ups in the Witness Protection Program and if I can possibly swing it, I'll see if they will throw in a vacation cabin by a lake."

Monte and Sylvia fell silent for a moment as the reality of the situation sank in. Monte shook his head slowly in disbelief. Kathy was gone. Now his job at Truly TV had also apparently been taken from him. "I can't believe any of this is happening," he quietly muttered to himself.

"Monte, you goddamned idiot." Sylvia had lost her patience with him.

"Calm down, Mrs. Levine. We are going to take care of you. You are going to be completely safe. And I just want to assure you, Mr. Levine, that you have nothing to worry about. You'll receive a monthly stipend for living expenses, until your new job starts."

"Job?" Monte perked up when was Gannon mentioned that word. "What kind of a job?" he asked apprehensively, afraid what the answer would be.

"Oh, don't worry Mr. Levine, we've done this before. Lots of times. We try to find an occupation where the protected witness already has some skills."

"And I've been working on this one personally," said Gannon with a big smile. "Generally, protected witnesses get pretty routine jobs— hardware store salesman, fast food outlet manager, grocery clerk—jobs like that. But since you're in the entertainment business, I got creative with this one. I think you're going to like it a lot."

"You're going to be an Executive Producer…." And here Gannon paused to let it sink in.

"Executive Producer of what?" Monte asked.

"Of a very special dinner theater right in the town where you'll be living."

"A dinner theater?" Monte repeated with a puzzled expression. He had never set foot in a dinner theater in his life.

But Gannon was enthusiastic about the job he had found for Monte. "It will be perfect for you! Very creative. Right up your alley. It's a very special kind of dinner theater—all about medieval knights, kings and queens, with a royal banquet and real jousting and a royal banquet you eat with your hands. My wife and I went to one once. Trust me, experience of a lifetime. We loved it!" My wife and I went to one once. Trust me, experience of a lifetime. We loved it!"

"And the real bonus," Gannon continued, "is that this Executive Producer job we've gotten you pays sixty-five thousand dollars a year!"

Sylvia collapsed back into her chair. "Oh my God!" she said.

"Yeah, I know," Gannon responded. "Pretty amazing, huh?"

She ignored Gannon and glared at Monte. "Do you have any idea what this means?"

He only took a second to respond.

"Sure," he said. "We'll start a new life wherever they send us. And as for the dinner theater... just leave it to me to come up with some really great   ideas..."

CHAPTER 7
TRANSFORMATION

Eighteen-year-old Boston University freshman Wendy Levine felt like she was on top of the world—at least until she got a frantic phone call from her older sister Lauren down in New York.

"Listen, Wendy, Daddy's in big trouble," Lauren said.

Wendy gasped. "What kind of trouble? Is he hurt?"

Wendy had a hard time imaging her father being in big trouble about anything. He had always been such a wonderfully entertaining and benign presence in her life.

Has he been arrested? Is it the IRS? Is Mom OK?" Wendy asked Lauren in rapid fire, wracking her brain for all the likely possibilities.

"No, he and Mom are in hiding. A gangster has threatened to kill them. It has something to do with Daddy's new show. Anyway, the cops think that we may be in danger too. They are sending US marshals to protect us. Two huge armed guards are already with me here."

Wendy's mind reeled with all the implications—mostly the implications for her status at school and her relationship with pre-med student Alex Nutman. Would she be shunned by her friends and professors? Would Alex's high-society family demand that he cut off all ties with her?

But there was little time to worry about her own future and reputation. After a long walk around campus, lost in thought about what this all would mean for her future, she returned to her dorm room to find two large men in dark suits and ties wearing security earpieces, standing on guard in the hall on either side of her dorm room door.

"Miss Levine?" one of them asked, reaching into his suit jacket to show her his badge. "I'm Agent O'Herlihy, he continued, in a broad Boston accent. "Me and agent Fontaine are here to make sure no harm comes to you."

* * *

Back at an FBI safe house in Lower Manhattan, Monte had never seen Sylvia so upset.

"You fucking idiot! You fucking idiot! You fucking idiot!" She sputtered, pacing back and forth across the cramped living room and repeating it over and over again. She wasn't even talking directly to Monte. It was more of a self-soothing mantra to take her mind off the terrible fix they were now in.

Standing quietly to the side, almost blending in with the furniture as he had been taught to do, was Special Agent Paul Belcher. He was with the Federal Witness Protection Program and he was going to be the case administrator for the Levines. His job right now was to get them out of the apartment as quickly and unobtrusively as possible, get them to the Federal Witness Protection Program orientation and re-education center in Langley, Virginia without leaving a trail or a clue as to where they had gone. As he silently watched Sylvia pace and curse and Monte hold his head sadly in his hands, a text message buzz in on his phone.

"Mr. and Mrs. Levine," Belcher interrupted them from their respective funks, "I just got a text from our field operations. Your two daughters are safe. We have agents protecting them right now."

Sylvia stopped and glared at Belcher. "OK, Agent Belcher, that's nice to know. Now what about us?"

"Please call me Paul," Belcher softly answered, hoping to defuse Sylvia's impatience and anger. He liked to keep the relationships with his subjects friendly. He was the Levines' assigned case worker now, and he would be with them for the next three months until they were ready to be secretly relocated in Mountain City, Montana, where they would begin new lives. After that, he would only be in touch with them infrequently. In case of emergencies, he would be their only contact with the world they had left behind.

"We're taking you to a secret government facility," he said cryptically, "you'll be very well cared for. But you can only bring the single suitcase you brought here. And I'm afraid I'm going to have to ask you leave any personal things here—anything that could connect you with your former life. No photographs. No IDs, no phones or laptops. We will wipe them clear and issue you new ones at the protected witness orientation center."

At 3am that morning, Monte and Sylvia were hustled out of the safe house. Both were wearing heavy, high collared coats and large floppy hats to cover their faces. Other agents stood outside, with guns drawn, holding open the rear passenger door of a large black Suburban, and gruffly pushing Monte and Sylvia in. The door slammed shut and the Suburban raced to the West Side, through the Holland Tunnel, zipping past the looming Meadowlands Sports Complex, and arriving at the private airport at Teterboro airport in less than a half hour.

A private government plane was waiting on the tarmac and they were hustled inside. Two marshals already aboard the small private jet stared at them sullenly, closely watching their every move.

After takeoff, Monte adjusted his seat back into the recline position, clearly enjoying this private plane flight. He looked up at the soothing dome light. He twisted around in his seat to scan the whole passenger cabin, and leaned into the aisle to look into the unlocked and open cockpit, fascinated with the glowing dials and the chatter between the pilots and air traffic control. Sylvia frowned as she watched him admiringly run his hand over on the leather of his armrest.

"Isn't this great?" Monte whispered to Sylvia while two marshals dozed behind them. "This is the only way to travel. No security lines, no waiting for the bags. No boarding by zones. And look at these seats. Real leather. And they recline six ways. It's that little control panel on the armrest. See? You see it? I've got to tell you, Sylvia, I've always dreamed of flying on one of these private jets."

Sylvia stared back at him with a stony expression. "You are a fucking idiot, Monte," she said.

*　*　*

After being given sheets and blankets for the twin beds in their linoleum floored, dorm-sized room at Langley, Monte and Sylvia slept fitfully. The next morning, after a breakfast in a private room off the dining hall (none of the residents were allowed to interact with each other for security purposes), when Monte and Sylvia learned that they were on their way to Mountain City, Montana, both of them realized in their own ways that the world, as they knew it, was about to end.

"Your life will never be the same again," Belcher had told them back in New York, "but at least you will have your life."

They would spend three months at Langley receiving their new identities and being carefully schooled on how they would have to live for the rest of their lives.

In just a few days, the girls arrived, escorted by marshals into the high-fenced, razor-wire topped compound and were given government-issue sheets and blankets for their own dormitory room to share. When they were reunited with their parents, they both hugged Sylvia tightly and glared toward Monte. "How could you, Daddy?!" Lauren blurted out.

Wendy could only cry.

Sylvia could say nothing.

She had run out of insults and curses for him. He had robbed them all of their bright futures. While Monte had lived his life in a dream state, making up stories, and to her mind, lying to himself, he had left Sylvia with so many unfulfilled hopes for her life. When the girls were young, she found her life's fulfillment in being their mother. She drove them to ballet and skating lessons; she never missed a play or an art exhibition at their schools. When Monte was off on a shoot or an editing deadline, she often felt like a single mother, but she enjoyed it— encouraging both Lauren and Wendy to follow their dreams, not just fantasize about them like their dad.

Her greatest joys came with her daughters' achievements: National Honor Society, Class President, Chair of the Student Council, Editor of the Class Yearbook, plus a thousand other extracurricular activities. Lauren got early admission to Vassar and became the shining star of the English Department by the end of her sophomore year. After graduation, she snagged a prize job as an editorial assistant at the prestigious New Yorker—these were all sweet tidbits to share with her friends most of whose own children were just mediocre students, headed for the family business, no greater expectations than a nice house nearby in Scarsdale, a pretty wife or handsome husband, flashy cars and jewelry, and season tickets at Yankee Stadium.

Now that the girls had begun to build independent lives for themselves, Sylvia envisioned a very different life, one that involved as little contact with Monte as possible and travel to as many glamorous places as she could. But now all future hope seemed to be all over; she was going to be stuck with Monte in fucking Montana until she died.

* * *

The orientation program at Langley proved to be a tedious mix of safety warnings, career counseling, and high school Social Studies about the State of Montana. Belcher was the teacher in all of them. On the first morning, Monte and Sylvia sat in the front row of the small classroom and Lauren and Wendy sat in the back row, staring blankly at the ceiling or making a big show of putting their heads down on their arms on the desktop and pretending to go to sleep. Sylvia distractedly examined her fingernails and frowned to see how badly she needed a manicure. Monte just stared off into space.

Belcher cleared his throat loudly. "Excuse me," he would say politely but insistently, "You all better pay attention and listen to everything I'm saying. Because when we finally let you loose, the slightest slip up or mistake can easily cost one of you—or all of you—your lives."

As if to make the point stick in their minds, he pulled down a projection screen at the front of the classroom, hooked his laptop into a digital projector, and dimmed the lights. He had usually encountered reactions like this on the first day with all of his subjects. So he routinely began the first session with a film intended to scare the families into really paying attention. And it generally worked.

When the girls had been in high school, they had taken a driver's education course. On the first day of the course, they were shown a film called "Blood and Glass." It was filled with images of horrific automobile accidents and the even more horrific injuries that resulted. The intent was to scare teenagers into becoming careful drivers, and it worked. Sometimes students fainted during the film. A few occasionally threw up. It was graphic. No punches were pulled. It made the point horrifyingly real.

Now, to start their reorientation, Belcher clicked on a video file called "Slip-ups can be Deadly." It began with happy families in the program, success stories, all on screen talking about how wonderful the experience had been. Then, about fifteen minutes into the film, the script shifted gears. In the style of a 1950s educational film, it showed what happened when someone forgot to use their new name, or messed up on their background life story and how suspicious it looked. Rumors would spread among the neighbors about something being "not quite right" about the new family in town, and before long everyone was spreading the word.

Enter a shady character with five o'clock shadow, a heavy overcoat, and a suspiciously Mafia-like fedora. He would get wind of the rumors and be shown in the next scene scowling and covering his mouth as talked on the phone to someone off screen. Then the video dissolved to graphic shots of splayed bodies lying in the blood-soaked shag carpeting of a living room; smashed-in heads with their brains leaking out onto the grass of a picnic ground; and the shattered driver's side window of a station wagon, with the driver slumped back against the front seat with his eyeballs and half of his face shot out.

Sylvia and Monte straightened up stiffly in their chairs. Wendy gasped and Lauren began to softly cry.

"Those were families who had didn't follow the rules," Belcher intoned when the video faded to black, "families who thought the rules did not apply to them, who didn't pay complete attention to the things we taught them here."

"Everything you knew before, everything you thought, everyone you knew, every experience, every memory, all of it, is over. From now on, you are different people."

"You are all going to be assigned new identities, receive new driver's licenses, new social security numbers, new backgrounds that are entirely made up but totally searchable on public and even law enforcement databases. If anyone was to search them, and trust me, people will, they will all check out. And that means you will all have to get new names. From now on, you are no longer the Levines. From now on, you are the Lewis family. 'Sharon Lewis,'" Belcher said, looking at Sylvia. "Willow Lewis," he said, looking at Wendy. "Linette Lewis," he said for Lauren, and "Mark Lewis," for Monte.

Lauren and Wendy both spoke up. "Do we have any choice in selecting our names?"

"I'm afraid not," Belcher answered, "your birth certificates, driver's licenses, social security cards and passports have already been prepared."

*   *   *

In the days that followed, Belcher lectured to them about their new home in Mountain City, Montana, zooming in from a Google Earth satellite image of the whole state of Montana, to the metropolitan area of Mountain City, and finally into the suburban neighborhood and even down to the specific 2-bedroom 1-bath ranch house where they would live.

He went on to describe the basic facts and figures about Mountain City, which was almost like learning about a foreign country or some kind of cowboy fantasyland to the Levine family who would soon become the Lewis clan. He was determined to make them act like Montanans and teach them everything a Montana high school graduate knew.

The biggest employer is now Valkyrie Pharmaceuticals." He projected some recent pictures of Valkyrie's main manufacturing complex that employed thousands of Mountain City residents—from janitors to research scientists. "Pretty impressive, isn't it? They make everything from birth control pills to Viagra, and everything in between. Thanks to them they've helped the city recover. The average annual income is already over $37,000, and they've soared from the 961st place among US metropolitan areas all the way up to 333."

*   *   *

After two and a half months at Langley—as much as their parents were getting deeper and deeper into the orientation, "Willow" and "Linette" were getting more and more infuriated with the idea of living in Montana and were just about ready to jettison their names, forget about rodeos and cowboy hats, and run away to some distant, exotic place-- never to be heard from again.

"We've had it," said Willow-Wendy to Belcher one morning.

"There's no way I'm going to Montana," added Linette-Lauren. "I'd rather die than live a lie—and a really stupid lie at that."

"My sister and I won't let you take away both our past and our future. You better have marshals to spare, because the moment we get dropped off in Mountain City—I mean the fucking moment you finally bid us farewell—we're just going to run away."

Monte tried to calm them down. "I know you're upset, Princess, but this isn't necessarily going to be forever. The FBI has already dismantled plenty of underworld gangs and there's a good chance we'll get home someday."

"Yeah, someday, sure. When I'm forty-one, unmarried, and back with my parents in Scarsdale" Lauren-Linette snapped. "There is no way. I mean NO way. I am finished with this ridiculous charade." Wendy was still in the same state of shock she had been in since arriving at Langley, but ever the younger child, she was prepared to follow her older sister's lead.

Belcher saw he had a real problem. Gentle persuasion wouldn't work anymore. If these stubborn, headstrong Levine—er Lewis—girls went through with their threat not to cooperate with the strict rules of the program, there was a good chance that Monte and Sylvia would end up in a grisly homicide photo, and he would probably be demoted and end up with a cut in pay and reassignment in some federal courthouse as a security guard.

"Those two spoiled brats," he complained to his supervisor later that afternoon, after a disastrous fly-fishing lesson. "There's no way I can get them to cooperate and that will make all of us look bad."

"Let me think about this," said Chief Deputy Marshal William Peyton, who ran the Langley compound. "Let me make a few phone calls and see what I can do."

The next day, as Belcher was explaining the rules of rodeos to Monte and Sylvia, and Wendy and Lauren were sitting stone-faced in the back row, Chief Peyton peeked his head into the classroom, and motioned to Belcher to come outside and have a world with him.

"I think I have a solution," he told Belcher. "We have what you might call a cooperative agreement with the UK Protected Persons

Service. I've talked to their chief about a favor they owe us—you remember us hiding that informer from the Millennium Dome Heist gang in a coal town in Appalachia? Well, they are willing to return the favor."

Belcher smiled broadly as Peyton described the details of the arrangement that he had made. "That's perfect," Belcher told him, "Now we can finally get them off our back."

Belcher returned to the classroom and told Monte and Sylvia that they could take the rest of the day off and return to their room. "I want to talk to Linette and Willow for a few minutes about their bad attitudes."

"I've got new plans for you," he announced to the two young women, once their parents had left the room. "I've spoken to my supervisor and he's willing to make an exception in your cases and he's spoken with the proper authorities. You are both going to be sent to live in England under your new identities; the National Crimes Agency over there is going to place you both in an out-of-the way location as researchers in a big project the BBC is just starting. It will last at least five years, and when it's over, the Brits will check back with us and we'll decide what to do with you."

"What kind of project?"

"It's a big documentary and book publication project: *The Search for King Arthur*. Should fit both your skills just fine. And who knows, you two might even make careers for yourself in England and stay under the radar of Danny Locovita's gang—if you just maintain the new identities we've given you and keep your mouths shut."

"OK, I'll do it," said Linette Lewis. She turned toward her sister Willow.

"Me too," Willow agreed.

* * *

With just a few days to go in their reorientation, it was time to say goodbye. Sharon-Sylvia got all teary when she hugged both girls and urged them to stay alert and take care of themselves—and prayed that they would get back together some day. Monte also got teary as he gave his daughters chaste hugs and kisses on their cheeks. "This is going to turn out great," he told them. "Think of this as one of life's great adventures."

"OK, it's time to go," Belcher told the girls.

They returned to their shared room that they were happy never ever to see again and soon appeared at the front entrance, with their heavy backpacks containing all the clothes and personal possessions that they had been allowed to take with them slung over their shoulders.

Mark-Monte and Sharon-Sylvia stood just inside the doorway, determined to get a last glimpse at the two girls they had raised from infancy, through kindergarten, grammar school, bat-mitzvahs, high school triumphs, mishaps, and nasty breakups with boyfriends. They waved sadly as the girls passed them without a word.

Willow and Linette Lewis just looked straight ahead as they accompanied a marshal into the black Suburban that would take them to the airport. They looked back toward their parents one last time as they slid into the backseat of the huge government SUV.

"Have a nice life in Montana," they both called out to their forlorn parents, as they waved goodbye and the SUV pulled away.

CHAPTER 8
BLACK SUN

Dr. Jerry Stewart leaned back in his leather office chair in a mood of deep reflection. The cityscape of Mountain City, Montana stretched out below him as he idly scanned the horizon from the floor-to-ceiling windows in his executive suite. So much had changed here since his arrival in the late 1940s. Mountain City was then just a dreary mining and lumbering town. Today it was a bustling, if still dreary, service and manufacturing town where his vast fortune had been made. Mountain City was kept alive by his own efforts: by the labs he had founded to the world-renowned Stewart Institute of Biochemical Innovation, whose striking modern architectural design had won its architect the Pritzker Prize in the 1980s—and which he had completely funded from the construction of the building itself down to the salaries of everyone who worked there—from Nobel Prize winners to janitors and maintenance men. He had cleverly established it as a recruiting ground for brilliant young biochemists from all over the world whom he would pay handsomely to work in his largest enterprise and proudest achievement: the Valkyrie Pharmaceutical Company.

Valkyrie Pharmaceuticals would have been a colossus anywhere. But in Mountain City it completely dominated everything else going on in town, and for that matter, in the state of Montana. The other Big Pharma giants in the U.S. and Europe had nothing even as remotely impressive as Valkyrie's extensive complex of laboratories, offices, vast manufacturing units, and secure warehouses surrounded by razor wire fences and watchtowers equipped with motion detectors, infra-red sensors, and armed security personnel who ensured that no industrial spies or other intruders would ever come near. As Founder and CEO, Jerry Stewart saw to it that his facilities were equipped with cutting-edge technology in every phase of production—from research experiments to data collection to robotic manufacturing, to distribution of his products in his own fleet of intentionally unmarked tractor-trailers and cargo planes.

The Mountain City complex produced an astounding variety of medications—from aspirin to erectile dysfunction pills to insulin and blood pressure medication to the most complex and expensive cancer treatment drugs. There were always more medical miracles in the pipeline, but Stewart scrupulously avoided issuing press releases. He had no need to artificially boost share prices on Wall Street; Valkyrie was a private company: his and his alone. He insisted on personally supervising every facet of the business from the color of the corrugated roofs of the maintenance sheds, to the font used on the employees' bar-coded identification badges to the shape of the blister packs and bottles of the market-ready medications, each inscribed with a tiny circular symbol whose meaning no one but Jerry Stewart knew.

Even at the impressively advanced age of 107, he was still fit and active. Though he had slowed down in recent years, he remained until very recently, an inveterate hiker, still watched his diet carefully, and rose before dawn every morning to take a cold shower and then go through a routine of very old-fashioned calisthenics. His butler would lay out for him his unchanging work outfit: a black suit, white shirt, and black tie. Once dressed Stewart would descend a circular staircase and eat a spartan breakfast of two slices of dark rye bread, lightly toasted, spread with elderberry jam. At precisely 6:45 a black Mercedes limousine would pull up to the rear entrance of his imposing residence and Stewart would ride in silence down the winding road to the executive office building of Valkyrie. Of late, he had been confined to a motorized wheelchair, but that in no way slowed him down. And his mind was still razor sharp.

If there was one weakness Jerry Stewart would admit to, it was his obsessive love of everything medieval: suits of armor, tapestries, sword and other weapons, even illuminated manuscripts. Although he never left Mountain City, he was a well-known telephone bidder at all the big art auction houses in New York, London, Paris, and Geneva. His collection was enormous—almost as large as that of the Musée de Cluny in Paris. There was hardly another collector anywhere else in the world to whom Jerry Stewart would allow himself to be outbid. Yet he permitted no one ever to view the private collection that filled three full floors of his gigantic mansion, which he had proudly dubbed "The Castle." The collection was for his own enjoyment and edification—not for the noisy school groups and common people of Mountain City. It embodied the spirit that motivated him to achieve all that he had accomplished in his long life. And he had made the purity, discipline, and chivalry of the Middle Ages the guiding ethos of his massive pharmaceutical firm.

* * *

Jerry Stewart also harbored a deep, dark secret, one he shared with no one. He had been baptized Gerhardt Friedrich Adolph Stürmer in the small Bavarian town of Dinkelsbühl in the extraordinarily hot summer of 1915. Just two years later, his father was badly wounded on the Western Front in the Great War and spent most of the rest of his life drinking and raging at Germany's humiliation in the Treaty of Versailles. Meanwhile his mother supported the family by working as a maid for one of the handful of prosperous Jewish families in town.

Chaos, fear, privation, and uncertainty were the companions that Gerhardt grew up with. And by the time he reached his late teens, hatred and resentment joined the emotional mix. Hitler had come to power. The Jewish family his mother had worked for years suddenly disappeared. And by age 18, Gerhardt joined the other members of the Hitler Youth smashing the windows and setting fire to the small synagogue in the town.

Gerhardt Stürmer worked his way up in the Nazi hierarchy, joining the elite Schutzstaffel, or SS. Unlike most of the SS, who were thugs and cold-blooded killers, Stürmer was bright, articulate, and ambitious. It was not long before he was recognized by SS commander Himmler himself and put on his personal staff.

Gerhardt was exceptional among the young men in Heinrich Himmler's inner circle. His life's ambition was not just to strut and issue commands in his tailored black SS uniform. From his school days he had always dreamed of becoming a scientist, a medical researcher to serve the German nation and heal the illnesses and infirmities of the Master Race. And he was among the select few admitted to study at the Kaiser Wilhelm Institute for Medical Research under the brilliant biochemist Richard Kuhn, a pioneer in the study of the effect of enzymes and vitamins on human health. Kuhn was a loyal German—he had even refused to accept the 1938 Nobel Prize in Chemistry on Hitler's direct command that this award had already been given to too many traitors and Jews.

After only four years of intense study with Kuhn, Gerhardt received a doctorate in biochemistry with the highest distinction and returned to Himmler's staff with yet another favor to ask. Kuhn had entrusted him with some of his most important research results and he believed that he was on the verge of a major breakthrough that could extend human lifespans—a potentially crucial advantage for the Third Reich as casualties mounted in the east, in the wake of the Stalingrad campaign.

Much had changed in Himmler's administration of the SS since Gerhardt had been away. The SS operations center had shifted from Berlin to Himmler's Wewelsburg Castle in western Germany, a looming castle with three immense medieval-style round towers that rose above its massive fortification walls. Rumors had it that Himmler had grown increasingly obsessed with occult rituals and even believed himself to be the reincarnation of Heinrich I, an 11th century Germanic king. Gerhardt did not know what to expect from his commander, but he nonetheless commandeered an SS car and driver to travel from Berlin to Wewelsburg and state his request in person for a special assignment to continue his medical research.

Himmler had visibly aged since Gerhardt had last seen him. Gerhardt entered the Reichsführer's gothic-style office in one of the castle towers and stood rigidly at attention, extending his right arm stiffly upward, "Heil Hitler!" he dutifully blurted out.

Himmler motioned for Gerhardt to be seated in the medieval style oak chair in front of his desk. Gerhardt sat rigid in his formal black SS uniform with high leather boots and tightly buttoned tunic with a thick belt and diagonal leather strap across his chest. A bright red swastika armband was fastened tightly on his left arm.

"I understand you have accomplished some impressive medical breakthroughs," Himmler mused in his high reedy voice, leaning back in his own chair and distractedly fondling his favorite leather riding crop. "I also understand that you are here to ask for a special assignment." Himmler always had many sources to inform him about all the activities—even the intentions—of the members of the SS.

"Ja, mein Reichsführer," Gerhardt answered without fear or intimidation. "I would like to be reassigned to continue my medical research. I think that we can unlock the key to curing maladies of the human digestive system in an unprecedented way."

"I have examined your educational records closely and conferred with the all the greatest medical experts in the Reich. They all agree that you can make a great contribution to the health of the German Volk. I will personally equip a full laboratory for you here at the Castle. You may request anything you need for your important research."

*   *   *

Wewelsberg Castle contained a warren of dark chambers, cavernous halls, hidden passages, mysterious meeting rooms, and storerooms filled with looted art and medieval artifacts that had been looted from every corner of Europe under Nazi control.

On the ground floor of the castle's north tower was a round hall reserved only for the twelve highest ranking SS-generals. A round depression in was embedded in the middle of the marble floor decorated with a dark sun wheel later known as the "Black Sun." It marked the center of the castle and symbolized the center of the Nazi world empire that would inevitably come.

Above the Black Sun, Himmler placed a heavy oak round table. And just as King Arthur had chosen his bravest twelve, so Himmler arranged twelve high-backed pig skin chairs for his Obergruppenführers, each chair carrying the name of its illustrious occupant inscribed on a silver plate.

Gerhardt Stürmer paid no attention to this occult nonsense. He could read the signs of the collapsing Nazi war effort and he worked day and night in his underground laboratory to record all the formulas he had devised at the Kaiser Wilhelm Institute to perfect his secret life-giving drug. He worked with a large team of medically trained SS assistants, whom he dispatched in the dark of night out into the cobbled streets and isolated farmsteads that lay at the foot of the castle to drug unwary peasants and carry them back to Gerhardt's laboratory. He had instructed his operatives to concentrate on the elderly who lived alone, as their absence would not be missed.

Sometimes the formulas worked, but sometimes they didn't. In both cases the experimental subject would be put to death with the notorious efficiency of the SS and never be seen again. The formula for longevity elixir remained frustratingly elusive, but Gerhardt developed other medications that offered him more immediate rewards. Heinrich Himmler himself was a pathetic human specimen. His weak eyes and weak, scrawny body had disqualified him for combat service in the German army in World War I. Gerhardt knew precisely what maladies he needed to attend to. He spent time developing enzyme treatment for poor digestion, a formula of vitamins and antioxidents for poor eyesight, and mega-dose steroid capsules to increase weight and muscle mass. When he was confident that they were all safe and effective he presented them to Himmler.

The gradual change in Himmler's mood and appearance was so dramatic once he started to take Stürmer's medications that one day the silver plate on one of the chair backs in the Round Table chamber was hastily removed and its occupant reassigned to the Eastern Front. In its place came a newly engraved silver plate that read "Obergruppenführer Gerhardt Stürmer." He was now placed in charge of the entire SS medical corps and given access to all of its records. He no longer privately mocked the medieval rituals that Himmler conducted. Gerhardt Stürmer had arrived at the pinnacle of power. He was now a Teutonic Knight who dutifully paid homage to the sign of the Black Sun.

* * *

In May, 1945, the Red Army entered the suburbs of Berlin. Even for the true believers, it was now clear that defeat for Nazi Germany was both imminent and inevitable.

Deep under the Reich Chancellery, Adolf Hitler and Eva Braun committed suicide, rather than face capture. Joseph Goebbels, propaganda minster and his wife also committed suicide, after killing their children with cyanide. Himmler attempted to flee towards the Danish border, but was captured and taken to a British interrogation center. During a physical examination, he bit down on a specially prepared potassium cyanide capsule rather than submit to punishment by the subhuman Allies.

But not everyone was so committed to death for the doomed Nazi cause.

Gerhardt Stürmer, with his many still unachieved medical ideas, was not about to kill himself. Neither was he willing to be executed as a war criminal by the vindictive Allies or spend the rest of his life in a military prison.

Himmler had left explicit instructions that if the enemy approached Wewelsburg Castle, the remaining SS officers were to detonate high explosives in each of the towers, turning the massive fortress into an enormous pile of medieval rubble, destroying all evidence of what had gone on there. Gerhardt of course knew of the plan and pretended to descend into his laboratory to place half a dozen sticks of dynamite under the lab tables; instead, he grabbed five boxes of documents he had carefully sequestered as a kind of insurance policy, grabbed the keys to one of Himmler's Mercedes sedans and drove west, racing toward the advancing U.S. 3rd Armored Division.

Gerhardt Stürmer carried his own ticket to freedom in America in those five boxes. They were the records from his own experiments and the data from most important medical research carried out by Nazi biochemists across the Reich since 1933. As the war drew to a close, both the Americans and the Soviets were anxious to gather in as many pieces of advanced German technology and science as they could lay their hands on. For the Americans, medical advances, next to rocket technology, were the most sought-after trophies of victory.

Driving like a madman on a road cratered by bombs from British and American raids and overcrowded with streams of refugees also headed West, Gerhardt Stürmer knew it would be a miracle if he made it to the American lines in one piece. And if he did, what would the GIs do when they saw a Mercedes—an official SS Mercedes no less—barreling straight for them?

He pulled over to the side of the road and affixed two white cloths to the small flagpoles on the front bumper of the car that used to carry the swastika, and hit the gas, scattering groups of starving refugees as he plowed westward, and surrendering to the first American troops he could find.

With the GIs' guns trained on him, Stürmer emerged from the Mercedes with his hands held high. As they jostled him to search for hidden weapons, he announced his rank and politely asked them to take him to their commanding officer, where he explained who he was and what he had to offer. Realizing the value of this prisoner's information, the American lieutenant colonel invited Stürmer into the house he had requisitioned as his headquarters and offered him a freshly opened can of C-rations for lunch.

* * *

Gerhardt Stürmer was constantly kept amused by his long, winding odyssey from the temporary headquarters of the 3rd Armored Division in Occupied Germany across the Atlantic to the United States. These Americans, boastfully naïve as they were, were apparently never quite sure that they hadn't been hoodwinked or made some terrible mistake, he thought to himself, as he was shuttled from one American installation to another. Gerhardt smiled and shook his head in amazement—no torture, no pistol held to the prisoner's forehead, none of the proven SS techniques. Mindless repetition and endless carbon-copied bureaucratic forms seemed to be the Americans' most potent weapons for getting information out of an enemy who had fallen into their hands.

Another source of Gerhardt's amusement was the wide-eyed amazement of the various American medical officers called in to look over the documents in his five precious boxes. First in Frankfurt, then in Paris, then finally at the 250th Station Hospital in England, the officers of the U.S. Medical Corps always seemed to say, as they read the manuscript pages filled with chemical formulas and statistical records, could this really be true? A whole range of synthetic antibiotics with strange names: erythromycin, tetracycline, terramycin; the antimetabolic formula methotrexate to be used as chemical treatments for certain types of cancer; a preparation of combined estrogen and progesterone to be used by women as oral contraceptives; even a detailed protocol for transplanting organs to a living recipient from a deceased donor. Stürmer's five boxes were a treasure trove of medical advances, if properly tested, they could utterly transform health care in the United States. Some of these documents he shared eagerly, others he kept for himself, for use when just the right opportunity arose. A great deal of his most sensitive information of course remained unwritten and invisible, held in his prodigious memory.

Once his potential value to American society was official recognized by the military chain of command, Stürmer was quickly shipped back to the United States under heavy guard and in total secrecy aboard on a Navy supply ship. After being processed on his arrival in New York at the Staten Island Naval Station, he was handed over to the custody of two FBI agents, who accompanied on the long train ride to Langley, Virginia—which even back then was a place for the American penchant for transforming identities.

There Stürmer joined the hundreds of captured German scientists, engineers, and technicians with specific knowledge and know-how that had been brought back to the United States. Stürmer spent days in intense debriefings with the top scientists from Pfizer, Roche, and Johnson & Johnson, allowing them to examine his notes and discuss possible further possible developments with them. The American pharmaceutical companies immediately understood that the source of all these new formulas must remain secret. They were the results of experiments that not only could never be repeated, but in fact could never even be made public, having their source in the murderous SS.

Once the pharmaceutical companies were satisfied that they had understood and recorded all of Stürmer's experimental successes, they had no more use for him. Yet unlike his roommate, a brilliant young rocket scientist named Von Braun, who would soon become a national celebrity, Stürmer's close association with Himmler made him an obvious target for prosecution as a war criminal. The OSS officials at Langley thought it more prudent that his identity be completely reinvented and he be allowed to live his life in anonymity as a productive medical researcher in some remote corner of America.

Indeed, Stürmer would spend almost a year in the Langley compound, learning to speak perfect, accent-free colloquial English. He would learn about American history, about American Big Band music, about Hollywood stars, and even about those two current superheroes of America's eccentric national pastime, Ted Williams and Joe DiMaggio. With a Virginia driver's license and new Social Security card, he had become a new person. Obergruppenführer Gerhardt Stürmer was now dead and buried, killed in the blast that destroyed the Wewelsburg Castle. He was now Jerry Stewart, born in Iowa Falls, graduate of Iowa Falls High School, and graduate of Iowa State University with a master's degree in biochemistry. He had all the paperwork and diplomas, and more important, so did the US government, which supplied them to Iowa Falls High School and Iowa State University. Even the State of Iowa complied with the request to enter Jerry's birth in the Vital Records Archive—as well as the birth and death certificates of Jerry's fictional Mom and Dad. And for his part, Jerry Stürmer had brought his intense German SS sense of discipline to becoming the best American he could be.

*   *   *

The transcontinental train taking Jerry Stewart to the new home the OSS had arranged for him seemed to take forever. Up from Washington and changing at Penn Station in New York, he quickly switched seats to distance himself as far as he could from an Orthodox Jewish couple, who thankfully got off in Pittsburgh. Darkness fell and dawn arose by the time he reached Cleveland and after changing trains the next day in Chicago, he began to appreciate America for its sweeping landscapes as the train rumbled westward across the Great Plains. At each stop passengers departed and passengers boarded. Jerry couldn't help notice that their accents and the brims of their hats broadened as he traveled further west. No Jews, not even any city people except for the occasional traveling salesman; Jerry thought to himself that he could get to like this place.

After several more days of crossing the prairie, the terrain grew more rugged. Thick forests covered the hillsides and whitewater streams and rivers ran beside the tracks. Jerry looked at the Northern Pacific Railroad map he had picked up at one of the stops. He knew he was getting close to his destination and felt an uncharacteristic rush of excitement. He stared intently out the window trying to memorize every detail as they finally slowed and entered a railyard. The conductor strode through the cars announcing loudly, "Northern Pacific Depot, Mountain City, Montana this stop."

Jerry pulled his single suitcase down from the overhead rack and descended the step steps at the back of the car. The station looked deserted, just a couple of haggard old men in well-worn cowboy hats sitting together on a wooden passenger bench passing the time of day. Jerry passed through the entrance doors out onto the sidewalk. He started walking and found what he was looking for just a block or so down North Higgins Avenue. The weathered neon sign read "Belmont Hotel" and on a front window "Steam heat, telephone service, hot and cold-water baths, reasonable rates by day or week." This was the beginning of his new life. He gripped the handle of his suitcase tightly and walked inside.

At the desk, a young woman looked up from the movie magazine she was reading. "Can I help you sir?" she asked.

"I have a room reserved here, Janice," he said, reading her l name tag and using his best all American accent.

"Name please?" she asked in an annoyingly cheery American way.

"Stewart," he said. "Jerry Stewart."

The girl at the front desk ran her finger over a registry book.

"Ah, Mr. Stewart. We have been expecting you. How was your trip?"

"It was fine," he said curtly. "Just fine." As he spoke, he suddenly pondered whether she could ever possibly grasp the million-mile voyage he had just completed from the Round Table in Wewelsburg Castle to this dingy Montana town.

"And how long are you going to be staying with is?" she asked.

"The rest of my life," he said.

She chuckled to herself, assuming that Jerry was just joking. "Well, that's real nice Mr. Stewart, because I hope that I won't be spending the rest of my life here."

She slid the door key over to him. It was affixed to a gigantic block of wood with the number 34 painted on it in black.

He took the key and looked at it.

"Room 34?"

She nodded.

There was no elevator, so he climbed three flights of stairs.

He opened the door to number 34 and stepped inside. The room was small and deeply depressing. There were two twin beds, both made up with a single pillow each and a pink bedspread, neatly made. There was a desk and chair shoved into the corner, and an overstuffed green parlor chair with matching ottoman footstool. He pulled back the curtain to reveal the view down North Higgins Avenue, the heart of downtown Mountain City. This was his prison now, as cruel a penitentiary as any he would have been sentenced to at Nuremberg.

He did not unpack.

Instead, he lay on the bed in his traveling clothes and stared at the ceiling.

His memory drifted back to his beloved laboratory in the basement of Wewelsberg castle. To the work. To the research. To the miracles he had achieved. If America was indeed the Land of Opportunity as his OSS supervisors at Langley constantly insisted, he would take full advantage of that opportunity.

The OSS had placed $10,000 in his checking account at the Mountain City First National Bank to tide him over and find a place to live and buy a car. Tomorrow he would withdraw that money, rent a place for a lab and resume his biochemical research. With his own efforts, scientific brilliance, and ambition, he would go on to build the greatest pharmaceutical company that America had ever seen. He smiled to himself in self-satisfaction at the enormity and seeming impossibility of that dream. And he pledged to himself, right there and then, in Room 34 of the Belmont Hotel, that all of his pills, capsules, syringes, and bottles would bear a tiny, almost imperceptibly small image of the Black Sun of the Teutonic Knights—as a secret sign that no one could ever vanquish him.

CHAPTER 9
DAY FOR KNIGHT

Monte Levine had always tried to make the best of a bad situation, but now, in his new identity as Mark Lewis in Mountain City, Montana, this was about the worst situation he had ever been in. He already missed his old life at TrulyTV. He missed the solace his Stratocaster had offered. He still felt heartbreak and guilt about Kathy, and immediately after moving with Sylvia into his new house on Schoolhouse Drive in the seedier west side of Mountain City, he began to peer nervously out of the windows every time a car drove down his street—wondering whether one of Danny Locovita's hit men had already found him and would mutilate and murder him in the same awful way that Danny Locovita had described.

But when he first got a glimpse of the brightly painted battlements and Cinderella's-castle-type towers of "Teutonic Nights"—his new place of employment—set back behind a large parking lot and hedged in among the fast-food drive-thrus and used car dealerships on the western edge of town, Monte-Mark felt a strange kind of fascination. It was a total dump, of course, but that meant there was so much he could do to make it western Montana's premier dining and entertainment attraction. Of course, he didn't know anything about the restaurant business, or even knights in shining armor. But he was a born tale spinner and audience pleaser. And however bizarre and hopelessly optimistic his feeling might have been, he was actually excited about the prospect of getting back into the entertainment industry again.

As he approached the main entrance to the castle, a lowered fiberglass drawbridge suspended by thick plastic chain links to the faux-stone wall of the façade, he was met by a surrealistic scene: a knight in shiny armor, with a smoldering cigarette drooping from the opening in his helmet's visor, was trying without success to kickstart a Harley-Davidson. A princess with a tall conical hat and dark tattoos showing through her gauzy sleeves was cursing at the knight who was obviously attempting to flee.

"I'm finished with you, you motherfucker! Don't ever talk to me again! Don't you even try to deny that you've been banging the Queen!" she shouted at him.

Mark-Monte watched the unfolding show before him with amusement. He had not produced Wife Swap Extreme for years for nothing. These were his people. In a strange way, he was more convinced than ever that he could make this cockamamie version of the Middle Ages into a live action reality show. He deftly sidestepped the squabbling knight and princess and walked across the wobbly drawbridge. It crossed a shallow moat, of sorts, that surrounded the castle. The copper glint of coins thrown into the moat shone alongside a scatter of crumpled beer cans and a few floating fast-food wrappers; it was clear that no one at the Teutonic Nights dinner theater made much of an effort to keep it clean.

He was already five minutes late for his first meeting with Dolph Stewart, the owner of Teutonic Nights and his new employer. The main entrance door to the castle was open but no one inside the lobby paid any attention or even seemed to care. Workers in jeans and Teutonic Nights logo T-shirts were emptying huge bags of popcorn into the medieval style dispensers at the snack bar while others were restocking the gift shop from cardboard cartons of newly arrived plastic swords and shields.

He examined the suits of armor on either side of the entrance to the "Knights" restroom and the faceless mannequins in chiffon dresses and puffy sleeves standing guard outside the "Miladys" restroom. Crossing the shiny linoleum floor of the lobby, which bore fanciful coats of arms and smelled strongly of Lysol, Monte-Mark approached the double doors marked "To the Tournament" in Old English Letters. Pushing the doors open, the annoying smell of Lysol and stale popcorn gave way to the earthy, acrid odors of horse urine, manure, and human sweat.

In the center of an arena the size of a hockey rink, armor clad horsemen hurtled toward each other, with the horses' hooves kicking up the soft sod and the riders shouting and cursing at each other more like rivals at a rodeo than medieval knights. Passing dangerously close to each other, they galloped to the opposite ends of the arena, wheeled around and galloped toward each other again.

The ground literally shook as they passed only a few feet from him, all muscle, all power, all thundering hooves. His mind began to reel with a hundred ideas about how he could boost the profits from a natural spectacle like this in ways he never could do with Reality TV.

Mark turned his attention to the empty rows of audience seats around the oval, fronted by narrow formica tables, with room for about a thousand people if the arena was sold out. At $49.95 for the show and dinner, Mark thought to himself, that would bring in almost $350,000 per week of seven shows and a matinee, not counting the snack bar, alcohol sales, and overpriced souvenirs. That would make $1.4 million a month; $16 mil a year. Not great by TV standards, but out here in Montana, Mark figured that you'd certainly have to consider this medieval-style dinner theater a dependable money-making machine. But he was convinced that it could be so much more than that.

As he turned to go back to the lobby, he was met by a young woman, perhaps in her early 20's, dressed in a long skirt and low bodice—basically a Hollywood caricature of a medieval serving wench. No wonder the place was so popular, he thought to himself.

"Can I help you, good Sire?" she asked in character.

"My name is Mark Lewis, I'm here to see Mr. Stewart."

"Oh, Mr. Lewis. Welcome. We've been expecting you. Let me take you up to see the boss." She led him back into the lobby and opened a hidden door between the restrooms and the gift shop. Mark followed her up a steep, narrow staircase that smelled of spilled beer and stale tobacco smoke. At the top were some file cabinets, covered with unopened mail, receipts, and unfiled documents in total disarray. Beyond was the Boss's office, in even more of a mess.

Dolph Stewart was deep in conversation on his phone, reclining far back in his tattered leather chair with his bargain basement gold-buckled loafers up on the desk. "Yes, yes, yes, next Tuesday, I promise," he shouted into the phone.

Noticing Mark enter the office and navigate his way around an overloaded coatrack and piles of magazines and broken pieces of armor on the floor, Dolph motioned to Mark to come in and make himself comfortable in the rickety folding chair next to his desk. Dolph smiled widely and moved his phone away from his ear, so Mark could hear. All he heard was the sound of a woman shouting at the top of her lungs. Dolph comically mimicked her rage with his facial expressions, showing Mark that it was all just a big joke to him. He ended the call abruptly. "Damn suppliers," he said, "I'm already overpaying for her turkey drumsticks as it is."

Dolph stood up to greet his guest properly. And as he rose from behind his desk, he looked like he had just stepped out of an 80s disco movie: black hair sprayed in place, Elvis-style sideburns, tight slacks, and a flowing silk shirt open with a shiny gold medallion swaying from a gold chain around his neck. Here was a guy who obviously loved bling. He enthusiastically reached out his hand toward Mark's, with gold bracelet swaying and a ring in every finger glistening dully in the office ceiling fluorescent light. Mark shook it cautiously and Dolph warmly covered it with his other hand as they shook.

"So great to have you here, Man," he said.

Back at Langley, Monte-Mark had been thoroughly briefed on the business. He was told that it was a huge success—that people came from miles around, sometimes hundreds of miles around, to have dinner and, what the glossy promo brochures said was "The Experience of a Lifetime." He had even been shown a feature article in Forbes about what the magazine called a Montana Medieval Miracle; a real success story with a full-page photo of Dolph on horseback in a full suit of armor and describing him as something of a genius in crafting this combination of eating and medieval entertainment, starting the place at only the age of 22.

But now sitting in the chaos of Dolph's office, Mark could see that the writer for Forbes had vastly exaggerated Dolph's "genius," because the man sitting in front of him with all the jewelry and an orangish tanning salon complexion was, well, not all that bright. So be it. Monte-Mark had spent his life in the TV business dealing with people like

Dolph every day. Programming executives. Upper management. So easy to manipulate.

"I am so, so, so delighted to meet you," Dolph repeated, as he poured them both a drink into Teutonic Nights-branded glass tumblers ($49.95 for 4 down in the giftshop) from the half empty bottle of Wild Turkey that he kept under his desk. "I've been waiting for you to arrive. We really need you. I think you can help me solve a few problems we have here."

"I've heard great things about you, Mr. Lewis. Great things."

"The stuff you did in Branson was amazing," Dolph said.

Monte-Mark was confused for a second, then quickly recalled the back story that the Feds had bult for him and tried to remember all the memorized details. According to that story, Mark had taken over the Tex Ritter Dinner Theater and Rodeo in Branson, Missouri, after it had been levelled in the terrible 2012 tornado that ripped through town. At least according to the carefully scripted story, he had supervised the rebuilding of the theater from the ground up, wrote and produced a new show and even designed all the costumes. By 2018, "Tex's Place" was totally destroying the competition. It was standing room only every night

"Oh sure, Branson is a lovely town. And I did pretty well there," Mark said in mock modesty. "You know, when I first got to Branson, I knew Tex's Place was in trouble, but I could see the potential a mile away." Same exact situation here. And we're going to fix it together—you and me."

"Well Mark, Mountain City isn't Branson..." Dolph countered, taking a long gulp of the Wild Turkey, nervously lighting up another cigarette.

"Not yet," said Mark, now totally getting into his role as a successful dinner theater producer.

Dolph grinned in at Mark's apparent confidence. That was exactly the kind of executive producer he needed. "I think I'm gonna like you, Mark," he said.

Dolph refilled his glass and topped off Mark's, holding his Teutonic Nights tumbler high for a celebratory toast.

"To the Middle Ages!"

"To the Middle Ages!" Mark Lewis enthusiastically chimed. in.

Monte Levine, now Mark Lewis, was finally feeling like his old self again. He was convinced that he was about to change this guy's fortunes and eventually find a way to maneuver himself out of this bizarre Witness Protection Program life.

*　*　*

Sylvia-Sharon was fanning herself with an old copy of People Magazine when Monte-Mark returned from Teutonic Nights that afternoon. All the windows of their new house on Schoolhouse Lane on the west side of Mountain City were open but it was still stifling inside.

"You may just have to kill me," Sylvia shouted out to Monte as he passed the cramped living room on his way to the cramped kitchen to find something to eat. "The toilet keeps running," she said as she approached Monte in the kitchen. The toilet she mentioned was a yellowish pink color with rust stains in the bowl and a fluffy cover on the seat lid. The whole house smelled musty and the tiny backyard was filled with used tires and the last occupants' junk.

Why don't you come with me tonight and get a decent meal?" Monte said to Sylvia as he munched on a supersized bag of Doritos that he had picked up at a nearby gas station the day before. "I need to go back to the theater tonight to see the show. My boss wants me to come up with a new script. Please join me. It'll be good for you to get out of the house for a while."

Sylvia did not protest. She had just about had it sitting in the scuffed La-Z-Boy chair with yellowed wallpaper all around her, watching a snowy black and white portable TV. She went upstairs and changed out of her sweatsuit into the only decent dress she had been allowed to bring with her, came back down the creaky stairs, locked the front door, and joined Monte in the front passenger seat of the banged-up '99 Toyota Camry that the Feds had provided for them.

By the time they reached Teutonic Nights at 5:30, the parking lot was still empty except for a few abandoned cars and a delivery truck unloading cases of beer through the side door.

As they parked the Toyota and crossed the wobbly fiberglass drawbridge to enter the Great Hall, Sylvia could not help but let out a laugh. Monte-Mark shushed her. Not wanting anyone to know he had been hired to run the place, he slid his credit card under the plexiglas to a bored young woman chewing gum and wearing what looked like a Robin Hood hat. She roughly swiped the card through the machine.

There were a few wild children running around, shouting and attacking each other with the plastic swords their parents had just bought them at the gift shop. The Hall of Arms was now open, with displays of a wide variety of medieval weapons from halberds to swords, maces, axes and long bows. Fake wooden doors were also open to the "Torture Chamber,"—a dark hallway, dimly lit with red light bulbs, where crude mannequins with horrified faces were posed in grotesque displays of medieval tortures like the Rack, the Iron Maiden, boiling in oil, or being burnt at the stake.

In the center of the lobby stood a radiant queen, heavily made up, with a rhinestone crown bobby-pinned to her high beehive hairdo, waiting expectantly with an embarrassed-looking photographer in a court jester's costume. For $10, arriving guests could have their photo taken with The Queen. For $20, they could be knighted—touched gently on each shoulder with a golden sword—an act recorded for posterity with a polaroid mounted in a commemorative Teutonic Nights cardboard frame.

Monte and Sylvia waved off the jester and made their way right into the arena to get good seats for the show. As they entered the arena, they were immediately greeted by a teenager with a bad complexion, dressed a green felt tunic and yellow tights. He spoke to them in a faux English accent so bad that it sounded like a speech impediment, but Monte and Sylvia were able to make something about "milord" and "milady" as he took them to their seats. They were seated in the red section, and as they read the menu and "historical guide" that served as their place mats, they learned they were expected to root for the Red Knight when the battle and jousting came.

There was of course no silverware on the placemat, just a gilded piece of cardboard wrapped in cellophane. "And what the hell is this?" Sylvia said, picking it up, examining it from all angles, reluctant to tear the cellophane.

"That's your crown. Open it and put it on," Monte whispered loudly. "Look around the place, everyone is wearing their crowns. Put it on, we don't want to stand out."

Sylvia opened her own cellophane packet and donned her crown at a jaunty angle. "Mountain City royalty, I guess," she smiled.

The house lights lowered, and a spotlight illuminated two thrones at one end of the arena—apparently the royal box. The purple velvet curtain behind it parted and a King and Queen, emerged, holding their hands clasped high above their heads. The Queen was a beauty in a kind of all American way: tiny waist, ample breasts, and long blond hair falling in ringlets over her ermine cape. The king was tall, slim and thickly bearded. He kissed the Queen's hand and led her to her throne. He then approached the railing of the royal box and bellowed to the crowd.

"Welcome to Teutonic Nights, my loyal subjects! Let the feasting begin!"

A closing fanfare sounded. The king took his seat. Monte's eyes widened with a sudden sense of recognition. There was no mistaking that voice. That crazy bastard, Dolph Stewart, his boss, had put on a false beard and lots of makeup and was playing the king!

As if on cue, serving wenches carrying large trays came down the aisles. They placed an overloaded paper plate and a large plastic chalice in front of every guest. The chalice, the placemat said, was "filled to the brim with freshly slain dragon's blood." Monte and Sylvia frowned as the lifted their chalices and sniffed it. It had the smell and consistency of reheated supermarket tomato soup.

On the plate was a huge turkey leg, dry and overcooked. An ear of corn slathered with margarine. Some greasy fried potato chunks. And a huge slice of garlic bread, about the size of a quarter loaf of Wonder Bread.

"I cannot eat this," Sylvia said in a low voice to Monte. "It's disgusting."

"Just take a few bites," Monte said, "Please try to look like you're enjoying it."

Apparently, some of the kids in the opposite Blue Section shared Sylvia's opinion. An ear of corn came hurtling through the air across the arena and knocked the crown off the head of one of the old folks sitting in the Red Section. Monte and Sylvia gasped and ducked as a food fight between the Reds and the Blues began.

The food stopped flying and a smattering of applause greeted the sound of another ear-splitting fanfare and King Dolph rose to declare, "Let the Tournament begin!"

A narrator, dressed as a court page, reading from a large scroll, stepped into the spotlight at the center of the arena and announced, "Good ladies and gentlemen, what you are about to see is living history. All of this actually happened, as you see it. This was the time of Lords and Ladies, knights in shining armor fighting for the right and the just. A world based on honor, chivalry, justice and God. It is a world that no longer exists, except here, at Teutonic Nights."

The show that followed, Monte had to admit, was impressive. The background story was conveyed in a narrated soundtrack accompanied by the pantomimed movements of costumed performers who quickly filled the arena as the page scrambled off. The story line was simple and straightforward. The King and Queen ruled over a happy and prosperous kingdom, as indicated by the wide smiles of the dancing maidens and squires who pirouetted, waltzed in couples, and then formed a large circle, holding hands, as a series of court jesters trotted into the middle of the circle performing acrobatic stunts, juggling axes, and placing flaming torches in their mouths. The audience oohed and ahhed at each stunt, but some of the older children just wanted to make mischief, lobbing fried potato chunks at the performers. A serf hurried down the aisle to warn their parents they would be ejected from the theater if they didn't control their kids.

A mounted troop of knights in shining armor galloped into the arena as the maidens and squires scurried away. They pranced in formation toward the King and Queen, lifting their helmet visors and raising their armored fists.

"We pledge our eternal allegiance to you, O Great and All-Powerful King Arthur and to you Fair and Wise Queen Guinevere," they shouted in unison.

The King rose to accept the fealty of his noble knights, as one of them rode toward the Royal Couple and handed Queen Guinevere a rose.

Suddenly there was a commotion at the entrance curtain at the back of the arena. A herald entered in a state of high agitation. "An evil usurper has attacked the boundaries of this fair kingdom." he shouted in alarm. "The royal falcon will deliver the enemy's ultimatum to the king." A falconer emerged and released his huge bird who swooped threateningly over the audience before handing on the arm of another falconer who emerged behind King Arthur's throne. He removed a folded piece of parchment from one of the falcon's leg and handed it to the king. The king rose to read the threat aloud.

"To King Arthur of the Britons, I, Heinrich the mighty king of the Saxons swear that I will conquer your realm and humiliate your pitiful knight champions. I will claim your Queen as my own bride. So, prepare to lose all that you hold dear."

Suddenly a troop of Blue Knights burst through the curtain into the arena, swords raised, and galloped toward the Red Knights beneath the Royal Box. The sound of swords clashing with swords, shouts of rage and agony, and the fearsome neighing of horses played on a high-volume soundtrack, so loud it made the undrunk Dragon's Blood chalices vibrate and some of the younger children in the audience to cry. The mounted knights in the arena, tried their best to simulate the melees, with their own swords swinging, and some of the knights falling off their horses and convulsing in mock death throes.

The king rose in anger and held up his hand. "Halt! I command you to halt!" he screamed. "We shall settle this act of aggression through the noble rules of chivalry. I bid that the bravest knight on each side wield their lances." All but a few Red and Blue Knights remained while the rest exited through the curtain and the dead knights quickly rose and ran after them.

"We shall have a tournament as our solemn rules of warfare dictate," the King continued. "A joust! A joust! Best three out of five!"

And so, the highlight of the evening followed, with the two sides at the two ends of the arena, and squires running out with long wooden lances, each painted in the color of their side in the conflict. Pairs of Red and Blue Knights, one after another, galloped toward each other with lances aimed straight ahead. In some cases, they missed each other and wheeled around and made another run toward their opponent until the lances crashed and splintered and one knight tumbled onto the ground.

A mock-elderly Wizard with a long grey artificial beard and a high pointed hat and a robe decorated with stars and moon crescents, set up a large easel to keep score. "Red 1 – Blue 0," he croaked in a high-pitched voice as the first joust came to an end. The tournament predictably reached a 2 to 2 tie. Before charging at his opponent, the last of the Red Knights approached the royal box. The King placed a large medallion around the Knight's shoulders and the Queen daintily handed him her perfumed handkerchief which the Knight gently kissed and tucked into his armor.

Armed with the blessings of the Royal Couple, the Red Knight raced toward the last of the enemies and with an acrobatic flair he lifted himself on his saddle and twirled his lance above his head timing it perfectly to strike the last Blue Knight squarely on the breastplate of his armor and send him tumbling to the ground.

"The kingdom is saved!" exclaimed the Wizard.

"May no enemy ever darken our kingdom again!" the king proclaimed. "And to all you noble subjects," he continued, waving his arm regally at the almost empty stands, "I wish you a good eventide, each and every one, and pray you will come visit us again."

*   *   *

Monte and Sylvia rode home in silence. Monte was clearly annoyed when Sylvia chuckled to herself about what a disaster Teutonic Nights was. She just didn't grasp the potential. There was no point in trying to persuade her about the theater's potential once he redesigned the performance by rewriting the script and getting a major star to headline the show. As usual, he had sold himself another impossibly perfect story and confused it with reality. The truth was that there were only about thirty-five people in the audience, not the nightly thousand he had counted on. This medieval dinner theatre in the middle of western Montana was not only a bad joke, but also a total financial disaster. And had either Monte or Mark been thinking clearly, he would have recognized that there was no way that he alone would be able to keep it alive.

Fortunately, the next day was Saturday and Monte-Mark had the day off and didn't have to go into work and tell Dolph what he thought of the present show. He stayed at home, wandering from the house into the trash strewn backyard and cautiously opened the door to the shed.

Inside were a few shovels, some garden tools and a gas-powered lawnmower from Sears. He pulled out the lawn mower with great effort. Why not give it a try? One yank on the ignition cord. Nothing. Another yank and he thought he heard something. Another yank and it sputtered briefly and then started to run.

All his neighbors seemed to take pride in their front lawns, as small as they might be. His lawn was overgrown and badly neglected. He thought for a moment and realized exactly what Mark Lewis would do. He pushed the mower around the side of the house and tore into the thicket of dry grass and weeds in the front yard.

Across the street a tall, stocky neighbor was clipping his hedges. Noticing Monte struggling with the lawnmower, and he put down his clippers and crossed the street to introduce himself.

"Howdy there, I'm Freddie Rich," he said extending his large, calloused hand, "Welcome to Schoolhouse Lane." Monte dutifully shook Freddie's hand. "I'm Mark Lewis," Monte countered, "Me and my wife Sharon just moved here from Branson, Missouri. Looks like a friendly neighborhood. Glad to be here."

"Branson?" Freddy was clearly intrigued. "You must be in show business."

"I am indeed," Monte-Mark proudly said.

"Well, it's real nice to have you as a neighbor," Freddie continued, "why don't you and the little lady come over for a drink later, we'd love to hear all about your life in Branson. My wife Susie and me just dream of being able to go there some day. Why don't you come over around 5?"

Monte-Mark nodded. He couldn't risk being standoffish to the neighbors and calling attention to Sylvia and himself. He shut off the lawn mower and pushed it back to the shed. He'd finish the front lawn later and maybe buy some fertilizer at the local hardware store. He imagined that was probably what his landscaper back in Scarsdale would do.

As he entered the screen door to the kitchen, Sylvia-Sharon was putting away the groceries that she had bought that morning at the Safeway out at the shopping center by the highway.

"Hey, listen" he said to her, "Our neighbors across the street, Freddie and Susie Rich, invited us to come for a drink."

"Oh, that's nice," Sylvia shot back. "Good to hear that at least some people in this broken-down neighborhood are rich. What can we bring?"

"I have some cheese and crackers; will that be ok?"

"Sure," Monte answered as he went up the creaky stairs to take a quick shower behind the cheap plastic shell and seahorse shower curtain in the antique bathtub.

*   *   *

At 5 o'clock Mark and Sharon crossed the street, went up the stairs, and rang the Rich family doorbell.

Freddie opened the door with a broad smile. "Come on in!" he said.

The Rich living room looked almost exactly like their own. Pastel shag carpet, faded wallpaper, a TV, La-Z-Boy and a sofa.

"Well, let me make the introductions," said Freddie, turning to his tiny wife. "Susie, meet Mark and Sharon, our new neighbors." He put his hand to his mouth to make a mock-secret aside to Susie. "They're from Branson, maybe they'll give this neighborhood some class."

Susie smiled coyly and scurried off to the kitchen, bringing back a tray with six ice-cold cans of Bud Light, their tabs already popped.

Sylvia-Sharon placed her own tray of Stoned Wheat Thins and sliced Jarlsberg cheese on the coffee table in the middle of the room.

"These look good!" said Susie as placed a slice of cheese on a cracker and then handed the beers to everyone as they settled in on the sofa and Freddy took his usual place, regally stretching out on the La-Z-boy.

"So what's your line of work, Fred?" Monte-Mark asked politely.

"What do you think? I live in Mountain City," Freddie answered with a chuckle. "I work as a sales manager for Valkyrie Pharmaceuticals. Just about the only show in town."

"And speaking of show business…" Freddie quickly changed the subject, "I mentioned to Susie that you two have moved here from Branson. If you don't mind me asking, what brings you folks to Mountain City?"

Sharon-Sylvia spoke up with apparent pride about her husband, though it was really meant to be a sarcastic, private jab at Monte. "Oh yes, Mark has spent his whole life in show business. And he's here to make his biggest splash yet: as the Executive Producer of Teutonic Nights!"

"Wow! We LOVE that place!" squealed Susie in delight. "I took Freddie there for his birthday two years ago. It was amazing! Like history taking place right in front of you."

"Hey Mark," Freddie said, grabbing another beer, "I bet you didn't know this, but in a way, we actually work for the same company."

Mark seemed confused.

"Your boss is the son of my boss," Freddie explained. "Your boss, Dolph Stewart, AKA King Arthur, is the son of my boss, Jerry Stewart, founder and CEO of Valkyrie Pharmaceuticals, a multi-gazillionaire, if you know what I mean—the richest man in Montana—and in the whole world for all I know."

That Stewart family connection was something that the Feds at Langley had neglected to mention.

"I probably shouldn't mention this," Freddie continued, "but it's a shame that Dolph has had such a hard time in life. Big disappointment to the old man. Well, actually a lot more than a disappointment. Heavy drinker. Pot smoker. Got thrown out of one school after another. Not exactly a chip off the old block, if you know what I mean."

Freddie leaned back in the La-Z-Boy and took a long slurp from his brewski. He reached for a napkin and wiped his lips and chin before he went on.

"Well, see about a dozen years ago, old Jerry sets up Dolph with this Teutonic Nights thing. Builds the whole thing for the kid. A lot of us thought that it was probably Jerry's idea. Mr. Stewart is a total nut about the Middle Ages. Rumor has it he's got a giant collection of old armor weapons and stuff, up at his huge mansion that everyone calls The Castle. Makes sense that the king and knight business was something he thought up to spread his ideas. That's what we hear anyway."

Monte suddenly put two and two together. That's how Teutonic Nights could stay in business with such a large cast and so few paying customers.

"And let me give you a friendly piece of advice," Freddie added. "Never get on the wrong side of Jerry Stewart. Just make his son look good and you can bet your bottom dollar that he'll take care of you."

CHAPTER 10
A TWIST IN THE STORY

On a late August morning at the Big Sky Tavern in downtown Mountain City. Billy Osmund, one of the city's most colorful and notorious personalities, was the only customer sitting at the bar. He held his bald head in his beefy hands, sighing deeply. Had anybody come into the Big Sky that morning and approached the bar, they would have immediately recognized the broad back of Billy's ragged and sleeveless jeans jacket, embroidered with the image of a charging knight and the slogan "Everything for the King." Billy's ample backside hung over the sides of the barstool. Bob Howard, the longtime Big Sky bartender, briefly stopped wiping the mahogany bar, leaned on one elbow, and listened to Billy's tale of woe.

"How could he do that to me?" Billy said, not really expecting an answer. "Thirteen years through thick and thin and this is what I deserve?"

Bob the bartender just shook his head in shared sorrow. He reached around to the row of bottles set up beneath a line of dusty rodeo and bowling trophies and grabbed a half-empty bottle of Wild Turkey. "How about a refill, Billy?" he asked. And before Billy could even answer, he poured Billy another double shot.

Like so many people in Mountain City, Billy and Bob had known each other for a long time. Both of them had graduated from Stewart High School, though a decade apart. Both of their family roots in

Mountain City were long and deep; their forebears had arrived here decades before the foundation of the town in 1830. The patriarchs of both families were rough and rugged fur trappers, but in the passage of time both families had settled into the routines and careers of Montana city folk. Billy had been Bob's Social Studies teacher in high school. In fact, he had been almost everybody's teacher in the years he taught at Stewart High and directed each year's senior play. "Guys and Dolls," "My Fair Lady," "Oklahoma," and "The Music Man" had all been smash hits, with costumes and scenery made by the students themselves.

Billy was undoubtedly the most popular teacher among the students and their parents—at least until the fateful production of the Class of '87 was performed. That was the year that Billy chose "Hello Dolly!" It all seemed to be going fine until Billy fell madly in love with Dolly, who actually happened to be 18-year-old Mary Beller, daughter of "Chief Ted" Beller, head of the Mountain City police force and one mean son-of-a-bitch if there ever was one. To make matters worse, Billy got Mary pregnant and although she was barely showing on the night of the final performance, Chief Ted angrily pinned Billy against the wall of cafeteria during the closing cast party and threatened he would make Billy a wheelchair jockey for the rest of his life unless he did the respectable thing and took his daughter to the altar and made her Mrs. Osmund, despite their unfortunate difference in age.

From there, things went downhill for Billy. He was fired from his job at the high school, and was given a job as an auxiliary cop by his father-in-law at minimum wage. Directing traffic, writing parking tickets, and collaring jaywalkers did not agree with him. The only thing he liked about the job was meeting for doughnuts and coffee for honest-to-goodness real cops. They all seemed to admire Chief Ted's uncompromising ideas about how to deal with strangers and juvenile delinquents in "his" town. But he still missed show business—or at least what passed for show business in Mountain City. The costumes. The music. The story. And the joy he felt from the sound of cheers and applause on opening nights.

His big break came from one of his former students, Dolph Stewart, son of the owner of Valkyrie Pharmaceuticals. Dolph had played the Devil in Billy's 1983 production of Damn Yankees; he had stumbled through the rehearsals, forgetting his lines, and over acting or underacting, depending (Billy suspected) how much pot he had smoked that day.

But when Dolph stopped Billy on the street one day, Billy's fortunes suddenly changed.

"Hey Mr. Osmund!" Dolph said as he reached out his multi-ringed hand to shake hands with Billy, "I've been looking for you everywhere."

Long story short: Dolph explained that he had a great business opportunity for Billy. He was setting up a chic dinner theater in Mountain City—something that was really going to put the place on the map. "Of course, there has to be great entertainment," Dolph added, and that's where you come in. Everybody remembers the fantastic shows you directed at Stewart High."

"Just one, catch," Dolph interrupted. "It has to be a performance set in the Middle Ages. With King Arthur and the Knights of the Round Table. Beautiful maidens, brave knights in shining armor, swordplay, jousting... all that stuff."

Billy was confused. "King Arthur in Mountain City?

Dolph was insistent. "That's your challenge. I want you to create something that will be as popular senior class shows. But it has to be about King Arthur. No if and or buts about that. Let's just say I have a silent partner—um, I think you call it an 'angel' on Broadway. Paying for everything. And if he wants a show about King Arthur, that's what it will be."

Billy shrugged in resignation.

Dolph held out his glittering hand again, as if to seal the deal. "How does $35,000 a year sound—plus all the turkey legs you can eat?"

That was the way the whole Teutonic Nights castle and dinner show started but now, after thirteen of his happiest years in show business, Billy's return to the stage had ended as quickly as it had begun.

"And he just fired you, just told you were done?" Bob the bartender asked in disbelief.

Billy stared into his glass.

"Yep. Just like that," he said, snapping his fingers to emphasize the suddenness of the shock. "I had no idea it was coming. Just like that." He snapped his fingers again.

"Did you do something to make him angry?" Bob the bartender

asked.

"Nope. It wasn't anything I did," Billy answered, "Dolph just seems to have hired someone else behind my back."

"Someone else?" Bob was incredulous at the idea that anyone else in Mountain City could possibly equal Billy's directorial skill.

"Yeah, some big shot from Branson. Dolph told me that he wanted to move in a more 'professional' direction and he hired him. But I guess he's got a point," Billy sadly admitted," the box office has been a bit on the slow side for the last three or four years."

Bob listened carefully. He thought silently for a moment as he wiped the bar again.

"Something doesn't make sense," he finally said to Billy, "why would some big shot from Branson come all the way here to Mountain City to direct a two-bit medieval show—no offense intended—and not stay there with all the stars and big money in Show Business City, USA? I smell a rat. He could be an informer for the FBI."

Billy had never thought of that. He shot back another drink that Bob had just poured. It made sense. The Deep State cast a shadow over everything these days. And the red-blooded patriots of Mountain City did and what they believed in was their business. The last thing they wanted was some undercover federal agent sniffing around.

Billy's face suddenly grew red with anger. Self-pity was instantly replaced by rage. "Mark Lewis. Branson big shot. My foot. You're absolutely right, Bob. There's something very fishy going on here and I'm gonna find out exactly what it is."

*   *   *

Folks in Mountain City liked stability. They didn't like change. Dolph had learned this lesson the hard way. At some point he tried to change the dinner menu at Teutonic Nights to bring in more customers. Instead of the usual turkey legs, he tried barbequed ribs. This was a big mistake. First, all turkey legs are pretty much all the same size, but rib portions can vary a lot – big ribs or small ribs. Fist fights had broken out the first rib night, which was also the last rib night. So the meals went back to turkey legs and the show remained unchanged.

Mark knew nothing about menu planning, certainly not in Montana, so he left the medieval cuisine alone. But the story definitely needed changing. Something had to be done to make the show more exciting—and most important of all to put more medieval-loving asses in the seats.

As soon as he started to work at Teutonic Nights and had seen how only a few dozen paying customers showed up at every performance, Mark-Monte recognized that, with a cast of nearly a hundred, the pitiful box office revenue would sooner or later spell doom for Dolph's dinner theater. And if Teutonic Nights went under, he understood that there was more at stake here than just another job. He had to make a success out of this crazy medieval pageant because Mountain City was the only relatively safe place that he and Sylvia had to hide. But he knew he could do it. Monte had supreme confidence in his own ability to make this whole Teutonic Nights thing really, really big.

The basic show itself would not be that hard to fix. The current show was a mess. The script could have been written from the material in a children's book about King Arthur, which, though Mark-Monte didn't know it, was Billy Osmund's main source. Violence on horseback, Monte had to admit, had obvious potential. Of course, there were downsides to galloping horses in an enclosed arena, particularly when food was being served. But besides that, the show's story line was fairly simple and straightforward. What was needed, Monte realized, was an eye-popping spectacle with an unexpected twist. That's what he did back at TrulyTV; he put together a grab bag of familiar story elements to create a totally mind-blowing idea.

One night after work, Monte sat down at his formica kitchen table with a yellow legal pad and began to jot down some notes. What made Real Housewives work? What made people obsessively watch Real Life Cops? What made any reality show work? Vivid characters that people either loved or loathed—nothing in between. Exotic, dangerous, or opulent surroundings. Lots of violence and sexual titillation. And an unexpected twist in the plot. Yes! That what was lacking. The twist. The surprise ending. The unexpected hook that would keep the audience coming back for more.

Monte realized that the pieces for something much better were already there. He just had to re-arrange them and turn up the heat. And then, it hit him. King Arthur and the Knights of the Round Table meet

WrestleMania. Camelot meet Hooters. If he could just turn up the heat a bit and cater to the lowest common denominator rather than medieval pomp and ceremony, he'd have something that thousands of Mountain City people from 9 to 90 would unfailingly pay cash money to watch.

Monte-Mark knew audiences well enough to see that Mountain City could never support a cliched medieval drama. He knew that Pro Wrestling in armor and on horseback was exactly what the public wanted, whether they admitted it or not. If a buzz could be started among New York and LA fan magazines and websites, who knows how many RVs, Harleys, hot rods, and limos would roar into town. And who knows, maybe the Universal Wrestling Network and the Macho Channel would start a bidding war for the television rights. Now this was a business he understood. Starting with this small seed in Mountain City, he felt certain that he could grow a Medieval Reality show into a major cable TV franchise and sell it to Discovery or Netflix. Why not? Even under his assumed name and identity, he could be back in business in no time—and besides, this Locovita thing wouldn't last forever.

A few phone calls the next morning set the wheels in motion. He knew he was taking a risk and breaking FBI protocols, but it was worth it. He knew just what to do and he knew just who to call. In the TV business, as Kathy told him a thousand times, casting is everything and so a new star was quickly recruited, but his identity would not be revealed until opening night.

When he had finished the new script, he gathered the Teutonic Knights cast together.

"I want to tell you how happy I am to be working with you," he began. "I have had the pleasure of seeing you perform night after night, and I want to tell you what an outstanding job, what a truly professional job you do. Every one of you."

"But I have to tell you, I think you are all capable of even greater things. Amazing things. And that is where I am going to take you, if you are willing to take the show to the next level."

Mark began to explain the new plot.

"From now on, you, Laurel," Mark said looking at his 22-year-old Queen Guinevere, "have a very unhappy marriage to the King. Very unhappy. Lots of fighting."

"You are going to fall in love with a new knight who has come to the castle to serve the king."

"The Black Knight."

"He's from a faraway land. No one knows him. He's the ultimate villain who becomes the hero, He's a superhero who can do amazing things."

"So the Black Knight woos the Queen away from the King, they fall in love and in the last scene of the show, Laurel, you lift his visor to kiss him really passionately."

Here, in Mountain City, in the unlikeliest of venues, Monte-Mark had at last found complete freedom to create the wildest, wackiest reality extravaganza that anyone had ever seen. It was hunky competitors for the hand of The Bachelorette in armor on horseback fighting with swords and lances instead of sweet words and bouquets of roses. The concept, he felt, pure genius. Radical enough and crazy enough to get him back on Fox, even if it had to be under an assumed name.

Dolph had led Monte-Mark to understand that he could not have cared less what he did with the show's choreography and plot, as long as the audience—and box office take—substantially grew. So long as the crowds kept coming, kept putting on their paper crowns, kept buying the beers, t-shirts, plastic swords and maces—and kept paying $20 to be knighted by Queen Guinevere in the lobby, or have their photos taken with her, everything would be perfectly fine with him.

And so, the cast of Teutonic Nights proceeded with their regular show, day after day, but late in the evenings and on weekend mornings, they secretly rehearsed the new spectacular that Monte-Mark had dreamed up—with stand-ins for King Arthur and the mysterious Black Knight—until it was perfect. Everyone on the team agreed it was great and no one spilled the beans. In just a week, on Saturday, the gala premiere was going to be a big night for them all.

* * *

On Wednesday, the Black Knight finally appeared at a full rehearsal. Everyone else in the cast was wearing their jeans and T-shirts for the run-through, but the Black Knight came in his full costume: a dark head-to-toe set of spiked armor, down to the pointed metal boots and razor-knuckled gloves. The closed visor of his helmet bore a menacing visage. His imposing height, deep voice, and massive frame scared everyone.

"Jesus Christ," one cast member yelled on seeing him. "It's Darth Vader.'

That was the image that he projected. He was big. He was powerful. And he was physically frightening—just the effect that Monte-Mark had wanted to achieve.

"How come he's in costume?' someone asked Monte-Mark during a break.

"Method actor," Mark said in a knowing whisper. "You know, like Marlon Brando, Daniel Day- Lewis, once he accepts a role, he never leaves character."

On the day of the premiere, Mark met with Dolph, not to divulge the secret, but to tell him that Branson was coming to Mountain City. "Better than Branson," Mark said with a smile. "We're going to feature a new star straight from Broadway."

"A real Broadway star?" Dolph asked.

"Straight from the Great White Way," Monte assured him.

"Who is it? You gotta tell me," Dolph playfully pleaded.

Monte-Mark lifted his fingers to his tightly closed lips. "That would spoil the surprise."

As soon as Mark left the office, Dolph got right on the phone. He put in calls to The Mountain City Tribune; The Billings Gazette; KPAX Channel 8; Montana Magazine; Fish and Stream Weekly, Gunns and Ammo; and any other media outlet he could think of, to invite their entertainment reporters to cover opening night.

Dolph's last call was the most important. He closed the door and punched in a private cell phone number he had not used in years. After three rings, a familiar voice answered.

"Papa," Dolph stuttered. "I would like to invite you to the premiere of our new show this Saturday night."

"A new show?" Jerry Stewart answered in annoyance. "You promised me that you would not corrupt the noble legend of the Round Table. That's why I keep your pitiful theater alive."

Jerry Stewart had never been to a performance. Not once. Not ever.

"Nein, mein Adolph. I cannot make it. But I will send a trusted representative to make sure you have not dishonored the values I hold dear."

* * *

Saturday came fast. While it was not a full house, it was a good turnout. And Monte-Mark was confident that the stands would be packed for months to come. Word had gotten out that something huge, new, and spectacular was coming to Mountain City. The Missoula press was there. The papers, TV, radio. It was going to be the biggest event in many years.

The show opened with the blinding glare of strobe lights and laser beams. stage smoke rose from the arena, as heavy metal music, played at AC-DC volume, vibrated through the stands. Heads turned as a white spotlight illuminated the royal box. Lauren, playing the Queen with a sudden fierceness, waved a golden dagger in the air as she screamed at King Arthur for his laziness, stupidity, and cruelty.

The crowd seemed to love it.

A shower of turkey legs and ears of corn rained down on the startled King. Dolph—playing King Arthur as usual—had no idea what was happening and quickly grabbed his shield to shelter him from the flying medieval meals. The bickering between king and queen escalated to slaps, hair pulling, and punches between them, with King Arthur Dolph now genuinely angry and giving as good as he got.

Any remaining trace of chivalry quickly vanished, as the crowd cheered wildly when a steel cage was lowered from the rafters brought for a death match between a red and blue knight. Excited blow-by-blow commentary, laced freely with curse words, boomed through the PA system in the now strangely manic voice of the royal scribe.

"And so, discord, not harmony, reigned in the court of King Arthur who for years only cared about himself and his own riches, and not the welfare of his people." the scribe concluded, as the king and queen's argument grew more raucous, and they eventually came to blows. The audience was by now going crazy, seeing their own daily frustrations and disappointments at the hands of their supervisors and managers taken out against the king.

"But one brave knight came to save the people and the Queen," the announcer intoned.

The arena suddenly went dark and the roaring crowd gradually grew quiet as the Darth Vader theme from Star Wars blared out. A single spotlight illuminated the opening curtains at the back of the arena as the enormous figure of the Black Knight galloped onto the scene, with his huge silver sword drawn and held high above his head. The crowd went wild, cheering at the top of their lungs.

The Black Knight circled the arena as the other cast members scattered, finally riding boldly toward the royal box and challenging the by-now trembling King to a duel. Dolph's instinct was to flee backstage from this huge, threatening figure, but he grabbed his own sword and descended from the royal box to the arena floor. The scrawny king exchanged blows with the Black Knight, until Dolph's instinct finally took over and he beat a hasty retreat back up into the royal box and disappeared backstage. The crowd booed loudly and burst into wild applause.

The Queen ran down to embrace the Black Knight who had saved her from her life of misery with the king. The Black Knight dropped to one knee to show his fealty to Guinivere then rose to his full height to embrace the Queen.

"Take leave of him, milady, and come away with me," the Black Knight said in a deep, manly voice, loud enough that even the spectators in the uppermost rows of the arena could hear.

"I will. I love you," the Queen sang in her beautiful soprano voice. Then she reached up to lift his visor and kissed him deeply and passionately, just as Monte-Mark had planned.

The crowd, which had been wildly cheering for the Darth Vader character, suddenly let out a gasp of surprise as the Black Knight turned to the audience, his visor now completely raised.

The Black Knight, played by the up-and-coming film star and Tony-award winning actor John Milldale, just happened to be Black.

Sitting in the front row of the Red Section as Jerry Stewart's designated observer, Billy Osmund, former director of the Teutonic Nights production, grinned at Mark Lewis's miscalculation. He knew exactly what his new boss what Jerry Stewart felt about People of Color and about ridiculing knighthood. He would now report the happenings at Teutonic Knights to his new employer, confident that he would finally get his revenge.

CHAPTER 11
MISSING PERSONS

In her hours of loneliness and isolation, Sylvia often wondered about the people who had lived in this house on before. Telltale signs of the former occupants were all around them: the framed portrait of the blonde and blue-eyed Jesus above the TV, the homemade knotty-pine cabinets in the kitchen, the flowerpots stacked neatly in the backyard shed, the roll-top desk in the second bedroom, with a straight-backed wooden desk chair. This house was not just a furnished rental, but clearly somebody's home. She imagined them as an American Gothic couple—older, stoic churchgoers, parsimonious senior citizens, who remained self-sufficient to the end.

And what could have happened to them? An old age home? Off to live with their children in some other city? Or maybe they had both passed away? Their departure must have been sudden, because everything had remained in its place. The kitchen drawers were still filled with forks, knives, spoons, and old-fashioned gadgets. The shelves still held a lifetime's mix of places, cups, and mugs. And up in the linoleum-floored bathroom, the medicine cabinet was still filled with old bottles of aspirin, laxatives, and Pepto-Bismol that Sylvia had quickly thrown away.

The ghostly presence of the former residents was matched by Sylvia's own lonely, spectral existence. She rarely ventured out and spent her waking hours in isolation. Monte left early for work and returned late in the evening—especially during the weeks he had been working on the new show. So left to her own devices, without a job, a car, or even a friend she could really confide in, she surrendered to a lonely, empty existence of watching hour after hour of daytime TV.

Early one afternoon, just as Judge Judy was about to make her final ruling, Sylvia heard the sound of a woman's footsteps coming up the front porch stairs. She panicked. Monte had warned her never to answer the door for anyone she didn't recognize. The sharp ring of the doorbell sounded twice. Sylvia rose cautiously from the sofa and peered into the tiny front hall. The woman at the front door pressed her hand against the glass pane of the door to see if anyone was inside.

Sylvia hesitated but there was something kindly and innocent about the woman. Attractive and stylish in a Montana sort of way. She warily opened the front door. "Can I help you?" she said to the stranger.

The woman seemed surprised to see Sylvia. "Sorry to bother you, ma'am, are Mr. and Mrs. Gunther at home?"

"No, no one named Gunther here. I'm afraid you have the wrong address," Sylvia answered. "This is the L-L-Lewis residence."

She stuttered out the answer, trying her best to maintain her cover, living in deathly fear of letting any telltale detail about who she really was slip out. Monte could live this deceptive life much more easily than she could. He was a natural manipulator; he honed his skill in years of producing Reality TV. But Sylvia could never do that. Robbed of her true identity and given a false history concocted by a white bread U.S. marshal, who knew nothing and cared even less about who she was and what she cherished; she had lost everything she had held precious in life.

The visitor seemed puzzled at Sylvia's answer. "That's so strange," Elizabeth said, checking her notebook. "According to my records, the Gunthers have lived here for fifty years."

She looked at Sylvia in an apologetic way. "You'll have to forgive me. I am new to this assignment. Elder care was handled by Mr. Pearson for as long as I can remember. Sadly, he passed on a few weeks ago, and I have been asked to take over his duties. I am sure I made a mistake." Her voice trailed off as she sensed Sylvia's discomfort. She reached out her hand toward Sylvia.

"I'm Elizabeth Beller, the neighborhood representative of the

Mountain City True Kingdom Free-Will Church. We like to keep an eye on our older members. I'm so sorry to hear that the Gunthers are gone."

"I suppose you're new in town," Elizabeth said, trying not to pry.

Sylvia nodded.

"Well, if there's anything I can do for you, here's my name and address and some information about our church." Elizabeth handed a glossy brochure with a Teutonic Jesus preaching to a group of blond children on the cover. "It must be lonely for you living in a new place. I just know you would enjoy meeting some of the members of our wonderful church."

As Elizabeth turned to leave, Sylvia closed the front door gently and watched her walk down the front stairs. She knew the importance of maintaining her distance from strangers. She had had that lesson drilled into her in Langley and Monte repeated the mantra pretty much every night when he came home. "We're in hiding until the danger blows over," he used to say. "I don't like it either, but we have to keep silent." Sylvia heard those words and understood them, but she was just so tired of the silence and loneliness of living an identity that wasn't hers.

She thought for a moment. Her loneliness was painful. She opened the door and stepped outside. "Excuse me, Mrs. Beller," she called out. "If you have a few minutes, I'd love to have you come in for a cup of tea."

* * *

That same morning, Monte-Mark faced his own surprise, but a much less pleasant one. He had been running the previous night's spectacular premiere of the new show over and over in his mind. What a show! What a riotous audience response! If he could add more strobe lights and pyrotechnics and start to promote the stars of the show like wrestling superstars, Teutonic Nights would pack the house every night and expand their line of merchandise from cheap plastic swords and armor to action figures, posters, trading cards, and who knows what else. Even here, at the end of the world, he had once again pulled the fat out of the fire.

As he drove down to the theater, he loudly hummed the Darth

Vader theme. He felt very pleased with himself.

Suddenly his cell phone buzzed him out of his elation. He pulled it out of his jacket pocket and stared down at the text message at the next red light. It was from Dolph and was written in all caps: NEED TO SEE YOU IMMEDIATELY.

A rush of adrenaline shot through Monte-Mark's body. No more humming. No more dreaming. When the light turned green, he stepped on the gas.

When he arrived at the theater to find out why he had been summoned so urgently, he quickly crossed he lobby, pulled open the hidden door next to the restrooms and bolted up the narrow stairs to Dolph's lair.

The office was as cluttered and disordered as ever, but he had never seen such a thick fog of cigarette smoke or such a strong smell of booze. Dolph was hunched over his desk with his face buried in his folded arms. When he heard Monte-Mark enter he looked up as if in a stupor, his eyes bloodshot and bleary and his tousled comb-over revealing how bald he really was.

"It's over," Dolph blubbered. "My father is pulling the plug."

Dolph lowered his face back into his arms. His shoulders bobbed up and down slightly as if he had started to cry.

Monte-Mark lunged toward the desk and grabbed Dolph by the shoulders and forced him to raise his head. "What the fuck is going on?" Dolph sniffed back his tears and reached for an almost empty bottle on the table behind his desk to pour himself another drink, but Monte-Mark grabbed it away from him.

Dolph took a deep breath. "OK. My father hates the show. He's absolutely furious. He's going to close down the theater and turn it into a warehouse for Valkyrie."

Monte-Mark was stunned. "But every seat was filled last night. The first time in years. The crowd loved every minute and I guarantee that they'll come back again and again. From what I hear, your father is a brilliant businessman. Doesn't he get that?"

"It's not the money," Dolph answered as he rose, reached across the desk and grabbed back the bottle out of Monte-Mark's hands. "No, it's something much more valuable to him."

"And that is…?" Monte-Mark was impatient to get to the bottom line.

"Chivalry," Dolph responded through tears.

"What?" Monte said, not really understanding.

"The Legend of King Arthur and his Knights of the Round Table. Chivalry. Honor. Victory."

Monte-Mark's jaw dropped. "You gotta be kidding. Teutonic Nights is cut rate dinner theater that serves tomato soup and turkey drumsticks and paper crowns to teenagers and working-class families. They watch horses run back and forth. The only goal is to put butts in the seats and to sell as much plastic shit as possible in the giftshop. Where's the chivalry, honor, and victory in that?"

"You just don't understand," Dolph said as he emptied the bottle into his glass and lit another cigarette.

"My father is old school. He grew up believing in something. When he was a young man, he was proud to be part of a tradition that stretched back hundreds of years. All the people he admired idolized King Arthur. More than Jesus Christ even. They dreamt of being knights sitting around the Round Table. Defending castles. Fighting for Right. Making a better world…"

Monte-Mark was amazed to hear Dolph rattle on about the medieval ideal of knightly honor, when he knew his main concerns were dating women half his age and getting the best wholesale price for turkey legs.

"And your father thought this place embodied those ideals? Come on. Get serious. Did he ever come down here and see the show?

"Never," Dolph answered. "He didn't have to. He wrote the script himself. He didn't care who came to see it. He didn't give a shit what they bought or what they ate. It was all about the story. Almost like a mystical ritual that had to be repeated again and again. King Arthur sat on his throne and reigned over a prosperous, orderly kingdom. Everyone knew their place and were ready to die for the kingdom. And when the enemy approached everyone rushed to defend their leader and his realm."

Dolph paused as he stubbed out a cigarette in the overflowing ashtray on his desk and lit up another one.

"That's ridiculous," Monte said.

Dolph suddenly turned on him, his face filled with anger.

"My father built his company from nothing by believing in the ideal of King Arthur. And you… you turned it into a joke."

* * *

Over tea and cookies in her 1950s-style knotty pine kitchen, Sylvia made her first true Mountain City friend. Elizabeth, ten years her senior, told her how she had been born in Mountain City, gone to Mountain City High School, married Ted, the football hero and homecoming king; she had been the homecoming queen, had three children, two grandchildren now and still worked at Valkyrie. And she proudly recounted the long, hard-won career of her husband Ted, from starting right after military service as an auxiliary policeman to becoming Mountain City Chief of Police.

Sylvia had memorized the details of her personal life history, and when Elizabeth asked about it she mentioned only the Tex Ritter Rodeo in Branson, which her husband Mark managed for a dozen years. But when Elizabeth asked about her children, she skated a bit, just a wee bit, closer to the truth.

"Willow and Linette," Sylvia said.

"Such lovely names," Elizabeth said. "And where are they now?"

Here, a red flag went up in Sylvia's mind.

"They're both overseas," she said, and having said it, she could see the look of surprise on her new friend's face. Hardly anyone in Mountain City had ever been out of the country for pleasure. The idea that your children, both of them, would be in another country could mean only one thing.

"Military?" she asked.

"We are just so proud of the girls," was all Sylvia could say. That had been close. Maybe too close.

"And you, do you have any children? Sylvia asked cautiously.

"Oh, yes two boys and a girl," Elizabeth answered. "Christopher and Wesley both work for Valkyrie in the shipping department and our daughter Mary is happily married to Billy Osmund, who used to teach drama at Stewart High. He worked at Teutonic Knights for a while, but he now works for Jerry Stewart himself."

"That's so nice. It must very comforting to have your whole family close by."

"It is. Our church community keeps us all together," Elizabeth added. "We are all family. I mean if someone needs a helping hand in hard times or a sympathetic ear when they're going through problems, we're all here for each other. Our goal is to always to expand our patriotic white Christian community. I don't suppose you didn't have that kind of a welcoming Christian fellowship in a big show business town like Branson."

"No, we lived pretty much on our own. Our friends and family were so far away. And they're even farther away now" Sylvia's eyes teared up and could barely get out those words. She tried to keep her composure, but there was something so comforting about having someone she to talk to that she let her emotions pour out and she began to cry.

Elizabeth reached across the formica tabletop between the teacups and dish of cookies and tenderly took Sylvia's hand. "Let's pray together," she said as she bowed her head.

"Lord Jesus, the world is so full of lonely people who are weary and burdened, alone and afflicted. Be gracious to my new friend Sharon Lewis. I ask that she can find comfort and succor in You, who came to earth to carry our burdens, heal our brokenness, and set us free from the bondage of Satan and the Deep State. I pray You will never ever leave us nor forsake us. I ask this in Jesus' name. Amen."

As a Jewish girl growing up on Long Island, Sylvia had always felt uneasy at the mention of Jesus, in school, on the radio, and TV. Her faith was permanent barrier to her full participation in American society. But now she didn't even have the warm embrace of New York Jewish culture to serve as substitute kind of citizenship. So, she was ready to take the next step in a process of assimilation that began the moment her Polish great-great grandparents landed at Ellis Island. Once they got to America, they became, as did so many others, Jews in name, but in fact, once exposed to life in America, aspired to be more WASP than the WASPs they encountered in the New World.

Elizabeth patted Sharon-Sylvia's hands and rose from the kitchen chair. "May Jesus offer you comfort in this difficult time," she said, "And I hope you'll come to the church and join our congregation. But I have to be going. There are many elders I still need to check on today as part of my lay ministry."

Sharon-Sylvia felt a pang of regret about parting from the first person who had offered her real sympathy in months. She looked toward Elizabeth with a pained expression.

"Would you mind if I came along?" she asked.

* * *

By mid-afternoon, the commercial trucks had already pulled up at the rear loading docks of the Teutonic Nights Theater to haul away the leased vending machines and refrigerator cases from the snack bar. Wholesale costume and toy dealers were taking inventory of all the merchandise left in the giftshop. The horses had been loaded on carriers to be taken off to auction and the entire cast sat in stunned silence in the empty arena as Monte gave them the bad news.

"I would say I feel like I let you all down," he said to the knights, jesters, monks, and ladies-in-waiting filling the first three rows of one side of the otherwise empty arena, "but the truth is I really don't understand what's going on here."

"You were stars, every one of you.

"You'll all be paid through last Saturday night. But that's it. Until further notice Teutonic Nights is closed. Good luck to all of you."

The members of the cast had all seen the trucks loading up the theater equipment and furnishings—and loading up the horses—so this announcement didn't come as a surprise. But it was a cause of sadness for many of them, not just because they were losing their jobs. As they filed out of the arena, Mark-Monte had a kind word for all of them, and more than a few of the departing cast members shared what Teutonic Nights had meant to them.

"Mountain City's going to miss this place," said one of the court jesters.

"I guess I'm going to have to trade in my tiara for a stupid Big Burgerz cap," said a lady-in-waiting.

"From Camelot back to the hog farm for me," said one of the Red Knights.

Last in line were Laurel Beeman and John Milldale—Queen Guinevere and the Dark Knight who rescued her from King Arthur— approached Mark-Monte, holding hands. Laurel's eyes were red from crying. Her blond hair was disheveled, but she also had a tearful smile on her face.

"Oh, Laurel," Mark-Monte said to her as he gave her a big hug and a fatherly kiss on the cheek.

Laurel turned toward John with a look of total devotion. "It's like a blessing that you invited John to come out here from New York. Meeting him changed my life. I can see now that there's a future for me outside of Mountain City."

"It's almost like a cosmic miracle," Laurel said in gratitude and wonder. "We'll be leaving for LA next week. Yesterday John got a call from his agent. The Disney people want him to do a screen test for the lead role in Black Panther, The Musical. Mr. Moskowitz says it could be even bigger than Lion King. And John has asked me to go with him."

Monte stood motionless leaning on the arena railing, dreaming of what might have been. He did not consider how bleak his prospects now actually were—how he would support himself and Sylvia and how he could maintain his cover now that he had enraged the most powerful man in Mountain City by playing around with his favorite myth.

A bloodcurdling, cackling laugh suddenly broke the silence of the now empty arena. Monte turned with a start toward the source of laughter at the top of the aisle stairs. Silhouetted against the light streaming in from the lobby was the stumpy, pot-bellied figure of Billy Osmund.

His loud laughter at Mark-Monte subsided to a loud chuckle. "I'm baaack!" he screamed in a taunting falsetto. His words sounded like those of a killer in B-list horror movie. And that's exactly what Billy Osmund intended to be.

$*\quad*\quad*$

At the end of a long day of visiting run-down houses, nursing homes, and hospice facilities around Mountain City, both Elizabeth and Sharon-Sylvia were emotionally drained and shocked to their very souls. The healing power of Jesus seemed unable to penetrate the fog of mysterious disappearances that had apparently swallowed up a large number of senior citizens all over town. Nothing like this had ever happened to Elizabeth before. Her monthly "Elder Ministry" book made no mention of the large number of supplicants who apparently had vanished. "I can't understand why Mr. Pearson didn't mark any of these down," she said. New to the job, she had made up a list of all the senior citizens she was scheduled to visit, written in a spiral bound notebook in the neat cursive handwriting she had been taught by the stern teachers at the Valkyrie Elementary School.

Two neatly drawn columns ran down every page to the right of the names, each awaiting a checkmark of either "Blessed" or "Deceased." "Blessed" indicated that Elizabeth had listened to them, prayed with them, and praised their righteousness. "Deceased" meant they had gone to heaven to abide with the Lord. Elizabeth's list that day contained 36 names of faithful Methodist parishioners, but by the end of the day, as the sun was setting, only eleven names had been filled in.

It had started with the Gunthers, the kindly old couple who had resided for fifty years in Sharon's house. Gone without a trace and without an explanation. But they were only the first. After that, Elizabeth and Sharon-Sylvia walked over to the Happy Pastures Long Term Care Facility just behind the Chevy dealership on Stewart Boulevard. Elizabeth had a list of eight parishioners to visit there. When she stepped politely up to the receptionist behind the glass partition in the main lobby, she learned that six of the eleven people she had come to ministered to were no longer there.

"Have they passed on? Have they been transferred to a hospital?" Elizabeth politely asked with genuine concern.

"I'm afraid that information is confidential," the new receptionist answered icily, "unless you are next-of-kin."

"But I'm their lay minister," Elizabeth insisted.

"Well, you're not entitled to that information," the receptionist responded, "But you are welcome to visit Mr. George in 308 and Mrs. Singleton in 412." With that, the receptionist slid the glass partition closed, stared into her computer screen, and pretended that Elizabeth and Sharon-Sylvia were not still standing there.

Unfortunately, neither Mr. George nor Mrs. Singleton were in any condition to willingly accept God's blessings, much less shed any light on the sudden disappearance of the other six.

Mr. George sat silently in a chair in his small plain room. His thoughts were almost entirely focused on his army service during World War II almost eighty years ago. He mistook Elizabeth and Sharon for two USO girls he had met behind the lines at the Battle of the Bulge and burst into a wide smile. "We'll beat those Nazi bastards, don't you worry." Elizabeth tried to engage him in conversation, but Mr. George remained in the cold forests of Belgium at the Battle of the Bulge. Having no alternative, she clutched Sharon-Sylvia's hand as she read from a prayer card.

"Pour your grace, O loving God, upon all suffering with the burdens of age and infirmity. It is frustrating not to recognize one's friends and family; it is fearful to live only with distant memories. Bless Mr. George to bear these burdens with patience and to live out his life peacefully until he is called to the heavenly gates. In Christ's name we pray."

"Amen," Elizabeth and Sharon Sylvia said in unison.

Mrs. Singleton was even less responsive. She lay still on her bed, eyes closed with labored breathing, sleeping or simply unable to speak. Elizabeth held her bony, arthritic hand gently and whispered to her about the births, marriages, and other happy occasions that were taking place at the church. When she read the prayer for divine grace to the aged, Sharon-Sylvia thought she saw Mrs. Singleton's eyes flutter while Elizabeth rose and tenderly replaced Mrs. Singleton's hand by her side.

And so it went all through the afternoon of caring for the elderly congregants of the Mountain City True Kingdom Free-Will Church. Those who suffered from grave dementia or total loss of consciousness were all there to be prayed over, while some of those who had been alert, talkative, and in good spirits had mysteriously disappeared. Elizabeth shared her realization of this strange pattern with Sharon-Sylvia and by the last few visits Elizabeth could uncannily predict who on her list would be there and who would be gone.

"It's so strange," Elizabeth said. "I always thought that Pastor Pearson was so conscientious about his lists and the ministry."

Elizabeth examined her notebook again.

"Well," Sharon-Sylvia said, "I suppose you can always ask him what happened."

Elizabeth looked at her for a long moment. "That would be hard to do," she said.

"Why is that?" Sharon-Sylvia asked.

"Strangely, Pastor Pearson simply vanished from the congregation las month. He lived alone, but I believe he had a sister in Arizona. We all thought he had gone off to be with her." And she made a note in her notebook. She would have to ask her fellow church members if any of them had heard from him.

As they trudged back from their final visits at the Mountain City Hospice, Elizabeth invited Sharon-Sylvia to have dinner at her home. "Why don't you call your husband to join us?" Elizabeth asked, "I'd love to have him meet Ted and get to know him. If your husband's half as nice as you are, I think the men will become good friends."

Sharon-Sylvia shook her head. "No, I'm afraid he'll be working late again."

"Well then it's settled, I'll make spaghetti and meatballs for the three of us. That's Ted's favorite meal.

Elizabeth's husband Ted—or "Chief Ted" as everyone in Mountain City called him—was a strapping six-footer. His police uniform was unbuttoned at the collar and he had taken off his holster and service pistol. He greeted Sharon-Sylvia with a big smile.

"Oh, you're Sharon Lewis," Chief Ted said in a sudden flash of recognition. "Yes, I heard about your arrival here in Mountain City. I understand your husband is doing a great job over there at Teutonic Nights. We're glad to have you folks here."

While Sharon-Sylvia and Chief Ted made small talk in the living room, Elizabeth went into the kitchen to prepare dinner. Sharon-Sylvia offered to help, but Elizabeth stubbornly refused. "No trouble at all, I can make this meal with my eyes closed. Within just a few minutes, Chief Ted ushered Sharon-Sylvia into the small dining room as Elizabeth brought out a steaming platter of pasta with tomato sauce and a bowl of microwaved meatballs. The Chief smacked his lips and loaded everyone's plates. Sharon-Sylvia lifted her fork and began to dig in. As she did, Elizabeth gently grabbed her hand and caught her eye. The Chief grabbed her other hand. Elizabeth grabbed the Chief's hand completing the circle.

"Oh Lord, bless this house, thank you for this wonderful meal and bless you Jesus, for bringing Sharon into our lives. May she help us build the Kingdom of God right here in Mountain City"

"Amen," he and Elizabeth said.

"Amen," said Sharon, and they all began to eat.

"So," The Chief asked, "how did the elder ministry go today?"

Elizabeth put down her fork and looked intently into Ted's eyes. "Something very strange is going on," she said.

She explained about the mysterious disappearances and how they seemed to follow a pattern, and how no one could—or would—offer an explanation.

Chief Ted frowned deeply as he took his first bite of a meatball. It was clearly something he didn't want to talk about. "Well, I'm afraid there's not much a small force like ours can do much about that. We have all we can do just writing out parking tickets, arresting drunken drivers, and picking up teenage shoplifters down at the mall. This is something for the G-men, if you can trust them to be anything other than stooges for the Deep State."

Elizabeth shot him a glance.

"Well, it's true. Listen Sharon, there are people in this country who are dead set on turning this into some kind of socialist nightmare. I'm talking about elitists from New York and Hollywood. We have to do all we can to protect and defend our Constitutional rights."

"Ted," she said, "Mark and Sharon have two daughters, both serving in the military right now, overseas. Now that's what I call a family of true patriots."

"Well God bless you and your family," he said. "Sorry for getting on my political high horse there. You're clearly one of the good guys. My apologies."

After the dinner was finished and Elizabeth cleared the table, the three returned to the living room where Elizabeth led them all in prayer for the souls of the disappeared.

Sharon-Sylvia looked at her watch and suddenly gasped. It was already 9:30 and she really had to get home. Chief Ted wouldn't allow her to walk home in the darkness and offered to drive her over in his squad car. "You never know who or what can be lurking out there," he said.

She did make it home safely but discovered an even more frightening situation when she entered the house. It was now past 10 o'clock and Monte was nowhere to be found.

CHAPTER 12
A VISIT TO THE CASTLE

Monte waited silently in his car in the parking lot of Teutonic Nights until the very end of the day.

Under darkening skies, he watched from a distance as the construction crew went about their work of not only closing the theater but making it almost as inaccessible as a nuclear waste disposal site. First the metal workers arrived with their acetylene torches and welders' masks toppled the towering neon sign at the entrance like some great sheet metal tree. When it hit the pavement, its Old English neon letters shattered and the golden crown that had been at the top broke off and skittered across the asphalt coming to rest against a graffiti-covered abandoned car. Next the carpentry crew came to board up all the entrances and remove the fiberglass bridge that crossed the trash-filled moat. Then came the fence crew who pounded in the vertical posts for a ten-foot cyclone fence that surrounded the building and topped it with razor wire. Last was the van of a security firm, whose uniformed officers posted ominous placards that read:

**PRIVATE PROPERTY OF THE VALKYRIE
PHARMACEUTICAL CORPORATION**

ABSOLUTELY NO TRESSPASSING

THIS SITE IS MONITORED WITH SURVEILLANCE CAMERAS

VIOLATORS WILL BE PROSECUTED TO THE FULL EXTENT OF THE LAW

As the security van pulled away, its occupants glared at Monte, leaning on the hood of his Ford Fiesta, indicating to him that the time had come for him to leave the premises. He got the message and got inside the car and turned the ignition key. But where would he go?

He could just imagine how Sylvia would react. Once again, she would say "I told you so." He needed a next step, a plan, before he talked to her. So instead of going home he drove aimlessly through the streets of Mountain City. He was never much of a drinker, but he eventually wound up sitting at the bar of the downtown Big Sky Tavern, where the bartender Bob Howard was the closest thing to a job bereavement counselor that Mountain City had.

"What can I get you, Mr. Lewis? It was part of his job for Bob Howard to know everyone in town. He wiped down the bar in front of Monte's stool and tossed Budweiser coaster there.

"Oh, I don't know," Monte answered. "What do you recommend for a person whose life has just gone up in flames?"

"That bad?" Bob the Bartender countered.

Monte nodded.

"OK, here's a double shot of Wild Turkey. Tell me when you want a refill. That should do something to dull the pain."

The Big Sky Tavern was a place where people mostly came to drown their sorrows with booze and other diversions and discuss their resentment of those damn liberal Hollywood celebrities and the strings secretly being pulled by the Illuminati and the New York elite. Meanwhile, a group around the pool table was arguing over the rules of 8-ball and another cluster of drinkers was looking up at the snowy picture on an old TV arguing loudly about whether the University of Montana or Montana State would have better football team in the coming season. And almost drowning out all the ruckus was the voice of Patsy Cline singing "I Fall to Pieces," booming from the Wurlitzer jukebox near the bar.

Monte's cell phone rang just as he motioned to Bob for his second refill. He had to press the phone hard against his ear to block out the background noise. Dolph was on the other end.

"Mark, it's worse than I ever expected," Dolph whispered in a desperate, panicked voice. "I'm pretty sure both our lives may be in great danger. I want you to meet me at midnight at the Shrine of Ten Thousand Buddhas. I'm serious. Our lives may depend on it. I can't talk more."

The connection suddenly clicked off.

The Shrine of Ten Thousand Buddhas? Here in Montana? Monte, himself a bit drunk, assumed that Dolph had totally gone off the deep end. But just to make sure, Monte googled the name "Shrine of Ten Thousand Buddhas" on his phone and sure enough it came right up as a religious shrine in a remote mountain valley about an hour and a half drive out of town.

It was almost ten o'clock. He had to get going. Monte tossed two twenty-dollar bills on the bar and told Bob to keep the change. "Just pray for me," he said.

* * *

The night was dark and foggy. The road was winding. And Monte clung to his steering wheel with white knuckles, deathly afraid that he would be pulled over by the Montana Highway Patrol. He turned over and over in his mind the very strange phone call from Dolph. Was he right to drive off almost a hundred miles into the darkness? Had he drunkenly embarked on a fool's errand? Was his life really in danger? How could he escape from one false identity into another? He had now reached the outer limits of his existence—all because of a stupid reality TV series and an even more idiotic medieval-themed dinner show.

After nearly two hours of driving, he finally spotted the reflective sign for the Garden of a Thousand Buddhas, and as he turned off the main road and onto a gravel drive that to a small parking lot, he realized that he would soon find out exactly what kind of mission he was on.

The entire site was shrouded in darkness as Monte felt the first drops of rain fall. Yellow security lights outlined a huge circle of white lotus-form sculptures with lines of white buddhas within the circle converging on a central shrine like spokes on a wheel. The whole area was empty and silent. Monte walked fearfully toward the central shrine, a towering image of a female goddess, who, he could see even in the darkness, was smiling down with perfect peacefulness on him.

Off to the side of the mandala-like circle was a long wooden structure, with what appeared to be a pinpoint of orange light dancing and growing brighter then dimmer inside. Monte was terrified as he wandered through this surrealistic scene, too frightened to call out Dolph's name and pierce the eerie silence that enveloped him. But he felt drawn toward the building and walked as silently as he could toward the tiny orange light.

As he pushed open its creaky wooden door, a banshee-like shriek pierced the silence. Monte nearly lost his footing as he reacted in terror, as a tall, robed figure approached.

"Jesus Christ, man, you're going to give us both heart attacks." It was Dolph, draped in a monk's robe, taking a deep drag on his cigarette. Its burning tip glowed bright orange and illuminated his haggard face.

Monte's heart was still beating hard as his terror suddenly turned to anger. "What is this all about? Why are you here? What is this place anyway?!"

"Look, I had to get away," Dolph answered. ""When my father heard about the show the other night, he exploded in a way I've never seen before. And believe me I've seen him explode many, many times in my—erm—fucked-up life. Teutonic Nights was his message to the people of Mountain City: that the King would always rule his kingdom and defeat all invaders and enemies. He didn't give a shit about the way it was packaged. He didn't give a shit about the souvenirs we sold or the turkey legs we served. He didn't even give a shit about the money.

"I came out here because this is one place where I knew he wouldn't find me. When I was young, we—I mean they—used to burn crosses and have secret meetings here. Years later, I dated a girl who was a groupie of the cult guru who bought this place. They're gone now. This is the last place my father's thugs will look."

A sudden flash of lightning and a low boom of thunder interrupted Dolph's agitated ramblings. He paused and took a deep drag on his cigarette.

"Listen man, there are things that go on in this town that you would not believe. Dangerous people. Sometimes even I can't believe them, and I grew up here. But that doesn't matter now."

"Dolph," Mark-Monte said insistently, wanting to put an end to all of this self-pity. It was not going to get them anywhere. "All I need is fifteen minutes with your father and, believe me, I can make everything all right."

Dolph stared at him. "You don't know my father," he said.

Monte smiled. "Do you have any idea who you are talking to?" He said in teasing outrage. "Do you have any idea how hard it was to convince Tex Ritter to sink millions into his tornado-flattened dinner theater in Branson? You can always rely on Mont... err Mark Lewis me to deliver a convincing pitch."

Suddenly Dolph brightened. A ray of sunshine in his otherwise darkened world. "Do you really think you can do it?" Dolph asked.

Monte smiled. "I know so. I can sell to anyone. The hard part is getting your father to agree to talk to me."

"I can arrange that," Dolph said. He   pulled out his cell phone and turned on the screen, which illuminated his haggard face with a green glow. He started punching in numbers.

"Wait a second. Are you sure you should be calling him now?" Monte reached out his hand to grab Dolph's cellphone from him. "Do you have any idea what time it is? It's quarter-past one!"

Dolph waved him off. "Don't worry, my father keeps strange hours," he said pressing his phone tightly to his ear. He nodded to indicate the call was going through.

"Pappa? It's Adolph. Yes. Yes. Of course. It doesn't matter where I am right now. I'm here with Mr. Lewis, our new executive producer, and he would very much like to talk to you. To apologize for any misunderstanding... and ask for your forgiveness..."

Monte shook his head vociferously and waved his hands in front of Dolph's face. "No way! That's not what I said!"

"Yes. Yes. Absolutely," Dolph dutifully said into the phone. "I appreciate your kindness, Pappa. He'll be there by 3 am."

*   *   *

Everyone in Mountain City knew exactly where Dr. Stewart lived. The Castle dominated the landscape, perched on a high hill approached by a heavily guarded entrance gate and surrounded by closed-circuit TV cameras, motion-activated floodlights and alarm system, and high-voltage electrified wire. Some years back, a few teenagers had attempted to scale the fence as a graduation prank; three of them were electrocuted and the other six sustained such serious injuries to their nervous systems that they would remain in vegetative states for the rest of their lives. Of course, Dr. Stewart paid generous compensation to all of the families and even built a new wing of the Stewart High School Library in their memory and honor. But needless to say, no teenagers ever tried to enter Dr. Stewart's property again.

In fact, even though a full 48% of Mountain City's workforce was employed by Valkyrie Pharmaceutical Corporation, and his presence, his name, and the fruits of his genius were felt everywhere in the city, no one, in fact, had actually seen Dr. Stewart in person in years.

An ominous shroud of secrecy enveloped Dr. Stewart's castle as well as his pharmaceutical empire. And now, in the middle of a dark night, despite the fact that Dr. Stewart was expecting him, and Monte would never have admitted it to anyone, he was nervous about making a pitch to someone who held his very future in his hands.

When he finally turned up the drive that led to Dr. Stewart's castle, he hit the brakes when he saw the lights and the heavy metal barrier of the gate house up ahead.

Monte expected to be stopped and questioned before he passed into Dr. Stewart's compound. But as he rolled slowly toward the guardhouse with its banks of blinking alarm monitors and TV surveillance screens, he was shocked that no one was there.

"Hello?" he shouted, "Anybody in there? I'm here to see Dr. Stewart."

"Hello?" he shouted even louder. "Hello?"

No one appeared. He waited for a moment and then shouted again.

A loud beeping suddenly broke the silence of the night. Revolving lights spun on the roof of the guardhouse. The heavy barrier in front of his car slowly swung upward and another one he had not noticed behind him blocking the backward path of the car. Monte silently admired this remote-control security system, completely unaware that his window for escape had just slammed shut.

Monte put his car back in drive and rolled into the compound. As he drove up the hillside, he got his first close-up glimpse of the Castle. Occasional flashes of lightning illuminated the building, with its turrets, crenelation, and forbidding entrance, straight out of an old horror movie. . Monte stared in wonder; this place could be a goddamn movie set, he thought to himself. It was not like Cinderella's castle at Disneyland with graceful towers and an air of magic, but a forbidding fortress with the look of Dr. Frankenstein's castle—a place where, audiences might imagine, terrible things went on.

Monte parked the car and walked quickly across the gravel drive toward the front door to find shelter from the rain. The place was absolutely silent except for the occasional booms of thunder and the crunching sound of gravel under his feet. As he got closer, the elaborate carved stone entrance, surmounted by a strange circular sun-wheel symbol, was shrouded in darkness. Undaunted, Monte stepped up to the entrance and rang the bell.

There was an ominous silence. The stone walls and oak door were so thick he could not hear the bell ring. He rang the bell again and waited.

Then, just when he was about to back away from the entrance, Monte heard a loud click and a disembodied voice so clear it could not have come from an intercom. It came from somewhere above.

"Open the door, Mark."

"Just push on the door."

With the slightest push of his fingertips, the heavy door simply came open.

Monte cautiously entered. The floors were marble. The high Gothic-arched ceilings were crisscrossed with elaborately painted ribs that converged at strange circular symbols, just like the one he had seen over the entranceway. A forest of giant stone columns rose toward the arched ceilings and a series Gothic pointed arch windows lined the outer walls. What struck Monte more than anything else was the silence. The only sound he heard as he slowly walked into this strange structure was the soft creak of the giant entrance door as it swung closed with a resounding boom followed by the metallic clicks of a series of deadbolts snapping shut, sealing him in.

An astonishing collection of medieval arms, armor, and precious works of art lay before him. As he wandered farther inside, he marveled at the paintings, the sculptures, the tapestries, the suits of armor and the medieval weapons– swords, axes, lances, maces, and halberds—all so beautifully conserved and presented in the glass cases that lined the stone walls.

A faint whirring sound broke the silence and grew progressively louder. Monte looked toward the source of the noise and saw a hunched figure in a motorized wheelchair approaching him. It was a very old man, obviously badly crippled, navigating the chair with a bony, crooked finger on a small joystick at the end of one of the arm rests. The rest of his body was draped with a grey blanket. Long, stringy white hair fell to his shoulders. He wore rimless glasses from an earlier time. The chair moved ever closer to Monte, stopping just a few feet from him. The man lifted his head with great effort, and then spoke.

"Mister Lewis, I deeply apologize for the ungracious welcome. I instructed the staff to absent themselves for your arrival. As usual, they do exactly what I say. I expect that both of us will want our very serious conversation this evening to be conducted in the strictest confidence."

Monte was ready to go. He had at last met the famous Dr. Stewart face-to-face and was eager to deliver his pitch to save Teutonic Nights.

"Doctor Stewart," Monte replied in his slickest salesman voice "it is truly an honor to meet you."

"Oh, Mark, please call me Jerry. Dolph has told me all about you. I consider you to be almost a member of the family."

"As you may have already noticed, Mark, my skills as a host have badly declined. I don't receive many visitors up here anymore. Please follow me."

With that, the old man maneuvered his wheelchair down one of the corridors that led off from the gigantic main room. The floors here too were polished marble. Dr. Stewart's wheelchair glided silently past more glass cases filled with precious and dramatically lit medieval artifacts.

Monte could hardly keep from glancing into the cases as the glint of gold and silver caught his eye. But there was no stopping Dr. Stewart's motorized wheelchair. Down the long corridor they went, past arched doorway after arched doorway. Finally, the chair slowed down, and turned right, entering what seemed to be a massive library.

There was a roaring fire in a fireplace large enough for a man to stand inside, big enough to warm a chilly castle. Huge logs were piled high inside and they crackled in the flames.

"Please have a seat," Stewart offered as he rolled toward the huge fireplace. "As you can see, I already have mine." He chuckled loudly at his joke. Monte smiled nervously. He was beginning to sense that this was going to be a much tougher sell than he thought. He took his place on a large silk covered couch that Stewart had motioned toward, one of two that faced each other in front of the roaring fire.

"May I offer you a cup of green tea?" Stewart asked.

Monte nodded. He had already drunk too much alcohol that night.

Stewart awkwardly moved his right hand from his wheelchair's toggle control, and pressed a small button on the armrest. In a few moments, a man in a full tuxedo appeared with a tray with a pot of hot tea and a glass of water on it.

"Thank you, Thomas," Stewart said to the man who appeared to be his butler. "I simply could not function without Thomas here," Stewart said to Monte, as Thomas poured a bit of the tea into a cup and handed it to Monte, placing the teapot on the small table before him. He handed Stewart the glass of water and helped him grasp it in his arthritic hand.

"The finest Japanese Green tea in the world," Jerry told Monte. "I hope you enjoy it."

Monte took a sip. It was good. He took a long drink and emptied the cup.

"Alas, at my old age, this is all I can now enjoy," said Jerry, sipping at his glass of water, which the butler had handed to him.

"I understand you have come to speak with me about the legend of King Arthur," Stewart said almost casually. "It is particular interest of mine, as you probably know."

Monte's body tensed. Here it comes. It's showtime. Just pretend you're pitching to the bigshots at Netflix, he thought to himself.

But Jerry Stewart was clearly not interested in hearing a pitch or being lectured to about profit. He was a million times the salesman

Monte was. And besides that, he was entirely preoccupied with lecturing his guest about questions of history and myth.

"The literature dealing with King Arthur and his Knights of the Round Table poses several interesting challenges for the scholar," Stewart began, "some even say that he never existed, which I simply cannot believe."

Monte could only nod politely. He saw his chances for making a successful pitch quickly fading away.

"True enough," Stewart continued, "the literature we now have was written centuries later. We really know very little about what the real King Arthur was like. All the medieval bards and poets that wrote of his exploits undoubtedly added a fair measure of imagination. But there is one repeated feature of all the legends that remained constant through all the centuries."

Suddenly Stewart turned Monte. "Wagner. Do you like Wagner?"

Monte didn't have the foggiest idea who he was referring to but was reluctant to reveal his ignorance. "Wagner? Oh, of course!" he said with a wave of his hand as if he were at a highbrow cocktail party. "Love the guy! One of a kind!"

Stewart could see that his increasingly uncomfortable guest was lying, but he ignored it, He began to hum a Wagnerian operatic theme louder and louder as he waved his spindly arms in the air, imitating an opera conductor in full musical euphoria.

"Ah, to hear Parsifal performed once more with a full orchestra. Sadly, I have not attended the festival in Bayreuth in many, many years. It is only the great Wagner who fully grasped the essence of the Arthurian literature." He continued to hum the stirring overture from memory.

"It is the story of one of Arthur's knights, the greatest of his knights, in my humble opinion, who quested for the Sacred Lance and the Holy Grail. And he recognized that it was not an earthly treasure, but a sacred possession, the key to eternal life."

"That has always been my own quest too," Stewart confided, "to discover some great secret of heaven and earth that will help me restore order and dignity to our very troubled world."

For a moment, Stewart seemed lost in his own thoughts, then he focused.

"So let us begin to talk about why you are here."

Monte saw his opening and finally launched into his businessman-to-businessman pitch.

"Dr. Stewart, I have very much enjoyed working for your son. He's a wonderful manager, but I think that I can help him run the business much more profitably."

"Mark," Stewart began sternly, "Let's not play games. My son Adolph is an incompetent. He does not run the business at all. From what I hear—and you can trust me that I have many reliable sources of information—he just sits in that filthy office of his and chain smokes cigarettes, thinking only of sex with cheap women and feeding his constant need for alcohol and drugs. The business, in so much as it is actually a business, is really more of a hobby, my hobby by the way. So, if we are going to be friends, and I hope we will, we must, start by being honest with each other."

"You see, Mark, the reason I set up Teutonic Nights, and the reason I have been more than happy to underwrite it these many years was not to provide an entertainment venue, nor simply to provide my idiot son with a job, though it did not hurt..."

"No Mark, my purpose was far greater... far greater..."

Stewart paused and seemed to stare far off into the distance, as though taken by some mystical vision of the future.

"My purpose here was not entertainment. It was—it is—an all-encompassing approach to life."

"It is my wish that this collection someday become an inspiration for the people of Mountain City. You have already done enough damage with your trashy television reality shows."

"Reality shows?" Mark-Monte sputtered in surprise. "You must be confusing me with someone else."

Stewart smiled broadly. He took out a cigarette, placed it carefully in a long cigarette holder and lit it, inhaling deeply.

"No Mark," he said, with a small laugh. "Perhaps it is you who is confusing yourself with someone else."

"I don't know what you mean sir," he said.

"Oh, come now," Stewart replied. "Surely you know what I mean. As a successful television producer, you know as well as I do that millions of people have learned many lessons about life from watching your shows, even if they didn't realize it. Am I correct, Mark, or should I say, Monte?"

At this, Monte's face turned deathly pale.

"I don't know what you are talking about sir."

"Oh, come now, Monte, of course you do. I know more about you than you do."

Monte could only stare at the old man, stunned. Finally, he was able to speak.

"But how did you know?"

"Let's just say that we billionaires have access to government information sources that most people don't even know exist. That's why I was able to request that the FBI place you here. How do you think you ended up here, of all places? And with this, he waved his hand. "But it doesn't matter. I should have taken the time to educate you myself. But perhaps it is not too late, yes? Would you like a bit of education Monte? Care to learn a bit about how the world really is?"

For the moment, Monte could only stare at him, dumbfounded. Then, at last, when he had found his voice, he said, "Yes... Yes, I would."

"Good," Gerhardt said. "Then follow me."

He spun his motorized wheelchair around and headed down the long, polished marble floor, with Monte walking briskly beside him.

"Try to keep up, Monte," he said. "We have a lot of territory to cover."

As he spoke, they entered a great hall. It was unlike anything Monte had ever seen or imagined, certainly not in someone's home; perhaps in a museum, for there before him was the greatest display of medieval art and armor anywhere on earth, greater, in fact, than the massive medieval display in the Metropolitan Museum of Art in New York.

Stewart paused to let Monte take it all in.

"Beautiful, isn't it?" Stewart asked.

"This is my great passion, Monte. This is my life's work."

And here, he reached out to touch a suit of armor, one of fifty or more that stood at rigid attention, lining the long corridor. He touched it with an almost religious respect, and in doing so, closed his eyes, as though to commune with a deep and lost past.

"These were the knights of the round table, Monte. They were men driven by a higher purpose, the highest purpose – chivalry, honor, God. They weren't driven by a lust for money or power. They were driven by a deep desire to make a better, purer world. Honor, Monte, honor and respect. Do you understand what I am saying here?"

Monte said nothing. He could only dumbly nod his head.

"This was the pinnacle of Western Civilization Monte. The pinnacle. These men were pure of heart. There has never been anything like it before or since." And again, Stewart closed his eyes, deep in thought. "Think of what could have been Monte. Think of the world that they could have created. But it was not to be. It was all lost. The story of King Arthur, of the Knights of the Round Table, all of it, is no myth, no Lerner and Lowe musical. It was real, Monte. It was real. So real. What might have been, Monte. What might have been."

Monte was struggling to take it all in. Even he had to admit it was all a bit overwhelming, like nothing he had ever seen or experienced before.

"So that was why you created the Teutonic Nights?"

Here Stewart looked up, his eyes flashing brightly.

"Yes Monte! Yes! To teach people, to teach all the god-fearing white Anglo-Saxon inhabitants of this town and this county about their own history. Although they do not know it, they are the heirs to this greatness. They are its children, the heirs of a great tradition.

"Yes sir, I understand," Monte said, not believing any of it, but reluctant to make any waves.

"You have no idea how glad I am to hear that, Monte," Stewart said with a menacing smile.

With that, Stewart's withered hand slid the toggle forward and the chair rolled out across the broad hall with Monte by his side.

They silently rolled through room after room of medieval armor, of weapons, of halberds and lances and swords, of medieval artwork. Finally, they entered into another chamber, but this one had no exhibition cases. It was an empty, chapel-like space with two thick candles burning at each side of thick velvet curtain. Behind them, on a wall were the strange circular symbols, with crooked spokes revolving around a small circle that Monte had seen carved above the Castle's entrance door.

Stewart sat silently, reverently in his chair. A gold cord hung beside the velvet curtains.

"Pull the cord Monte," Stewart said, "Pull the cord and learn the future."

Monte stared at him for a moment, then stepped gingerly toward the cord. He gave it a tug and the velvet curtains parted, revealing a massive painting behind it. It was a painting of a knight in full armor, on a horse, carrying a lance.

"Step back Monte," Stewart said. "Step back and take it in in all its power."

Monte stepped back and stared.

"Good God," Monte said. "The knight looks exactly like Hitler!"

"That," Stewart said, "is because it is Hitler." And here, Dr. Stewart raised his withered right arm in what looked for all the world to Monte like a 'Heil Hitler' salute.

Monte gasped at the large heroic painting the open curtain had revealed—of Adolph Hitler in a full set of gleaming silver armor, mounted on a noble steed with an unfurled red Nazi flag bearing a swastika in its white circle, filling the painting's background.

"That painting, my dear friend, is known as *Der Bannerträger*." He pronounced the title in a flawless accent, as if German were his mother tongue. "In English, that would be something like 'The Standard Bearer,' because that is precisely what the Führer was... This magnificent painting remained too long in the hands of the U.S. Army at a heavily guarded warehouse at Fort Belvoir, in northern Virginia, as forbidden enemy property.

Fortunately, some of my attractive female representatives were able to establish, shall I say 'friendly relationships' with some key military officials at the Pentagon and accumulated enough photographic evidence and audio recordings of their 'meetings,' that they were able to arrange for the transfer of the painting here, where it could be properly appreciated."

Stewart's voice trailed off as he turned to gaze reverently at the painting. "King Arthur was real, as real as Hitler. Of that I have no doubt, because I saw his reincarnation with my own eyes. Do you understand what I am revealing to you, Mr. Levine?"

Monte stared at the painting in shock, then stared at Stewart. "You've got to be kidding. Really, Dr. Stewart is this some kind of a sick joke? You are an intelligent man, a highly educated man. I am sure you know, you must know, what a monster Hitler was."

At this, Stewart stared at Monte with a suddenly cold eye.

"Monster? My dear Monte, sixty million Germans did not follow Hitler because he was a monster. They followed him, loved him, worshiped him in fact because he was their savior, a once in a thousand-year miracle for mankind. Hitler was not the frothing-at-the-mouth madman that you and your kind have taken such satisfaction in depicting him in your films and history books. Lies, all lies.

"Hitler was a noble leader, the reincarnation of King Arthur himself. And the Reich that he established, like Camelot, was a brief shining moment in which the greatness, the purity, of Western Civilization could be at last be recaptured and restored.

"He took a broken and shattered society, bankrupt, defeated, destroyed. In only a few years he took it to greatness. He took a rotten society, the decadent and perverse Weimar Republic, and demanded that honor, decency, family, chivalry be restored. He restored to the German people their confidence, their power, their honor, their proper place in the world– at the pinnacle of humanity. He was no madman; he was a genius. No Monte. His was not the work of a monster. It was the work of God."

Monte stared at him utterly dumbfounded.

Stewart smiled again, reached into his breast pocket and extracted another cigarette, placed it in its holder and lit it. He inhaled and blew out the smoke before speaking.

"Never expected to meet a Nazi sympathizer? Don't worry Monte. You have not met a Nazi sympathizer. You have met a genuine, lifelong member of the Nationalsozialistische Deutsche Arbeiterpartei," he said, pronouncing the words effortlessly, "In other words a real Nazi."

"What?"

"Like you Monte, I have also assumed a false identity, one that I have revealed to no one until this very moment. You see, you portray yourself to the world as Mark Lewis, when you are actually Monte Levine. Well, the world knows me as Dr. Jerry Stewart, but in reality, I am actually Gerhardt Friedrich Adolph Stürmer. I proudly served in the SS as Heinrich Himmler's medical aide-de-camp. It was Himmler who first introduced me to the sublime Arthurian epic and I am still honored to say that I was given a place at the Round Table that Himmler established in his castle in Wewelsburg. I have many fond memories of the place.

"I often think I spent my best years there. But Himmler was not the king I held in the greatest honor; it was the Führer himself. He ruled a kingdom where might and right were the highest values; where loyalty to the leader was more precious than life itself. His Reich would have lasted forever, if he had not been betrayed by the Bolsheviks and the Jews. The world would have been cleansed of the filth and perfidy of inferior races. I think you know what I mean, Mr. Levine..."

Monte was reeling.

And now we enter the third, and sadly, the last part of your education."

With that, Gerhardt pushed a button on his wheelchair.

Almost instantly, Billy Osmund appeared in the room, wearing his tattered jean jacket, embroidered with a charging knight and the slogan "Everything for the King."

"Let's take Mr. Levine down to the exfusion room, shall we?"

Billy roughly grasped Monte by the arm and led him down to the end of the corridor to a large elevator, with Stewart-Stürmer gliding in his wheelchair close behind.

Billy breathed heavily in eager anticipation as the elevator doors closed slowly. Stewart-Stürmer closed his eyes, smiled to himself, but remained silent.

When the elevator gently jerked to a halt and the doors opened, Monte's jaw dropped. Before him was the most gruesome scene he had ever witnessed in his life.

CHAPTER 13
PAIN'S HARVEST

The vast fluorescent-lit underground hall looked at first glance like a massive mortuary. Table after table, dozens of them in regular rows, extended all the way to the distant back wall. On each table was a single individual, many of them dressed in their Sunday best, as if they were on their way to church when they were suddenly brought here, without even a moment to change their clothes. They were all old people, some still appearing healthy and vital, others with sunken cheeks and pallid complexions.

"Good God, are they dead?" Monte asked.

"No, but I bet they all wish they was," Billy answered immediately.

"Billy!" Gerhardt sharply rebuked him. "We must not frighten our guest."

"Sorry doc," Billy answered rather sheepishly, but Gerhardt waved him off. "Let's go."

And they rolled into the room.

As they drew closer, Monte could see that they were not dead at all, but semi-conscious—in a half-awake, half-asleep state.

Each motionless occupant was hooked up to an IV stand and a vice like apparatus was attached to one of their body parts.

White uniformed orderlies scurried from one table to another, listening to heartbeats through stethoscopes, tightening the screws on the attached apparatus, and replacing the IV bags when they were full. Soft moans could be heard throughout hall.

Three supervising doctors briskly approached Gerhardt's wheelchair and gave him stiff Nazi salutes. "Heil, Führer!" they said in unison, in broad western American accents, making the German title sound for all the world like the word "furor," which of course it was.

Gerhardt turned his wheelchair toward Monte.

"I see you find this upsetting, Monte. You shouldn't. What you are looking here is science, pure science, perhaps the purest science at work."

A sudden shriek from one of the cots rose above the background murmur of moans, as an orderly tightened the screws on one of the hall's occupants, perhaps a turn or two too far.

Gerhardt looked toward the source of the noise and frowned. He motioned to a nearby orderly to go over to see what the matter was. "We like to keep things well-ordered and highly regulated here," he said to Monte.

"You know of my love for King Arthur, well, just as King Arthur led his knights on a difficult quest for the Holy Grail, so too I have spent most of my life searching for the ultimate pharmaceutical prize. It is my Holy Grail: a chemical formulation that would offer the possibility of eternal life. And I am now on the verge of achieving my lifelong quest, thanks to the good people of Mountain City, who you now see lying before you. Do you recognize any of them?"

Most of them were strangers to Monte, but in Row 3, he did recognize an older man who had worked in the ticket booth of Teutonic Nights, a woman who had worked in the gift shop, and another man who had sometimes filled in as an usher who would chase rowdy children away from the arena rail.

Gerhardt rolled forward to a set of tables, Monte, escorted closely by Billy, followed him.

"Perhaps you recognize the Gunthers," Gerhardt said.

Monte simply stared; shell shocked.

"No? Too bad. You're living in their house." And again, he gave a small laugh. "You see, they are benefit not just to science, but also to you and the lovely Sharon, or should I say Sylvia."

At the mention of his wife's name a cold shudder ran down his spine.

Monte stared at him, barely comprehending what he was seeing.

"You're a murderer. A Nazi bastard murderer."

Gerhardt smiled.

"Murder? Not at all my dear Levine. These people are all alive. Admittedly, in a state of semiconsciousness, but very much alive. They would be of no value to me dead. You should consider yourself privileged; it is not everyone who gets to see where Valkyrie's greatest scientific discoveries are made."

While he was speaking to Monte, Gerhardt was also working. He observed a metering device attached to Mr. Gunther and turned to a white coated assistant. "Tommy, Mr. Gunther's C rating seems a bit low. Can we increase the pressure just a bit please?"

And with that, the assistant turned a screw and Gunther let out a small whimper. As he did, the numbers on the meter jumped.

"Yes, that is much better, thank you."

Gerhardt turned from his attentions to Mr. Gunther and rolled close to Monte.

"Did you ever hear of chloroquine? No? It's the cure for malaria. Our brave German troops were suffering in the North Africa campaign. Malaria was killing more men than the British army. But I discovered the treatment. Saved millions of lives. Valkyrie still holds the patent. And how did I discover it? Using human subjects like these."

"Animal," Monte scoffed.

"Oh! Animal! Come on Monte. What were the lives of a few dozen prisoners of war, Russians, no less, when you think of all the lives that I have saved with my medical breakthroughs? And let's not get too arrogant. I am sure you know about your Tuskegee experiments in which your own Black Americans were used as medical guinea pigs. Happens all the time."

"Do you realize that cholesterol-lowering blood statins were my discovery, based on experimentation with on the livers of live sausage-eating, beer guzzling Bavarian peasants? How else do you think that obese oaf Goering made it all the way through the war? And anti-depressants? Fortunately, I was given free rein to do as I pleased in an insane asylum in Westphalia. Without my chemical handiwork, that sour-faced, chronically-depressed Goebbels would not have made it through a single day as the confident, serpent-tongued Reichsminister of Propaganda that we all came to know and love. And of course, Valkyrie holds the patents to those-- those and over one hundred over treatments that people use every day. That's science in the service of humanity."

"But those drugs, and hundreds of others, all of which I hold the patents to, were mere child's play compared to the idea of extending human life. Think about it Levine. The Bible tells us that the days of our lives are but threescore years and ten.

"Threescore years and ten was the ideal age to live to three thousand years ago, and still no progress," Gerhardt continued. "I knew we could do better, so I got to work. Himmler was delighted with my work, as was the Führer himself. And you may wonder Monte, how we Germans, known for our planning, our efficiency, our attention to detail, could have a government under the Führer with no plan for succession."

At this moment, Gerhardt reached for the vinyl collection bag connected by a tube to Mr. Gunther and held it aloft.

"Here is a foolproof succession plan. Eternal life for the Führer. Or at least a good 200 or 300 years. Now that is Nazi science at its best!"

Monte was shocked but could still answer. "Well, you were a bit late for to do anything for the Führer, weren't you?"

Gerhardt stopped and stared at him.

"Yes, Monte. Sadly, that is true. Something I shall regret for the rest of my life. A true tragedy for mankind. However, all is not lost. Here we have cracked the code. There can arise a new Führer whose life I can extend for at least a good 150 years, maybe more. In the meantime, I already have lots of eager customers. A few American billionaires, Mr. Putin in Russia, Mr. Xi in China. All happy to pay me $5 billion for the treatment. Of course, we don't accept Medicare or any other kind of your private health insurance. Too much paperwork." And again, Gerhardt let out his raucous laugh. "And of course, my number one patient for this treatment is my good self."

After he spoke, Gerhardt went back to monitoring the "patients." From time to time he would stop, motion to someone and give them instructions on what to do and when.

"You're insane. You're a monster. You should be in prison."

Now Gerhardt stared directly at Monte.

"Oh please. Enough with this "You, Nazi monster" nonsense. Surely you have heard of Dr. Wernher von Braun, winner of the famous Langley Gold Medal in Science? The Great American Hero?" And Gerhardt lingered over the words, laced with contempt.

"Let me tell you, von Braun's V1 and V2 rockets killed a lot more people than my experiments ever did. Von Braun never saved a life in his entire career. And when you Americans landed on the moon, that wasn't American science up there. That was German science. Nazi science! And every drug you have ever taken, every antibiotic, every treatment. German science. GERMAN NATIONAL SOCIALIST SCIENCE!" Gerhardt was almost shouting. The assistants in the room stopped what they were doing to stare.

Gerhardt regained control of himself.

"Sorry, but as you can see, I tend to take this personally. I apologize."

"But I digress. The process is quite impressive. Let me explain it to you. Look here." Gerhardt motioned to some nearby orderlies to turn an elderly victim on his side.

Tubes had been inserted into two bloody incisions in his lower back. "These drain raw cortisol from the adrenal glands on each of his kidneys," Gerhardt explained with the patience of a medical instructor, "Cortisol, by the way is a hormonal steroid produced by stress. That's why we constantly tighten the vice on his ankles. Keeps the cortisol flowing in a steady stream."

Gerhardt motioned to the orderlies to lay the comatose victim back and pointed out the two sets of tubes ran from his head: one set was inserted into a hole drilled at the side of his nose; another attached to a stent on the side of his skull.

It was all very gruesome to Monte. But Gerhardt viewed his surgical handiwork with undisguised pride. "You see," he pointed toward the victim's nose, "these tubes follow a hole neatly drilled through the right maxillary sinus to drain stress-induced trophic hormones from his anterior pituitary lobe. They have an amazing effect on one's cognition and memory. I sometimes take it in small doses myself when I need to recall some obscure Arthurian text.

And the final ingredient in my pharmaceutical masterpiece is dehydroepiandrosterone. This stent here on the side of Grandpa's skull catches it as it pools in certain areas of the brain. It gives the gonads a jolt, if you know what I mean. I'm sure Lancelot was drowning in the stuff the first time he made love to Guinevere."

"Now here's the really puzzling thing, Monte," Gerhardt mock whispered, "when the human body is placed under special stress, the three hormones take on a special quality. A specially prepared chemical cocktail of all three has the rather remarkable effect of not just halting, but in fact reversing, the aging process of human cells. And even if aging has already occurred, it reverses the process. That's why I have dubbed it Merlinium!" Monte stared blankly at Gerhardt, biting his fist against the urge to vomit.

"Merlinium! Merlin!! Merlin the Wizard!!! Don't you get it, man? King Arthur's favorite magician famously lived his life backwards. As he grew younger and younger his memories were all of the future—thus his amazing prophetic abilities were uncannily accurate. I too want to have that eternal dream of possessing the wisdom of age and the energy of youth, but I have yet to fully achieve it.

"The main problem I have encountered," Gerhardt explained, "is that the effect so far is only temporary. I have to inject myself with a good dose every day or it will begin to go away. That's why I have to keep finding new sources of raw materials."

"Because the special hormones are produced by organic human reactions to intense stress, I must have living subjects. Corpses or test tubes are useless. And being the employer of almost everyone in the city, no one would dare suspect me of harvesting human subjects. Believe me I have experimented on every age group, from babies to teenagers to the hapless, motionless pensioners you see before you. The bumbling police force in this city knows very well that people regularly go missing, but for one reason or another..." Gerhardt paused dramatically to emphasize his point, "they simply fail to investigate. I cannot imagine why. And again, Gerhardt laughed.

"That Monte, is why we are here. Since you ruined my Arthurian drama and were foolish enough to come here, I clearly can't let you go now, not with all you now know."

He motioned to Billy, lurking in a corner, to approach him. "Put him on a table," he ordered. And with that, he grabbed Monte in a headlock, leading him to an empty cot. Monte tried to struggle but could not break Billy's hold. Billy threw him down roughly on the empty table.

Suddenly, there was a disturbance at table 34. One of the inmates was screaming and writhing uncontrollably. Instinctively, Billy bolted for table 34. Monte saw his moment. He leapt off the table, grabbed the IV bag stand that awaited him, and instead hit Gerhardt with it then jammed it into the wheels of his wheelchair, immobilizing him.

Gerhardt screamed "stop him!", but it was too late. Monte had enough time to run across the room and bolt toward the elevator. The doors closed just at Billy approached.

When the elevator came to a halt, Monte found himself back on the main floor. He started to run, but the place was so massive, he had no idea where the exit was. Running down a few corridors, he found a small space between the display cases to hide in. He crouched down and pulled out his phone. He still had a signal and dialed 911. A woman answered.

"Mountain City Police Department. How can I help you?"

Speaking as softly he could, Monte said, "My name is Mark Lewis. I'm being held captive at The Castle, Dr. Stewart's place. He's trying to kill me. Please send someone to rescue me right away!"

"Will do, Mister Lewis," the woman said, "Now you have a nice day." With that, she hung up.

Monte stared at the phone and cursed the Mountain City police. A bunch of total buffoons. Afraid of making too much noise, he quickly tapped out a short text message to Sylvia: AT STEWART CASTLE. GET HELP. He hit send.

At that moment, Monte heard footsteps approaching.

"Oh Mon-tee."

It was Billy.

"Oh Mon-tee. Come out, come out, wherever you are..."

Monte held his breath.

"I'm going to find you. You better just come on out and make it easier on yourself. Otherwise, the doc really knows how to make it hurt. Come on out Monte."

Monte's breath came faster and faster. He could feel his heart racing. And he could tell from Billy's voice that he was getting closer all the time.

"Oh Monte. I know I am getting close. I can practically smell your fancy New York aftershave. You know Monte, the doctor warned me about you and your kind. You find a nice decent family show like we had at The Teutonic Nights and you bring in your sex and your perversions and you destroy good people. But you won't do that ever again, will you, Monte. You people won't replace us, the way you tried to replace me."

Monte could smell the beer on Billy's breath, he was so close.

He reached behind the open back of the display case and grabbed a mace. This was his one chance. He would only get one shot. He leapt out from behind the cabinet, knocking it over. The noise distracted Billy just long enough for Monte to swing the mace and catch Billy across the face, knocking him down. He ran as fast as he could down the corridor, past the many suits of armor, down through the great hall and made it to the door. He was worried that it would be locked, but instead it opened with ease.

"Thank God," Monte muttered to himself.

Opening the door, he ran out the wind-driven sheets of rain now pounding onto the driveway, just in time to see a Mountain City Police car, lights flashing, siren wailing, race up to him. It was Chief Ted.

Monte ran up to the Chief.

"Chief Ted, thank God you got here," Monte said, breathlessly, now totally soaked to the bone. "You can't imagine what is going on in there."

Chief Ted stepped out of the car and pulled down the brim of his police cap, trying to keep the pouring rain out of his eyes.

Chief Ted motioned to two of his deputies, who had just arrived in their own squad car.

"Cuff him." Ted ordered them.

The deputies grabbed Monte and put him in handcuffs.

"What are you doing?" Monte said.

"Mark Lewis, I am placing you under arrest."

"Under arrest? For what???" Monte cried.

"Attempted murder. You have the right to remain silent, but anything you do say may be used against you in a court of law. Do you understand your rights?"

"Wait!" Monte screamed at the top of his lungs as his arms were roughly twisted behind his back.

Words tumbled madly out of Monte's mouth. He was trembling with excitement and fear. "Doctor Stewart is not who everybody thinks he is. He's a Nazi. A real honest to God Nazi and he is carrying out horrible medical experiments in there. It's a nightmare."

The chief stared at him coldly, as if he were drunk or a psychiatric case.

He reached for the radio transmitter that was clipped to his vest. He had to speak in a loud voice to make himself heard.

"Hello, Doctor Stewart? Yes, I've got him. Yes sir. I'm bringing him back now."

The Chief pointed his gun directly at Monte and motioned with the barrel toward the castle.

"Start walking," Chief Ted said.

As they entered the main hall, Gerhardt rolled up to meet them.

"Hello Ted," Gerhardt said.

Ted tipped his hat. "Dr. Stewart."

"He won't get away again sir," Ted said.

Gerhardt turned to two orderlies. "Take him back downstairs."

* * *

The sharp pain of an injection into his neck almost instantly calmed Monte down. He was back in the exfusion chamber, strapped securely to a table. A surgical light now shone brightly in his face. He could make out a few blurry figures hovering over him. He then recognized Gerhardt's threateningly kindly voice.

"You should feel almost completely paralyzed by now, am I right, Mr. Levine? Can you try moving your arms and legs just a bit? Your breathing will begin to slow down a great deal."

Monte could barely breathe. And he his arms and legs were completely numb.

Gerhardt, his face bruised but now back in his wheelchair, took out a small flashlight and shined it into Monte's eyes, lifting the lids.

"Good," he said, "Very good."

"Good ocular response," continued Gerhardt, "you are perhaps stronger than I had a first thought. You will make an excellent experimental subject."

"We were regrettably forced to give you a rather large dose of curare. Quite potent and fast acting. It's a wonderful drug actually. It's derived from a wild plant of the moonseed family, and used by the indigenous hunters of Central and South America to paralyze their prey."

"Here's a fun fact," Gerhardt continued, as the color drained completely from Monte's face, "it's said that the Macushi tribe of Guyana can bring down a wild boar with this stuff on a dart from their blowguns at 40 meters. Quite amazing, no?"

Billy pushed his way into the circle of faces hovering over Monte. He handed a large surgical drill to Gerhardt. The light glistened off its foot-long drill head. Monte screamed in horror, but no sound came out of his mouth.

"Welcome to your new home, Mr. Levine. I am sure you will be of immense assistance in helping me perfect the formula for Merlinium." Gerhardt poised the point of the drill slightly to the left of Monte's nose.

"But before we begin to harvest the life-giving nectar of your pituitary gland, I think I do owe you a few words of explanation. After all, you were so gratifyingly attentive as I showed you my Arthurian collection and my shrine to the Führer. And except for your unfortunate attempt to escape the Castle, you have been an absolutely perfect guest."

"Now I shall tell you the happy ending to the story that took such an unfortunate turn in the Führerbunker in Berlin in May 1945. The dreams of chivalry, nobility, and perfect loyalty were crushed as the barbaric Soviet troops approached. But that dream will never die. It has blossomed and grows daily as noble Caucasians everywhere have again begun take pride in their heritage and unashamedly greet each other with the familiar stiff-armed salute. Bright Aryan men like Billy here have joined forces with other like-minded Anglo-Saxons to resist the forces of darkness and vice. That would be you and your kind."

Gerhardt's voice grew louder and more passionate. "The time is right for a new renaissance, a new Middle Ages, in the most positive sense of those words. I intend to create an Arthurian Kingdom here in Montana. A Rocky Mountain Camelot, if you will. No blacks, no Jews, no Asians, no Indians, in fact absolutely no one whose skin and whose soul are not lily-white. As the employer of thousands who all owe their livelihood to me; as a master of pharmaceuticals who can immobilize millions with the tiniest change in my mass-produced formulas, I have power in this drug-addled world that no one has ever possessed before. Except King Arthur. And Hitler."

"But mortality was the undoing of both. Arthur had no heir except a treasonous son. Hitler had no heir at all. I have an heir, but he is a buffoon and a fool. I am on the verge of perfecting Merlinium, don't you see? When my experiments have reached a successful conclusion, when I find just the perfect mixture of cortisol, dchydroepiandrosterone, and the other stress-induced hormones, I will rule forever over my own secure, racially purified, knightly domain.

Yes, those Broadway Jews Lerner and Loewe had one thing right, at least." Gerhardt smiled and began to hum a few bars of the famous theme before breaking into song:

"The rain may never fall till after sundown
By eight, the morning fog must disappear
In short, there's simply not
A more congenial spot
For happily-ever-aftering
Than... here... in Ca-me-lot."

The assembled orderlies nodded and clapped in amusement. Billy burst out in a broad, gap-toothed grin.

"Enough nonsense," Gerhardt said suddenly turning grim. "Let us begin." An orderly marked a small "X" on Monte's left cheek and Gerhardt took up the drill again. Monte's eyes opened wide with terror as the spinning drill bit disappeared into his face. First came the strong odor of burnt bone, followed shortly by a spray of blood and a bloody rivulet, which an orderly dabbed away with gauze as Gerhardt continued with his procedure.

Withdrawing the drill, he inserted a rubber tube with a barbed metal fitting into the hole in Monte's face.

"Perfect," Gerhardt said, as another orderly affixed the tube to a plastic exfusion bag and hung it on a hook on the side of the cot.

Monte let out a groan as his eyes slowly closed.

"Ah, yes, the cortisol is now flowing," Gerhardt said as he looked toward a meter attached to the exfusion bag. "But the volume of the flow is much too low."

"We must increase the flow, and for that he must be conscious." He motioned to Billy to inject him with the curare antidote.

Monte's eyes fluttered open as soon as the antidote entered his bloodstream.

"I have an idea," Gerhardt said to those gathered around him. "I want to try something a bit more—um-- 'impactful' than the cheap hardware store vises we use on all our other subjects. Billy, please bring me artifact 3001 from display case B-21."

Gerhardt closely watched the exfusion meter until Billy returned.

"This mischievous Jew knocked over the display case, but the artifact seems to be intact," Billy said as he handed a bizarre wooden screw device with ivory spikes to Gerhardt.

"Excellent, even though it's not strictly Arthurian, we'll use it. I purchased this piece some years ago at an auction in Madrid. The catalogue claimed that it had been personally used by the Grand Inquisitor Torquemada himself."

Monte, though paralyzed, stared in horror as Billy tightened the screws.

Monte's entire body tensed with pain.

"Now we will see how much cortisol a human body can produce and still remain alive."

The meter on the exfusion bag rapidly twitched upward until it reflected maximum flow levels. Gerhardt could not stifle a chuckle.

"These New York types," he said to himself, "their mere fears of personal injury exceed the stress levels that most other races experience at the actual threshold of horrible physical pain. During the war, we tried to extract cortisol from Russian prisoners on the Eastern Front. We worked on tens of thousands of them. Worthless. You could tear their fingers off one by one. You could pull out their toenails with pliers and they barely produced a drop of cortisol. But you and your kind," he said directly to Monte, who was wild-eyed and trying to struggle against the restraints, "… a regular cortisol factory."

"Look at you. We've barely gotten started and already your stress levels are up 300%. Excellent!"

Monte tried once again to free himself to no avail. Regaining the use of his vocal chords, he vainly screamed for mercy—and then pitifully pleaded for help.

"Monte, don't waste your breath. We are a good 100 feet below the ground here. The walls are three feet thick, and anyway, no one can hear you. Why tire yourself out?"

With that, Gerhardt helped an orderly slip the spiked wooden device onto Monte's right leg.

"Now, here's an interesting device that the medieval torturers loved to use," he explained. "You would probably have seen it had you ever bothered to visit the Museum of Torture over at Teutonic Nights. But then you were too busy trying to undermine the moral of the King Arthur story, weren't you? This is from my collection. An original. All the things in the Museum of Torture over there were exact replicas, but here, I insist on using authentic artifacts.

"Do you know what this is?"

"This is one of my favorite pieces. It's called a knee splitter. I am sure a bright fellow like you can figure out how this works."

With that, he placed the knee splitter around Monte's right knee and began to turn the screws.

"Now, the nice thing here is that most of these medieval torture devices won't kill you. When you are torturing someone, the last thing you want to do is kill them. It kind of defeats the whole purpose of the exercise, if you understand the usefulness of medical experimentation on live subjects."

"Amazing these medieval technologies. I have no idea how anyone can possibly think the inventors of these devices were primitive."

And with this, Gerhardt began to turn the screws and the spikes began to split Monte's knee.

A loud cracking sound could be heard. Monte's agonized shriek was earth shattering. But Gerhardt was just beginning.

"Let's see how high we can go," he said with sadistic anticipation.

An orderly quickly replaced the vinyl exfusion bag. The first one was already full.

"Amazing! It usually takes at least six weeks for a normal subject to produce this much fluid. Tighter, tighter, tighter" Gerhardt screamed.

The orderlies now took over to twist the screws with all their strength. The ivory spikes now penetrated all the way through Monte's leg, with their sharp tips appearing on both sides of the joint, completely pulverizing the bone and tearing the ligaments apart.

It was a bloody mess, but the second exfusion bag was filling quickly.

Monte's eyes began to flutter. His arms and legs fell limp.

And then, for Monte, in the midst of the indescribable pain and stress he was experiencing, everything suddenly went black.

CHAPTER 14
HURTLING THROUGH TIME

Monte had the sensation of tumbling, turning, and spinning into an inky blackness. "This is what death must be like," he thought to himself. Fully conscious, but totally confused about where he was and what was happening to him, he felt himself falling, falling, falling, finally coming to rest on what seemed like a soft carpet of damp grass.

A brilliant light shone through his closed eyelids. He hesitated to open his eyes, afraid of where he was and what he might see. But the light was so bright, his eyelids almost involuntarily fluttered open. And instead of being in a torture chamber, in hell, or in heaven, Monte looked around and saw that he was lying under a tree in an open field. The excruciating pain in his knee had miraculously vanished and when he reached up to his face to feel where the tube had been inserted, he realized that it too was gone.

Above him was a cobalt blue sky. He could hear birds singing and see the dappled sunlight between the green leaves. He pulled himself up and cautiously looked around to see an astonishingly beautiful vista of green forest and open fields. Off in the distance he could hear a rooster crowing; a herd of reddish-brown cows was grazing in a nearby field. The faint scent of manure wafted toward him. A twist of white smoke twirled upward from a distant chimney. He looked around frantically, trying to figure out exactly where he was.

A muddy path ran close by and Monte shakily rose to his feet to get his bearings. He patted his pants pockets for his wallet and car keys. They were gone. All he had were the clothes he was wearing: An Oxford button-down shirt and a pair of chinos, which he had been wearing since the previous morning. Both were rumpled and spattered with his own blood and sweat. So, he started walking, following the rutted path toward the cluster of wooden houses a few hundred yards away. If he could just get to a phone, he would call somebody, maybe Sylvia. She might know what to do. But as he approached the small village, he recognized that there was something very, very strange about this remote place he had been transported to.

It was the thatching on the roofs of the houses that first drew his attention. The thick bundles of reed, neatly trimmed and rounded at the eaves, like thick straw blankets thrown over each shed, home, and hovel, made the tiny village resemble a set from the Lord of the Rings. From the distance he could see young people in homespun costumes busily going about their chores of washing, weaving, hauling water in buckets, tending to small vegetable gardens, and filling the troughs for the few filthy sheep in wattle pens and mud-crusted pigs in their stys. Crazy historical reenactors, Monte thought to himself. He waved his hands to get their attention as he approached a rough-hewn fence.

"Hey, I need help," Monte shouted. "It's a long story, but I'm lost and I need to get back to Mountain City. Does anyone here have a cell phone I can use?"

A young man looked up from chopping wood. He seemed not to understand the question.

"I'm lost," Monte raised his voice and spoke more slowly, as if that would get his message across. "Does anyone here have a phone I can borrow? It's an emergency."

Others gathered with suspicious looks on their faces. They murmured among themselves and grabbed rakes, pruning hooks, and wooden shovels waved them threateningly at Monte, to keep him from coming any closer.

"I mean you no harm," Monte pleaded, "I'm lost and I just want to go home."

One of the villagers put the fingers of his right hand to his mouth and whistled loudly. A boy ran toward them and was given a quick command. He ran off at full speed toward the steep hill that towered over the village. A wooden watchtower was built at its top.

"OK, OK," Monte said to the wary villagers, "I get the message. I didn't mean to disturb you. I'll get help from someone else." He backed away from them and slowly, then walked briskly further down the path. As he passed the foot of the hill, he heard the creak of a wooden gate opening and the sound of hoofbeats galloping down the steep slope directly towards him.

A sudden twinge of pain shot through his knee. It lasted only for a moment, but it made Monte wonder whether he was still strapped to the table in Gerhardt's laboratory, still connected somehow to that awful past. He stopped to rub the throbbing knee. That seemed to make the pain go away. Besides, he had an immediate threat he had to deal with. After the hell he had been through in the last twenty-four hours, almost anything could happen. As the riders bore down on him, he tensed his body. What was going to happen next? Monte's initial instinct was to run away from them, but he had no idea which direction to take. He would have liked to head for the nearest highway and flag down the first passing car. But there were no highways or cars in sight. So he froze and waited for the horsemen to arrive.

As they got closer, Monte's eyes widened. Their chain mail, helmets, swords, and even their lances were just like the stage props the cast had used in the dinner shows at Teutonic Nights. Could it be that this was all just an elaborate practical joke?

The riders pulled their horses to a halt and surrounded Monte. "Who are you and what are you doing here?" their leader demanded in a voice that Monte did not recognize. "What business have you in this territory?"

The leader of the group was dressed in a coat of chain mail, with his face hidden behind the closed visor of his helmet. With his fully mailed hand, he grabbed Monte by the scruff of his neck and lifted him off the ground.

"Speak now, you wretch. Reveal wherefrom you have come and what evil mission you have come on. This is our territory. Reveal your intentions, before I cut you to pieces."

The helmeted figure tightened his grip on Monte. No, this was definitely not the cast of Teutonic Nights come to rescue him. Monte scanned the faces of the other riders and recognized none of them. "Jesus Christ Almighty," Monte shouted at the top of his voice. "Put me down! I've done nothing wrong, for Christ's sake!"

Someone in the gang screamed in outrage. "He takes the name of our Lord, in vain! Dispatch him to the pit of Hell, Sir Galahad. Let us see his wicked blood flow!" The others nodded in agreement. The helmeted rider threw Monte to the ground and lifted his visor as he held the edge of his sword against Monte's throat.

The man's face was pale white with a scraggly red beard. A crude tattoo ran down the side of his neck. "On your knees, sinner!" he shouted. Monte meekly obeyed.

"Sir Kay," the helmeted rider shouted to one of his comrades. "Bind this intruder behind you. We will let our lord, King Arthur, decide if he lives or dies."

Kay did as he was instructed, jumping off his horse and roughly tying Monte's hands behind him. Two others helped him lift Monte to the back of Sir Kay's saddle. Kay remounted as the troop spurred their horses and set off at a gallop, with Monte bouncing helplessly and painfully with every stride of Sir Kay's horse.

*   *   *

Monte's ride on the back of Sir Kay's horse across the rolling terrain of forest, fields, and rocky hillsides was as uncomfortable as it was revealing. The road was clogged with peasants transporting the fruits of in the same direction. Donkeys groaned under the weight of overfilled baskets of grain. Swineherds led fatted pigs ahead. A crude cart was loaded with apples; a herd of cattle, pushed forward by cowherds who beat them with switches, led the way. None of the peasants seemed happy; it was harvest time and if they did not get to the castle before sunset with their offerings to their lord and master, they knew there would be hell to pay.

The troop of riders galloped past the peasant convoy. As they bounced across the landscape, Monte winced in pain with every stride. Monte grew even more confused about this strange place where he had landed. He had not seen a single telephone pole, or high-tension wire; not a car, not a road, not a shopping center, not a sign in the whole time they were riding. Not a single airplane passed overhead. The landscape was clearly not of Montana. The Rockies were nowhere in sight. Nor did he know long how long they had ridden. Without his watch and phone, he now had to rely directly on his senses. When they had set off from the first village the sun was strong and high above him. But now, as the sun sank toward the horizon and the shadows of the horses and riders grew longer, they finally came to a stop.

"Get down!" Sir Kay ordered Monte, before simply tossing him on the ground. "Behold!" Sir Kay proudly announced to his prisoner, "The impenetrable fortress of Camelot!"

Camelot? Could he really be in Camelot? Monte had always imagined that the real Camelot to be dominated by a great castle, with turrets and battlements just like in the movies, or at least something approaching Cinderella's castle at Disneyland. Instead, what he saw was more like a frontier fort with from the American West, built of rough-hewn logs raised and lashed together, with their pointed tops serving as a defensive barrier. There was no moat, no drawbridge, no thick stone walls. What kind of a medieval castle was this?

"Open the gate!" Sir Kay shouted toward the stockade. Two wooden doors wobbled open, pushed open from within. "Move!" Sir

Kay shouted, prodding Monte with the tip of his sword. The others riders followed closely behind. Monte would soon learn their names: Sagramore, Pellinore, Gawain, and Galahad.

And so, Monte, stiff and sore from the horseback ride and dazed and confused about where he was, stumbled into the court of King Arthur. This was very much not the Camelot of the Lerner and Lowe Broadway musical with Richard Burton and Robert Goulet singing their hearts out. Nor was it the Nazi paradise that Gerhardt Stürmer dreamed of. This was Camelot as it had actually existed in southwestern England sometime around in 500 AD. And as Monte would soon see for himself, it was a small, filthy, and dangerously violent place.

*　*　*

Inside the open courtyard, arriving peasants were being pushed, shoved, and cursed at as they handed over their tribute to the king. Under shouts and beatings by royal overseers, they dumped their heavy baskets of grain into large, stone-lined silos. They piled their apples, pears, and vegetables into huge wooden crates. They herded their cattle, sheep, and pigs into fenced enclosures, knowing well that they would soon be butchered for the feasts of the king and his men. It was hard enough to wrest enough food for their own families from the land, but the demands of King Arthur and his thugs made it even more difficult. But they had no alternative; the king's warband had the power to destroy their fields and orchards and zealously protected them from the raids of gangs from neighboring territories.

Monte himself was just another kind of offering brought to the court. His clothing marked him as an intruder—and anyone found in the territory without a good reason for being there was assumed to be a thief or a spy. As soon as he stumbled into the courtyard, Monte was handed over to a crowd of the king's enforcers who would show him what happened to intruders in Camelot. Forming a circle, they begin to push him between themselves. Back and forth, back and forth, cursing and taunting him. But Monte clearly was not a common peasant turncoat; his strange clothing suggested that he had come from some unknown, exotic place. The crowd eagerly stripped him of his shirt, his belt, his pants, his shoes, fighting amongst themselves who would get to keep each item for themselves.

The ruckus brought Galahad to see what was happening with the prisoner, now stripped down to his Brooks Brothers boxer shorts. Sometimes Galahad had no patience for these hoodlums, even though they provided the muscle to make the whole system work. They would never be knights just low-level enforcers and village bullies. "Take him inside the royal hall," he commanded them gruffly. They knew their place in the organization. Chastened and with heads bowed, they took the prisoner away.

They led Monte stumbling and shivering into a large wooden building in the middle of the compound. This was a royal hall? To Monte it looked more like a tumbledown barn than anything else. Still with his hands tied behind him, he was taken to the back and tossed into a muddy, excrement-filled pen among pigs, chickens, and goats. "Let's see how the king's butchers and cooks prepare this pitiful cut of meat," one of them quipped as they left him in the filth and went over to join the circle of men sitting cross-legged around a roaring fire in the middle of the hall.

All of a sudden, a loud fanfare of rams' horns stilled the voices of the seated knights and assorted court hangers-on. "The king!! The king!!" a court page shouted and everyone rose to their feet. From the parted back curtain, two burly guards marched before a short squat figure. He nodded and passed by the standing group and plopped his own meaty frame into the wooden throne. He motioned to the others to sit down and listen to him. As they did, the firelight from an open hearth illuminated his face.

It was the King himself, King Arthur. Through the fence of the animal pen, Monte struggled to get a good look at him. But this was not the King Arthur of the legends, the movies, the Broadway shows. Monte gasped in both terror and amazement. This King Arthur was, in fact, bore a striking resemblance to Danny Locovita, wrapped up in rough cloak with a crudely made crown on his head.

The guests rose to their feet for a long round of cheers and warlike hooting, holding high their drinking horns and filled goblets as a tribute to Arthur, their chief. They were his people, his loyal subjects, his vassals, his army. Among them were men who had bullied more villagers, struck more insolent children, and assaulted more beautiful maidens than any other warband of any local leader in the land.

As the guests in the royal hall dived back into the greasy platters and resumed their heavy drinking, Arthur waved off a serving girl who had come to bring him his own heaping platter and called for his minstrel. "I must be entertained before I eat!" he shouted.

A scrawny minstrel rose from the crowd to approach the king. Acting more like a madman than an entertainer, he hopped around like an animal, made a variety of funny faces, shakily juggled some brightly-colored balls, and sang a few ditties in a high, squeaky voice. Monte watched this pathetic performance through the animal pen fence. He cringed at the rousing peals of laughter and rounds of applause that the minstrel received. Monte thought to himself: this talentless guy couldn't even get a show on public access cable in the middle of the night. And this guy they call "king"-- he has no idea what real entertainment is.

As the minstrel departed, Sir Galahad quickly sprang to his feet. "I know it is your majesty's practice," Galahad boldly announced to King Arthur, "to also have some stirring story of adventure related to you before you begin to eat. And this evening, I shall be your second minstrel and will offer you an exceedingly strange tale."

"This very afternoon, my humble colleagues and I captured a dangerous spy lurking about one of your villages. He was certainly up to no good. When we confronted him, he put up a tremendous fight and battled us with the strength of twelve giants. He was armed with a great scimitar, a spiked mace, and evil magical powers. After subduing him with great difficulty we bound him and interrogated him. He admitted to being a spy for a most dastardly prince who the Frankish king. His name—if indeed it is his true name—betrays his Frankish origins. From what I can make out from his strange accent he comes from wine country and is apparently the lord of a high hill rich with vineyards. He calls himself Monte Le Vine."

"Bring him before me," King Arthur demanded.

Galahad turned and motioned to the guards stationed at the pen in the back of the hall. They stood Monte up and dragged him from the animal pen to the presence of the king.

"Good God, he stinks!" said Arthur, holding his nose. "Clean him up."

At this command, there was a sudden commotion behind the curtain and two servants soon emerged with a large wooden tub of water which they raised with great difficulty and dumped over Monte's head. The water flooded the floor around the royal platform and left Monte shivering, standing only in his boxer shorts.

"And this is the wretch that fought with the strength of twelve giants?" The king turned to Galahad with a skeptical stare.

"Well maybe three giants," was Galahad's reply.

King Arthur turned back to Monte. "You must know that our ancient laws demand the torture and execution of spies."

At this point Monte saw his life flash before his eyes. Had he come this far just to die? "But I am not a spy, Your Majesty," he cried.

Arthur stared at the strange figure, repulsed but at the same time somewhat amused.

"Then what are you? Arthur demanded.

"I'm a.... a.... a.... television producer," Monte said, not knowing what else to say.

"A what???"

Monte tried to think quickly of another way to describe it. "A-a-a member of the media," Your Majesty," he said nervously.

King Arthur was clearly getting annoyed. "Can you say it in English, perhaps?"

The crowd tittered, clearly enjoying Monte's discomfort.

But suddenly, miraculously, his discomfort vanished. Monte recognized he was in a very familiar situation. "I am a storyteller," Monte proudly blurted out.

At this, Arthur slapped his knee and laughed loudly. "A storyteller, are you?" he smiled. "Well then, show us your craft. Tell us a tale. But be warned, it had better be good. If ye be lying, our next entertainment will be to see your severed head rolling on the floor."

The crowd roared with approval at the King's cat-and-mouse game. Clearly this spy was lying, and Arthur had called his bluff. A few of the knights drew their swords in eager anticipation of the bloody amusement to come.

Monte heard the sound of the swords being drawn and knew his life now depended on what he said. His mind was racing, trying to think of a story that even the toughest audience would love. He knew exactly what to do.

A servant brought out a roughly woven cloak and draped it over Monte's shoulders. As they did, his brain was spinning like a slot machine to hit the jackpot with just the right combination of elements.

"OK," Monte said, raising his hands to get the attention of the crowd. The room began to quiet down. Monte's brain was racing, but he had already decided on the story he would tell.   He took a deep breath and began to speak.

"I shall tell you a tale, Your Majesty, of the man who.... became... a spider.

The assembled warriors were intrigued by this intro. The men poised to execute Monte quietly slid their swords back into their scabbards and sat down. Arthur leaned forward, now thinking that this might indeed be a good story. "Do proceed Le Vine," he commanded.

The room grew silent. The king and his men leaned toward Monte to hear every word. For them, the spider was a holy and mysterious creature, whose webs revealed mystical patterns, of Creation, of the Future, of the sun, moon, and the stars. They listened closely to learn how a man could take on this sacred form.

"In a far-off kingdom called America," Monte began.

"Where?" the King demanded.

"It is an island, my lord, somewhere west of Ireland," Monte replied, not missing a beat.

"It must be Iceland he speaks of," said Gawain, the most learned of the knights.

"Pray continue," the king said.

"In that far-off kingdom lived a weak and timid young man named Peter Parker, who, despite his fears of fighting and physical combat, had an unquenchable passion for wizardry. One day, he visited a great wizard's cave and as he rummaged through the mysterious vials and cages, a spider of enormous dimensions suddenly leapt upon his arm and gave him a deep and painful bite. Peter soon fell ill and the people around him feared he would die. But when he awoke many days later an amazing transformation had occurred: Peter now had incredible super powers: he could see great distances with perfect clarity and he now had a muscular body unequalled by any man alive."

The king and his followers were mesmerized by this set up, but Monte knew that the best was yet to come.

"This would have been a great miracle," Monte continued, "but Peter Parker had not only become a great warrior, he had inherited the wiliness and skills of a spider in human form. From his wrists, he could shoot the silky cords of spider webs and swing on them effortlessly."

"With these powers, he fashioned a unique set of armor, not of metal or chain mail, but a thin layer of magical cloth that clung to him like a second skin. Bright red and blue in color, it also covered his face, to hide his true identity. Like a spider he could scale walls and scamper across ceilings. These unique powers aroused the jealously of the rulers of this kingdom, who are unable to kill or capture him."

The crowd was clearly captivated by the story. This gave Monte even more courage to continue. He paused, and the dramatically walked to the center of the room. He was back in his element, pitching an alternate kind of reality to his rapt audience.

"Look up!" he suddenly shouted and all heads quickly craned upward to the cobwebs in the rafters of the royal hall. "Imagine the power of a Spider Man suspended up there in an intricate web of his own making, ready to pounce suddenly on any one of you."

The crowd gasped as if they could see the superhero themselves.

"The Spider Man's only weakness," Monte continued, "is a beautiful young woman, something that I think every man can sympathize with." The king and guests nodded in agreement. No storyteller had ever drawn them in to a tale as simultaneously lifelike and dreamlike as this.

"So, the evil powers capture the young woman, and dare the Spider Man to come rescue her. With extraordinary strength and reflexes, the Spider Man rescues his beloved and entraps the villains in a deadly spiderweb. And from that day forward the Spiderman vows to fight for the cause of justice and like your own leader, the great King Arthur always does."

When he was finished, there was silence, soon broken by the sound of thunderous applause by everyone in the royal hall.

"A truly unforgettable tale!" King Arthur proclaimed. "I must hear more about this Man Spider. Approach the throne."

"I am going to let you live, storyteller." And at this the king smiled, "So long as you keep telling me such wonderous tales as the spider man."

Monte breathed a sigh of relief.

"Let us hope you have some more, for if the only tale you know is of the spider man, then like a spider, I will crush you under my foot!"

The assembled crowd laughed at the king's brutal sense of humor.

"Now, take him away."

Two burly guards grabbed him under his shoulders and marched him out of the hall. They passed close by the Queen and her ladies-in-waiting sitting off to the side in the shadows.

Monte had already been stupefied by uncanny resemblance of King Arthur to Danny Locovita, but his legs now wobbled and his head began to spin when he got his first good look at the face of Guinevere. She looked exactly like a young Sylvia.

CHAPTER 15
SECRETS OF THE WIZARD

Was this all a dream? A hallucination? An alternate reality he had entered? Or was he dead? Was this the vivid mashup of former acquaintances and life events that people experience when they've passed on? These disturbing thoughts were all that Monte now had to go on. At this point, he was living from moment to moment trying with all his might to prolong his survival in this medieval-themed immersive reality, whenever and whatever it was. For the first time in his recent life, he actually wished he was back in Montana, where the craziness was easier to understand.

The two burly guards hustled him out of the royal hall and across the pebbled paths of the stockade courtyard to a thatched Hobbit house, barely six feet high. Monte had to duck his head as they pushed inside and slammed the wooden door behind him, cursing him as nothing but a Frankish dog. The room inside was completely dark, and Monte felt around like a blind man.

The floor was covered with straw and the night chill blew through two tiny windows just below the roof on either side of the single room. There was enough light from the torches burning outside for Monte to be able to see that this was not the best room in the place. But he was dead tired. Sleep came quickly as he lay down on the floor with his rough-woven robe wrapped around him. Scratchy as it might be, he was grateful that at least he had something to cover himself with.

His eyes fluttered open just a few hours later as light and the sound of birds chirping filled the room. But Monte only became fully awake and sat up in the straw when he heard the sound of a loud argument going on outside.

"Let me in there, damn it!" a raspy, irritated voice shouted, "I must interrogate the prisoner!"

"We have our orders, sir. He is to be kept in isolation until the feast tonight. No one is to see him. No one is to talk to him. That is King Arthur's command." Monte recognized the voice of one of his guards.

"Don't make me cast a spell and make your lives a living hell," responded the raspy voice, clearly getting increasingly annoyed. "I have a good mind to turn you two into warty toads who will just hop away. Do you nincompoops have any idea who am?"

"Indeed, we do, sir."

"Then open the door or I'll rip it open myself!"

At that moment Monte was startled as the door flew open, banging loudly against the outside wall. A short, stocky man with a broad face and a voice that would never take no for an answer, pushed his way past the guards into the room. In the darkness, and perhaps because he was already in a delusional state, Monte thought, for a moment, that Sam Brinkman had come to rescue him.

"Sam?" he said, barely able to rise from the filthy floor. "Sam, is that you?" He squinted in the darkness, trying desperately to focus on the distant yet strangely familiar face. Clearly, he thought, he was dead and perhaps this was hell.

"Well, well, well," the stranger said as he entered the room, "what do we have here?" As he looked with disdain down at Monte sitting cross-legged in the straw, Monte saw a face he had seen so many times before.

"I don't know who this Sam is," the strange figure said, "But I can see you are no French spy. In fact, I've never seen such a pitiful excuse for either a spy or a Frenchman in my life."

The man paced with heavy steps around Monte, examining the walls, the windows, kicking the straw, and even looking down at the rusty chamber pot placed near the prisoner. "What a complete shithole the king's men have prepared for our distinguished guest. I must mention to the king that you will need a proper bed and a full wardrobe, if you are to remain here for any length of time."

Monte was at last beginning to focus.

"Well, who are you?" he asked at last.

"Let's just say that I am an advisor to the king, and at the moment, the only friend you have here. And trust me, you are going to need a friend."

Monte stared at the man.

"Can you tell me where I am?" he asked at last.

The man pulled up a rough-hewn wooden chair and climbed up on it with his short, stubby legs.

"You, my young friend, are in Camelot."

Monte could only stare. This tiny man, whoever he was, was clearly out of his mind.

"Camelot?? Are you insane?"

The old man smiled. "Insane?" he said, tapping his ancient head, "No, I don't think so." And he smiled again. "You have, no doubt, heard of Camelot and King Arthur."

Monte stared at him with an incredulous look. Of course, he had heard of King Arthur, Camelot and the Knights of the Round Table. Who had not? He had even seen the movie. He had even rewritten the script about the fate of King Arthur at Teutonic Nights.

"What year is this?" Monte asked.

The old man stared up at the ceiling, making some quick mental calculations. "Why, this is the twelfth year of the reign of King Arthur. If I am correct, you may also know it as the Year of Our Lord 522—or in other words 522 AD."

"That's impossible," Monte said.

The old man stared at him. "And why may I ask?"

"Well, first of all," Monte said, increasingly sure now that that he was simply hallucinating in Gerhardt's laboratory, "This place looks absolutely nothing like Camelot. Everyone knows that King Arthur lived in a magnificent castle, just like in the musical. This place is a dump. This looks more like a set for *How the West Was Won*. A wooden stockade? Come on. King Arthur didn't live like this."

The old man chuckled to himself, "How the West was Won... It has such a nice ring. I shall have to remember that one." Then, in a suddenly deadly serious tone, he turned to Monte. "Now, listen to me Mister Le-veene," he said, stressing the modern pronunciation of Monte's name, "and listen carefully. The story you told the King last night, about the man who was a spider, was truly a masterpiece of storytelling—weaving a web of mystery, if you don't mind my saying so. But don't underestimate the danger you are in. Your life here hangs by a thread more slender than that spun by your spider man. "

"So long as you continue to tell great stories, the king will let you live. But falter, even once, and..." At this moment, the old man drew his finger quickly across his throat. "Do you understand what I am saying?"

Monte nodded. "I do," He replied.

"Good," said the old man. "And now I must depart. I look forward to hearing the story you tell tonight. Truly I do."

And with that, the old man arose, prepared to leave.

"Guard," he yelled. "I am done here. Open the door."

"I have just one question," Monte said, rising to his feet.

The old man turned.

"Why are you helping me?" Monte asked.

The old man held his hand up, slowing the guard opening the door.

"You don't realize it yet, but it is you who will be helping me."

And with that, he was gone.

* * *

As darkness once again fell, the guards flung the door open again and hustled Monte off to the royal hall for his second night's command performance. All he had eaten that day were some greasy scraps from the previous night's feast that had been tossed into his prison cell. Yet despite the queasiness he now felt in the pit of his stomach, Monte girded himself for action. He knew that there were only two possible outcomes of this evening: either he told another great story or would face immediate execution. This was the TV business stripped down to its barest essentials he thought to himself. So, he had spent the whole day rehearsing a story that he hoped would save his life.

Inside the royal hall the torches were lit, the warriors' shields were hung on the walls, and the hearth fire was roaring. Seated around it was the same crowd of hoodlums who had been screaming for his blood only the night before. Talk about tough audiences; this had to be one of the worst. But Monte understood that if he could please the king he would please all of his toadying followers. And as the guards released Monte from their grip and pushed him onto the low stage in front of King Arthur's throne, he bowed deeply and began to tell his tale.

"Your Majesty, may I introduce you tonight a man who ran faster than a speeding arrow and was able to leap over the highest hills in a single bound. He could even fly in the sky. And the peasants who watched him soar high above them would cry out in amazement, 'Is it a bird? Is it a falcon?' while others would answer, 'No, it is a super man!'"

"How did he get such powers?" the King asked. "Was he too bitten by a spider?" The crowd roared in laughter at this sarcastic question. But Monte had a comeback that quickly silenced everyone in the hall.

"Oh no, My Lord, his powers came directly from God, who we all worship and would never, ever dare ridicule. You see this man I speak of came from the heavens, from a place high in the celestial spheres called Krypton, which lay close to the Garden of Eden, which the Almighty had hidden there until the End of Times. This man was born as the only son of a mighty archangel named Jor-el, who was even mightier than Gabri-el or Uri-el. I am sure you are aware of the power of those angels in leading armies to victory on earth."

The King nodded enthusiastically, fervently believing in the power of angels, as did every member of his warrior band.

"Well then just imagine an archangel so powerful that he could be humbled only by the Devil. And that is exactly what happened. The Devil cast a spell upward towards the heavens, blasting an enormous hole in the celestial spheres where all of the angels and archangels dwell. The mighty archangel Jor-el saw the fiery wave of satanic destruction approaching Krypton and desperately sought to save the life of his beloved baby son. So, he quickly cut down an enormous tree trunk from the Garden of Eden, hollowing it out to fashion a secure vessel for his dear infant. And with all his might, he hurled it to safety down on the surface of the earth."

"And do you know what happened then?" Monte asked the King, who shook his head slowly, obviously eager to know.

156

"The heavenly tree trunk landed with a might thud just outside the small village of Smallsville in Kent, where an elderly couple were passing by. The old man and woman discovered the child inside the tree trunk, adopted him as their own, and named him Clark. Clark of Kent, perhaps hoping that he would become a royal clerk someday."

"Now, as the years passed, it became clear that young Clark of Kent had special powers, far greater than those of a mortal man. Even as a small boy he could lift enormous weights and hear even the tiniest sound at a distance of miles. As he grew to manhood, he developed an amazing ability to see through walls. At age 18, he learned that he could fly. And when he first stepped on a field of battle, the enemy's deadly arrows harmlessly bounced off him."

"Amazing!" said the King himself, clearly captivated by the story.

"And what did Clark of Kent do with his vast powers?" King Arthur now asked, sitting on the very edge of his throne.

"He wandered the world, a freelance knight, seeking out a King who he could serve."

"Every King would want Clark of Kent as his knight," said the King. "Who did he serve?"

"He chose to serve only those kings whose hearts were pure and who had the love of Jesus in their souls and practiced God's word every day," answered Monte, changing the story to please his potentially dangerous listeners.

King Arthur stood up. "You shall live to see another dawn, Monte Le Vine. You now may repair to your quarters and we shall see you again tomorrow eve."

At that, the guards approached Monte to hustle him off, but the King held up his hand. "There is no need to guard our court storyteller any longer. Unhand him immediately. My wizard Merlin will accompany him from now on."

To Monte's astonishment, it was the short, stocky old man.

Merlin emerged from the shadows at the back of the hall and strode toward Monte.

"Right this way, my good man," he said. Merlin turned and proudly paraded out through the audience with Monte close behind. The crowd parted before them, displaying sudden respect for the man who had the power to repeatedly entertain the king.

Merlin led him back to the cottage, which had been completely refurbished in the hour or so he had been away. The straw had been swept off the floor. A proper bed and wardrobe had been delivered, and the rusty old chamber pot had been replaced by a shiny ceramic one.

Monte slowly opened the wooden doors of the wardrobe to reveal several sets of minstrel costumes—of silk, velvet, and linen—fit for the court bard of any kingdom in the world.

"You did well, young man," Merlin said, folding his arms across his chest, "But this is no time to rest on your laurels. Your story was good, but it could definitely have been better."

Monte had learned a long time ago that no show was perfect its first time out. Things needed fine tuning. "Like how could it have been better?" he asked.

"Well to start with there was no romantic interest. True love is a must for courtly tales. Couldn't this super man of yours, with all his powers, attract a single woman?"

"Sure, the tale does include a woman. Her name was Lois," Monte answered, I'll include her next time.

The wizard continued. "And two more things were missing: mystery and danger. The mystery could come in the form of a secret identity or something like that. Maybe he lives his everyday life as another character and only reveals his powers when someone needs help. And there should also be a source of constant danger—something that can take away his powers. Maybe a kind of rock that has also fallen from heaven that makes him suddenly weak. An excellent prop that gives him another challenge to overcome."

"I'm just telling you," Merlin warned, "if you don't add a lot more razzmatazz to your stories, they're going to grow tired of you—and you know what that will mean." Merlin once more quickly drew his finger across his neck. In TV that gesture meant it was time to end the program; in Camelot it apparently meant that real daggers would slit your throat. Yes, this guy Merlin was starting to remind him more and more of Brinkman every day.

*   *   *

And so it went on night after night, with Monte telling tales of his Lordship Bruce of Wayne who when darkness fell, dressed himself as a bat and swooped down on the enemies of the King. "These are the kinds of vassals I need!" shouted Arthur. "Tell us more of this Bat Man." And so it, went, night after night, with Monte entrancing the king with amazing tales of the kinds of superheroes that Arthur would have liked to have among his own men.

By the flickering light of the torches that burned in the Great Hall for each night's feast, Monte told of the mild-mannered man who turned green and hulk-like when he got angry; of a wolverine man who used his razor-like talons to attack his enemies; even of a powerful woman who wore a tight-fitting red and blue costume, with a gold belt around her waist, a gold tiara on her head, and magical, arrow-repelling gold cuffs on each wrist. But it didn't take long for Monte to exhaust all the Marvel and DC Comics characters he remembered from his own childhood.

And just as Merlin had warned and predicted, the king and his court became increasingly restless at the evening entertainment that Monte provided to them. It was all so formulaic, so repetitive; even the mightiest super heroes lose their power if they are presented in the same way again and again. Merlin watched in dismay as the royal yawns became more frequent and the audience grew more interested in the platters of greasy meat than in the tales being told.

Even in the sixth century, Monte thought, it's all about the ratings. You live and die by the ratings, but in this case the death was a bit less metaphorical than in the TV biz.

"Look, my dear man," Merlin said to Monte after one particularly lackluster performance, "Your stories remind me more of cow dung than poetry. They have become boring... boring... boring... They're even putting me to sleep. You need more action, more twists and turns, more family intrigue, more violence, more lust for power. You're taking an enormous risk by just giving them the same thing over and over again."

This was not a revelation to Monte, of all people. He had seen several of his own reality shows get great ratings one year and tank the next. Apparently, people had as short attention span in the 6th century as they did in the 21st. He had to rev up the action. He needed something new.

But what?

Having run the spectrum of Marvel and DC comic book characters, Monte fell back on some of his favorite movies and TV shows but realized that most would not work. The seven castaways on Gilligan's Island – no. The wise-cracking battlefield medics of M*A*S*H—no. The visit of a cute extraterrestrial to some kids in the suburbs—no, they didn't know about life on other planets, or even suburbs for that matter. The shark that kept eating people? Hmm, no. These people had never seen a shark and the concept of a summer resort community on the beach was at least 1500 years in the future. Then, suddenly, he hit on an idea he knew the audience would love.

"My Lords and Ladies," he began. "Let me tell you the sad story of a mortal man who, without realizing it, married a beautiful, blonde-haired woman named Samantha, who turned out to be a witch."

As soon as he began to tell this story, he saw Merlin cover his face with his hands. The audience began to murmur and grow restless. And the deeper Monte got into the story – with his detailed description of Samantha's secret magical abilities and how her mother, a Queen of Witches, moved in with the hapless couple, only enraged the audience more.

"Heretic!" they yelled. "Devil worshipper! The man should have burned that evil woman," one man yelled.

"Burn the storyteller instead!" someone else in the audience cried.

The king and his followers had gotten their fill of Monte's stories. The murmuring grew louder. They began to throw food.

Just like Montana, Monte thought, as a goose leg hit him in the head.

"What blasphemy!" shouted one. "Let's kill him," screamed another. King Arthur sat silently and did not raise a word of protest, implicitly giving them the go-ahead.

The king rose from his throne in outrage and the sound of swords being unsheathed in the audience made the imminent danger to Monte's life all too clear. He turned pale, closing his eyes in resignation, awaiting a shower of cold steel to plunge into his flesh. But just at that moment Merlin suddenly leapt on the stage.

Merlin held up his hands to still the murmuring crowd and turned to address King Arthur. "Your Majesty, I am afraid that your court storyteller is not feeling very well this evening. It must be the venison stew that the cooks made for him today. And we all know that the cooks do sometimes use meat for the court staff that is—how shall I say it—somewhat passed its prime. The audience knew exactly what he meant and broke out in laughter.

"So I beg the indulgence of your Majesty and your faithful liegemen," Merlin continued, "to tell you all a story that the court bard Le Vine has told me this very day. It is an amazing, unforgettable story. I think you will enjoy it more than any other story he has told.

He glared at Monte."I am sure, Le Vine, you will recall this amazing story you told me just this very day."

Monte seemed confused. He did not tell Merlin any story that day. He had no idea what kind of tale Merlin would now tell in his name. The stakes were enormous. He knew that his own life was now on the line.

As Merlin began to tell the story, the King sat back down on his throne and the audience slipped their swords back into their sheathes. "This is a tale about a great and wondrous King, not unlike our own beloved monarch who earned the grateful loyalty of his subjects and struck fear into the hearts of any who would dare oppose him. Because his power was so great, he was called by friend and foe alike, the Godly Father. And he ruled his realm with a generous spirit and an iron fist. When a noble horse breeder refused to accede to his wishes..." And here Merlin once again stared at Monte as a cue to continue the tale himself

"Tell us, Le Vine. Tell His Majesty just how the Godly Father dealt with this errant horse breeder How did he teach him a lesson he would never forget?"

Monte stared dumbfounded, first at Merlin and then at the King and the assembled. They were waiting for his answer, and like a nervous schoolboy, called upon in class and uncertain if he had done the required reading, stammered "he put a horse's head in his bed?"

Merlin smiled. His student had done well.

"He did indeed my Lords. The horse breeder awoke to find the head of one of his best stallions in bed besides him."

The assembled roared with approval.

The King was intoxicated with the story. Clearly this Godly Father was a King to be feared—and this was a quality that he deeply admired.

"Pray, tell us, Le Vine, what happened then?"

Monte stared, then began, slowly at first, but gaining steam has he saw his audience was captivated by the tale.

"This king had three sons, three princes of the realm, each of a different nature," Monte continued, "and he had to decide which of them would succeed him to the throne. The eldest son was the obvious choice. His name was Santino, but he was hot tempered and impetuous and was killed in an ambush by his enemies on a remote highway. After his tragic death, the King saw to it that he was canonized by the local bishop and henceforth was known as Saint Sonny, the beloved son.

The next son, who had been sickly and weak since his childhood, was named Alfredo. Although he loudly claimed that he was smart and could do things—in contradiction to what other people said—he was given little responsibility in the family's affairs. Indeed, he was sent off to the west country where he was given an inn and ale house to manage, where he seemed more interested in the serving wenches than in the business at hand.

"The youngest of the sons was named Michael..."

"Like the archangel." Arthur yelled.

Merlin smiled.

"Exactly. And after faithfully serving as a young knight, he withdrew from the world of court politics and warfare, but his sense of loyalty to the family kept drawing him back. Protecting his father in a time of grave crisis, and bravely killing those who plotted against the family, Michael eventually inherited the title of "Godly Father himself."

The king and his warband loved the story and broke out in applause. "Perhaps we owe our story teller Le Vine an apology," the king announced. That was truly a great story!"

"Well put," said Merlin, "Just wait until you hear him tell you Godly Father Part II."

*   *   *

They walked back to Monte's quarters, Merlin leading the way. Monte followed a few steps behind, but walked in silence.

As they entered the room, Merlin said, "that was a close one Levine. I don't want to have to do that again."

Monte just stared at him for a long time. There was silence between the two of them. Then, at long last, Monte got up, closed the door and turned to Merlin. He put his face inches from Merlin's and spoke slowly but distinctly in a threatening voice.

"What...the...fuck...is...going...on?"

Merlin stared back at him.

"What are you talking about?"

Now infuriated, Monte grabbed Merlin by the throat and held him up against the wall. Monte was not, by nature, a violent person. In fact, he had never in his life hit anyone, but now, he felt a wave of rage.

"How do you know all this stuff? The Godfather, for chrissake! Superman. Kryptonite. And you're the only one who calls me Levine, not Le Vine. Who told you that? If you don't tell me what's going on here, I'm going to fucking kill you!"

Merlin, his eyes bulging from Monte's tight grasp, relented.

"OK. Put me down and I will explain everything, but you're not going to believe it."

Monte released Merlin, walked across the room and sat on the edge of his bed, now with his head in his hands. He stared up at Merlin.

"You know what I think? I think this is all a dream. I think I am going to wake up at any minute and this is all going to be some kind of crazy dream."

Merlin walked up to Monte, so close that his own increasingly agitated face was only a few inches away from Monte's. Merlin spoke in an angry whisper so no one except Monte could hear.

"You really think this is a dream, huh?"

Monte nodded.

"And would you like to wake up?"

Monte nodded, again, his head still in his hands. He felt almost childlike now.

"And do you really want to wake up and find yourself back in Colonel Stürmer's laboratory, strapped to that table, with cortisol being extracted from your brain?"

Monte lifted his head and stared at Merlin, his mouth agape. For a few moments, he could not even speak.

"How do you know about Stürmer?" he finally asked.

Merlin placed his hands on Monte's shoulders.

"How do I know about Jerry Stewart, the pharmaceutical genius who is really a Nazi?"

Monte could only nod to indicate that was, for the moment, the most important question. Weird, juxtaposed images of past and present flashed through his mind. Brinkman. Merlin. Danny. King Arthur. He was now almost certain that he had simply gone insane.

"And how do I know about the plot of The Godfather? Or Bewitched, for that matter? Not to mention, Wife Swap Extreme."

Merlin let the title of Monte's last show linger in the air for a moment.

Monte was speechless.

"No! No! NO!" Monte at last cried out. "It's not possible."

"Oh, but it is," Merlin said. And here, he grabbed a roughhewn wooden chair and pulled it close to Monte. "You are the storyteller here but let me tell you a story instead. I think you'll find this interesting. Maybe there's even a TV series in this," Merlin said with a laugh. "Or maybe even a hit Broadway musical." And here, Merlin broke the tension by bursting out in a raucous laugh.

Monte just stared, dumbfounded. At last, he was able to get out a few words.

"So tell me the story..."

Merlin rubbed his hands with glee. He didn't get to tell this one very often.

As you know from your own childhood, nothing grabs people's attention like superheroes. Particularly when they discover their unique superpowers for the first time... Well, when I was a child, I, like Superman, Batman, the Incredible Spiderman, and all the rest of them, found that I had a special kind of super power myself. I discovered that unlike everyone else—and I mean everyone else since Creation—I was living life backwards."

"What do you mean backwards?" Monte asked.

"I was born at the end of time and have grown older while the world got younger. I live in reverse to everyone else."

"You're kidding," Monte said in disbelief.

"I wish I was. Believe me, I wish I was. Some kind of weird genetic anomaly, I suppose. In any event, I have seen all of the future, I have the curse of knowing all that is going to happen, and now I am hurtling into your past. That's my future. But your future—and everyone else's-- are my own still-vivid memories"

"That's amazing," Monte said.

"Amazing indeed. Or perhaps something of a nightmare. You try living like this some time. Stuff you took for granted one day is gone the next."

"What do you mean?" Monte asked.

"Well, one day you have a chip implanted in your head that allows you to hologram yourself to anyone on earth. Next thing you know, the chip is gone and you have an iPhone. By the time you figure out the iPhone, that's gone and a dial up phone is hanging on your kitchen wall. And, before you can dial 911, it's been replaced with a telegraph. Then, smoke signals. Do you see what I am saying here?"

"I guess that could be difficult."

"Difficult? Difficult? Let me tell you about the day that flush toilets vanished."

Merlin paused before he revealed his most amazing secret of all.

"At any rate Monte, there's a reason I conjured you up here. There's a reason I saved you from a fate, quite literally worse than death, at the hands of Colonel Stürmer. I need your help."

Merlin smiled slyly. "You, my friend, are far more valuable to me alive than dead. That's why I stuck out my neck and rescued you tonight. That's why I tele-transported you here from Mountain City."

"Tele-transported?" Monte said.

Merlin looked at him. "Simple twenty-fourth century technology. You wouldn't understand. Doesn't matter... at any rate, I have a secret plan, and I think if we put our heads together, we both stand to gain."

Monte was totally confused. "What kind of plan are you talking about?"

"First, let me explain to you, what is going on here, because you are still clearly in the dark," Merlin calmly answered. "What you see around you is no prank or practical joke. I can assure you that there are no historical reenactors here. You are indeed at the court of King Arthur— the famous King Arthur of literary, theatrical, and cinematic fame. But peel all those layers away and what you have is a band of thugs and bullies who have taken it upon themselves to profit from others' misfortune. There's no government here to speak of. Since the departure of the Romans with the fall of their so-called empire, it's been total chaos here. No law, no order, just the survival of the fittest, you might say—but only if the "fittest" means the roughest, toughest, meanest bastards in the neighborhood."

"As for my own role here," Merlin continued, "yes, I am a wizard. But I have far greater powers than just casting spells. In fact, I am responsible for your presence here across the vast gulf of time that separates your own era from this one. Let me put it more plainly," Merlin solemnly admitted, "You have been transported here to the Age of King Arthur, to help me with an enormous world-changing task. Don't ask me the mechanics, I just wished for it to come true and in the blink of an eye you tumbled out of the clouds. I also know what will come out of our—um—close collaboration. You and I will assist Arthur, the real, authentic King Arthur in..." Merlin hesitated and then blurted it out, "getting his head out of his ass."

"You see he's just a garden variety gang boss right now, but I see a great future for him and the dozens and dozens of generations of Englishmen, Europeans, and Americans that will come after him. They will be swept away with the intoxicating image of the Knights of the Round Table and the legend of Camelot. They will launch fleets, mobilize armies, rule whole continents in the belief that they are the chosen ones and that might—their might—makes right everywhere. The noble image of King Arthur will animate Crusaders, explorers, colonizers, and it will change politics. The legend will result in Magna Carta, in the United States Constitution, in the concept of democracy all the way up to the Kennedy White House—and even beyond. But in order for that history to unfold as it must, Arthur must be delicately and diplomatically guided to transform his image and that of his followers, from extortionists to paragons of chivalry."

By this time, Monte's head was spinning.

"And to answer your obvious question, which you would surely ask if I let you get a word in edgewise," Merlin added, "Why you? Why did I choose you of all the millions and billions of people who have existed from this time to yours? Well, I have to admit that I've been a great fan of yours for well over a thousand years. I thought Real Life Cops was a real breakthrough. Emergency Room Hell was breathtakingly bloody. Wife Swap Extreme was amazing, and Thou Shalt Not, I mean what can I say? It changed television forever. There's nothing I need more than an experienced Reality TV producer to transform Camelot and everyone in it from a robbers' den into a place of legend and myth.

"In every epoch of human history," Merlin continued, "there is a craft in which those who live in it excel. Here, of course, it is hand to hand combat, rather primitive, but they are the world's best. In the Renaissance, it would be writing great literature, sculpting, and painting in oils. In yet another era, commanding great sailing ships, something you could never do. But in your own era, humanity reached it apex in the art of storytelling. Your entire era was based not in building or philosophy or warfare, but rather in telling stories. You took it to a high art – Hollywood, cable, Netflix. It was probably inevitable that your civilization crumbled when everyone spent all their time living in a world of pure fantasy. Particularly after Zuckerberg introduced Meta, it was like opium in China. People abandoned the real world forever.

Anyway, I know you have a singular talent to magically transform reality into fantasy. And I know that you can do it now on a far vaster stage than ever before. Screw Fox and the Discovery Channel, man! You and I are going to make history!"

At this, Monte looked askance.

"Listen Merlin. I have been in the storytelling business for my entire life. It's nothing but stupid entertainment. In the end, it's all sound and fury, signifying nothing."

"MacBeth," Merlin said. "You see how you remember it, even though it was written nearly 500 years before you were born. That's great storytelling."

Monte laughed.

"Yeah, well trust me, I am not Shakespeare. Maybe you should have conjured him up. But anyway, it doesn't matter. I know that this is all one huge freaking hallucination. I am sure that I'm still strapped to Stürmer's table, unconscious from the excruciating pain. You, my friend, are but an illusion. Entertaining to be sure, but still unreal."

Merlin sat quietly for a moment, thinking. Then, he spoke.

"Listen to me, Monte, because this is important. You may believe, if you wish, that all of this is a dream, an illusion. That's fine. It's understandable. In your own not too distant future, a great new religion will sweep the world, based on the idea that all of human reality is nothing but a computer game being played by beings of vastly superior intelligence. The idea was conjured up by a man named Elon Musk, a storyteller if ever there was one. People will believe anything. But even if this is an illusion, I need you to trust me. What have you got to lose?"

Monte thought for a moment. It was true. What did he have to lose? The only thing he knew for certain was that if he did suddenly wake up in Sturmer's laboratory, he would awaken only to wish he was dead. Maybe he should just shut up and play along.

"Human beings live by their stories.," Merlin continued with his monologue, not really caring if Monte was paying full attention or not. "Their stories have power. What is Christianity but a story? The story of Jesus. What is Islam but a story, the story of Mohammed. What is Judaism, Hinduism, Nationalism, Communism, and even the belief in human progress? Yet how many millions, hundreds of millions, billions in fact, will bend their entire lives to the sweeping narratives that justify each of them? How many will live by a particular story; how many will die by it? No. It is stories, not facts, that shape history. And you and I, my friend, are about to become two of the greatest storytellers in all of human history."

Monte thought for a moment.

"So, as I understand it, you want me to create the Arthurian myth, is that right? The noble King Arthur? The knights of the round table? Is that what you want?

Merlin smiled.

"Yes, I do. Think of this as your greatest production."

"And it's going to change history?"

"It already has," replied Merlin.

"What do you mean?" Monte asked.

"It already worked. It's what created the myths, the stories, the history that you know. You have seen it yourself. On Broadway. At the movies. Camelot! JFK for chrissake!"

"I did all that?" Monte said, somewhat shocked.

"Oh yes, and even more. Add the Crusades, the European domination of the world, and the idea of the quest for perfection and perfect harmony by mankind. That is, if you get it right from here on in."

"And if I mess it up?" Monte wondered out loud.

"In that case," Merlin said, "the dark ages will last not for a thousand years, but for six thousand years. Probably forever. So you better not fuck this up."

CHAPTER 16
PRODUCING A LEGEND

Despite Merlin's great masterplan for rewriting history, Monte would need a lot of tutoring. Most of what he knew of the myths and legends of the Middle Ages he had learned at Teutonic Nights and from the occasional movie and TV show. Those caricatures of a caricature were useless raw material for the creation of a lasting myth. They were just distant reflections of something much more profound. When Monte suggested to Merlin that Dragon's Blood soup be added to the menu of the nightly feasts, the wizard simply ignored him. When he suggested that a gift shop might be a useful addition to Arthur's compound, Merlin smacked the back of Monte's head with his magic wand.

"Get serious, man!" Merlin bellowed. "No more stupid ideas. We're not going to open a dinner theater here; we are going to create a legend that will live for centuries. For that, you're going to have to get out of this damn fortress and weave some compelling stories about what you see. Learn about the villagers in the countryside; get to know how these knights actually operate. And then give the public what they want and need: some real-life stories that make King Arthur's men seem noble and even heroic. I want you to really get to know your characters so you know exactly what to include, what to conceal, and what to change in the final version of our great Arthurian tale.

Monte nodded.

"So, here's your first assignment," said Merlin in the stern voice of the tutor he was quickly becoming. "Tomorrow morning, a few of the knights are going out to raid some nearby villages. You're going with them. I've arranged a mount for you and I've let them know you're coming along. They loved the Godfather story told and they now want you to include them in the same kind of thing."

"But I don't know how to ride," said Monte, whose lifelong fear of large animals now rose to the surface. "I've never ridden a horse in my life."

Merlin smiled.

"The boys know that. I already talked to them. They're going to take care of you. And I've arranged for you to have a special saddle. All you have to do is sit there and hold on. The horse will take care of the rest. Trust me, you'll be fine. And I think you're going to find this very interesting."

"You just jot down the observations you make, and when you come back here, you'll weave them into a story. When I think it's right, we'll hire a scribe from St. David's monastery just down the road to put it all down in fancy calligraphy on the finest parchment and maybe add a few tiny illustrations in the margins. People in the future always loved that stuff."

"You got that?"

Monte shrugged his shoulders. "I'll give it a try," Monte said, "what other choice do I have?"

Slapping Monte on the back, Merlin turned and walked out of Monte's quarters. Growling over his shoulder as he left, he said, "I know you'll figure it out, Levine."

*   *   *

Monte could see his breath as he waited outside the corral under the slowly brightening dawn sky. Off in the distance, the crowing of roosters, the distant mooing of cows, and an unusually strong smell of manure filled the air. The birds chirped loudly and the horses in the pen neighed as they were brought out, one by one, by the royal grooms. The grooms saddled each of the horses with strange-looking leather seats. Now those are going to be uncomfortable to sit on, even standing still,

Monte thought to himself. But his inner neurotic ruminations were rudely interrupted by the sudden squeaking of boots, metallic rattle of chain mail, and raucous joking banter of Galahad, Kay, and Gawain.

"Ah, here you are, Sir Monte," Galahad said with a nasty smirk.

Monte felt no kinship with these men and in fact he found their physical presence, especially up close, more than a bit intimidating. They were tall and muscular, and it was clear that they prided themselves on the advantage their physical prowess gave them over everyone else. They spent endless hours each day practicing the arts of war – riding, jousting, sword fighting, and refining their deadly aim with a bow. Never before had Monte felt so like a clumsy, weak city-boy, trying to pass amongst Olympian demi-gods in human form.

"Are you ready to make some trouble with us, Sir Monte?" Galahad asked. The other two knights laughed.

"Look, Sir Monte, here's your noble steed," Sir Kay shouted as one of the stable boys brought out an old but safe nag. Strapped to her back was more of a chair than a saddle. "Lift him up boys," Sir Kay shouted to the stable hands, who collectively lifted Monte into his chair.

Monte turned to one of the boys as he fitted him into his seat.

"Are you sure this is right?" he asked.

"Oh, yes, my Lord. You'll be perfectly fine here. This saddle is normally used by a woman, but we were told to outfit it for you. Now, here are your reins. Pull left to turn left, pull on the right to turn right, and pull both together to make her stop."

"I'll try to remember that," Monte said, a bit nervously.

"Don't be frightened sir. She knows what to do. All you really have to do is sit there and not fall off. You'll be fine."

Meanwhile, on the ground, Kay, Galahad and Gawain were doubled over with laughter. They suddenly fell silent when Merlin unexpectedly arrived.

"What's so funny?" Merlin demanded.

Upon seeing Merlin, the knights snapped to attention. They all knew that Merlin had the ear of the king.

"Nothing, Sir," Gawain said. Galahad and Kay guiltily nodded in agreement.

"Now listen boys," Merlin instructed. "Sir Monte here is accompanying you on the orders of the King himself. Bring him back in one piece or don't bother coming back. Have you got that?"

Gawain touched his forehead with his hand. "Got it, Sir," they said.

"Good, then be off."

The three knights leapt effortlessly on their steeds, kicked their sides, and trotted off toward the stockade gate.

Monte's horse remained still—waiting for his rider's command.

"C'mon, Sir Monte! My stomach's already rumbling for a hearty breakfast. Let's get going down the valley to the blacksmith's village of Ironbound!" Galahad said.

The grooms both sharply slapped Monte's mount on the haunches and the horse took off with a start. Reaching the others, he broke into a gallop down the road to the nearby valley, keeping pace with the other horses, stride for stride. Monte was just a helpless passenger, holding on for dear life. The landscape bounced crazily around him and he had a hard time making out what the knights were saying among themselves.

Kay pointed toward a village ahead and they raced toward it, finally coming to stop outside a small shed with thick black smoke billowing out of its tumbledown chimney. Monte limply collapsed on his horse's neck and desperately trying to catch his breath and regain his composure. Galahad put the index finger of his gloved hand to his lips, indicating that they all should remain silent. He hopped off his horse and silently approached the shed, raising his boot to kick the wooden door open.

Inside, a burly blacksmith froze in mid strike of his heavy hammer. His eyes widened as he recognized Galahad.

"Well good morning to you, Goodfellow William," Galahad said as Gawain and Kay appeared behind him in the doorway. "It seems that your harvest offering to His Majesty King Arthur was a bit on the light side. And the court clerks don't seem to have recorded any iron goods at all."

The blacksmith dropped his hammer and put his sooty hands together in a gesture of supplication. "Please, Good Sir, it has been a terrible year. I swear I will make it up to you."

Galahad clicked his tongue. "I'm afraid King Arthur is a very impatient man. If he allows you to shirk your obligations, then he will have to allow all his subjects to become lazy shirkers. Now that wouldn't be very good for the kingdom, would it?"

"I beg of you..." the blacksmith pleaded.

By this time, Monte had slid off his horse and walked stiffly toward the others just as they turned from the blacksmith's open shed door and headed toward the nearby house. Monte followed behind them. After they had walked a few paces, the blacksmith burst out of the shed and ran ahead of the knights, desperate to defend his wife and children.

Kay drew his broadsword out of its sheath and struck the blacksmith with the sword's flat side full against the blacksmith's face. The blow toppled the blacksmith unconscious to the ground, with blood streaming and from his mouth, nose, and ears.

Galahad bowed and made a mock chivalrous gesture to Gawain, offering him a chance to do the honors. Gawain bowed in return and lifted his boot to kick in the door of the house. Inside was a haggard young woman with her gaggle of young children clinging to her long skirt. They were all frozen in fear.

"My men are hungry, Goodwife," Galahad shouted. "Make them some food."

With a trembling hand she picked up a knife and a began to slice a round, crusty loaf of bread, but suddenly lunged at Gawain who was standing closest to her. He deftly grabbed her wrist and forced the knife out of her hand. It clattered harmlessly to the floor.

"Now that is certainly no way to treat your honored guests, Goodwife," said Gawain as he released the woman and stuffed a thick slice of bread into his mouth. Meanwhile the other knights were rummaging through the pottery jars that held the family's meager provisions. Galahad found a small jar of honey which he poured on his bread, then hurled the jar against the wall, where it shattered with a loud bang, with a sunburst of honey, slowly dripping down to the floor. The wailing of the terrified children grew shriller; the moaning of the father outside could now be heard.

When the knights had eaten their fill and destroyed all the leftovers, they returned to their horses and set off. "Follow me," Kay told the others as they trotted further down the road.

Monte was getting used to the pace of the horse and relaxed more in the saddle. Because the horse was so well trained, he found he could even make a few notes as he rode.

I feel like one of those war correspondents, he thought. Yeah, that was it. He was simply an observer making notes for history.

In a mile or two, they came upon a cluster of thatched houses, built so close to each other they almost touched. A large vegetable garden spread out in front of the houses, and a figure dressed in light blue crouched among the parsnip, carrot, and onion plants. The three knights and Monte approached, and Kay let out a loud whistle.

The figure among the garden rows lifted her head. She was a strikingly beautiful woman with dazzling blue eyes and golden ringlets of hair falling to her shoulders. Her simple blue dress with low bodice made her even more alluring to the visitors.

Kay motioned for her to approach them. She dutifully obeyed.

"Are you lonesome, fair maiden?" Kay said with a grinning leer. "The four of us have come to keep you company..."

He hopped off his horse and approached the young woman, reaching out for her hand. She pulled her hand instinctively away. The other knights had dismounted and now surrounded her. Monte remained on his horse.

"Don't be nervous, just come with us to the forest across the road," cooed Galahad, and we'll show you how real men can make you feel."

The three briefly turned and looked up towards Monte, still sitting in the saddle. "Come join us, Sir Storyteller," Kay urged, "You'll have some fun and also have a great tale to tell."

The young woman seized the momentary diversion to run off past the houses and into the thick underbrush beyond. The knights did not bother to chase after her. They would get their release in another way.

"Bitch!" snorted Kay.

"Witch!" sputtered Gawain.

Kay stepped toward one of the nearby houses and took out a piece of flint and a small block of steel from his belt pouch. He reached up toward the edge of the roof thatching and struck the flint against the steel. A spark flew into the dry, reed material and a slight twist of white smoke drifted upward. In a moment it had burst into an open flame. The flame grew and quickly spread across the roof, soon igniting the adjoining the other houses as well.

"Our work here is done," declared Galahad in satisfaction as he remounted his horse and led the group to their next stopping place.

And so it went for the rest of the day, with Galahad, Gawain, and

Kay making as much cruel mischief as they could. They chased down a runaway dog and slayed it, taking special pleasure in seeing it writhe in pain before it died. They cut out the tongue of a teenage boy who dared to curse them. And they roughly stole a ring from a blind beggar. It was the only possession of any value that he had.

With darkness falling, they headed back to Camelot, supremely satisfied with a full day of knightly work.

* * *

Merlin was waiting for Monte as soon as he had returned to Camelot. As Monte came through the door of his own room, Merlin was lying on his bed, reading a scroll of magical formulas.

"How did it go?" Merlin asked.

Monte was visibly shaken.

"My God," Monte said at long last. "These people are animals. Criminals. Rapists."

"Murderers," Merlin interjected, not looking up from his scroll.

Monte glared at him for his apparent nonchalance.

"You knew? You knew what they were like? What they were up to?"

"Of course I knew. Everyone knows. You can't go around raping and pillaging and burning villages to the ground and keep it a secret."

"They're terrorists!"

"The originals," Merlin responded, finally putting down his scroll and staring at Monte. "That's how they stay in power. Terror."

"And Arthur?" Monte said.

"Merlin smiled. "The worst. The King of the Terrorists. Osama bin Laden's got nothing on him. Think of them as gangsters. As mobsters. But they're not alone. All of Britain, all of Europe is like this. Run by warlords, terrorists, gangsters. That's why we have to change the narrative. That's what you're here for. You have to create a different story, and if it's good enough, people will repeat it and repeat it until it becomes fact."

"I don't see how it's possible...." Monte said, almost trembling. "Some stupid story is not going to change history."

Merlin sat up and moved to the edge of the bed and began to sing some lines from the Broadway musical.

"Ask every person if he's heard the story
And tell it loud and clear if he has not.
That once there was an ancient wisp of glory
Called Camelot... Camelot..."

Ironic, no? That's the power of storytelling. That's how we're going to end this reign of terror.

Now, tonight you're going to do your usual storytelling entertainment. But tomorrow night, you're going to begin to tell the wondrous tales of Camelot, the way it should be, not the way it unfortunately is."

"I don't think I can," Monte said.

"Of course, you can," Merlin replied. "Spinning gold from dross. What the hell do you think reality TV is? You take a bunch of mediocre social misfits and turn them into national heroes. Think Real Housewives. You can do this. Come on. Give it a shot."

"Pick up your notes and just give me a rough idea of how the story is going to run."

Monte took this as a challenge. Despite being tired and sore, he was supremely confident. He knew he had the goods of an amazing pitch for Reality TV. He picked up his wax tablets and just started riffing the storyline.

"In the Kingdom of Camelot, power was everything, no matter who it helped or who it harmed. Might made right and might over the weak was more precious than gold…"

Merlin furrowed his brow; he didn't like where this was going.

"Try this," he said,

"Setting off from their impregnable fortress at the first light of dawn," Merlin continued, "three bravehearted knights—Galahad, Kay, and Gawain—rode across the kingdom on their steeds to faithfully carry out the wishes of their wise king."

Monte began to sweat. He wasn't stupid. He suddenly had to reconsider his idea of what exactly "good" storytelling was.

Merlin could see that he was making Monte uncomfortable. That was how he needed him to be. They had an enormous challenge ahead of them: to construct a myth that people would be retelling for hundreds, even thousands of years. He had to show him how to turn raw reality into stories of nobility, heroism, and triumph over evil that people in every era can believe in."

"Listen to me, Monte," Merlin said in an eerie contradiction of the words Brinkman once spoke to him and had served as his watchwords throughout his career. "You have to take control of the situation. You think mythmaking is just showing up and writing down what you see? Nothing could be further from the truth. You have to direct. You have to become a mythmaker. Like Homer, like Moses, like Matthew, Mark, Luke, and John. Like Steven Spielberg. You have to make everything your heroes do seem noble, even if they are actually out of their minds or committing war crimes. Get the concept here?"

Monte nodded.

"I do," he said.

"Good," said Merlin. "Because you have 24 hours to get your story together. If you appear at the royal hall tomorrow night and don't have a great tale that makes King Arthur's gang sound like the Delta Force, the Royal Marines, or even the Salvation Army, I'll make sure your head is rolling around in the sawdust on the floor.

*   *   *

Sure enough, by the next evening, Monte proved that he had learned his lesson and created the first tentative episode of the King Arthur myth. Once again Merlin introduced him to the crowd and allowed to sink or swim on his own. But he had also whispered in the ear of the king and gossiped among all the knights and courtiers that Le Vine was going to be telling a new kind of story—still filled with surprises and acts of strength and daring—but the difference was that his amazing tale was going to be about them.

Human nature being what it always was and always will be, everyone reacts to stories personally, as if it were about them. But when the hero is actually about the listener, the attraction is irresistible. Whether it's an appearance on TV, an awards dinner, or even bulletin boards filled with photos taken by a cruise ship photographer, there is something hypnotic about self-representation. This, after all, was the very basis of Facebook. And so it was that evening in the royal hall. King Arthur and his knights actually looked forward to Le Vine's story. It was not just after dinner entertainment; it was a chance to see themselves as others saw them. Monte was about to create the world's first selfie, fashioned entirely out of flattering words.

Monte mounted the platform in a new costume, with a cape, silk shirt, and floppy feathered velvet hat. He was now a respected member of the court, and no one ever suspected him of being a spy any more. He was also washed and rested, having a day to recover from his ride through the countryside. "Your Majesty, noble Knights and courtiers of Camelot," Monte announced proudly and confidently as he mounted the low platform in the royal hall. "I have come to praise your greatness tonight. I have also come to tell you a story—a story that merely begins to tell of the full glory of Camelot and its wise king."

"It is an extraordinary tale. Each and every one of you have created a realm that will be remembered forever, and I hope that my humble tale, committed to writing and passed down from generation to generation both here in Britain and in every corner of the world, will inspire countless souls to admire your achievements and aspire to be as noble and righteous as you."

King Arthur leaned back in his throne to hear the story, clearly pleased with the prospect of being admired forever. The audience leaned forward in rapt attention. There was absolutely no conversation; the royal hall suddenly became so silent for Monte to begin his story that you could have heard a greasy meat fork drop.

"Camelot is a place where laws are cheerfully obeyed," Monte started, "and where the knights and noblemen have great compassion for the poor. It is a land of perfect justice, where all the hardworking peasants love their King. Yesterday, for example, I saw how the king's heroic knights traveled through the land, helping the destitute, punishing evil doers, protecting the realm from fearsome monsters, and helping the halt and the blind."

"I watched in great admiration as three of Camelot's noblest knights—Galahad, Gawain, and Kay—permitted me to accompany them on a tour of the territory and I shall relate what I saw. They first called on a loyal blacksmith named William in the village of Ironbound. The court clerks had noticed his absence at harvest time and the knights rode out to check on his welfare. Was he sick? Had he fallen victim to an accident? No, they found him in good health and grateful that King Arthur's noble knights had taken time from their many official duties to call upon him."

"In gratitude, he invited the knights to share a humble meal with him and his family. Unfortunately, he slipped and fell and could not join them, but his lovely wife welcomed the knights into their home and their children screamed in excitement to see such imposing men. The family had little to offer—certainly not the quality or quantity of the food generously provided to us here at Camelot. But the knights did not want to offend the poor family and happily broke bread with them in order to both honor the humble generosity of their hosts and to better understand what the simple folk do. A memorable time was had by all at this modest farmstead and the knights departed, confident that all was well."

"Their next stop was to take on a far more dangerous mission in a far more dangerous place. Rumors in the neighboring villages reported that demons flew through the air around midnight; frightening ghosts and evil spirits visited peasants in their fields and workshops; a recurrent curse caused apples to rot on their trees. This was clearly a case of witchcraft and Sir Kay led the way to investigate. When the knights arrived, a beautiful maiden rose out of the earth. When they approached her, she turned into a horrible hag. None of the knights was able to grab ahold of her and she disappeared into thin air. Luckily, it was Sir Kay who had the presence of mind to bring along a firebox that he used to burn the witch's lair to the ground."

Hearing the stories, Galahad, Gawain, and Kay first nodded their heads in agreement, then smiled delightedly and at last, smacked each other on the back and cheered Monte on. Yes, they thought, he's got it. We are indeed great and noble men.   And as the rest of the audience repeatedly reacted with oohs and aahs of admiration, and even the King himself nodded approvingly at the heroes of Monte's story, they all came to believe it themselves. Monte's story became a reality far more believable than what had actually happened. This was the way it had been, they were all convinced.

"So let us raise our mead cups high in salute to King Arthur and the knights who serve him," Monte shouted as he held his own cup aloft. "For this is only one story of which there are many, many more—as many as the stars in the heavens—that record the wonders and amazing feats of daring that take place every day in this marvelous land of Camelot."

After the crowd mobbed Galahad, Gawain, and Kay to congratulate them for their great acts of kindness and heroism, the three men approached the king and kneeled before his throne.

"O great King Arthur," they said almost in unison, "all praise belongs to you. You have given us the honor of serving your kingdom where our might is used only for good."

Monte stepped off the platform and sidled up to Merlin who was standing in the shadows, with tears of joy streaming down his face.

CHAPTER 17
IF EVER I SHOULD LEAVE YOU

Queen Guinevere was unhappy, profoundly unhappy. She had been married to King Arthur for more than fifteen years and she knew how much he adored her. But he proved to be a never- ending source of disappointment to her. He was not the heroic figure she thought he was when they had wed.

Guinevere loathed the boorish knights that gathered in the royal hall and her idea for the Round Table was really nothing more than to get their filthy asses of the floor and onto chairs. Since childhood, she had been brought up in a proper royal court—where the guests did not fart or burp at dinner; where her father the king was interested in many more things—the rules of chivalry, philosophy, theology, and alchemy—than filling his coffers and his belly in raucous nightly feasts. Her father was a man of spartan habits and enormous generosity. He had seen that the future of his kingdom lay in prosperity for all, down to the lowliest peasant. And instead of intimidating them and bleeding them dry of their crops and their possessions, he encouraged them all to work together in a great enterprise of developing the kingdom into a prosperous realm of stone carvers, basket weavers, sheep rearers, and overseas traders in precious works of art and tapestries.

So now left to her own devices, without a child, without a mission in life, without a friend she could really confide in, Guinevere surrendered to a lonely, empty existence. Going through the motions of being Arthur's consort and helpmate, she appeared at feasts and seasonal celebrations, public executions, and witch burnings as a queen was expected to do. But she really wasn't all there at any of these occasions. Her once warm heart had turned to stone. She lived in a state of nearly complete emotional withdrawal, blocking out the violent, cruel reality that surrounded her.

In fact, she was not even aware of the uproar that erupted among King Arthur's knights and squires when a mounted stranger in full battle armor appeared unexpectedly outside the main stockade gate. He spoke in a strange accent but made himself understood. He had come to offer his services to King Arthur. His name, he shouted out to the sentries, was Lancelot.

* * *

It was tough for Merlin to break the news to Monte, after all he had been through already. He had now ridden for weeks with all of King Arthur's knights on their daily circuits. He had been forced to witness the bloody banality of their evil, cutting off heads, crushing testicles, raping, stealing, and destroying to keep the peasantry in a total state of fear. Worse yet, he had to transform that daily crime spree into the stuff of legend, and—to put it most simply—the legend wasn't going anywhere. It was essentially the same story every night. King Arthur's men were noble, righteous, and had excuses for everything. Everything they did was to carry out the orders of their sovereign and for the good of all his subjects, from the noblest to the lowliest.

Unfortunately, popular legends had at least two things in common with Reality TV: first, repetition breeds boredom, which will drive even the most faithful audience to away. And second, if the ratings fall, the show is cancelled, and as a rule, the producer is axed.

Those were exactly the traps that Monte had fallen into at the very start of his medieval mythmaking career. He should have known better after all his years in the dog-eat-dog world of Reality TV. But Merlin, for his part, knew that it was at least partly his own fault, for insisting that Monte appear night after night to the same audience of hoodlums and mouth breathers, and essentially telling the same lying tale over and over—about riding through the countryside and helping everyone. Merlin had by this time grown quite discouraged about the extent of his own powers. His life lived backward in time had merely taught him the utter unpredictability of how things had actually begun. The romantic legends of knights in shining armor he had learned as a child were no more authentic than the stories of Santa Claus or the Easter Bunny. These guys and even Arthur himself would never be moved to abandon their rough and rowdy ways by mere fairy tales. In fact, Monte's mythmaking gave them a cover to act even more cruelly, having an in-house propagandist to provide them with a heroic cover for their crimes.

After one night's performance, Merlin approached Monte, tapped him on the shoulder, and motioned for him to join him outside. They sat down together.

"Monte," he said grimly, "I thought I was going to be able to change these guys into something more noble than hitmen. But they're only getting worse. My powers of backward prediction have failed me. Sure, the myth of Arthur will gradually develop and spread around the world, but not based on anything that actually happened in the Middle Ages and certainly not as a guide to a more moral and just society. It will all be just a cover for slashing and burning and taking from the poor to give to the rich."

"It was stupid of me," Merlin continued, "to ever think that a made-up, heroic image of King Arthur could ever be anything more than a big con. Every dictator starts out as a small-time grifter with great PR. But the PR eventually slams into reality and the slogans can't delay the inevitable forever. I mean did Lenin create a Communist worker's paradise? Did Hitler's Reich actually last for a thousand years? Did Saddam Hussein make American soldiers drown in their own blood? Of course not. Even though all of them had temporarily convinced their most faithful followers to believe that they could change history."

Monte had never seen Merlin so disconsolate before. It was usually himself who needed cheering up. He tried to wrap his mind around what Merlin was saying, but Merlin suddenly made it all terrifyingly clear.

"Well, what happens now?" Monte asked.

"I've made a terrible mistake in bringing you here. Even your considerable storytelling skills aren't powerful enough to persuade these guys to do anything more than sink deeper into their own couches, munching on rich snack foods, and making fun of others' misfortune. That's what we've done here. We've just created another kind of mind-numbing Reality TV. I've decided to pull the plug on this whole crazy idea and send you back to your own century."

Monte wasn't expecting that Merlin would give up on his masterplan after only a few weeks.

"You've got to give it some time," Monte responded.

"What? You're afraid if I send you back, you're going to wake up on Stürmer's torture table? Don't worry about that. I can send you back to any time or place you want."

Flickering light suddenly illuminated Merlin's downcast face, as a drunken knight stumbled out of the side door of the royal hall, apparently to puke somewhere in the darkness. When the knight had disappeared into the night, Monte leaned into Merlin's face with the same intense stare that he had often received from him.

"There's no way I'm going anywhere," he insisted. "You've taught me something I never realized before. I never took my story ideas very seriously; they were just a way to pay the bills. All I ever did was take other peoples' order or copy what everyone else was doing, whatever was hot at the moment. Here, I have the chance to do something really new."

"Not only new," Monte continued, "but something that could make a difference. I know how to make this work.

"What exactly do you have in mind?" Merlin asked.

"A complete change in the medium."

Merlin seemed confused. "Look, I've been through more technological changes than you can shake a stick at," he insisted. "Every single medium you've ever heard of from social media to the telegraph to carrier pigeons—and plenty more that you have not lived long enough to see. But it all comes down to one essential quality, no matter what the technology may be. And the quality is always the same: Entertainment, that feeling of wonder and enjoyment of being a part of a group—or should I say part of an 'audience.' Exactly what kind of "change in medium" do you have in mind?"

"Oh, I'm not talking about technology," Monte said with a dismissive wave of his hand. He was acting like the teacher now. "What I have in mind is changing our key demographic, as we say in the TV biz."

"Right now, we're aiming at exactly the wrong audience," Monte continued. Up until now, we've been playing just to the King and his knights. That's our mistake. That's like writing The Godfather and giving the only copy to Don Corleone. We've got to go public, big time."

"Well, who else is there that really matters?" Merlin asked, furrowing his brow. "You can't really mean the peasants..."

"Of course! They are the only people who'll love the story and pass it on."

"I dunno," Merlin said.

"Listen," Monte implored. "We're also gonna change the format."

"What do you mean?"

"I mean, a story is OK, but we need something with legs. Something that will last. Something that has stickiness. Something that can go viral."

"And what would that be?" Merlin said skeptically.

I'm talking about Camelot!" Monte quickly snapped back. "Not this shithole that goes by that name, but the real Camelot—the Camelot that ran for almost a thousand performances on Broadway and God know how many tens of thousands of performances in revivals, touring companies, and senior class plays. And that doesn't even start to count the millions who saw it at the movies, on DVD, and Netflix."

"Don't be ridiculous," Merlin screamed back, red in the face. "We're living in the fucking Middle Ages! How in hell do you think you can put on a goddam musical?"

"The peasants will love it," Monte smiled broadly, as if he were already planning his next move.

"Just leave it to me."

* * *

It had to happen sooner or later. Monte Le Vine, at the height of his prestige in King Arthur's court, had fallen in love. He still could not be sure that what he was experiencing was a dream or hallucination, but there was something about the twinkle in the stunning green eyes of one of Queen Guinevere's ladies-in-waiting that was real enough for him. It was a dream he actually wanted to have. She seemed amused at a subtle joke he had inserted into his story, a joke that revealed that he was really parodying the epic genre, a joke that no one else in the royal hall apparently got.

"King Arthur," Monte had said in the course of one of his stories, "entered the witch's lair to defend the entire kingdom from her wicked curse. No man alive had as much courage to confront as the great king. The witch's wrinkled greenish face was horrible to behold and her loud cackle would have frightened a lesser man. But as King Arthur boldly reached for his weapon, the hag smiled widely, exposing her rotten teeth and exclaimed 'Is that Excalibur in your pocket or are you just happy to see me?' At that, Arthur whipped out Excalibur and plunged it deep into her."

The knights, all of limited capacity to grasp double-entendre, cheered wildly at the account of another great feat of heroism of their king. But Monte tried to stifle his smile as his eyes and the handmaiden's met. From then on, Monte would intentionally insert a wisecrack or pun into his stories. He hardly even noticed that the interest of the knights in his stories was slowly waning, because he was more concerned that the interest of the lady-in-waiting with the green eyes and the flaming red halo of hair steadily grew.

Her name, he later, learned was Katarin, and she had come to King Arthur's court as a prisoner of war. She had been the wife of an Anglo-Saxon warrior chief who had fallen in battle with King Arthur's forces, and had been captured when the surviving enemy troops had panicked and fled. She had come to the field of battle because she was the eldest daughter of a powerful Saxon king. And it was because of that royal connection that she was not harmed, but added to Queen Guinevere's retinue in the hope that someday her father would ransom her for a hefty reward. The ransom never came, but as a few years passed, she grew close to Queen Guinevere. Though Katarin still spoke with an eastern accent, they shared stories of the love that they both held for their distant royal fathers, and both shared a distaste for what was going on in Camelot. In time, Katarin became Guinevere's closest advisor and social secretary.

Monte was entranced not only by Katarin's beauty but her enormous intelligence. He began to request chaperoned visits with her, and since she came to Camelot as a captive, not an heir to a local noble, the request was granted. He would sit with her in the benches in the Queen's Garden, far from the smelly animal pens. It was a small rose-scented island of tranquility in the otherwise muddy and chaotic stockade.

The two seemed a perfect match for each other. Katarin laughed at Monte's jokes and Monte quipped that Katarin that the Dark Ages were a little bit brighter for him, having had the pleasure of meeting her. Katarin told Monte her whole story, of the dark forestland she had come from, where the people were as tough and uncompromising as the cold winter wind.

"You know we could be related," Monte joked at one of their meetings, "My people come from Eastern Europe too."

"Were they warriors?" Katarin replied in all seriousness.

"Let's just say they were worriers," Monte replied with a smirk.

As the months passed, Monte and Katarin grew closer and they were eventually permitted to go off on their own. Monte never expected to get back to the twenty-first century, so he figured he would be beyond the reach of any bigamy laws if he and Katarin should wed. Indeed, he cherished the time they spent together, making love or just talking about life. Merlin was too mercurial to offer much intellectual stimulation and no one else in Camelot—except perhaps for Queen Guinevere—had any brains at all.

In fact, he had first turned to Katarin when he faced his problem of declining popularity at the court. He explained his idea for sharing his stories with the kingdom's peasant population, she immediately told him that she thought it was brilliant, though of course she had no idea—at least at first—of what a "musical" was. But it was an idea that eventually captured her imagination as over the course of the next week or so Monte explained the plot of Camelot to her and even sung a few of the catchiest tunes.

"I think Queen Guinevere will love it. And of course, she will insist on playing herself," Katarin predicted, "and there's this new knight that arrived, so strange that his name is also Lancelot, just like the actor who played that role—what did you say his name was?"

"Robert Goulet," Monte answered, "but later he was King Arthur in the road company."

Katarin was totally confused. "Oh never mind," she said, "I've already sent word to the abbot of Glastonbury and he has agreed to lend us his choir for the musical backgrounds."

So, it was all set. Katarin persuaded Guinevere that performing in a play-- "a royal pageant," she called it—would be good for her. It would give her something to do and something to look forward to. And it would only help the King by improving his image among the peasants. Though Arthur would have rather killed a few more of his subjects than stage a cultural performance to boost his powerful reputation, he always agreed to Guinevere's every whim.

That evening, King Arthur announced to his knights and the assembled crowd in the royal hall that Sir Monte Le Vine the royal storyteller would be taking a leave of absence. He was preparing a surprise that would entertain everyone. In the meantime, the King announced there would be alternate entertainment in the evening: he had already acquired the services of a sword swallower, a fire eater, a juggler, and even a troupe of wrestlers.

The audience rose to their feet and gave a deafening cheer. That kind of entertainment was much more their liking.

* * *

The loud pounding of iron hammers and shouts of the workers echoed throughout the valley as a bizarre wooden contraption rose on the steep slope of Camelot's stockade hill. Like a huge box with its front ripped open, it rose to a great height and its brightly painted inner walls were laid bare for all to see.

Monte stood on its smooth floorboards with Katarin, closely supervising the progress and quality of the construction, checking every detail against the sketches he had drawn on an oversized parchment scroll. From time to time, Katarin approached the artists who were painting large wooden cutouts of castle turrets and faux stone walls of an elaborate royal hall adorned with swords and shields.

Nearly everyone in the kingdom—from knights to clerks to servants to swineherds were intensely curious about the reason for this open structure, and everyone had their own theory about what it was for.

"The King must have an important announcement," Galahad

announced with an air of ambitious expectation, "perhaps he is going to declare his successor to the throne."

"No doubt there will be a public execution in the coming days," said a worried farmer to his wife. "And it can be any of us."

"I suspect that this is all Merlin's doing," said one of the newly hired wrestlers to a juggler, "he's just trying to show us up. He always has something up his wizard's sleeve."

"Perhaps there will be a great wedding of one of the Queen's ladies-in-waiting," said a jealous serving girl to a scullery maid."

When a column of silent monks marched two-by-two up the steep path to the stockade gate, a wave of panic swept through nobles and commoners alike. King Arthur was never known to be a particularly religious man—and the arrival of the clergy could only mean one of three things, all of the bad: the king was on his deathbed, a plague had arrived in the kingdom, or the End of the World was Nigh.

What none of the members of the court or any of its victims could possibly imagine was that a stage was being prepared for mass entertainment, something that they had never experienced themselves. Centuries before, the Romans had perfected rule of the masses through bread and circuses, holding spectacular shows and distributing food for the hungry. But that was far in the past. Now entertainment was delivered in private for the self-glorification of the rich and powerful; those outside the charmed circles of the rulers were left to tell each other stories by the hearth and the campfire and to tremble with fear when the king's emissaries came to deliver a message to them.

But Monte was determined to draw the peasants en masse to the foot Camelot's slope and to put on a performance they would never forget. He was only eight when his parents took him to a performance of Camelot on Broadway, and he never forgot the music, the costumes, and the impression that it made on him. Although he did not remember many of the plot details, he knew the main story: Arthur was a wise and noble king who created a utopian kingdom with the help of his wise and understanding wife. He was the model king and idealist, the perfect leader and generous leader who created one "bright and shining moment" of perfect justice in his kingdom of Camelot. But that moment was not destined to last forever. Evil schemers sought to undermine his rule and grasp power. His beloved wife Guinevere fell deeply in love with his most loyal knight Lancelot. The peace and tranquility of Camelot crumbled into chaos. But King Arthur, true to his noble nature, recognized that humanity's greatest ideals are not destroyed by failure. They live on to inspire future generations to do better—to remember that "bright and shining moment" as a goal that may someday be reborn.

This was the opposite of the Reality TV that Monte had spent most of his professional life producing, where the basest of human instincts and actions drew the greatest ratings and applause. But if he now, with the help of Katarin could use his persuasive powers and Reality TV skills to engineer a dramatic transformation of King Arthur's real kingdom, the ideal and the reality of Camelot might converge right back here in the sixth century AD. And if that happened the Arthurian ideal would become a historical reality, not just a romantic fairy tale.

This, Monte came to realize, was the real power of storytelling in human history. It was not the work of Kings or Emperors or Popes that decided the path of human advancement, it was rather the stories that were told about them and repeated generation after generation.

The cast was assembled, and intensive rehearsals began. Guinevere would play herself in the "pageant," guided by her own desperate desire for true chivalry, true love, and a noble husband who would—unlike Arthur—understand. Merlin would, of course, play Merlin, and the handsome young knight who had appeared unannounced at the gates of the stockade would play his namesake Lancelot. The casting of Arthur, though, posed a serious problem. Arthur was no Richard Burton, not even an actor, and both Katarin and Guinevere knew it was going to be impossible to get the boorish, impetuous king to remember his lines, much less stay in tune during his many songs.

Even more worrisome was his likely reaction to the moral of the story. The main themes of Camelot were idealism and self-sacrifice, and the real King Arthur could not possibly understand, much less sympathize with either one. For him and his band of thugs, power and machismo were the ultimate virtues—and to ask Arthur to willingly play the cuckold, and to nobly accept his beloved wife's love for another man and her happiness over his own was more than anyone could expect from him.

Yet casting the role of King Arthur was obviously critical to the success of the play. Not only because he was the leading character but also because the whole purpose of the royal pageant was to change the real King Arthur's image in the minds of his subjects, his knights, and naturally in the mind of King Arthur himself. If storytelling could ever have an effect on reality, then staging Camelot in Camelot could perhaps prove it was possible. Monte and Katarin were given the Queen's permission to recruit all the artists, jewelers, and costumers in the kingdom to ensure that the production would be spectacular. Riders were sent out to all the villages of the realm to declare a public holiday on the day of the performance, and to urge them to attend—even offering free refreshments and a 10% reduction on their yearly tribute if they did.

Arthur remained blissfully ignorant of the details of the upcoming royal pageant, egotistically confident that Guinevere's promise that it would celebrate the king's greatness before all of his subjects was actually true. In the meantime, Monte, with Katarin's help, was busy from dawn to dusk with rehearsals inside the royal hall—which the Queen had demanded was strictly off-limits during daylight hours to anyone not in the cast.

Training the monks to provide just the right musical background was Monte's first challenge. Their monotonously droning chants turned Lerner and Lowe's catchy, uplifting tunes into funeral dirges that all sounded the same.

"Come on guys," Monte pleaded with the hooded monks, "up-tempo! Pull back those hoods and sing with smiles on your faces! This is entertainment not vespers!"

Monte could quickly see that this was going to be a problem. You can't have a musical without the music, and while Lerner and Lowe had a 42-piece orchestra for the Broadway production, all he had was this grim assembly of chanting monks. But he had to work with what he had to work with. Along with the monks, the abbot had sent his musicians. They had lutes, psalteriums, drums, cymbals and a harp. That was it.

Monte waved his arms to a faster beat and encouraged them with and exaggerated smile. But still they grimly droned through every song Monte had taught them, making "How to Handle a Woman" sound absolutely indistinguishable from "What Do the Simple Folk Do?" The fact that the monks had no experience with women and little experience with the joys of peasanthood did not make things any easier.

Finally, in his frustration, Monte called for silence. Then, he began to clap rhythmically.

"Come on boys, clap along with me." And, with great reluctance, the hooded monks began to clap as Monte clapped.

Once he had set the tempo with the clapping, Monte began to sing. He knew he had to keep it simple at first.

"A-a-a...men." he sang.

They looked up. This they could recognize.

"A-a-a...men... A-a-a...men, Amen, Amen," with his voice steadily rising in volume and pitch, clapping and swaying like a gospel singer incongruously dressed in medieval garb.

He encouraged them to join in the chorus, which they did, at first hesitatingly and then with increased gusto. This was, at least a religious song and it had an infectious rhythm. Soon the room was filled with the soulful musical response of the congregation at a revival meeting.

"A-a-a... men, Aa-a... men, A... men"

At this point, Monte began to run up and down the aisles, like a TV evangelist, urging on the monks with a counterpoint verse.

"See the baby Jesus... A...men

Laying in the manger....A...men

Oh Christmas morning...

A...men, amen, amen

Hallelujah!"

Soon the room was rocking. The monks were clapping and stamping their feet and singing along at the top of their voices.

"See him in the Temple....

Talking to the elders...

Who marvel at his wisdom...

Amen... amen amen..."

At the conclusion of the song, the room burst into wild applause. Katarin sidled up to Monte.

"That was incredible," she said, with tears coming down her face.

"Oh, Otis Redding did it way better. Now that was a man with soul," Monte replied.

"Who?" Katarin asked. She stared blankly into Monte's eyes.

Sometimes she didn't have the vaguest idea what he was talking about, but she did not care. Monte was the most amazing man she had ever met.

Having won over the loyalty of the monks, Monte proceeded to turn them into first class performers. He began by taking the lute from one of the court musicians.

"You don't mind, do you?" he said, and proceeded to re-tune the lute to his familiar 6 strings of his Stratocaster. As he held the lute, his fingers pressing down on the strings, he closed his eyes, and for a moment, he was once again transported to another place and another time.

He began to play, and to sing.

"There's a lady who's sure
All that glitters is gold
And she's buying a stairway to heaven. "

The great room, which had only a few minutes ago been alive with excited chatter now fell completely silent as Monte, in a kind of trance, played on.

"And it makes me wonder
If there's a bustle in your hedgerow, don't be alarmed now
It's just a spring clean for the May queen
Yes, there are two paths you can go by, but in the long run
There's still time to change the road you're on"

"Yes, yes!" the monks were yelling.

"There's still time to change the road you're on! It is never too late to find salvation."

Katarin watched all this with amazement. She had never heard someone make music like this. There was love in her eyes.

Within a few weeks, the monks and the court musicians were perhaps not good enough for Broadway, but they definitely were good enough to sing backup for a high school musical. And that would be enough for an audience who had never seen a stage play in their lives.

Next were the actors and the rehearsal of the plot, with its poignant ending. The matter of casting King Arthur was still a problem, so Monte played the role as a stand-in, at least until a final casting decision was made.

Finally, Monte's Arthur was found. One of the monks in the chorus had a particularly good voice, and, at 5'8, he was far taller than the rest. The perfect King, Monte thought. King Arthur at only 5'1" was always self-conscious about his height. This would surely flatter him. Put a crown on his head and we're done.

"What's your name, brother?" Monte had asked the monk.

"Lewellyn," the monk replied, more than a bit nervous.

"Well, today is your lucky day, Lewellyn. You're going to play King Arthur."

Day after day they went through the story: From the arrival of Guinevere in Camelot to wed King Arthur to her escape from the kingdom with Lancelot. Guinevere understood her role deeply. It was after all the life that she lived and the dreams that she had. But she knew that Arthur would grow furious when he heard another man sing love songs to her. But she had to do it. She had to announce to her husband in the presence of all his subjects what a great king and an ideal kingdom could be.

*   *   *

Considering all the difficulties he had faced in producing the show, the performances slowly improved through the weeks of rehearsal. The only slight problem was Lancelot, who unwittingly revealed that he was actually not a French knight at all. The first sign of trouble was when he seemed utterly incapable of correctly pronouncing the lyrics to his character's trademark song "C'est moi." He tried and tried but every time he musically professed his desire to become a knight of the Round Table, it came out more like a Welsh peasant than a French noble. Because that is exactly what he was. Tired of living the miserable life of a peasant he had come to try to better his lot in life.

"Say Moy, Say Moy," he would sing, trying his best to twist his tongue into a passable French accent, amusing Guinivere and all of the cast. He was handsome. He was earnest. He was idealistic. In a strange way, and certainly carried by the sheer romance of the show itself, Guinevere began to realize that here, in this noble peasant were all the traits she had sought for so long and never found in her husband. And Guinivere actually soon found herself falling in love with him as they rehearsed their romantic duets.

So, by the day of the grand premiere of the "royal pageant," everything was ready. The huge stage on the slope was completed, the elaborate scenery was painted, the costumes were finished and fitted to each of the actors, the monks had become really quite good with their singing, and soon after dawn on the great day, the first of the audience began to arrive in the grassy area beneath the stage on foot and in creaky oxcarts.

By noon, the whole area was filled with peasants, shouting, singing, dancing, and generally celebrating on this, the first official day off they had been given in seventeen years. Monte and Merlin peeked out toward the crowd from the wings of the stage and smiled broadly in great satisfaction at the sheer numbers who had gathered to watch the play.

"It's a fucking medieval Woodstock!" Monte exclaimed. "Let's just hope the message gets through loud and clear."

At two o'clock the court trumpeters played a loud fanfare as the King and his knights took their places in a special box built just for them. His royal wave to the crowd was greeted with jeers and catcalls, to which he responded with an angry wave of his fist.

The curtain rose. The crowd was expectant. King Arthur leaned forward and the knights surrounding him watched his expression carefully to see how they should react. The audience gasped as they got their first glance of the opulence of the stage. As the monks sang the overture, the stage was filled with knights, horses, and maidens like none they had ever seen before. The knights wore shiny metal suits, not the rusty chain mail that King Arthur's real knights wore. The maidens were refined and moved gracefully, greeting the knights with charm and respect. The eyes of the onlookers widened to take in the spectacle; this was a version of the Middle Ages imported straight from the twentieth century that could hardly dream of. Needless to say, they had never seen anything like it before.

The milling actors parted, and Merlin appeared on stage and took a deep bow. He called to the stage King Arthur and announced the imminent arrival of his beautiful bride-to-be Guinevere. In the royal box, Arthur leaned back in his throne and smiled nostalgically.

"She really was the most beautiful princess in all of Britain," he said as his faithful knights, following that cue, nodded enthusiastically.

At that moment, Guinevere herself appeared on the stage, dressed in a long blue velvet dress with sparkling gold applique. The crowd murmured at the sight of the Queen, who though now middle-aged retained her beauty and grace. Though initially hesitant to meet her royal groom, she realized that her future would be bright as the monks sang out the famous lyrics.

A law was made a distant moon ago here:
July and August cannot be too hot.
And there's a legal limit to the snow here
In Camelot.
The winter is forbidden till December
And exits March the second on the dot.
By order, summer lingers through September
In Camelot.
Camelot! Camelot!

The audience began to sway from side to side in rhythm with the tune, that described the way they all wished Camelot would be. The king and his companions smiled broadly at what they now expected would be a wonderful show.

The curtains briefly closed and the scenery was quickly changed to reveal an opulent royal hall that bore little resemblance to the smoky barn where Arthur held his nightly feasts. Lewellyn, playing the king, announced his wish that Camelot would soon be greater than any kingdom on earth. He and his faithful knights would create a new age of prosperity and toleration in Camelot, no longer pillaging the countryside, levying unbearable taxes, or using violence against their subjects to collect it, but establishing a peaceful realm with justice and dignity for all.

At these lines a murmur swept through the close packed audience of peasants that soon grew into and enthusiastic roar. Here and there commoners who had suffered at the hands of King Arthur's knights rose to applaud the surprising sentiments.

"Long live King Arthur!" they shouted. "What a great and noble king!"

In the royal box, the real King Arthur and his knights exchanged nervous glances. None of this visionary balderdash was in their plans.

And when the offstage King Arthur announced that he would establish a great Round Table where all knights and even the King himself would be brothers and equals, concerned only for the kingdom's welfare not private gain. The audience roared even louder and the real King Arthur's face began to redden with rage.

But worse—much worse—was soon to come as the handsome Lancelot strode on stage. He had come "from France" to join the Knights of the Round Table, he proclaimed and broke into song about his knightly achievements. "C'est moi" still came out in his flat Welsh accent, but no one in the audience, living their entire lives within the kingdom, even noticed or cared.

Exciting jousts, joyful dances, jesters' acrobatics, and royal ceremonies now followed, filling the stage with a series of colorful spectacles that wowed the crowd of peasant spectators and further unsettled the occupants of the royal box.

Monte, standing offstage, could hardly contain his own excitement. "My God, this is better than anything I ever put on in Teutonic Nights," he said out loud to himself.

If this was all just a dream, Monte thought, it is the best I have ever had. But that beautiful dream quickly turned into a horrible nightmare, as it became clear that in the play Guinevere and Lancelot had fallen in love. Both proclaimed in song and tender dialogue that they were torn between their passionate love for each other and their loyalty to the wise and noble King Arthur. But no matter the consequences, love would prevail.

As the handsome Lancelot took Guinevere in his arms and sang "If ever I would leave you, it wouldn't be in summer"-- or winter, or spring, or autumn for that matter—there was a sudden commotion in the royal box. King Arthur and his knights rose angrily from their seats, swords drawn, ready to leap over the railing onto the stage.

Lancelot embraced Guinevere tightly then quickly backed away to draw his own sword.

"Traitor!" screamed one of the approaching knights with murder in his eyes.

"Harlot!" screeched King Arthur as he struggled to maneuver his royal pot belly over the rail.

Without a moment's hesitation, Sir Guy swiftly beheaded the trembling Lewellyn, knocking his wooden crown to the ground as his head rolled after it. This was not in the script.

Lancelot skillfully parried the sword blows of the first of the approaching knights and grabbed the bridle of a fully armored steed standing at the edge of the stage. With a single sweeping motion, he grabbed Guinevere around the waist and hoisted her into the saddle, quickly leaping onto the horse himself.

The slashing swords of the knights bounced harmlessly off the armored haunches of Lancelot's steed. Lancelot turned the horse toward the edge of the stage and slapped the reins to urge it to leap onto the grass below. The crowd of peasants parted in panic and amazement as Lancelot and Guinevere galloped away. They would never be seen in Camelot again.

CHAPTER 18
ESCAPE FROM CAMELOT

"We have to get out of here immediately," Katarin whispered loudly to Monte, grabbing him roughly by the arm. They had hidden themselves behind some of the scenery in the right wing of the stage and they both knew they needed to make a quick escape before Arthur and his knights discovered them. Quickly donning the costumes of happy peasants, they looked around them to make sure that they had not been observed and jumped off the stage to mix into the frightened, milling crowd.

The knights were by then dispersing the peasants with curses and threats of violence.

"Get out of here, you filthy maggots!" shouted one.

"Go back to your miserable hovels," said a furious knight, raising his sword above his head in a menacing gesture.

"And forget about the 10% reduction in tribute!" screamed another knight still standing on the edge of the stage.

Mass slaughter ensued with those in the crowd who were not quick enough on their feet, but unsatisfied with the punishment inflicted on those who had attended, Arthur bore a special hatred for those who had participated in this debacle.

"Anyone who was a part of this insult to me," Arthur announced, "shall have a sentence of death passed upon them."

For those who had been in the cast, for those who had been in the chorus, for those unfortunate monks who had learned the songs or played in the orchestra, there was no going back to Camelot or their old lives.

Instead, they took to the road, got as far away as they could, never to return, and over time, found they could make a living as traveling troubadours, singing the songs and telling the story of Camelot, as Monte had taught it to them. Thus was the story spread all across England, to be repeated over and over, generation after generation.

Meanwhile, the panicked flight of the crowd provided Katarin and Monte the perfect cover to get away. The grassy field quickly emptied for all except lost children and the halt and lame who were being mercilessly kicked and beaten by the knights of Camelot.

They followed closely behind a group of young men and women who had broken into a run to get away from the chaos, and after a while they slowed back down to a walk as the distant sound of screaming and beatings faded away.

By the time they had put some distance between themselves and chaos, maybe three or four miles of steady walking, the sun had risen high in the sky and the group sat down in the shade of an elm tree to pass a waterskin around and relax now that the danger had passed.

One of the young men looked over toward Monte and Katarin and not recognizing them as either neighbors or kinsfolk, offered the waterskin to them. Monte took a long drink and Katarin just a sip.

"Why thank you, Goodfellow," Monte said as he handed the waterskin back.

The young man nodded, smiled, and started to hum a catchy tune from the pageant they all had just seen. After a few bars he broke out in a rich baritone.

Oh, what do the simple folk do,
To help them escape when they're blue?
The shepherd who is ailing, the milkmaid who is glum
The cobbler who is wailing from nailing his thumb...

The rest of the group joyfully hummed along, as he sang laughingly joining in at the catchline at the end of the verse,

"Oh what do the simple folk do?"

"If only we lived in a kingdom like that," one of the young women said, "where the king and queen thought of us as real people, not just sheep to be sheared down to the skin and then led to slaughter."

Everyone in the group nodded in agreement. Monte and Katarin remained silent.

"And where may ye be headed, Goodfellow and Goodwife?" Another young man of the group asked them, "I don't believe I've seen either of you before and reckon you're not from around these parts."

Monte remained nervously silent, but Katarin confidently replied.

"We're headed for the sea, our path to freedom and greener pastures."

"Aye, the sea," someone else in the group answered, "my grandfather told me about the stormy grey waters that extend for as far as the eye can see—and the long dark ships that depart for lands unknown."

"Will you help us?" Katarin asked.

"But how?" The young men and women looked at each.

"Take us into your families," said Katarin. "Hide us from the knights and pass us along from house to house, from farm to farm, until we reach the great shore of the eastern sea."

"But that must be a million miles away," objected one of the group.

"So what?" Katarin retorted. "You, 'the simple folk' you sing of, are as numerous as the stars in the sky. You cover the earth as the stars cover the heavens. You have the power to do many noble things. Please help us escape."

The young men and women quickly looked at each other, deciding what they would do. On the one hand the fear of King Arthur and his knights had been drummed into them since they were children. Every move they had made in their lives included a silent calculation of whether the knights would permit it or reward it with a sharp smack of their swords—or worse.

But at this moment. They asked no questions. They knew clearly what was right and what was wrong. Two fellow human beings were begging for help in gaining their freedom. It was something that all of them could understand.

One young man rose, apparently the group's leader. "All right," he said, "we'll do it. Because that's what the simple folk do."

*　*　*

For the next two weeks, Katarin and Monte were ferried under the cover of darkness from village to village, moving steadily eastward. The ties of family and friendship among the poor farmers, shepherds, and craftspeople were their underground highway to freedom, invisible to the knightly thugs and bullies who ruled the land and were actively searching for them. Guided by eager men, women, and sometimes children who were inspired by the plot of the musical, they crossed the borders of duchies, counties, and even tiny Dark Age kingdoms that were technically at war. But those boundaries were really nothing more than the limits of gang territories of hoodlums who imposed separate identities of Britons, Mercians, Angles, Jutes, and Saxons on their subjects—to keep them all living in fear of war and invasion, helpless to resist their real enemies. As Monte and Katrin moved across this landscape of knightly extortion, the romantic ideal of that "fleeting wisp of glory" became ever more powerful.

Each night, hidden in a barn or a stable, under a craftsman table or a cramped attic, the villagers would gather to hear Katarin and Monte sing one of the memorable songs. After weeks of rehearsing, Monte could sing each lyric without stumbling, as he had once sung so powerfully with his beloved Stratocaster guitar. Katarin's voice merged in gentle soprano harmony to pass the message along from one village to the next.

"I wonder what the king is doing tonight," Monte sang to a village of sheepherders whose scrawny flocks that were left after the local knights had claimed the strongest and fattest, could barely keep them alive.

"Well, I'll tell you what the king is doing tonight!" Monte ended the chorus, "He's scared! He's scared!" It gave a sense of confidence to the villagers gathered around him, not only because Monte's voice was strong and melodic, but also because now for the first time they had found someone who gave voice to their anger and hatred of the king.

And so it went night after night as Monte and Katarin were led to a new village way station, the message became viral among the people of broad swathes of territory—people who proved not to be so simple after all. During daylight hours, the fugitives remained hidden and undiscovered by the roaming knights sent out from Camelot to capture them and bring them back to Arthur for the punishment he believed they so richly deserved. But if there had ever been anything like medieval toothpaste, it was as someone might say centuries later, already out of the tube. The human frailties of the knights and nobles that the peasants had been taught to believe were invincible, became all too evident as the clever lyrics and catchy Lerner and Lowe tunes spread through the countryside.

As they neared the coast, Monte and Katarin were almost afraid to mention the obvious fact that, despite all the odds, they had made it across all of Britannia with the help of local guides who cared more for helping them evade royal authority than guarding the so-called boundaries of the warring factions and rival domains. One more day's journey and they would make it to the waterside emporium of traders where Katarin was convinced they would make contact with some of her own people from Eastern Europe who regularly landed there and be smuggled out among the trade goods on one of the long boats that crossed the North Sea.

That would mean one more night and one more day secretly hidden by villagers. So, with their spirits as high as their hopes of imminent escape, they sought to make the most of that time that remained to them to spread the musical tale of Camelot to the people of the land who had already suffered for so long. Before the dawn's light they were guided to a clearing in a deep highland forest by a cowherd from the village where they had spent the previous night. This was, he explained, a community of woodsmen and their families made their meager living cutting timber for the houses of the wealthy traders that lived at the coast and for the boatbuilders that made their wealth possible.

As Monte and Katarin approached the village, the smell of freshly-cut wood hung thick in the morning mist and the sounds of axes chopping into trunks provided a rhythmic percussion to the rising chirping of the forest birds. As they drew closer to the village, they could see high piles of neatly stacked longs, towering walls of smooth planed planks, and gigantic bundles of long, branchless tree trunks waiting to become masts for sailing ships. Wood was this village's medium; trees were its crops. Monte and Katarin marveled at the range of colors, surfaces, and ring patterns as they were led through the labyrinthine lumber yard.

"Welcome, honored guests!" came an old man's voice from somewhere in the middle of the wooden maze.

"Halloooo!!!" Monte, Katarin, and their guide responded. "How do we get inside? We're lost!"

As they felt their way along the timber walls, repeatedly coming to dead ends and false turns, a wizened old man with long white hair and a beard suddenly appeared. "It's our little means of protection," he said with a laugh. "They can come and steal our wood, but they never can find us. We're all long gone by the time they find their way in."

The old man offered his hand to Katarin and led her though the narrow aisles until they came to a sheltered clearing where the village houses were built. And what houses they were! Carved ornamentation and a rainbow of colors made each dwelling distinct from its neighbor, an embodiment of each family's spirit and skill. Unlike many of the villages they had passed through, this one was the very picture of order. And as the sun rose higher in the sky, a long table was set for the whole community to set an afternoon's repast with special places at the center of the long table for the special guests.

"You must be hungry," the old man said, ushering Monte and Katarin and the guide who had brought them toward the table. The men and the women of the villages all took their places standing behind the finely carved wooden chairs. Some of the children gathered to stare at Monte and Katrina, whose stage peasant clothing, wrinkled and torn in places where they had been ripped on bushes and brambles, showed the wear and tear of a long frantic escape.

"I am Gildas," the old man said, "we have lived here since the Romans ruled the land. We once supplied the emperors and the imperial army with the oak and beech wood to build their mighty sea-going galleys, to build their river-spanning bridges, and, yes, the elm and adder wood to build their terrifying catapults. But that was in the time of my grandfather's father's father—before the devastating droughts and famines and invasions that forced the Emperor Constantine to order the legions to leave. We were faithful Christians and imperial subjects then, and now we are the helpless victims of roving bands of half-pagan knights."

"But I have detained you long enough with my ramblings about days long gone by," Gildas said as he raised his cup high to salute Monte and Katarin and then bid everyone to be seated at their places at the table. "Let us welcome you among us as our guests as you prepare to set off tomorrow and leave this land of suffering behind."

The lunch was a happy one with a generous larder of wild game caught from the surrounding forest, freshly gathered mushrooms, and a cornucopia of fruits and vegetables grown by the villagers themselves. The conversation was lively, interrupted by song. For as with every place they had been hidden across the country, the songs—and message—of Camelot the musical had arrived before them, and Monte and Katarin basked in the amusement and joy among the "simple folk" that those melodies had spread.

"You and your companion have brought great joy across the entire country," Gildas said to Monte said as the others nodded. "We deeply appreciate what you've done. We here in the forest try to keep our distance from our own king and knights and stay true to the old ways, but that's not always possible."

"The old ways?" Monte asked.

"Yes," Gildas answered the old ways when there were Roman laws and customs that everyone accepted and obeyed, not just the greedy whims of the king's hired bullies. It's the same here in Essex as it is in Camelot. Knights in every kingdom are all birds of a feather; they owe allegiance to only two masters: Violence and Greed. But the lessons and hymns from the Gospel of the Saints Lerner and Lowe that you've been preaching all over the country have given people the courage to resist the present kind of might-makes-right rule."

"Let me show you something," Gildas continued. He motioned to one of the other village men in the workshop to help him pry up one of the floorboards. With a creak, the old oak plank bent upwards revealing a narrow wooden compartment in which lay a heavy sword. Gildas leaned down to pick it and hold it by its narrow grip, his hand trembling from its weight. It had a strange form, much different and deadlier than the swords now carried by the knights. Its blade was much wider with sharp edges along both sides for slashing, with a wide triangular point at the tip—for stabbing an enemy great force.

"Those knights' swords would snap like a twig compared to this one," Gildas said proudly. "This one was passed down to me from my father's father's father, who served as an auxiliary with the last Roman garrison before they abandoned Britannia a hundred years ago. But he didn't flee with them. He was a brave man and survived in the forest, always keeping this sword by his side. He handed it down to my grandfather—even after such arms held by peasants were declared illegal by the new bandit kings. He said 'Hide this well my son, and pass it down the generations, for it is both a battle-tested weapon and a reminder of the orderly, civilized times when it was made.'"

"Look here," Gildas said, slowly running his gnarled finger along the surface of the blade. It was inlaid with spidery silver Latin letters: GLADIUS EQUITIS NOBILISSIMI. "That means 'Sword of the Noblest Knight of them all.'"

Monte took the sword in his hands to examine the inscription closely, when the door to the workshop flew open with a bang. A grey-haired woman stood in the doorway, obviously shaken. "Come quickly, Gildas," she said.

*　*　*

Kay, Gawain, and Galahad had frantically ridden throughout the kingdom with blood lust in their eyes. Their sacred duty—ordered by King Arthur himself—was to capture and kill the evil lady-in-waiting and the perfidious storyteller who had instigated the sedition that had now spread through the land. They had torn apart village houses, tortured any peasant who looked suspicious, but still failed to uncover any trace of the miscreants who had caused King Arthur such a loss of face. Guinevere and Lancelot had already fled across the Channel into the arms of Arthur's most powerful enemies. It seemed likely that Katarin and Monte were headed in the same direction, so the knights of Arthur's Round Table asked—and were given permission—to pursue them across Wessex, Sussex, and Essex to find them and kill them before they reached the water's edge.

But so far, they felt as if they had been chasing phantoms. And that only made them even hungrier to devour their prey. Whenever village informers let them know that the couple had been seen hiding in a barn or in a cottage, the gates of Camelot opened, and the knights came galloping out. As the reports filtered in from more distant places, King Arthur's faithful knights ordered their squires to gather up all their equipment, tents, and weapons and prepare to accompany them on an extended campaign. Yet the farther they wandered from Camelot on their chase of the fugitives eastward, their luck did not improve. Worse still were the frightening sounds that plagued them every night at their campsites as they finished their evening meal and sat around their campfires.

Carried on the breeze or echoing through the valleys were the maddening strains of the song that mocked them from afar. The distant sound of villagers tormented them and everything they lived for as the far-off peasant voices sang off a more perfect world to come.

Each evening, from December to December,
Before you drift to sleep upon your cot,
Think back on all the tales that you remember
Of Camelot.
Ask ev'ry person if he's heard the story,
And tell it strong and clear if he has not,
That once there was a fleeting wisp of glory
Called Camelot... Camelot! Camelot!

That damned song was a provocation to ride harder and search more frantically for the traitors who had transformed the name of Arthur's kingdom into something it was not. Their frustration mounted as they continued toward the sea. They began to argue with each other. They roughed up every peasant that had the misfortune to cross their pass. At last, they came to a strange village in the hills overlooking the coastline, nestled in a clearing in dark woods. Around it was a strange fortification of felled timbers, wooden beams, and oaken planks that rose to an impressive height. The knights slowed their steeds as they approached this curious sight. And as they did, they could not help see beautiful young women laughing, singing, and darting in and out of the gaps in the tall piles of stacked wood.

Kay let out a loud whistle and motioned for them to approach. Their eyes grew wide with fright and they disappeared into the wooden labyrinth. Kay was in no mood for games or evasions. He had only one thing on his mind. He dismounted his steed and ran after them.

The girls had disappeared and Kay grew furious. He raced wildly between the high timber walls, following the aisles and turning sharp corners, again and again reaching dead ends and having to reverse his path. He could hear the frightened shrieks of young women near him, but could not find the path among the woodpiles that led to them.

Galahad and Gawain, still mounted on their horses, soon lost their patience waiting for Kay to return. They could hear the rattle of his chain mail, his heavy breathing, and his cursing as he bumped into another dead end.

"Come on out, Kay!" shouted Galahad, "We have no time for your randy games. You'll have plenty of fair virgins to deflower, once we catch and kill the prey we are after."

No answer, just the sound of more of Kay's bumping and cursing within the labyrinthine lumber yard. Galahad and Gawain were clearly exasperated.

"Go on, play your games. There is nothing but woodsmen, sawyers, and their families here," shouted Gawain.

"Blast you to hell, Kay," Galahad sputtered, as he spurred his horse onward, with Gawain close behind. We're going to make our way down toward the seashore and will catch those treasonous bastards on our own."

As Kay heard his fellow knights gallop away from the woodsmen's village, he grew more frantic and enraged. He finally found a passage through the stacked lumber and came upon a group of girls and young women, huddled together paralyzed in fear. Kay lunged to grab one of them and have his way with her.

"Stop!" a man's voice shouted out behind him. Kay spun around to see old Gildas tightly gripping a sharpened axe that he had used to fell many towering trees. "I'll cut you down at the legs and chop you into bloody kindling, if you don't join your friends and ride away."

Kay towered over the white-haired woodsman, hunched his shoulders back and let out a violent, unhinged laugh. "Why you silly old man," Kay taunted, you can barely hold that axe in your hands. I'll take what I want from these damsels after I put you out of your misery."

He unsheathed his sword and slashed Gildas's right arm, slicing through the old man's flesh and forcing him to drop the axe, as he collapsed in the growing pool of his own blood.

The young women gasped at the gruesome sight and escaped around a pile of huge logs, as Katarin stepped out from behind it to face Sir Kay herself.

His eyes widened to see her. He leered at her, undressing her in his medieval mind. At last, his prey was in his grasp.

"I am the one you are after. Come with me around the corner," she said, shamelessly unlacing her bodice. "At least let this poor old man die in peace."

Kay followed eagerly and turned the blind corner as the blade of a stout sword swung out to meet him and sever his head. The knight's tall headless frame sunk to its knees and toppled over, pumping crimson rivulets of knightly blood on to the ground from the jagged bone and flesh of his open neck. Katarin gasped and looked with relief toward Monte, who still grasped the now bloody sword in his hand.

Monte felt a strange rush of elation as he looked down at Sir Kay's head resting against a pile of freshly sawn beams. Kay's face bore a confused expression, now covered with a bizarre mask of sawdust. He had defeated an enemy with action, not stories—with a display of courage to save someone he loved. Stories were easy; navigating reality was hard, but infinitely more fulfilling. For perhaps the first time in his life, he felt truly alive. Monte averted his eyes from the lifeless face of the knight and looked up at the dark sky, feeling heavy raindrops begin the splatter on his face. He loosened his grip on the heavy Roman sword with the Latin inscription and let it fall to the ground.

＊　＊　＊

By nightfall, when Katarin and Monte reached the shoreline, the wind had picked up and the rain continued to fall. A dozen or so longships were beached on the sand. As the rain pelted down, the captains and crews all huddled under their well-oiled sails, all pulled down from the slender masts because of the freshening wind. In normal times this costal inlet would be a beehive of activity, even at night—especially at night. Traders, courtesans, craftspeople, criminals, spies and royal envoys from the powerful Frankish kingdom just across the channel would mingle, drink together, lie to each other, at this sandy beachhead where people of many cultures met. But now it was eerily still, pitch black, with the sound of heavy raindrops pounding down on beached ships and sand. An occasional flash of lightning illuminated the scene followed by ominous rumbles of thunder when the darkness returned.

But Monte was deep in thought about what had taken place in the last village.

"Monte, do you hear me?" Katarin said loudly, as if she was repeating herself. "Monte?"

Monte looked up.

"We need to find Adolphus quickly. Arthur's knights can't be far behind."

"Adolphus?" Monte didn't seem to recognize the name.

"Adolphus, my brother."

Monte knew the plan, even if he had momentarily forgotten the name. They were going to meet Katarin's brother on a ship that would take the two of them across the sea to Katarin's father's kingdom on a distant shore of the North Sea. But for Monte, something fundamental had now changed. He had defeated the knight who had once terrified him. He had taken on a King who terrorized his subjects and roused them to resist. Maybe Merlin was right after all. Maybe he had in fact begun to change history.

Katarin trotted her horse down a sandy slope toward the beached vessels with Monte following close behind. She dismounted and tied her horse to the rib of a wrecked boat half-buried in the sand and made her way to each of the beached vessels, lifting up their sailcloths and quickly looking inside.

A hairy arm grabbed her at the first ship. "Come in here out of the rain, goodwife, and spend some time with us! We've got plenty of ale for you and plenty of men."

Katarin angrily pulled her hand away and frantically moved on among the other beached boats. Most of the crews huddled under the sails were harmless Dutch traders, come to England exchange their Continental baubles, knives, and exotic vessels of glass and fine pottery.

"We have to find the ship that will take us back to my father's kingdom. There they will appreciate the ideals of Camelot. We have to hurry," she said as she walked briskly desperately craning her neck toward each boat's carved wooden figureheads, desperate to find the one she was looking for.

A dragon. No. An eagle with its wings spread, its beak poised to devour its prey. No. A bear. A horse's head. No. No. And then she saw it, illuminated brightly for an instant, before a deafening crack of thunder exploded over the beach.

It was a carving of the Black Sun, the Sonnenrad, the sunwheel of bent swastikas that would be a symbol of the darkest, bloodiest evil for centuries to come.

Katarin smiled broadly and pulled Monte by the hand under the shelter of the sail. A few small oil lamps, hardly bigger than candles filled the covered space with smoke and an eerie flickering light. She embraced the man she had been so frantically looking for: Adolphus the Younger, a tall thin man whose fingers were bejeweled with gaudy rings and who wore a thick gold medallion of the Black Sun around his neck.

Katarin embraced him tightly. "Thank God you're here, Adolphus, we almost didn't make it. I want you to meet Monte, who will save our kingdom" she said, turning to introduce him.

But Monte was gone.

When Monte had first seen the Black Sun symbol on the sail of the ship, he knew. He knew what he had to do. He had seen that symbol before, on every pharmaceutical product that Valkyrie had ever made. He had seen it embedded into the floor of Dr. Stewart's castle. And now, here it was again, not only on the figurehead of the ship he was being asked to get aboard, but tattooed on the neck of Katarin's brother, Adolphus. Monte's mind was now made up about his next course of action. He lifted the dripping edge of the sail and steeped back outside in the rain.

When Katarin realized that Monte had disappeared, she frowned deeply. But she put on a brave, tightly smiling face when Adolphus introduced her to a tall blond-haired, blue-eyed knight. "This is Percival—ach I speak too much English—Parsifal is what I should call him in our Saxon tongue. He has come to protect our cargo, now made even more precious with our beloved princess aboard."

Katarin excused herself briefly and ventured out into the torrential rain again. Monte was standing outside, his back turned to the boat, his arms folded across his chest, his head lowered deep in thought.

"What in the pit of hell is the matter with you?" she shouted, grabbing Monte by the shoulder and turning him around to face her by force. "These are my people, the faithful servants of a glorious Reich. And they will soon be your people too. The myths you will spin, the tales you will tell of the Reich's greatness and the nobility of its rulers and subjects, will help it last for a thousand years or more."

"I'm not going with you, Katarin. I have come to the end of my own story. I can no longer live in this twilight reality. You go back to your people. I am staying here to meet whatever fate destiny has prepared for me."

"Have you gone mad?" Katarin screamed, the veins in her slender neck bulging with anger her face turned deathly pale in outrage. "After all that we have gone through? After all that we have achieved. We have given hope to the peasants across all of Arthur's kingdom—all of England—that tomorrow belongs to them."

"You have begun something that cannot now be stopped," she screeched, she implored.

As the rain continued to pour in sheets, Monte had to raise his voice to make himself heard. He repeated the decision he had taken. She should go. He wasn't leaving. He was tired of running away – of running away from Brinkman, of running away from Danny, of running away from Colonel Stürmer. But now he realized that he didn't have to live in world of fantasy any longer. He was so tired of telling stories for other people with some ulterior motive in mind. Whether it was for money or for idealism, it all ended the same. The stories took on a life of their own after they were first uttered and no one could ever really tell what effect they would have on history—whether they would end up helping someone or doing great harm.

Katarin's face turned hard. "You fool! You coward!" she shouted. "You traitor to all that is noble and good. It's all been a charade, hasn't it? You wove that story and staged it for a huge audience as if it were just a silly game. It's not a game to me. I intend to bring that story to inspire generation after generation of noble Teutonic Knights, who will establish a great Reich that will endure for thousands of years.

She spun on her heels, as the Saxon sailors began to raise the sail. Katarin took Parsifal's helping hand to climb up into the longboat. The sailors around them silently steeled themselves for the dangerous voyage. They had been taught to obey orders, no matter how difficult or cruel those orders might be. They hoisted the sail to its full height. It billowed immediately in the high wind, violently shaking off the rainwater that had collected within its folds. Four crew members hopped off the stern to push the boat off the sand. When the boat began to move, they hoisted themselves aboard.

The rolling waves grew higher as the Saxon boat plowed through them, its mast and sail bobbing in and out of sight behind the roaring wall of the North Sea. Monte stared silently as it finally disappeared from sight, paralyzed by shock and sadness that Katarin had left without a parting word of understanding, without one last embrace.

Monte was so distracted that he did not hear the heavy footsteps approaching from behind.

It was the familiar melody that suddenly drew his attention. A croaking, off key-voice startled him. His heart was pounding as he quickly turned around.

Don't let it be forgot
That once there was a spot…
For one brief shining moment that was known
As… Ca-me-lot…"

A flash of lighting revealed it was Galahad.

And the last thing Monte saw that night was the glistening blade of Galahad's sword slashing toward him—just before it ripped his skull apart.

CHAPTER 19
BACK TO THE FUTURE

"Check his exfusion tube!" Gerhardt shouted frantically to the nearby orderly. "He seems to be having a violent hallucination of some sort." He had already taken Monte's pulse and his comatose heart rate had suddenly rocketed from a stable 25 beats per minute to over 150. After five weeks of steady cortisol production, stimulated by periodic turns of the spiked vise on his knees, the precious liquid was now overflowing. It was now being pumped with such pressure through the vinyl tube inserted into Monte's cheek that it dribbled out of the hole drilled in his skull and ran down the side of his ashen face.

"Splendid! Wonderful!" Gerhardt exclaimed. "I've never seen a human produce this much cortisol before! Rivers of it! Buckets of it! Maybe you turned the vise a few turns too much," he quipped sarcastically to an arriving doctor. "You know we must be careful with these New York types. They are obviously over-sensitive to stress."

"Ach, so many great discoveries have come as the result of accidents and blunders," Gerhardt confided to his white-coated protege, "Just think of Louis Pasteur's discovery of human vaccines by playing around with sick chickens. Think of Alexander Fleming's chance discovery of penicillin from mold on his lab bench. Think of Albert Hoffman's discovery of LSD by mixing chemicals willy-nilly. But this is a thousand times greater than any of them. Imagine! Extracting fully purified cortisol—the essential ingredient for extending human life indefinitely by being so sloppy with the torture of a patient! This would have undoubtedly won me the Nobel prize, if the damn Nazi party hadn't overreached during the war."

"But," added Gerhardt, "before we pop any champagne bottles, we must closely examine the chemical composition of the cortisol that Mr. Levine is producing in such great quantities." Normally in such sensitive cases, he would submit the samples to the room-sized mass spectrometer in the laboratories of Valkyrie labs. But he was eager to get some preliminary results as soon as possible. He urgently motioned to Billy, who scurried obediently toward him. "Bring me my portable mass spectrometer," he barked, "it's in one of the cabinets in the library, in a green leatherette carrying case."

As Billy ran off, Gerhardt held a half-full beaker of Monte's light greenish cortisol up to fluorescent lights of the exfusion chamber's ceiling and admired what he saw. It would take a month to collect a quantity like this from the fifty or so wizened senior citizen bodies that lay on neat rows of tables all around him, with their vinyl tubes yielding cortisol one drop at a time.

Suddenly the sounds of loud popping outside could be heard through one of the ventilation shafts. The doctors and orderlies stopped what they were doing and looked up in concern. Gerhardt glared at them and paid no attention to the distraction, assuming the sounds to be of bored Mountain City teenagers playing with fireworks—or perhaps even foolishly trying to climb the high-voltage perimeter fence again. He was confident that his laboratory was secure and was elated that he finally had a great enough concentration to synthesize Merlinium on an industrial scale.

Gerhardt waited impatiently for Billy to return. He was losing his patience as a series of loud blows—sounding like the impacts of a heavy wrecking ball or battering ram shook the stone walls of the exfusion chamber. The lights flickered. Dust drifted down from the ceiling. Now even Gerhardt was becoming concerned.

Upstairs in the corridor outside the library and the chapel, Billy was in a panic. When he first heard the sounds of the popping, he had snatched the portable spectrometer, as Gerhardt had directed, then rushed to the security room to see what was going on. Looking up at the bank of surveillance monitors that covered every inch of the Castle grounds, he watched the operation that was now unfolding with military precision. Dozens of SWAT team members in full body armor were swarming through the entrance gates, leaving a handful of Valkyrie security personnel shot dead, lying on the ground. Behind them rumbled an armored personnel carrier, painted in an olive military color, with the large white letters "FBI" stenciled on its side.

As the SWAT team members scrambled up the steep driveway and took their places as snipers all aimed at the Castle entrance door, the armored vehicle rumbled directly toward it, with a thick iron prow aimed at the heavy carved oak door.

Billy stood paralyzed as the door was pounded inwards, eventually giving way. SWAT team members streamed through the shattered doorway, jostling Billy as they ran past him, apparently knowing exactly where they were headed. It suddenly dawned on him that his world was crumbling when, in the midst of the shouting and confusion, he felt a tap on his shoulder.

"William Francis Osmund Jr.?" asked a man in a dark suit standing next to another. They both flashed their FBI wallet-style badges.

Billy looked at them dumbly.

"You are under arrest," they said, as they firmly twisted his arms behind his behind his back and clicked the handcuffs shut around his wrists. Billy was in shock and did not try to resist. The portable Spectrometer case fell to the marble floor.

Down in the exfusion chamber, Gerhardt finally realized that something was terribly wrong. At the sound of heavy footsteps pounding the corridor above, a crowd of Valkyrie doctors and orderlies, scrambled for the elevators, not realizing that they had already been disabled by the arriving SWAT teams. Gerhardt frowned at the cowardice of his underlings but at this moment he cared about only one thing: preserving the precious vial of superior quality cortisol that had flowed so plentifully from Monte's brain and adrenal glands.

The first of the heavily armed invaders began to appear at the foot of the spiral stone staircases that were now the only way out of the exfusion chamber. But their eyes widened when they caught their first glimpse at the horrible sight of dozens of comatose bodies stretched out on tables with tubes coming out of their skulls.

The lead officer of the commandos raised his hand, signaling the troops behind him to stop. Stifling his own urge to vomit, he spoke loudly into the wrap-around microphone attached to his helmet. "We're going to need massive medical assistance," he radioed to his operation headquarters, "send as many ambulances to the target site as you can."

Gerhardt, in the meantime, had injected himself in the thigh with a hypodermic needle and rose calmly from his wheelchair. He had synthesized enough of his secret formula to provide him with brief periods of youthful vigor. He arose from his wheelchair and walked nonchalantly toward the SWAT team commander, he was confident that his dose would be sufficient to calm the situation and diffuse this unfortunate unpleasantness.

"I am Dr. Jerry Stewart," he said, extending his hand toward the officer. "Without my immediate help all these people will die in a matter of moments. So, if you have the slightest concern about the lives of these people—or the reputation of your unit—you will let me go about my work."

Despite the extensive training in hostage situations that the SWAT commander had gone through, he now realized that he did not know what to do. It would take at least half an hour for the first of the ambulances to arrive from the surrounding towns. The emergency medical teams at the nearby Jerry Stewart Medical Complex could hardly be trusted; he had a federal warrant for the arrest of Dr. Stewart tucked inside his kevlar vest.

He remained silent and motionless as Gerhardt turned on his heel and walked briskly back toward the exfusion tables. The few orderlies who had not attempted to flee stood at attention, waiting for Gerhardt's instructions.

"Remove the tubes and bring them out of their comas with the standard reversal procedure," he shouted, "and do it slowly until their body temperature reaches ninety-five degrees and their heartbeats increase to seventy BPM."

The SWAT team watched helplessly as the orderlies followed Gerhardt's instructions. What they did not see was Gerhardt slip a sealed test tube of Monte's cortisol into a hidden compartment beneath the right armrest of his wheelchair. He was confident that this small sample of the unique hormone, now in his hands, could be precisely synthesized.

Not a word was spoken in the exfusion chamber as the orderlies went about their grim task. Time seemed to move at an excruciatingly slow pace. Five minutes. Ten minutes. Twenty minutes. At last, the distant sound of sirens could be heard approaching, with only about twenty of Gerhardt's elderly victims opening their eyes and showing slight signs of movement and consciousness.

As the sirens grew louder, and the first EMT crews bounded down the stone stairways carrying oxygen tanks, defibrillator units, and heavy medical backpacks, the SWAT commander strode toward Gerhardt, with the arrest warrant in his hand.

"I'm afraid, I'm feeling a bit unwell," Gerhardt said softly to his captor as he slipped back into his wheelchair.

"Dr. Stewart, I am placing you under arrest on suspicion of murder, attempted murder, kidnapping, criminal medical malpractice, wire fraud, and tax evasion." As Gerhardt was handcuffed and rolled out toward the reactivated elevators, he smiled slyly.

He knew that his 20-person legal dream team, from America's finest law schools and most prestigious criminal law firms, would soon be on their way to Montana in a fleet of Valkyrie private jets, specially dispatched to Los Angeles, New York, Dallas, and Washington.

*　*　*

It would be ten days before Monte was released from the Intensive Care Unit of the Montana Neuroscience Clinic at St. Catherine's Hospital in Missoula, though he was wheelchair bound, and was allowed to have visitors in his private room. It was there that he watched the live TV coverage of Dr. Jerry Stewart's arraignment in federal court and the impromptu press conference of Stewart's lawyers on the courthouse steps. They expressed outrage at the Justice Department's overreach in disrupting the sensitive medical procedures of a man who had done more than anyone else in the country to improve the health and happiness of the American public over the last fifty years.

"Dr. Stewart is the embodiment of the American immigrant dream," said one of his lawyers, a famous criminal attorney, who starred in his own popular reality TV show.

"The Attorney General is clearly pursuing this case for partisan political purposes," said another of Gerhardt's legal team who had once served as Attorney General himself.

Monte pointed the remote control at the screen and turned off the TV. His head was pounding and the bone grafts and sutures to repair the wound in his skull throbbed with pain. He lay back on his pillow and closed his eyes, trying desperately to dispel all horrible images that flashed through his mind.

Swords. Blood. Gore. Medieval relics. Knights. Kings and Queens. Ladies in waiting. Cruelty. Violence. Cheap plastic suits of armor. Ridiculous paper crowns. Overcooked turkey legs. The thought of the Middle Ages made him want to vomit. He never wanted to have anything with that again—from the betrayal and murderous threats of the Tire King of New Jersey in his "Castle," to the ragtag crowds of children and drunks in Mountain City screaming for the garbage entertainment of Teutonic Nights.

And then, of course, there was the genocidal fixation of "Dr. Jerry Stewart" with the purity and order of the Arthurian myth.

He still could not decide if his adventures in King Arthur's England were real or imagined. But they were all so vivid that he could not completely dismiss the possibility that they had actually occurred. Or was it just the bio-chemical effects of Gerhardt's insidious experiment with his brain? The dank, fetid smell of the crowd gathered in the royal hall at Camelot; Merlin's annoying voice instructing him how to tell stories; Katarin's quick mind and soft and graceful body; even the smell of the wood and Sir Kay's bloody head rolling in the sawdust in the village in the forest clearing were all too real to his innermost feelings and senses that he could not dismiss them out of hand. And that sword that he himself had wielded with such instinctive ferocity in a moment of unbridled rage—that old woodsman's cherished Roman sword with the inscription "TO THE NOBLEST KNIGHT OF THEM ALL."

Monte vowed silently to himself that he would never again be a frightened yes-man, concerned only with bare survival, whatever the cost. He dreamed of the joy that his Stratocaster had once brought him, and although his body was still too weak to sit up—much less hold a guitar. But in his mind, he could still go to that place of happiness and contentment, imagining the weight of his leather guitar strap slipping over his shoulder; feeling the smooth wood of the neck against his open palm. In his silent, glazed stare at the ceiling of his hotel room, he could feel the pressure of the metal strings against his fingertips and replayed in his imagination the complex chord changes he would make in the opening bars of Stairway to Heaven, his favorite song.

What joy this bedridden daydream gave him after the months—or perhaps centuries—of nightmares he had lived through. Maybe, when he had fully recovered, he would give his musical career another try. It didn't have to be superstardom. He didn't need screaming girls, multimillion dollar contracts; just a regular gig that would give him a small audience to play to, to express his own creativity. Just a small stage somewhere, performing for people who appreciated his songs. He might even start writing his own songs and—who knows—maybe he could record an album or two.

Monte closed his eyes as he imagined this life and the pain in his face and skull at least temporarily went away. He allowed himself, just for the moment, the utter luxury of not having to fear anything or anyone. Humming softly to himself, he smiled and opened his eyelids, fantasizing that his amps were turned all the way up. He could almost feel his music vibrating, resonating, pulsing through his veins. He was about to imagine singing the second verse of Stairway when he heard a gentle voice calling his name.

"Monte... Monte... I'm so glad that you're looking better. Better every day. In just another few weeks the doctors say you'll be well enough to recuperate at home."

It was Sylvia. She sat down in a chair beside his bed and lightly touched his hand.

"I have some wonderful news," she said.

Monte had already heard from Sylvia the amazing story of how he had been freed from Gerhardt's torture chamber. When he had finally come out of his coma and the doctors assured Sylvia that he was fully conscious and could communicate freely, she just had to tell him. But she knew that he was in no condition to listen to understand all the details. She told it anyway because she simply had to tell the story—for herself as much as for Monte—of what and intricate web of evil the good folks of Mountain City could spin.

It had all started, Sylvia explained to a dozing, bandaged Monte, the night that he, Monte had disappeared. Her night was sleepless, listening carefully for, hoping for, the sound of the squeaky brakes of Monte's Ford Fiesta announcing that he had finally come home. A violent thunderstorm just before dawn seemed to be an evil omen. Something was terribly wrong. She knew Chief Ted would be up for the early morning shift and phoned him as much for reassurance as to ask for help. Then came Monte's garbled text message. When she immediately called back, Monte's phone just rang and rang and rang.

Sylvia wasted no time in calling Ted's wife to share her growing panic. Elizabeth's soft missionary voice turned hard. She promised she would call Ted immediately and phone Sylvia back with any news about Monte. But she concluded the call with the enigmatic words, "Perhaps it is part of God's plan which we all may soon live to see." That was the last that Sylvia heard from her. By noon, Elizabeth still hadn't called back.

There was only one number left to call—a number that she and Monte had been warned that should only be used in a life-threatening emergency. If there ever was a life-and-death situation, Sylvia thought to herself, this would be one. She suspected that somehow, some way, Elizabeth and Chief Ted were involved in Monte's abduction? Did Chief Ted show a surprising lack of interest in all the elderly people who had suddenly disappeared in Mountain City? Was she being paranoid? Was she missing a chance to save Monte's life? The possibilities raced through Sylvia's frightened mind. She would do it. She had to do it. She ran upstairs to retrieve the nondescript card they had been given before their departure from Langley and dialed the number printed on it with a shaking hand.

A brief conversation with the Duty Officer followed and once dusk had fallen, she was secretly whisked off to Missoula by the U.S. Marshall's Service and intensively questioned for the next five days. When had she last seen Monte? What mood was he in? Who was his employer? Did he have any enemies? She was put up in a dingy Knight's Inn on the outskirts of the city and waited every morning for a phone call from the federal building informing her what time they would come to pick her up.

At the end of the five days, the pieces finally came together. The Marshal's Service, after extensive detective work in coordination with the FBI and the Department of Homeland Security knew that they would have to work quickly. No, it had nothing to do with Danny Locovita and his hit men, they assured her. Something much more serious was afoot in Mountain City. A deep data sweep of the nation's top-secret intelligence network brought up a surprising pattern: Mountain City was the focus of a dangerous fundamentalist right-wing militia, who were kept under careful surveillance by the Department of Homeland Security with special electronic eavesdropping and digital decryption assistance by the FBI. After much work, the FBI had been able to penetrate Dr. Stewart's encrypted phone and internet network and observed a worrisome increase of activity in his Castle.

A court-ordered tap placed on the phone behind the bar at the downtown Big Sky Tavern revealed that it was a secret meeting place for white supremacists and neo-Nazis throughout the West. Even Dolph was photographed at a violent demonstration in Billings wearing a Camp Auschwitz T-shirt; his cheap jewelry and extravagant comb-over made advanced face-recognition software completely unnecessary. Elizabeth Beller, Chief Ted's wife, was a founder of the local True Kingdom Free-Will Church, whose charismatic national pastor, L. Randolph MacGuffin, lived in a heavily fortified compound in Lubbock, Texas—and was under suspicion by the ATF for hoarding thousands of assault rifles and millions of rounds of ammunition for "God's Army" and possessing silos full of ammonium nitrate. The chatter suggested that the group that called themselves "The Teutonic Knights" was preparing to attack all federal agencies within 50 miles of the municipal boundaries of Mountain City and set up an independent all-white Anglo-Saxon Christian kingdom that they would defend with their lives.

But in addition to Sylvia's panicked call to the Duty Officer at the U.S. Marshal's headquarters in Washington, the clue that clinched the case came from Billy Osmund's Facebook page. With the famous picture of a mounted Hitler in full armor as his cover photo and quotations from Mein Kampf sprinkled liberally in his posts and comments, his latest post was both incriminating and incredibly stupid. It showed a shaky picture of Jerry Stewart's castle with the caption "The

Eagle will fly in two weeks."

That was enough for the federal Inter-agency Taskforce on Domestic Terror Organizations to get a judge to issue search warrants throughout Mountain City—including the Castle—to arrest all the conspirators, and prepare an elite Swat team to enter Dr. Stewart's castle and seize all the munitions they expected to find. What they found were not firearms—but thousands of medieval artifacts and dozens of kidnapped senior citizens strapped to tables with strange tubes coming out of their heads.

So Monte was freed with the others and rushed to Montana's foremost neurosurgery center, where his life was saved and he received intensive medical care. But she had not come to visit Monte this day to repeat that story. Earlier that morning, she had received an unexpected phone call from Special Agent Paul Belcher, their case officer at Langley.

"I have some wonderful news," she repeated to Monte who was lost in his own thoughts.

"Can you hear me, Monte?"

Monte let out a soft groan to indicate that he could.

"Well, I hope that you will be as delighted as I was to hear that Danny Locovita was stabbed to death yesterday in the exercise yard of his supermax prison. You know what that means, don't you? When you're well enough to travel, we can finally go home."

* * *

The arrest and arraignment of Dr. Jerry Stewart had the entire town of Mountain City nervously buzzing. Thousands of local office workers, warehouse staff, chemists, truck drivers, and security guarded feared for their livelihoods should the massive Valkyrie Pharmaceutical Industry be closed. The mayor, John Stimson Gibbs, worried about public safety, now that a large proportion of the police force and fire department had been placed under arrest for their complicity in the militia's plot. And those who hadn't been arrested were busy destroying incriminating information and hiding their vast arsenal of guns. Because of Stewart's fatherly connection to most of the people in Mountain City, and indeed all of Montana, the federal prosecutors petitioned Montana's District

Court for a change of venue, since it seemed unlikely that a totally impartial jury could be found.

Normally, a petition to change venue was the prerogative of the defense. The conventional wisdom among defense lawyers was that residents of a jurisdiction where a heinous crime had been committed would have an inherent prejudice against the defendant and might be influenced by inflammatory news coverage—or just local gossip—to convict without judging the case fairly. But in this case, the conventional wisdom was turned on its head. The alleged crimes were certainly heinous, but since the trial was scheduled to take place in the federal district in Missoula, only 50 miles away from Mountain City, the prosecutors felt that no one in all of southwest Montana would ever vote to convict Dr. Stewart, who was the most prominent businessman and most generous philanthropist there. And so, the case had been moved to another city in the Montana district, Billings, the state's largest city that lay outside Dr. Stewart's patriarchal sphere of influence.

Yet a conviction there of Dr. Stewart was equally uncertain, for the eastern side of the state also had its share of white supremacist and neo-Nazi groups. But the federal charges filed against Dr. Stewart were daunting: three-hundred charges of federal cases of kidnapping under 18 U.S. Code § 1201, which bore a minimum sentence of thousands of years in a federal supermax prison—and that was even before the dozens of counts of attempted murder, conspiracy, wire fraud, and a whole range of federal Hate Crime laws.

Dr. Stewart was not held pending trial. He had friends in very high places and shocked the court authorities by having his record-breaking cash bond of $350,000,000 delivered to the federal courthouse the day after his arraignment by a fleet of Valkyrie Pharmaceutical armored cars carrying bond delivering 35,000 fresh $100 bills.

At the same time, Stewart dispatched his personal realtor to rent the most expensive house in Billings for the extent of the trial, which he expected would be brief. Valued at a mere $25 million, the mansion was the property of a notorious embezzler who had fled the country. Perched on a mountain overlooking the city, the house had 15 bedrooms, 25 bathrooms, an 18-car garage, a five-story elevator, an indoor shooting range, three swimming pools, and was surrounded by watchtowers and a high security fence. But the feature that immediately caught Dr. Stewart's attention was its design. Fashioned to invoke the style of "a modern-day castle," it boasted a high stone turret and a moat with a retractable draw bridge. He knew he would feel right at home while this tawdry trial got underway.

His first meeting with his legal team took place around the round conference table in the top floor of the turret. Arrayed before him were the best courtroom warriors that money could buy. The distinguished attorney in the pin striped suit had recently won acquittal for a Wall Street Ponzi scammer who had bankrupted thousands. Next to him was a slick lawyer in a burgundy suit and vest and paisley tie who had gotten a notorious Mexican cartel boss off scot-free. Next to him was a brash New Yorker with a ponytail dressed in a suede jacket who had done the impossible: freeing a notorious bomber from Guantanamo Bay. Finally, there was a tall Texan with a cowboy hat and string tie who was a famous TV personality, and there was also another prominent lawyer from Washington, DC, who had once successfully defended a former cabinet member from federal charges of bribery and child pornography.

Each of them was backed by a large law firm with dozens of bright young associates who could think of any possible technicality to get the charges dropped—or if that failed—make even the most hardened juror break down in tears of sympathy. This all-star team did not come cheaply. Each of them billed $2500 per hour. But money meant nothing to Dr. Jerry Stewart when his honor was at stake. And all of the celebrity lawyers had eagerly accepted the challenge of defending Dr. Jerry Stewart, medical genius, billionaire, philanthropist and apparently, kidnapper and white supremacist.

Each of the assembled counsellors had defended many, many unsavory characters, and even though they had all read the file, each felt confident that they could get him off in their own distinct ways. Of course, having a client with a personal fortune of more than $100 billion, who had personally found cures or treatments for a score of diseases, saved millions of lives around the world, and had universities, hospitals, and libraries named after him would not hurt either. But even though all of them had gone over the trial documents, they were all completely unprepared for their first meeting with Dr. Stewart.

Stewart was rolled into the meeting in a wheelchair. His long white hair cascaded over the side of his head. He was wrapped in a blanket.

As he was wheeled alongside the table, each lawyer respectfully rose and extended his hand in greeting. Stewart looked at them all with contempt and did not proffer his hand to any of them.

When he took his place at the far end of the conference table, Stewart glared at his world-class attorneys, "I know who you all are," Stewart said, "and I have absolutely no interest in any of your clever ideas for my defense."

Jaws dropped around the table.

"No," said Stewart, drawing the words out slowly and staring intently at each of the lawyers. "I intend to defend myself."

"This is my show. I decide what we are going to do. Your job is just to help me with the legal procedures and terminology. That's it."

The lawyers, all of them used to commanding the respect and total obedience of their clients, looked at each other in utter confusion. But none dared object to what Dr. Stewart had just told them or even roll their eyes. Self-respect was not worth twenty-five hundred dollars an hour plus expenses. And the clock was ticking. So they all sat like obedient yes-men, as their employer—not client—Dr. Stuart continued in his clipped and uncompromising tone.

"I have only one question to ask you," he said. "You've all presumably reviewed the accusations against me. I want you each to tell me what you think my chances are."

The same thought went through the mind of everyone else at the table. This man claimed to be 107 years old and looked every bit that old. It was 50-50 that he would make it through jury selection, much less the trial. But they ignored that grim probability, and each lawyer told Dr. Stewart what they thought he wanted to hear.

"Well, I think I can wear down your so-called 'patients' under cross examination and make them admit they thought you were a medical genius," the Wall Streeter from the white shoe law firm said. "That will make the jury wonder if they were kidnapped or merely sought treatment, so with some expert medical testimony that cortisol extraction is a legitimate therapy, that should take care of the most serious charge, and bring everything to about twenty years"

All eyes turned to the smooth talker in the burgundy suit. "What you need is a catchy rhyme, like in the OJ trial: 'If the glove don't fit, you must acquit.' And just say it over and over again so the jury pays no attention to the testimony and just remembers the rhyme. In your case, I'd suggest 'A doctor's cure, not a kidnapper's lure.' and I agree, twenty years tops."

The pony-tailed radical banged on the table. "The charges you face are outrageous! This is all a vendetta against science! And there's a matter of your right to free speech. As for the charges of sedition? Nonsense! You are defending the right to free expression of every-red-blooded American. I'd make it a constitutional issue! Twenty years. Maybe less."

The tall Texan, leaned back in his chair and clasped his hands behind his heat, just beneath his ten-gallon hat. "Well shoot, I've seen harder cases than this in traffic court," he drawled. We'll just concentrate on all the good you've done in your life. Upstanding citizen. Self-made man. Now the Deep State and the east coast elites are trying to take you down. No more than twenty years, I reckon."

Last to speak was the Inside-the-Beltway lawyer with close ties to the CPAC, AIPAC, and the NRA. I can take care of the whole thing with just one phone call."

He took out his cell phone and raised his hand to silence the other lawyers at the table.

He dialed and held the phone to his ear. The room was silent.

"Hello Marie, it's Jack Perkins. Is he available?"

A pause of a 30 seconds or so.

"Hello Sir. Yes, thank you. Saw you on the news last night. You looked great, as always. Thank you. Yes sir. I'm out in Montana and we've got a little problem. Yes sir. That one. I imagined you were already on top of it. Yes sir. Very much appreciated. Thank you, sir. And best regards to the little lady as well. Yes sir. Bye."

The tall Texan looked at him.

"That's it?"

"That's it," Jack Perkins replied. "Done."

"I sure would like to have that phone number, if you don't mind," the pony tailed New Yorker said. "Me too," said all the others.

Perkins smiled.

"I bet you would, but there's only about a dozen people on the planet who have this number."

Three days later, the tall Texan and Perkins were sharing a drink in the hotel bar when Perkins got a text message. It said the Department of Justice was dropping all of the charges of domestic terrorism against Dr. Stewart, the indictment would include only engaging in experimental medical drug tests without FDA approval.

Perkins showed his phone screen to the Texan whose eyes widened at the news.

"But why?" the Texan slapped his knee and asked in amazement.

"Because," Perkins quickly countered, "the DOJ knows that if they went after Stewart on all those political conspiracy charges, they would implicate people in high places all over the country. All hell would break lose. Nobody wants that."

"I suppose at least not yet," the Texan said, sipping his scotch.

"Exactly," Perkins replied. "And besides, at Stürmer's age, one conviction and a sentence of twenty years, which is about what he would get, well, it's a death sentence. Problem solved. We move on."

"I'll drink to that," said the Texan, and they toasted their very good fortune.

The next day, as the legal team met with Stewart and explained the situation, Stewart smiled broadly and motioned for his attendant to give him some oxygen. "Good. Very Good," he said as he placed the oxygen mask over his mouth and nose and inhaled deeply.

"Twenty years? I can definitely handle twenty years."

CHAPTER 20
JUDGMENT DAY

There was no escaping the inevitability of the painful moment, Monte thought to himself as he was wheeled by a skycap through the airport concourse, with Sylvia fussing with her handbag as they arrived at security. How could he, how would he tell her he was leaving her? The security check passed uneventfully for Monte, who was wanded in his wheelchair by a heavy-set woman in a TSA uniform with frown on her face. Sylvia, though, was forced to go through the scanner several times as she slowly removed all her jewelry, getting more and more frustrated, and keeping her eye on the plastic container into which the screeners had dropped her watch, necklace, rings, heavy earrings, and rhinestone brooch.

The flight from Missoula to LaGuardia, connecting through Minneapolis was going to be sheer hell for Monte; seven-plus hours in the air and in terminals with the woman he had spent his adult life with, waiting for just the right moment to tell her that he wanted to make a permanent break. Sylvia, for her part, was ecstatic to finally be out of Mountain City. She hardly noticed Monte's discomfort as she window-shopped the only store open at the tiny Missoula airport—a giftshop featuring sweatshirt, baseball caps, refrigerator magnets, and other tacky "Souvenir of Montana" merchandise.

"Oh well, I'm sure they'll have more upscale boutiques in

Minneapolis," she said. "I think I deserve to splurge on something nice."

A U.S. Marshal greeted them at the departure gate to make sure they boarded the plane without incident. Monte and Sylvia were allowed to be first down the jetway and an airline employee took over Monte's wheelchair and maneuvered him into the aisle chair for the short backwards roll to seat 4D. Sylvia took her place in 4C.

Monte remained sullenly silent while Sylvia chatted about all the great things that awaited them now that they were free. They would find out how to get in touch with Wendy and Laurel. "I just want to give them both a big hug. Mwah!" Sylvia said.

During their layover in Minneapolis, Sylvia shopped and Monte sat in their departure gate with his head bowed in his wheelchair. He thought back to all the regrets he harbored: not leaving to start a new life with Kathy; wasting his life making reality TV crap for ratings and money; doing all the things he did to make other people happy, and leave him to live in a childish fantasy world. He still could not figure out if his adventures in the Kingdom of Arthur were somehow real or a hallucination, but one memory was seared into his soul. He did not stop to think; he did not stop to worry about the implications when he beheaded Sir Galahad with the heavy Roman blade that bore the inscription "Sword of the Noblest Knight of them all." He did it because it was the right thing to do, even if it had all been in a dream. To defend Katarin. To stop something terrible from happening. And from now on, he vowed to himself for the thousandth time, he would live his life in a different way.

But would he break the news to Sylvia right now, before reboarding, right here at Gate E15 of Minneapolis-St. Paul International Airport? Would she become hysterical at his decision and make an embarrassing scene? And if that happened, what kind of special hell would the next flight of just over two hours be—sitting next to her in silence or in weeping—as they flew toward LaGuardia. No, he decided, he would spare her the pain in such a public place. He would wait until they arrived back in LaGuardia and tell her there. He would then at least accompany her home. As far as Monte was concerned, she could have the damn house. It held only unpleasant memories for him.

The first boarding call was announced from the podium and Monte craned his neck from the wheelchair to see if Sylvia was anywhere in sight. And there she came, walking as fast as she could in her heels, toting an armful of branded shopping bags, with a wide smile on her face.

"Sorry," she said, out of breath, "but there are some fantastic prices here, much lower than the Westchester Mall. Thank God we're back in civilization again."

Monte nodded perfunctorily and leaned back as an airport employee pushed him down the jetway, once again stiffly maneuvering him into a first-class seat. After takeoff, Sylvia enthusiastically raved about her bargains and rustled through the shopping bags at her feet while Monte dozed fitfully for the two hours of the flight with bizarre visions of Camelot dancing in his head.

When they landed in LaGuardia, they sat patiently as the other passengers deplaned and then made their way toward the baggage claim. At the exit into the terminal a scrum of limousine drivers who jostled to wave their signs at the faces of the arriving passengers eager to make a match with their assigned riders. As Monte and Sylvia rolled passed the drivers, they scanned the handwritten names; it was Monte who first spotted their driver. "Mr. And Mrs. Le Vine," it read. Despite his anxiety about breaking the news to Sylvia, he couldn't help but smile.

So, Monte decided he would delay the inevitable yet again. He would absolutely, positively talk to Sylvia after they got back to Scarsdale, to make sure that their house was still in one piece. Both of them rode in silence as the limo navigated out of the airport and eventually headed north on the Hutchinson River Parkway. They both worried what they would find. They had been away from the house since Danny Locovita's first threats more than two and a half years before. Now Danny was dead, but they had no contact with the housekeeper, the landscaper, the utilities companies, or, for that matter, with the tax office at the Scarsdale town hall.

And as the limo turned down Tryamon Drive, both Sylvia and Monte were shocked at what they saw. The house was exactly as they left it. Lawn mowed, shrubs neatly trimmed, and the swimming pool, with chairs neatly arranged around it, a sparkling, crystal-clear blue. Had the place been sold for back taxes? Was another family now in residence? The limo pulled into the driveway and Monte suggested that maybe the driver should stay. Surprisingly, Sylvia waved him off and asked him to leave their luggage and her airport shopping bags right in front of the garage. By this time, Monte gingerly got out of the car and walked behind Sylvia to the front door. It was unlocked. They stepped inside.

The dining room and living room were just as they had left them. The carpets were freshly vacuumed. The expensive family was still arranged in a corner cabinet, and Sylvia's glossy travel magazines were still arranged in neat piles on the marble-topped coffee table in the living room. No. No new family was living here. Someone had been looking out for them.

Now was the moment that Monte would tell Sylvia that it was time they ended their marriage and both went their own ways. She could travel. She could buy anything she wants. No more TV talk, no more listening to his guitar riffs. It would be better for them both.

Monte followed Sylvia into the kitchen to deliver the news that would change his life. She was leaning over the counter and had something large in her hands. Monte stepped closer. It was an enormous bouquet of red roses. In her hand was a handwritten card that read "To My Beloved. Welcome Home." Tears were running down her cheeks.

She spun around when she realized that Monte had approached her and faced him with a guilty face. "I'm so sorry, Monte," she said. "I just haven't gotten up the courage to tell you."

"Sam Brinkman and I were having an affair for several years before we went away. And he's the only person in the world that I kept in touch with while we were in Mountain City. I'm sorry, Monte. I want to be with him. It's time that you and I go our separate ways."

* * *

The trial of Dr. Jerry Stewart, aka Gerhardt Stürmer, turned out to be a media circus, as Judge Judith Greenstein had feared. Despite the fact that the prosecutors had been explicitly instructed by the Attorney General to drop all charges relating to sedition, insurrection, and domestic terrorism, the proceedings would, before they were over, make the OJ Simpson trial look like the deliberations of the College of

Cardinals.

Bob Jackson, the US Attorney for the District of Montana, would lead the prosecution. He was known as the straightest of straight arrows in the Department of Justice—and he had seen it all. Corrupt politicians. Narcotics kingpins. Human traffickers. Skimmers from tribal casinos. And of course, plenty of gun runners and self-styled "patriot" groups. But this trial was going to be a weird one. He had received specific instructions from no less a source than the Attorney General of the United States, who took his orders directly from the White House. He was told that National Security was at stake if certain information were made public. And he was warned that the American pharmaceutical industry—and needless to say the stock market—had already been teetering on the verge of a catastrophic meltdown when the news broke of Dr. Jerry Stewart's arrest.

"Just stick to one or two simple and easy to prove crimes," Jackson had been told on a secure phone line. "The guy is already over a hundred years old. Just look at him. He won't live another year or so. Get a quick conviction, get it over with quickly."

And so, Dr. Stewart was charged with only two federal crimes, both of them violations of the Federal Food, Drug, and Cosmetic Act, namely the use of medical devices not officially approved by the FDA and the manufacture or attempted manufacture of drugs that had not undergone formal testing and approval by the FDA. In most cases, these violations were usually treated as misdemeanors subject to large fines and possible loss of medical license. But because of the large number of victims and the obvious harm that they had suffered, Jackson was authorized to prosecute these violations as felonies, subject to imprisonment for 24 months for each violation and a seven-figure fine.

No sooner had the judge gaveled the proceedings to order than did the headline-grabbing shenanigans begin. Stewart's four attorneys, the Wall Street lawyer, the slickster, the radical, the beltway fixer, and the tall Texan, sat beside each other at a long defense table with Jerry Stewart, still in his wheelchair, at the end. The comical appearance of these five characters together might have been more appropriate in a TV lawyer sitcom than a real trial and even Judge Greenstein found it hard to stifle a smile.

The Texan rose to speak for the others. "Your Honor, the defendant has an important statement he would like to make to the court."

"Highly irregular," she replied, "but without objection from the prosecution?" She looked toward the prosecution table, with a quizzical look. Bob Jackson seemed equally surprised by this move and merely shrugged his shoulders, indicating that he had no objection and would like to see what the defense had up its sleeve.

"Without objection, then. The defendant may address the court."

Stewart rose slowly and shakily from his wheelchair, with his arms supporting himself on the edge of the defense table. Then, in a voice far stronger than what one would have expected from his feeble body, he said, "from now on, I do not wish to be addressed by this court as Dr. Jerry Stewart. My name is and always has been, Obergruppenführer-- or as you might say-- Colonel Gerhardt Stürmer. I served as chief medical aide to Reichsführer Heinrich Himmler of the SS during World War II. I was brought to the United States by the OSS and granted full American citizenship just like my distinguished colleague Dr. Werner Von Braun."

Everyone in the courtroom gasped.

Jackson turned and whispered to one of his assistants at the prosecution table. "They're obviously going for an insanity defense. Brilliant."

"I will also be defending myself," Stewart, now Colonel Stürmer, announced to the silenced courtroom.

"As you wish, Dr. Stewart—I mean "Colonel" Stürmer. I assume that you have discussed this dangerous strategy with your very competent legal team," Judge Greenstein responded.

The Wall Street lawyer, the slickster, the radical, the beltway fixer, and the tall Texan all nodded sheepishly.

"Thank you Judge…" and here, Stürmer took a long pause, "Green…. Steeeeen." And sat back down in his wheelchair.

The prosecution proceeded as expected and as Jackson had been instructed – short, specific and to the point. No direct witnesses were called in person. Instead, fifteen of the 300 survivors of the medical experiments, all well into their 80s, were interviewed via video, their age and their medical condition precluding them from testifying in person. In each case, the witnesses gave chilling testimony of the procedures they had been subjected to, and the injuries and mental suffering they had sustained.

Then came the expert witnesses—eminent professors of medicine from the University of Montana as well as world-famous neurologists from the Massachusetts General Hospital and the Walter Reed Army Institute of Research. Without exception they forcefully denied that the extraction of Cortisol from the human brain was entirely useless for any medical purpose whatsoever and that drilling a hole in a living patient's skull to access the pituitary gland was a gross and inexcusable breach of medical ethics, if not a crime against humanity.

Stewart declined to cross examine any of them.

"No questions, your Honor," he said, over and over.

The only witness who appeared in person was Billy. He could do little more than support the evidence that had already been offered, having apparently flipped to cooperate with the prosecution—to save himself from a certain life sentence on the charges of domestic terrorism, which he still faced.

In fact, Billy was the only witness that Gerhardt chose to cross examine. He rolled toward the witness stand and stared long and hard into Billy's face. He then posed only one question.

"Do you understand the concept of loyalty?" he asked a trembling Billy.

"I do," Billy responded.

"I think not," Gerhardt said, as he maneuvered his wheelchair to return to the defense table. "No further questions."

With that, the prosecution rested.

*   *   *

When the court reconvened for the defense to present its case, Bob Jackson was quite content that he had done as he was asked. During the emotional video testimony of the elderly victims, he observed several of the jurors dabbing their eyes with tissues. And when the expert witnesses described the grotesque human experimentation that Gerhardt had performed on Mountain City's helpless senior citizens, all of the jurors glared at the defendant in undisguised outrage. Jackson was therefore confident that he had made his case and that Dr. Stewart would soon be behind bars. And, at his age, God willing, it would not be for long. When the Grim Reaper came to take Stewart away, the US government, Big Pharma, and the Dow Jones Industrial Average would all be able to put this ugly matter behind them once and for all.

"Does the defense wish to proceed?" Judge Greenstein asked.

"We do," said the Wall Street lawyer. These were the first words he had spoken since the trial had begun.

"Then please go ahead."

"The defense wishes to call Herr Colonel Gerhardt Stürmer to the stand."

Almost immediately, Jackson rose to object.

"I will allow it," Greenstein said to the U.S. Attorney, "As Mr. Jackson must obviously know, the Supreme Court held in Bird v. Arkansas that the right of a defendant to testify at trial is not affected by his or her decision to defend themselves. I am simply facilitating this testimony."

Jackson sat down in silence. Dr. Jerry Stewart, aka Herr Colonel Gerhardt Stürmer arose from his wheelchair and strode to the stand.

"Do you swear to tell the truth, the whole truth and nothing but the truth?" the bailiff asked.

"I do," Stürmer said, placing his hand on the bible.

"Please be seated."

And so the Wall Street lawyer began, exactly as Jerry Stewart had instructed him.

"Can you give us your name please?" he asked.

"I am Colonel Gerhardt Stürmer."

"And where and when were you born, Colonel?"

"I was born in Dinkelsbühl, Bavaria in on August 8, 1915" Gerhardt said.

Murmurs of disbelief swept through the courtroom. Judge Greenstein gaveled the proceedings to order.

"I object," Bob Jackson said in a loud voice as he rose to his feet again. "Clearly, the defendant is merely trying bolster his insanity defense. Does he really expect us to believe that he is 107 years old?"

"But I am, Mr. Jackson,"

"Your honor, this is ridiculous…"

At this, Gerhardt sat up straight in the witness box, with almost a military bearing. He addressed both Jackson and the room. He knew his words would be published far and wide by the court reporters scribbled furiously on their notepads as he began to speak.

"I have seen many things, many things that you cannot imagine. That none of you here in this courtroom can begin to understand. I am old enough to remember when our glorious German troops under the direction of our beloved Kaiser brought the British Empire and the Russian Empire and the French to their knees. To their knees! Have you ever heard of the Treaty of Brest-Litovsk Mr. Jackson? Probably not. Probably like most Americans you know no history. You only know what you see on your stupid television. Well at Brest-Litovsk in the Ukraine, the hapless Russians surrendered the western half of their great empire to Germany. The Deutschland. To the Vaterland!

Through German blood and steel, we conquered Eastern Europe. We won Ukraine, we won Poland, we won all of the Baltic states. Millions of square miles of Europe were ours, out of the grasp of the barbaric Slavs and back into civilized hands. It was a great victory, bought at unimaginable cost with German lives. The war was almost over. But no. Then the Americans came. Your smiling Yankee doughboys, along with the perfidious Brits and their colonial subjects, held the great German armies to a draw and on the Western Front. So we signed an armistice, not a surrender Mister Jackson, an armistice."

"You will address the court and the jury," Judge Greenstein interrupted him. But Gerhardt was so passionate in his response that he simply ignored her.

"But did we get treated as an equal? We did NOT Mister Jackson. We were treated as dogs. We were stabbed in the back. Stabbed in the back by the Americans, by the British, by the French and worst of all, by the Jews."

Gasps of outrage could be heard in the courtroom, but Gerhardt was undeterred.

"We were broken and defeated and cheated. My own father, a hero of the First World War was reduced to begging in the streets. I saw families starve to death. We were destroyed, not by our enemies on the battlefield, but by internal enemies who wished to destroy Germany: Communists and Jews."

"But then, a great man, perhaps the greatest man who has ever lived, rose up amongst us – sent perhaps by God, for who else could imagine such a thing? And he took us from the depths of our despair to the very edge of world domination in but a few short years. A genius the likes of which mankind sees perhaps one every thousand years, and not even then. A messiah in his own right. Mein Fuhrer. Adolf Hitler. Sieg Heil!"

The courtroom erupted. The judge furiously banged her gavel, threatening Gerhardt with contempt. Three husky bailiffs dragged him out of the witness box. Reporters dashed out of the courtroom to file their stories. The trial in Montana became national news.

When order was restored, the defense rested, and the jury was empaneled. After only 41 minutes of deliberation, they found Dr. Stewart guilty on both felony counts of gross medical malpractice that caused so much suffering, in open defiance of the FDA.

Yet Gerhardt's speech had had a galvanizing effect on the right-wing groups, underground militias, and conspiracy fanatics all across America. Social media were all abuzz with rapturous expressions of honor and respect for a man who had finally been able to tell the truth. "At last, a breath of fresh air!" a smarmy cable TV host crowed. "Doctor Freedom!" the headline of a major metropolitan tabloid screamed, over a full-page color photo of the CEO of Valkyrie.

"I face my future with honor. I have no regrets for what I did." Gerhardt said in a final statement to the court. "You did not understand the Third Reich. "You are the victims of Jewish control of the media and Hollywood—and the satanic aims of the Deep State. We brought science and order to its highest expression in all of human history. We alone stood against Communism and Bolshevism. Do you know how many millions Stalin killed? Do you know how many millions Mao killed? All of this could have been prevented. Millions of decent lives could have been saved; diseases could have been cured; lifespans could have been extended forever, if only you had the courage to stand with us."

The jury found Gerhardt guilty. There had been no question about that. He had never denied who he was, and more importantly, he had never denied what he believed. And he knew, as he had learned throughout his life, that there was a strong audience for those beliefs in America, from the OSS agents he had lectured after the war to the audiences who had feasted on turkey legs at Teutonic Nights in Mountain City, to secret converts to his plans for an Aryan kingdom in western Montana. He would not be broken now. He would not grovel. He would not disavow the core beliefs that he had held since his distant youth.

His outrageously overpaid lawyers tried their best to persuade him to be contrite, apologetic, deeply sorry for his misguided medical experiments—and for past crimes committed so long ago, when he was a young and foolish man.

Gerhardt would have none of it.

"I will not lie. I will not recant the very foundation of all my beliefs of a lifetime to please a mongrelized America."

"Then you better be prepared for a long sentence," the Beltway fixer warned him with a clear tone of exasperation. "You could get as much as twenty-five or thirty years if you don't change your tune."

Gerhardt merely laughed.

"Doctor Stewart...." said the radical before he was corrected by his client.

"Stürmer...."

"OK, then, Mr. Stürmer...."

"Colonel Stürmer!" Gerhardt bellowed.

"Colonel Stürmer," the tall Texan tried to calm him down with his trademark folksy manner, "Let's face it, you're a nice fella. But you're well over 100 years old. You don't want to spend the rest of your life behind bars. Right, pardner?"

At this, Gerhardt only sneered derisively.

"Twenty-five, even thirty years are nothing to me."

*   *   *

Back in Scarsdale, Monte rose earlier than usual. It had been almost a month since he had returned and with daily physical therapy, his sense of balance was now normal and his tinnitus had disappeared. The wound on his left cheek had healed. But he had spent enough time living and sleeping in the finished basement, playing his stratocaster only for himself. The no-contest divorce papers had all been signed and notarized. He was tired of hearing Sam Brinkman's stomping footsteps upstairs in the kitchen. He had agreed to let Sylvia have everything except for a single suitcase full of his clothing and two pairs of shoes—and of course his guitar.

He silently padded up the carpeted stairs to the backdoor hall and stepped outside, closing the door behind him with a soft click. The early morning air was bracing. He hitched up his backpack straps on his shoulders and lifted the handle of his guitar case. He was on his way to Camelot.

EPILOGUE
A STORY THAT NEVER ENDS

Gerhardt Stürmer knew this would be his last morning in his luxurious rented castle in Billings and his butler Thomas had been carefully instructed how to make every detail memorable. After rising and taking his customary cold shower, Gerhardt toweled himself off and shaved himself with a straight razor as he had done every morning since he first joined the SS. He insisted on maintaining this wartime ritual as an essential part of his spartan lifestyle as all of the Nazi upper echelon had done. He donned a robe and strode into the small anteroom of his master suite to take his breakfast—before dressing for his sentencing at the federal court.

On this day of all days, he sought to turn back the clock to a time when order and discipline was paramount and when the world—for one bright shining moment—made sense. On a small table in the carpeted anteroom, Thomas had precisely arranged the china and silverware exactly as both Himmler and his Führer insisted that their breakfasts be served. On a small serving dish lay two lightly toasted slices of rye bread and with a modest dollop of apricot marmalade on the side. Thomas returned with a silver carafe of coffee which he poured carefully into a delicate china cup. And just as the Fuhrer had done, Gerhardt dropped precisely eight sugar cubes into the cup.

Once the morning ritual was completed, Gerhardt rose and strode into his bedroom where Thomas had carefully laid his employer's outfit onto the bed. But first, Gerhardt stepped toward the dresser on which was a silver tray with a large medical syringe. He lovingly gazed at it for a moment before grasping it in his right hand. He then quickly plunged it into his thigh, exhaling slowly to take his mind off the pain. There. He had done it. He had injected himself with the purest form of his anti-aging elixir—not the short-term Merlinium that only lasted for a few hours, but the 10,000 times more concentrated Merlinium extracted from the brain of Monte Levine. Gerhardt chuckled to himself at the thought of a prison sentence of only three decades. This substance, the crowning achievement of a lifetime of pharmaceutical research would enable him to live for a thousand years.

He quickly dressed for court and admired his appearance in the full-length mirror in the corner of the bedroom. Before leaving the master suite, he bid Thomas farewell and assured him that he would be well taken care of while he was away. On the ground floor, black-suited security guards with ear pieces and lapel mics summoned the armored Suburban that would take Gerhardt to court. He arrived promptly at 9:30 and took his place next to his lawyers, this time without a wheelchair, standing in a stiff, almost military pose.

"All rise," the bailiff announced as Judge Judith Greenstein entered the courtroom and took her seat at the bench. As she did, Gerhardt took the long rain coat he had worn to court, revealing a jet-black uniform SS uniform, complete with death's head insignia, a red and white swastika armband, and the sign of the Black Sun.

Judge Greenstein's eyes widened. The observers in the public gallery let out a loud gasp. Gerhardt remained unmoved.

"Are you really intending to wear that—uh—costume in my courtroom for your sentencing, Dr. Stewart?" Judge Greenstein asked.

"Indeed," Gerhardt answered.

All four of Gerhardt's lawyers bowed their heads in embarrassment and shuffled nervously from foot to foot.

"Very well then," Judge Greenstein continued, "I will begin the announcement of my decision on your sentence by saying that you are undoubtedly the most despicable human being I have ever had the misfortune of having to judge. You have shown no respect for this court or even the norms of civilized behavior. Your choice of clothing today proves my point quite eloquently. I have taken your conduct and demeanor during this trial into account, along with the charges that the jury has found you to be guilty of."

Gerhardt sneered, confident that he would outlive any possible sentence by centuries.

"Therefore, I have decided that you will receive a three-year sentence for both charges of your indictment..."

Gerhardt smiled in triumph at that news. His tall Texan lawyer slapped the radical lawyer on the back in what turned out to be a premature celebration.

"Let me make this perfectly clear," Judge Greenstein continued, "three years for each of your 314 victims, to be served consecutively, bringing your sentence to a total of 942 years to be served at the Administrative Maximum Facility at the United States Penitentiary in Florence, Colorado. Even if you were to live for a thousand years in the incredibly harsh supermax conditions, it is unlikely that you will ever see the light of day as a free man again."

And with that, she banged her gavel. "Bailiff, take the prisoner away."

"Nein!" Gerhardt yelled as bailiff and court officers surrounded him to twist his arms behind his back and cuff him. "Nein!!!" he shouted even louder as they roughly hustled him out of the courtroom and into a holding cell.

* * *

Monte was grateful to have gotten his first steady gig in his favorite casino. He had traveled all the way across the country, sometimes by train, sometimes by bus, trying to conserve the money he had to find himself a decent place to live in Vegas.

The Camelot was not the fanciest place on the Strip. It could never compete with Caesar's or the Venetian for spectacular shows or long-term contracts for regular appearances by global superstars. It wasn't the fanciest casino. Far from it. The carpets were worn, the ceilings had water spots here and there, and the tacky medieval décor was hardly even noticed by anyone. The crowd here was mostly made up of folks who had scrimped and saved to spend their one week a year in Vegas. It was their time to feel free from their bills and bosses and everyday worries. They were his people. They came for a drink and some comforting entertainment; nothing more. He covered the songs they loved with no cover charge. And they loved him for doing it every night in the King Arthur Lounge. And every night, no matter how tired he was, he swore he would give them a show they would never forget.

With the small stage beneath his feet and the heat of a single fixed spotlight on his face, he basked in the affection of the Camelot crowd. There was no backup band. There were no other instrumentals, no bass guitar. No drummer, no soulful backup singers. No. It was just him. Just him and his Stratocaster. That was all it had ever been.

Monte Levine slipped the strap of the Stratocaster guitar over his shoulder and prepared to step out onto the stage.

For most of his life, this had been a fantasy, but now it was real. He felt the steel strings of the guitar pressing into his fingers as he fondled the neck. Real. He peered through the curtains and saw the assembled audience. They were real. The smell of beer and cigarette smoke permeated the room. That was real too.

He stepped out onto the stage and hit the first few notes.

Stairway to Heaven.

Ironic, Monte thought to himself. Up until now, he had lived in a world of fantasy. His reality TV shows were nothing in the end but a well-crafted illusion. His life with Sylvia had been a kind of fantasy as well. Pretending to be a rock star in his finished basement was a fantasy too. But of course, the biggest fantasy of all had been the dream he had had while he was under the anesthetic from Gerhardt Stürmer. The crazy story of King Arthur, the knights of the round table, the lovely Katarin, Merlin the Wizard. Crazy. What a fantasy.

But now he was awake. Now he was in the real world at long last, living a real life for the very first time.

In a strange way, the décor of the King Arthur Lounge was reassuring to Monte. It was such a kitschy, over-the-top Hollywood vision of the Middle Ages that it helped him to laugh off his frightening experiences in Mountain City and it reassured him that his equally traumatic visions of his adventures in the Middle Ages were all just part of a bizarre, pain induced dream. He was ok now. He had received a $3.5 million civil settlement from a class action suit by the victims of Gerhardt Stürmer's medical experiments, which Gerhardt's own slickster lawyer had initiated and skillfully piloted through the Montana courts.

Now Monte could just concentrate on his music. His five nights a week at the Camelot kept him content and just busy enough to enjoy life. So did his new girlfriend Katy, a single mom who worked at the Camelot as a waitress and insisted on catching Monte's act as often as she could. If this wasn't exactly a happy-ever-after ending, it was happy enough for Monte Levine.

As he played his set, he scanned audience, something he always did. It was a typical audience for the Camelot – firemen, policemen, EMS workers – real people, he thought. Real lives. Then, in the corner, at a back table, he briefly did a double take. There was a guy with a beautiful blonde, easily 30 years younger than he was. He looked just like Merlin.

Monte laughed to himself.

Dreams, he thought, the power of dreams. When he scanned the room again, the Merlin look-alike was gone. Just an illusion, he thought, just like the illusion of the whole King Arthur thing.

The audience, of course, loved Monte's performance. From time to time, they waved their arms or sang along. They always did.

His boss, Johnny Pastore, a former mobster from New Jersey, liked Monte and his music. And he also liked the whole medieval schtick.

That night after Monte's performance, he invited Monte into his private office for a talk and a drink. In his office he had a glass case filled with his small but growing collection of medieval artifacts. On his desk was a long wooden box.

"You won't believe this, but this guy called me and said he had a real sword from the time of King Arthur. I mean a real one, dug up somewhere in England by someone with a metal detector. It even came with one of those archaeologist certificates or whatever you call them. Ya gotta see this thing, Monte. I'm gonna put it up on the wall the way they do it over at the Hard Rock, you know, with the classic guitars. Hey, maybe one day your guitar will hang up there as well with a big plaque – Monte Levine."

Monte smiled. "That would be great," Monte said, but he doubted it was very likely.

Monte wanted more than anything else to get out of there. Katy would be waiting. He was pretty sure that whatever was in the box was a fake. The world was full of them.

"Wait till you see this thing," Johnny said as he opened the box. "I know you're not into all this medieval crap, but just look at this beauty. All the way from England. Cost me ten grand but it's worth every penny."

Inside the box was a corroded bronze sword. "Of course, I'm gonna have it cleaned up and hung in the lounge. It will look great," Johnny said. "Go ahead, take it out."

To be kind, Monte grasped the handle of the sword and looked down at the blade.

"It even has some letters on it," Johnny said proudly. "I think it's in Latin. But who the hell knows Latin? What the fuck am I, a priest?"

There, along the blade, corroded but still legible, Monte saw it.

The inscription read GLADIUS EQUITIS NOBILISSIMI.

"Sword of the Noblest Knight of them all."

Monte stared at the sword for a long time, until at last, Johnny got a bit concerned and asked Monte if he was OK.

Monte looked up at Johnny as if he had just awoken from a dream. "It's a long story," Monte finally said.

"Totally crazy. Almost impossible to believe. But if you want to hear it, just sit down, pour yourself a drink, and I'll tell you the most amazing tale you've ever heard in your life…"

ABOUT THE AUTHORS

Neil Silberman is an author and heritage scholar who has published widely on the power of the past in the modern world. Among his published works are *The Bible Unearthed*, *The Hidden Scrolls*, *Between Past and Present*, and *Digging for God & Country*.

Michael Rosenblum is the Founder and CEO of Rosenblum TV. For more than 25 years, he has been on the cutting edge of the digital 'videojournalist' revolution. Among his many published articles and books on media culture are *iPhone Millionaire* and *Don't Watch This*.

Printed in Great Britain
by Amazon